REVENGE WITH BENEFITS

CAT SCHIELD

A CONVENIENT SCANDAL

KIMBERLEY TROUTTE

MILLS & BOON

First Published in Great Britain 2019
by Mills & Boon, an imprint of HarperCollinsPublishers,
1 London Bridge Street, London, SE1 9GF

Revenge With Benefits © 2019 Catherine Schield
A Convenient Scandal © 2019 Kimberley Troutte

ISBN: 978-0-263-27172-0

0219

MIX
Paper from
responsible sources
FSC
www.fsc.org
FSC™ C007454

This book is produced from independently certified FSC™ paper to ensure responsible forest management.

For more information visit: www.harpercollins.co.uk/green

Printed and bound in Spain
by CPI, Barcelona

REVENGE WITH BENEFITS

CAT SCHIELD

Prologue

While the keynote speaker for the Beautiful Women Taking Charge event droned on, Everly Briggs contemplated Zoe Crosby and recognized the former Charleston, South Carolina trophy wife was the weak link in her plan.

Before the networking function Everly had researched the attendees and settled on two women recently wronged by the men in their lives. Over cocktails, Everly had chatted up both women, sharing her own tale of how her sister had been wronged by wealthy entrepreneur Ryan Dailey. In addition to Zoe Crosby, she'd encouraged London McCaffrey to pour out her heartbreak after Linc Thurston broke off their engagement.

"We've each been the victim of a wealthy, powerful man," Everly said, thinking that was most true of Zoe. Her ex-husband had hired Charleston's most ruthless divorce attorney and rumor had it that Zoe's settlement was going to be eaten up by her lawyer's fees. "Don't you think it's time we get a little payback?"

"Anything we try would only end up making things

worse for us," Zoe said, her hesitation grating on Everly's nerves.

Up until this moment, Zoe Crosby had been listening and nodding sympathetically. Before meeting her, Everly figured if anyone would want to take down a powerful man it would be a wife who'd been cheated on by one, then cast aside and forced to defend her honor in divorce court.

Instead, Everly was starting to understand why Tristan Crosby had treated his wife with such disdain. The woman was too soft, too passive. She lacked fire and purpose. Well, Everly would just have to stir up the socialite's indignation over how she'd been treated and drive Zoe into the revenge scheme.

"Not if we go after each other's men," Everly explained, gratified to see London McCaffrey nodding in understanding. Zoe still looked worried, so Everly continued to lay out her plan. "Think about it," she said, fighting to keep impatience out of her voice. "We're strangers at a cocktail party. Who would ever connect us? I go after Linc. London goes after Tristan and, Zoe, you go after Ryan."

"When you say 'go after,'" Zoe said cautiously, "what do you have in mind?"

Everly resisted the urge to roll her eyes. From the first she'd suspected Zoe would be too timid to make a good revenge partner, but at least the socialite could be manipulated into doing as Everly wanted.

"In Ryan's case, his sister is running for state senate," Everly said, deciding she'd better monitor Zoe's part of the plan to make sure Ryan Dailey paid dearly for putting her sister in jail.

After all, he was responsible for breaking Kelly's heart and driving her to act out against his firm by deleting millions of dollars worth of engineering drawings. If he hadn't led her on, Everly was convinced Kelly never would've snapped like that.

Zoe's frown deepened at Everly's suggestion that she go after Ryan indirectly. "I thought we were supposed to be going after the men. I don't feel comfortable."

"Since Ryan destroyed my sister's life," Everly explained with elaborate patience even as her irritation reached a boiling point, "it only seems fair that we ruin his sister's chances at being elected." Her pause was too brief to give Zoe a chance to argue further. "Getting at Ryan through his sister is the best way to go. Okay?"

Zoe's abbreviated nod didn't fill Everly with confidence. Well, if the socialite couldn't do what needed to be done, Everly would just have to take care of things herself.

One

Fingers biting into the armrest of the hair salon's cheap vinyl chair, Zoe Crosby—*Alston*, she reminded herself yet again—stared at her reflection. As of today it was official. Forevermore she would check the *divorced* box on every survey form or application that asked her marital status. Even though for the last year she'd told herself it wasn't her fault, the shame of failure sent heat rushing over her skin, leaving her feeling sweaty and miserable.

"Are you sure about this?" the stylist asked, her face screwed into doubtful lines. Penny raked her fingers through Zoe's long, silky hair. "Your hair is so gorgeous. The caramel color with the paler blond streaks. Are you sure you don't want me to take an inch off and call it good?"

Zoe set her jaw and shook her head. "No. I want you to shave it all off."

The stylist looked even more pained, if that was possible. "It's none of my business, and you are beautiful enough to wear your hair whatever length you want, but I wouldn't be doing my job if I didn't talk you out of doing something that radical."

Tristan had been very particular about her hair. He'd wanted it to end exactly at her nipples, deeming it the perfect length. She was not allowed to have bangs or layers. Just a silky, straight curtain with blunt ends. She hadn't been allowed to curl it or to put it up when he'd been around. It was just one of the many ways he'd controlled her.

Zoe sighed, her courage deflating. She'd marched into the hair salon after deciding to shave her head as a middle finger salute to her ex. Tristan couldn't control her anymore and that was empowering, but maybe getting rid of all her hair was a bit extreme. Still, she needed to do something to mark the day that she was utterly and joyfully free of Tristan Crosby. Her gaze swept the photos of women modeling various haircuts lining the walls, snagging on one in particular.

"What about that?" She pointed to a brunette sporting a short, spiky cut. "Only I'd like to go platinum blond."

The stylist looked relieved. "With your bone structure, that look would be fantastic on you."

"Do it."

An hour and a half later Zoe regarded her reflection and didn't recognize herself. Gone was the traditional wife of a successful Charleston businessman with her sweater sets and pretty floral dresses. In her place was an edgy replacement in a graphic T-shirt and torn black jeans. Zoe shivered as she raked her fingers through her new do.

Tristan would hate her dramatic transformation.

But then dismay flooded her. When would she stop running all her decisions through the filter of pleasing her ex-husband? All the more reason to make the change. She needed to think about what made *her* happy.

Plus, she had another reason for altering her appearance.

With step one of her transformation complete, Zoe exited the salon and popped into a drugstore to purchase lipstick and an eye shadow kit in smoky shades that Tristan

Crosby's ex-wife would never have been allowed to wear. In the parking lot, she sat in her car and applied the makeup.

Drawing confidence from her new look, Zoe put her car in gear and headed to the campaign headquarters for Susannah Dailey-Kirby's state senate race. She intended to volunteer for the campaign, making herself indispensable and gathering as much dirt as she could to take down Ryan Dailey's twin.

Everly had suggested the strategy to get back at him for Everly's sister, Kelly.

At the time Zoe had been happy for the input. She'd had absolutely no idea how one went about seeking revenge. Her time married to Tristan had been all about surviving his psychological battery, leaving her little energy for schemes or the gumption to carry them out.

Yet that wasn't completely true. As a safety net, she'd managed to siphon off tens of thousands of dollars from her allowance during her marriage. Having grown up not exactly poor but with a family that lived paycheck to paycheck, she'd liked the idea of financial independence that ready access to the secret stash offered her.

She should have realized Tristan would view any attempt at self-sufficiency as a threat to his power. When he'd found out, he'd reclaimed her stash and monitored her spending more closely. But instead of intimidating her, his actions had made her more determined, and less trusting of her so-called friends and allies.

The crushing loneliness of being married to Tristan was almost as bad as the emotional and psychological abuse he'd heaped on her. Maybe she shouldn't have let Tristan convince her to quit college after her junior year. But she'd chosen to plan an elaborate wedding instead of finishing her degree. Floating down the aisle mere months before her twenty-first birthday, she'd actually believed the rest of her life would be like a fairy tale. And in some ways it had. Only she hadn't been the lucky princess rescued by Prince Charming. Tristan had turned out to be more like the evil king who overtaxed the peasants and punished his subjects whenever the mood struck him.

She'd had no real friends, as was glaringly obvious in the wake of her separation from Tristan and subsequent divorce. No one had stepped up to support or to help her. She'd become a pariah in their tight social circles as Tristan had leaked false stories of her infidelity. No one had cared or believed her when she'd denied the allegations. It was one thing if a man strayed, but unseemly for a Southern woman.

Zoe came out of her reverie as she neared North Charleston. Susannah Dailey-Kirby's campaign headquarters wasn't far from the humane society where Zoe volunteered once a week, loving the time she got to spend with the animals. She'd grown up with dogs and cats, but Tristan had refused to allow her to have a pet.

After parking her car in the strip mall parking lot, Zoe strode along the sidewalk in the direction of the campaign's storefront. For the last week or so she'd been sitting at the fast-food franchise across the street, contemplating the comings and goings of the staff and gathering courage to make her approach. In the weeks since she'd agreed to the revenge bargain, her enthusiasm for the project had waned.

But she'd made a promise and staying true to her commitments was an intrinsic element of her personality she couldn't just set aside. She couldn't help it, even when that trait had kept her in a bad marriage past all self-preservation. She'd meant it when she'd stood before family and friends and pledged to love, honor and cherish Tristan until death. That he'd done everything to destroy her good intentions hadn't lessened her dedication to her vows. No doubt she'd still be married and miserable if he hadn't decided to cast her aside.

Some days it was hard for her to distinguish whether

the brunt of her anger over the failure of her marriage was directed at Tristan or herself. The rational part of her mind blamed Tristan's unreasonable expectations, but her emotions turned the fault on her shortcomings.

Approaching the campaign headquarters, Zoe took a deep breath and held it while she pushed all doubts and worries out of her mind. She needed to focus on the task at hand or everything would be lost.

She'd decided to keep her backstory vague, because she didn't want to talk about her ex-husband or the messy divorce he'd put her through. She was restarting her life as Zoe Alston and that opened up a whole range of possibilities. But first she had to see her commitment through.

Gathering a deep breath for courage, Zoe pushed through the front door, expecting the campaign office to be buzzing despite the election being a year off. But the space she entered was static and tense, as if she'd burst onto the scene of a tragedy.

A tiny bell had rung as she'd entered, but no one had noticed. The same chime sounded now as the door swung shut behind her. The campaign staff remained focused on a large TV. Feeling like an intruder, she advanced two steps into the room and then hesitated, unsure if she should continue or retreat. She'd obviously stumbled into something dire.

Four people stood in a semicircle surrounding a tall, slender man with thick, neatly combed gray hair. Phones rang at several desks but no one paid them any heed. In fact, the staffers' only reaction was to dial the TV volume up.

Zoe shifted her focus from the campaign workers to the news footage that held their attention. It took her a couple of seconds to realize that someone new had entered the race and apparently this was very bad indeed. Realizing this was not a good time for her to approach the campaign team about volunteering, she started to pivot back the way she'd come and promptly collided with someone.

Like the campaign staff, she'd been so focused on the television coverage she hadn't noticed the tinkling bell. Now, however, as her nose took a hit from the man's cologne, her senses went on full alert. She was still reeling from the masculine scent of him as her right shoulder impacted with his rock-solid chest. It was like hitting a wall. Zoe bounced off him like a kitten off a mastiff.

She stumbled and might've fallen had he not caught her by the arm. His fingers were strong. His grip firm and steadying. It sent her heart sprinting as he guided her back the way she'd come. Her brain struggled to catch up with the to-and-fro movements of her body and decode the electric jolt she felt when he'd first touched her.

Her gaze collided with pale gray eyes of incredible intensity. For a moment she was utterly mesmerized. And then recognition flared. She gulped in panic.

Ryan Dailey.

Less than thirty seconds had passed since she'd initiated her part of the revenge plot and already she'd bumped into her target. And what an unexpected encounter it was shaping up to be.

The man's sharp jawline, hawkish gaze, impossibly wide shoulders and sensual grin packed a solid wallop. Tingles raced across her nerve endings as heat built beneath her skin. It raced past her throat and exploded in her cheeks.

"You okay?" Ryan Dailey asked, his deep, rich voice rumbling against her eardrums and awakening queer flutters in her stomach.

"Yeah." It was all she could manage.

"I'm Ryan Dailey," he said, letting his focus flow over her white-blond spikes, dark plum lips and edgy bohemian outfit. "Susannah's brother."

While he checked her out, she took in his custom navy suit, white shirt and pale blue tie. Even with the four-inch heels on her ankle boots making her about five-nine, the man towered over her. Yet despite his imposing stature, she didn't experience the bitter taste of anxiety her ex-husband had often awakened.

But that didn't mean she felt calm.

"I'm Zoe…" Her mind froze before she could add her last name. For eight years she'd gone by Zoe Crosby. Those days were done.

"Nice to meet you, Zoe," Ryan said, smoothly filling in the awkward gap. The way his gray eyes sharpened with interest, he seemed to mean it.

"Nice to meet you, too." She couldn't seem to peel her gaze free, but had enough presence of mind to lift her elbow and alert him that she no longer needed his continued support.

His steely fingers relaxed and slid away, but her skin prickled beneath her black leather jacket as she continued to react to the pressure of his touch.

"You're new to Susannah's campaign," he remarked.

"What makes you say that?"

"If you'd been around before, I would've noticed you."

His comment reawakened those anxious flutters in her stomach. The interest in his eyes was a little too keen, so Zoe settled deeper into playing her role of eager volunteer with nothing to hide.

"I'm really interested in volunteering for the campaign, but it seems like today might not be the best day to be here." She indicated the cluster of staff and then glanced toward the front door. "They seem really busy. Maybe I'll come back another time."

"Don't go." His cajoling smile sent a lance of delight through her. "Come on. I'll introduce you."

Zoe found herself smiling in return. "How about I wait right here and if they have time, you wave me over."

Offering her a brief nod, he moved past her.

Zoe stared after him, appalled and thrilled in turns.

That was Ryan Dailey?

Despite her promise to stay, she slipped out the front door, sucking in a huge breath of air as she escaped the charged atmosphere. No wonder Everly had suggested Zoe focus on the sister. Taking down such a formidable man would've been beyond Zoe's abilities even if she hadn't been brought low by her ex-husband's cold-blooded machinations.

Yet, Ryan Dailey wasn't Tristan. He didn't seem the sort who took pleasure in being ruthless. That didn't mean he wasn't dangerous, especially given what had happened to Everly's sister, but Zoe didn't sense she was in peril.

At least not yet.

Interesting, Ryan mused. Bumping into her had stirred something that had been missing from his life for a long time. Lust. When was the last time he'd noticed a woman and wanted to put his mark on her? To take her to bed and satisfy a basic physical need, indulge in a whole host of dirty fantasies?

The chemistry between them had shivered across his nerve endings and rattled his bones. As he headed to the back of the office, he continued to be aware of her presence. He rubbed his chest where her shoulder had struck him. The spot seemed to buzz in the aftermath of the contact. In fact, the collision had started a chain reaction through his body.

But the uptick in Ryan's mood faded fast as he approached the campaign staffers huddled in front of the TV. The news segment on Lyle Abernathy entering the state senate race was over, but the strategizing about how to handle things was just getting started.

Ryan joined the group, noting Gil Moore's grim expression. "Hi, Gil."

"Hey, Ryan. I take it you heard."

"About Abernathy? Yeah."

"It's going to be bad," the campaign manager said.

"How's Susannah doing?"

"You know her motto. Never let them see you sweat."

Ryan acknowledged Gil's words with a nod. "Someone is here to volunteer. Her name is…" Ryan turned to where he'd left Zoe standing only to discover she'd gone. "Damn it."

He couldn't believe he was panicking. It spoke to the strong effect she had on him. Now that she'd bolted, he couldn't bear the thought that he'd never see her again.

"Looks like she took off."

"She didn't think her timing was right."

"Hopefully we haven't scared her off for good," Gil said. "Did you get a name?"

"Zoe." It wasn't much. Definitely not enough to track her down. "If she comes back, can you let me know? She has really short blond hair and a black leather jacket. Sort of a bohemian style."

Gil nodded. "We'll keep a lookout."

"Thanks." Ryan was grateful the campaign manager didn't ask any more questions. "I'd better go find out how Susannah's doing."

He headed towards his twin sister's office near the back of the building. On entering, he found her seated at her desk, staring at her computer. Her long black hair lay in a sleek curtain against her royal blue suit. Her beautiful face was relaxed; she looked not the least bit flustered that her campaign had just gotten that much harder.

Susannah looked up, her gray eyes narrowing. "What are you doing here?"

"I came to see if you're okay." Ryan knew it was a useless gesture as soon as he spoke. Still, he didn't regret rushing over. It had enabled him to meet Zoe.

"Oh, for heaven's sake! You and Mom. I just got off the phone with her a few minutes ago. I'm fine." And she meant it. Even when they were kids nothing had seemed to faze

Susannah. Her unflappability would serve her well in the months to come. "Lyle is barely more than a speed bump."

Ryan glanced over his shoulder to where her staff had fallen to conversing in low tones among themselves. "Gil doesn't seem to share your opinion."

"He likes to worry."

"You don't worry enough."

"What good would it do me?" Susannah asked, her brows coming together. "Lyle switched districts because he wasn't going to get elected to a fourth term, and he's too arrogant to believe that I won't be as much competition as Jeb Harrell."

"It's your first shot at running for state senate."

And you're a woman. Ryan knew better than to add the second part. Abernathy would throw dirt at Susannah any way he could. It was a sure bet he would use her gender against her.

"I'm a fantastic candidate for this district and everyone knows it." She paused and gave him a cocky little smile. "Including Lyle Abernathy."

"That'll just make him play dirty."

"I'm as squeaky clean as it gets," his twin reminded him. Then, seeing Ryan's continued doubt, she huffed impatiently. "There's nothing for him to use against me."

"That won't stop him. He'll make stuff up."

"We'll be ready."

Ryan opened his mouth to argue but decided he'd be wasting his breath. Susannah Dailey-Kirby was not a woman in need of his assistance.

The walls separating Susannah's office from the rest of the campaign headquarters were made of glass. Blinds had been added in case she needed privacy, but at the moment they were open. Ryan caught himself glancing a third time toward the front door where he'd last glimpsed Zoe.

Susannah followed the direction of his gaze. "Looking for something?"

"Someone. Your newest volunteer."

"I don't see anyone."

"With everything going on, she left before anyone met her. I was hoping she'd changed her mind and come back."

"My," his sister drawled, "she must've been something for you to be this interested. Was she pretty?"

"Yes."

Was he crazy to be so preoccupied with a woman he'd talked to for less than a minute? But then he remembered how bumping into her had short-circuited his system and knocked all thoughts of politics and Lyle Abernathy from his mind.

"Very pretty?"

"Very pretty. But she was different from the women I'm usually attracted to."

"How so?"

For a second Ryan wondered if he could put into words his unexpected reaction. He met hundreds of women a year. Why this particular one? While beautiful, she wasn't the most stunning woman he'd ever met and he hadn't spoken with her long enough to determine if she was bright or funny. Yet her impact on him lingered.

"She dressed like a badass. Black jeans and a graphic tee. Spiky blond hair and dark makeup. Sort of a 'flower child meets rock-and-roll' vibe." Yet beneath the tough-girl exterior he'd sensed her vulnerability.

"Seriously?" His sister made no attempt to hide her amusement. "You're right. That doesn't sound like your type at all."

He was tired of dating successful, sophisticated women like his sister—women who made it their mission to kick the world's ass. He wanted someone who could use his help.

A woman who wasn't afraid to need him. "Maybe what I need is someone totally different."

Despite his mistakes with Kelly Briggs, Ryan liked the idea of being someone's hero and he refused to shy away from the arrogance of being convinced he was right when he acted in another person's best interest. Sure, maybe in this day and age women didn't want to be rescued or helped. Maybe they demanded the power in their relationships be balanced and equal. Ryan wasn't opposed to that, but what was wrong with letting their guard down and letting a guy flex his muscles once in a while?

Zoe intrigued him. He'd glimpsed something in her eyes that triggered his protective instincts. Which might prove problematic, given what had happened when he'd tried to help Kelly Briggs. She'd misinterpreted his assistance as some deep emotional connection between them. When he'd explained his concern was strictly platonic, she'd struck out against his company in a vicious act of revenge.

"But this isn't about me," Ryan objected. "It's about your campaign. You need all the help you can get. Especially now that Lyle has joined the race."

"Sure." His sister gave him a wry smile. "You keep telling yourself that. I hope she comes back." Susannah's eyes twinkled. "For the campaign's sake, of course." She paused to let her ribbing sink in and then added, "What did you say her name was?"

"Zoe. Hopefully she'll come back."

"If she does, we'll make sure we get all her details. I don't want her to disappear on you a second time."

Ryan opened his mouth to deny his interest and sighed instead. "That would be great. I have to get going. Call me if anything new comes up."

Before he could go, Susannah caught his arm. "I love you, big brother. Thanks for worrying about me even if I don't really need it."

He covered her hand with his. "It's what I do."

"I know. And I worry about you in turn." She spoke in a low tone. "I hope your mystery woman comes back and that she's great because you deserve someone fabulous in your life."

"I'm fine," he said automatically.

"Of course you're fine," she countered. "But I want you to be fantastic and the right woman could do that for you."

Susannah had married the first man she'd ever dated and they lived the blissful life of the perfect couple. She and Jefferson had been married for ten years and had two beautiful children, Violet and Casey, ages six and eight. In addition to being a supportive wife and supermom, she was a corporate attorney with the top law firm in the city. Every day she strove to take successful to new levels and did it with grace and ease.

"Jeff is a lucky man to have you," Ryan said. "I'm afraid you might have set the bar too high for my future wife."

With a quick wave of her hand, Susannah dismissed his compliment. "We're a great team. I couldn't do any of this without him."

While Ryan wondered if that was true, he gave her a hard hug and took his leave.

Despite his sister's confidence that she could handle whatever trash Lyle threw at her in the senate race, Ryan didn't like this new development. It was time for him to pay his buddy downtown a visit. He might have a fresh take on what sort of dirty tricks they could expect in the months between now and election day.

Two

The day after Zoe's first attempt to join Susannah Dailey Kirby's state senate campaign, she returned to the storefront, hoping for less chaos and no Ryan. Although the atmosphere continued to buzz with activity and anticipation, the staffers were no longer in crisis mode. She was greeted as soon as the door closed behind her

"Hi, I'm Tonya." A pretty redhead in her midtwenties wearing jeans and a T-shirt emblazoned with Dailey for Senate approached Zoe. "Is there something I can do to help you?"

"Yes, I was here yesterday and—"

Tanya interrupted her. "Are you Zoe?"

That the staffer knew her name sent a shock through Zoe. Had she been found out already? Impossible.

"Yes."

"Wonderful. We're so glad you came back. Ryan mentioned that you'd stopped by but left before we could get any of your information."

"You all looked really busy," Zoe said, hoping her relief didn't show. "I just thought I'd try a different time."

"Well, we're really glad you did. Have you ever volunteered for a political campaign before?"

Zoe shook her head and Tonya began to describe the various activities volunteers could participate in.

"Why don't you come sit at my desk and I'll get some basic information from you."

While it was easy for Zoe to give Tonya her email and phone number, when it came to her home address, she was cagier. "I'm crashing with a friend at the moment. Can I give you a PO Box?"

Tonya looked doubtful but nodded. "I guess that would be okay. Are you looking for a permanent place?"

"That's the plan." Zoe pictured her cot in the back room of the retail space she'd rented a year earlier. That was before legal fees had consumed her divorce settlement and jeopardized her dream of running a consignment store that helped victims of domestic violence get back on their feet financially. "I just need something I can afford."

"Sure." Tonya went on to ask questions about what sort of work Zoe did and what she saw herself doing for the campaign.

While Zoe answered Tonya's questions, her gaze was drawn toward the large glassed-in office at the back of the campaign headquarters. From this angle, Zoe could see Susannah working on her computer. Zoe's gut tightened. She was dreading her first meeting with Susannah, knowing she was going to do everything she could to cause the woman harm.

Guilt gouged her conscience. She'd been so focused on getting through her divorce and being angry at everything Tristan had done to her that she'd barely considered the damage her bargain with London and Everly would do to an innocent third party. Zoe gave herself a mental shake. She couldn't start thinking like this or she'd never be able to go through with what she planned. Instead, she focused on Everly's justification that Ryan deserved to feel the sort of pain and frustration Everly had gone through because of what he'd done to her sister.

While she shied away from dwelling on the ethics of what she and her coconspirators were up to, Zoe heard the front door open behind her and noted how the energy in the room ratcheted up several notches. Tonya's attention shifted past Zoe and her expression relaxed into a relieved half smile. Alarm bells began to ring in Zoe's mind. Had she been found out? Was someone coming to haul her away? She balled her hands in her lap and dug her fingernails into her palms to fight down panic. Letting her imagination run amok wasn't going to make her job any easier.

"Hi, Ryan," Tonya said, her smile turning supernova. "How are you doing today?"

Learning that Ryan was the person who'd just arrived didn't calm Zoe's nerves at all. She'd bolted after meeting him the day before, determining she was too rattled by her sharp reaction to their brief encounter to stick around and pretend she was just an average campaign volunteer.

Now, feeling Ryan's approach in a rush of tingles over her skin, Zoe contemplated the younger woman and realized that Tonya had a crush on the handsome businessman. This gave Zoe a little breathing room. At least all eyes wouldn't be on her for now.

"I'm great," Ryan said in his velvet voice. "How are you doing, Tonya?"

The woman rolled her eyes significantly. "Way better than yesterday. The news about Lyle was such a shock. But of course Susannah calmed everyone down. She's so amazing."

The hero worship in Tanya's eyes might have amused Zoe if her own heart wasn't pounding so hard in reaction to Ryan Dailey.

"She is that," Ryan agreed as he stepped into Zoe's line

of sight. "You came back," he said, a warm smile curving his sculpted lips. "That's great."

Zoe's gaze drifted upward over his light gray suit, white shirt and peach-colored tie. Her mouth was practically watering by the time she noted the faint stubble on his chin that gave him a slightly rakish air.

While preparing to take down Ryan Dailey, Zoe had done extensive online research. Despite his wealth and business success, the man wasn't much for stepping into the public eye. She'd had only the headshot of him on his company's web site to recognize him by. That photo hadn't prepared her for the man's compelling presence.

By contrast, his sister enjoyed being in the spotlight. She was on the board of several charities focused on children's issues. With her husband at her side, she attended all sorts of events. Although Zoe had seen her many times over the years, they ran in completely different circles and never crossed paths. Zoe couldn't imagine what she could possibly say to engage such a brilliant, successful lawyer.

Whatever interests Ryan Dailey pursued in his personal life, he kept a tight lid on his activities. Zoe had found no trace of his love life in the media, but she suspected like so many wealthy and powerful men, he liked arm candy. Beautiful and sexy women that were meant to be showed off. They accentuated a man's virility.

But Ryan Dailey didn't need help in that department.

Zoe cursed as she noted her breathlessness. "Everyone seemed really busy yesterday," she explained.

"I'm glad you came back."

The fact that he sounded sincere combined with the keen interest in his gray eyes sent a shiver of awareness through her.

To Zoe's dismay, she recognized what lay beneath the shrilling of her nerves: attraction. It sizzled through her like lightning, awakening a fever she'd never known with her husband. Their marriage hadn't been a love match. He'd chosen her for reasons he'd made clear in the months following their wedding and in the beginning she'd been both flattered that he'd found her desirable and naïve enough to believe that feeling affection for her husband was enough for her to be happily married.

She'd never make that mistake again.

Zoe wasn't exactly sure what she wanted out of her next long-term relationship, but she'd never be with anyone who trifled with her emotions or damaged her self-esteem in any way.

"I am, too," Zoe said. "Tonya was just filling me in on some of the things I could do to help out."

"So you're going to be a regular?"

"I'd like that," Zoe said, glancing Tonya's way to escape his intense scrutiny.

The turmoil raging inside her from her subterfuge, her guilt and her body's chemical reaction to Ryan was a volatile mix. Zoe set her palms together and slid her hands between her thighs to hide their shaking.

"And we're happy to have her," Tonya said, her attention remaining fixed on Ryan.

"Hey, Tonya, could you come here a second?" a man called from across the room.

"Excuse me," she said, getting to her feet. "I'll be right back. Don't go anywhere." This last part she added with a wry smile in Ryan's direction.

With Tonya's departure, Zoe expected Ryan to head off, as well. Instead, he dropped into the chair Tonya had vacated and glanced at the paperwork Zoe had filled out. He glanced up and noticed her watching him. His lopsided smile made her pulse skip.

"I was afraid when you left yesterday that I'd never see you again," he said, the admission making her heart race.

"It just didn't seem like the right time to be here," she murmured, barely able to hear herself over the litany of alerts blaring in her mind.

"Do you want to grab a cup of coffee when you're done here?"

Her initial unguarded reaction was jubilation and she goggled at his invitation like a smitten fool. Ryan was an incredibly sexy man and any woman would be thrilled that he wanted to spend time with her.

But did it make sense that he was interested in her? Not Zoe Crosby the wealthy socialite, but plain Zoe Alston with her spiky hair and inexpensive clothing. In her current state, she recognized she wasn't in his league and he had to know that. So what was his angle and how did she go about finding out without tipping her hand?

Everly had warned her that Ryan was bound to be suspicious if Zoe came on too strong, so she intended to focus all her attention on getting on Susannah's good side. She'd never imagined that Ryan might be interested in her and this odd turn left her tongue-tied while she rethought her strategy.

"Don't look so alarmed," he said, misreading her hesitation. "I'm harmless. Ask anyone here."

"I'm not sure harmless is an accurate description of you," she said.

"No? Then what would you say that I am?"

Charming. Sexy. Irresistible.

Or if Everly was right, he was predatory, manipulative and cruel.

Zoe couldn't picture him like that.

"You seem quite nice."

He laughed. "The way you say that it almost seems like an insult."

"It's not." Her cheeks felt overly warm. "I like nice."

His white teeth flashed in a smile that heated her blood

and drew her in until she caught herself leaning into his space. Silver glinted in his gray eyes, mesmerizing her.

"Good," he murmured. "Because I want you to like me."

It unnerved her to discover that she craved his company and that her motivation wasn't due to any revenge plot she'd embroiled herself in. Zoe recognized that her interest in Ryan was purely female and driven by an instinct as old as time. She fingered her short hair and struggled against the pull of his charisma.

"I'm not sure how long they need me to stick around today," she hedged, glancing in Tonya's direction. The woman watched Zoe and Ryan with interest.

"I'll wait." His gray eyes remained fixed on her and their steadiness made Zoe fidget.

"I'm sure you have much better things to do than hang around and wait for me," she said. "Don't you have a company to run?"

He deflected her brush-off with a lazy grin. "One perk of being the boss is that I set my own schedule."

His utter confidence was turning her on. Zoe shifted in her chair. This would not do. There was too much at stake for her to become distracted by an attack of lust.

"Or if you'd prefer," he continued, his deep voice turning her bones—and willpower—to mush. "We could have dinner."

Zoe compelled her gaze to shift away from the determined glint in his eyes, but the damage was done. His unrelenting focus had struck a match to the dry tinder of loneliness she'd endured in her marriage.

"Sure." The word came out in a breathless rush before her thoughts caught up to her emotions. "I mean—"

A broad smile bloomed on his face. "Too late," he said, cutting her off. "Tonight at seven?"

"I'm busy tonight," she lied, remembering that she shouldn't appear too eager.

"Tomorrow?"

"You're awfully determined, aren't you?" She tried to act as if she wasn't flattered by his persistence while a traitorous thrill pulsed deep inside her, setting her nerves to jangling and twisting her stomach into knots.

"I'm used to getting my way."

Indeed. Which was why she'd be wise to keep her wits about her and her defenses on high alert. Her purpose in joining the campaign was to hurt him by causing his sister damage. An eye for an eye, Everly had said.

Zoe hadn't taken into account how difficult it would be to exact revenge on someone she found herself liking. She had to remember that Ryan was a bad guy like her ex-husband. Focusing on that would make it a lot easier to take him down.

Instead she caught herself daydreaming about his handsome face and gorgeous body. But more worrisome than her double-crossing libido was the way his wry humor made her smile and his easy confidence bypassed her defenses. Add in his devotion to his sister and he appeared to be quite the catch.

The question remained. If he was so wonderful, why was he still single? Everly insisted he lacked a conscience. That he had no qualms about using women and then throwing them aside. He'd certainly done that to Kelly Briggs.

And then he'd sent her to jail after she'd acted out, impulsively deleting engineering schematics that had cost his company millions of dollars. Everly wanted him to pay for leading her sister on and then turning his back on her. From the picture Everly had painted of him, Zoe easily perceived him as someone who deserved payback.

But how was she to reconcile that version of Ryan with the man she'd met? The disconnect worried Zoe and made her question the wisdom of what she'd joined Susannah's campaign intending to do.

"Where can I pick you up?" he asked, interrupting her train of thought.

Zoe shook her head. He would expect her to be renting an apartment or a house. Her living arrangements were far less conventional and he would ask too many questions she didn't want to answer.

"How about I meet you at the restaurant?" she suggested.

His eyes narrowed as he surveyed her. "How do I know you'll show up?"

"Why wouldn't I?"

"That's an interesting question." He leaned forward and his powerful presence enveloped her. "There's something about you I can't put my finger on, but you intrigue me."

His declaration gave Zoe goose bumps. And only some of them were the good kind.

"Me?" She huffed out a laugh and shook her head. "That's funny. There's not a single interesting thing about me."

"Let me be the judge of that. I'm looking forward to getting to know you much better. How about we meet at Charleston Grill at seven?"

The last thing Zoe wanted to do was to eat anywhere close to downtown Charleston where she might run into someone she knew.

"That's a little too fancy for me," she said, thinking fast. "How about Bertha's Kitchen at six?"

The iconic soul food restaurant was located in North Charleston and famous for its fried chicken and Southern sides. The hearty helpings of delicious soul food were served cafeteria-style on no-frills foam plates. Not necessarily a place she'd expect a wealthy businessman like Ryan to dine.

To her surprise, he nodded without hesitation. "I'll see you at six." He pulled a card out of his pocket and handed it to her. "Here's my number if anything changes." When she started to pull it from his fingers, Ryan tightened his grip. "But you have to know I'll be crushed if you stand me up."

She doubted that anything could crush him, but rushed to assure him. "I won't."

With a quick, heart-stopping smile, he got to his feet. "See you tomorrow, Zoe Alston."

"See you tomorrow," she echoed faintly, her whole body buzzing with energy. "Ryan Dailey."

Buzzing with satisfaction, Ryan headed for his sister's office. As he entered, Susannah leaned back in her executive chair and the springs creaked ominously. Although his sister had more than enough money to furnish her campaign office with all new furniture, she'd chosen to downplay her wealth by sticking to a strict budget.

"Thanks for calling me with a heads-up that Zoe had returned," he said, sliding into one of her guest chairs.

"I'm always happy to help out my big brother." Susannah was five minutes younger than Ryan, but her serious nature had always made her seem years older. "Did you ask her out?"

"I invited her to dinner."

Susannah arched an eyebrow. "And is she going?"

"What do you think?" He made no attempt to hide his smirk.

"That she's not exactly your type."

Ryan knew his sister was referring to the fact that all the women he dated came from their social circles. Interchangeable beauties that came from wealth. Good families. Good schools. Good manners. Good careers. By marrying any of them he would've fallen into a predictable pattern. He wanted a woman who riled his emotions and challenged him.

"I'll admit her style isn't what I'm used to, but I'd like to think I'm not that shallow." Ryan flashed a disarming grin. "She's mysterious and there's something tragic in her eyes."

"And deep down inside you have a knight-in-shining armor complex that gets you into trouble."

Susannah was talking about Kelly Briggs. He'd tried to help her out and the whole thing had backfired.

"Just because you haven't needed my help since middle school doesn't mean others don't appreciate some assistance now and then," he said. "And you're not exactly one to talk. No one likes to help out more than you."

"Help," she said. "Not rescue."

"Zoe doesn't strike me as a woman who needs to be rescued."

"Yet you just said there was something tragic about her. It worries me after what happened with Kelly."

It still bugged Ryan that he'd mishandled the situation with Kelly Briggs. Well, maybe mishandled wasn't the best description for what had happened. He'd taken her at face value and failed to look below the surface for what had motivated her.

From the first Kelly had shown great promise, establishing herself as a clever and talented member of his team. She was also beautiful and if she hadn't been his employee, he might've dated her. They'd had wonderful chemistry both professionally as well as personally. Several times he'd been tempted to cross the line, but he never had.

That wasn't to say things didn't get blurry from time to time. Especially after he'd discovered that Kelly'd had ongoing troubles with an ex-boyfriend who had refused to accept that they were done. Ryan hadn't considered there might be repercussions when he'd come to her rescue one evening in the company parking lot. Or that he might be sending the wrong signals when he'd offered to help her out if the guy came around again.

"What happened with Kelly was a brief lapse in my

judgment. And Zoe's different. She's wary and prickly. I think she's been through something difficult and hasn't fully healed."

He had a hard time picturing Zoe as someone who was going to fall for him just because he was nice to her. No, if he wanted Zoe, he was going to have to work damned hard to get her.

"Do you think it's a good idea to get involved with someone like that? Can't you find someone uncomplicated to date?"

"Uncomplicated is boring."

"As an old married woman who adores her husband and two darling children, I can tell you that uncomplicated is perfectly wonderful."

"So much so that you decided to run for office? If you were as completely happy as you claim, then you'd be satisfied with your brilliant law career and perfect home life."

She frowned at him. "That's unfair. Being satisfied doesn't mean you don't want more. Part of being happy with my life is challenging myself and growing as a person. Running for office is part of that."

A knock sounded and Ryan glanced around to see Gil standing in the open doorway. Susannah invited him in and he took the chair beside Ryan.

"What's going on, Gil?" Susannah asked.

"What do you know about the woman you were talking to?" Gil asked Ryan.

"Zoe?" Ryan glanced at his sister to gauge her reaction and saw she was equally puzzled. "I don't know anything about her. Why?"

"I was talking to Tonya and she says she's getting a bad vibe off of her."

"What sort of bad vibe?" Susannah asked, beating Ryan to the punch.

"She's just been very evasive about her background and

why she wants to work for the campaign." Gil fixed his gaze on Susannah. "She showed up the day Abernathy announced he was running in this district. I just think the timing is suspicious."

Ryan didn't like what the campaign manager was insinuating. "Suspicious how?"

"What if Lyle sent her here to spy on us."

"Seriously?" Ryan scoffed. "Does she look like a spy?"

"Of course not. That's what makes her so perfect. Tanya said she used a PO Box for her home address and asked a lot of questions about everybody who works here. I think we should do more research on her before giving her anything that would tip our hand about our strategy."

"You have to be kidding about this." Yet even as he continued to argue, Ryan noted a shift in his attitude. His twin's earlier concern that he was intrigued with Zoe reclaimed his attention. Was she another bad choice? Ryan hated that he continued to question his instincts. "Susannah, are you buying this conspiracy theory?"

Another way they were different was in her measured approach to all situations. Where Ryan tended to jump in and deal with the consequences later, Susannah waited, calculating all options before making a move. He liked to think they balanced each other out. She encouraged him to slow down. He persuaded her to follow her gut.

"You're having dinner with her, aren't you?" she asked him. "I agree with Gil that we need to learn a little bit more about her."

To his dismay, Ryan noted an uptick in his own doubts. This campaign meant a great deal to Susannah. She was sacrificing a run at making partner at her law firm and taking time away from her family to chase her political dreams. If something like misplaced trust in a campaign volunteer created problems that led to her losing to a hack like Abernathy, she would be devastated.

"I like this woman," he protested, knowing he would do everything in his power to protect his sister. "I'm not going to treat her like an enemy combatant."

"You don't have to go full-interrogation mode on her," Susannah said with a mocking smile. "Just use that special Ryan Dailey charm of yours and get to know her better." She arched an eyebrow.

"Fine, I will do my duty to the campaign and learn every single detail about her life." He paused, noting that Gil didn't look particularly happy with the exchange. "Why don't you give me a copy of her information form and I'll see what I can find out from Paul?"

Paul Watts, owner of Watts Cyber Security, had helped Ryan figure out who'd sabotaged his engineering firm to the tune of two and a half million dollars and had been instrumental in building a case against Kelly Briggs.

More importantly, he'd been Ryan's best friend since kindergarten. A fascination with technology had sparked a friendship between the two boys and kept them tight as adults. In addition to growing up in the same neighborhood, they'd attended the same schools through college.

Despite their many similarities, each man had chosen a very different career. Ryan had started his own engineering firm while Paul had turned his back on his family's shipping business, choosing a career in law enforcement instead. That had put him at odds with his father and brother, leading to bitter arguments and an estrangement that went back several years.

Unsure where he might find his friend at the moment, Ryan shot Paul a quick text, suggesting they meet for a drink. Paul was a self-proclaimed workaholic. Often he would get lost in his work and forget to eat and sleep. Things had gotten worse in the last year while he'd chased a gang of cyber thieves who had hacked one of his clients and stolen financial data on tens of thousands of their customers.

I'm home. Stop on by.

Ryan collected Zoe's information form and headed to his car. He looked for her as he strolled through the campaign office, but she was already gone.

After making a couple quick stops, Ryan stood on Paul's front porch armed with cold beer and a loaded pizza from D'Allesandro's. Paul was barefoot and freshly showered when he answered the door, but despite his well-groomed appearance, he had dark circles beneath his forest-green eyes.

"Geez," Ryan commented, shocked at his friend's paleness. "Have you been getting any sleep?"

"I worked all night," Paul muttered as he took the pizza and led the way into his kitchen.

"You do know it's five in the afternoon."

Paul set the box down and raked his fingers through his thick sandy-blond hair. He glanced at the clock on the microwave. "Is it?"

"I don't even want to ask if you're eating." Ryan pushed aside his own issues for the moment so he could focus on his friend. He popped the top on one of the beers and handed it over. "How's Grady doing?"

Grady Watts was Paul's grandfather and one of his biggest influences in life. A man who worked hard and played harder, Grady had been in failing health over the last several years. And things had really gone downhill after he'd suffered a stroke a month ago that affected his speech and paralyzed his right side.

"It's not looking good," Paul replied, his manner grim. He braced his hand on the counter, took a long swig from the bottle and stared off into space. "He just doesn't have the will to get better and I don't know how to reach him."

"Have you talked with your dad and brother about it?"

"What do you think?"

Ryan kept his opinion to himself. He loved his friend, but Paul had a black-and-white view of things that made compromise impossible. And although he'd never admit it, the way his family had refused to support his decision to join the police force had badly hurt him.

"That really sucks," Ryan said. Maybe it was being a twin or the fact that his parents were so supportive of everything he'd done, but Ryan couldn't imagine being estranged from any of his immediate family. "Is there anything I can do to help?"

A ghost of a smile crossed Paul's lips. "You're here with pizza and beer."

Ryan winced. "Well, it's not exactly an altruistic visit." He pulled out the copy of Zoe's information form and slid it along the marble-topped kitchen island toward his friend. "I have someone I need you to check out."

"Who is she?"

"Someone who recently joined Susannah's campaign and Gil is suspicious of her. He thinks she might be a spy for Lyle Abernathy."

"Why would that matter?"

"Have you come up for air at all in the last few days?" Ryan asked, his tone split between amusement and frustration. "Abernathy has switched districts and entered the state senate race against Susannah."

"I guess I heard something about it but didn't put two and two together." Paul grabbed a slice of pizza and took a bite while perusing the sheet of paper with Zoe's information. "So what do you think is going on with Zoe Alston?"

"I'm reserving judgment."

For a long moment Paul studied his friend. "Are you attracted to her?"

"Yes."

"So is this really about your sister's campaign or are you having me investigate her because of what happened with Kelly Briggs?"

"Maybe a little of both," Ryan admitted, hating that he no longer trusted his gut when it came to women he was drawn to. "Look, there's nothing wrong with erring on the side of caution. And I'm not the one who raised the alarm."

While that was true, it was also the case that he wasn't rushing to defend Zoe as innocent. Gil's paranoia had aroused Ryan's suspicions and they weren't going away without concrete proof that she wasn't a threat to Susannah.

"I'll check into her," Paul said. "Just promise me you'll back off if I turn up anything."

Ryan recalled the hit to his libido dealt by Zoe's delectable scent, lean curves and full lips. Something about her put his senses on full alert and he doubted he'd be able to walk away without getting her into bed first.

"I'll think about it," he said, knowing he would do no such thing.

Three

Zoe was fretting about the dinner date she'd made with Ryan Dailey the previous day as she walked through the front door of Second Chance Treasures. She'd opened the boutique featuring arts and crafts items made by women who'd been victims of domestic violence a year ago. The concept for the project had been inspired by the helplessness Zoe had felt while married to Tristan. Usually, the store imbued her with an uplifting sense of pride and accomplishment, but more and more lately she'd been weighed down by looming dread as her bank balance dwindled.

From fledgling idea to breaking even, the project had been Zoe's passion for three years. In that time she'd been able to help nearly a hundred women who struggled financially after fleeing their troubled marriages. With each month that passed, both her inventory and her customer base grew. Unfortunately, in getting to this point, she'd put everything she had into the store only to find it wasn't enough.

She was behind on her rent and on the verge of failing everyone who so desperately needed her to pull off a win.

The ever-increasing financial pressure was part of what had goaded her into entering the revenge plot with Everly and London. The possibility that London might find a clue that would point Zoe in the direction of the money Tristan had hidden offshore combined with longing to see her ex-husband suffer for the pain he'd put her through was what had drawn Zoe into Everly's scheme.

"Hey, Jessica," she called to her part-time helper standing behind the counter. "How'd we do today?"

"Something horrible happened," the twenty-five-year-old mother of two wailed, heartbreak in her voice. "And it's all my fault."

Zoe rushed to her, tamping down panic. The last thing she needed to do was to overreact. "I'm sure it's not your fault," she said, coming close enough to see that Jessica's blue eyes were rimmed in red. She'd obviously been crying. "What happened? Are you okay? No one hurt you, did they?"

"No." Jessica shook her head vehemently. "Nothing like that. All the cash that was supposed to go to the bank today is gone."

Zoe bit back a moan as she absorbed the financial hit and wrapped her arms around the distraught woman. "It's okay. Why don't you tell me what happened?"

"I wanted to catch Ashley's program at school so Maggie came in just before lunch to watch the store for me," Jessica began, her breath shuddering as tears began to fall.

Although Maggie had limited artistic or crafts experience, she'd helped out at the store whenever possible. Zoe had always found her reliable and trustworthy. "You think she took the money?"

Jessica's shoulders rose and fell. She looked miserable. "When I came back she bolted out of here and I thought it was really strange. It didn't occur to me until an hour later that I hadn't locked the cash into the bank deposit bag before I left. When I went into the back to check on it, the money was gone."

"It's okay," Zoe repeated even though that was the furthest thing from the truth.

Dozens of women were counting on her to pay them for the inventory they'd put their hearts and souls into and she'd promised the landlord she'd catch up on several months' worth of past-due lease payments. Zoe guessed there had been nearly five thousand dollars in cash ready to be deposited. This was all her fault. She'd been distracted by her work with Susannah's campaign and had neglected to get to the bank for nearly a week.

"How was Maggie acting when she came in today?"

"I don't know." Jessica scrunched up her face as she thought. "Maybe a little distracted. She's been that way a lot lately. I think something might be going on with her ex."

"Has she talked to you about him?"

Even as she asked the question, Zoe knew the likely answer was no. Domestic violence was a silent epidemic with many victims either too afraid or too ashamed to speak out against their abuser.

"No," Jessica said, confirming what Zoe had assumed to be the case. "You know how Maggie is."

Magnolia Fenton had three children and an ex-husband with a hair-trigger temper. While he'd never been physically abusive, his systematic belittling and shaming of Maggie, and the way he'd cut her off from family and friends, had taken its toll.

Add to that her lack of marketable skills that kept her from getting a job and saving money and Maggie had felt completely trapped. Her situation resonated with Zoe because of her own experiences and she'd tried sharing her story in an attempt to connect with Maggie. Over the last few months Zoe had believed she was making progress. And now this.

"I'm sure Maggie had a good reason for taking the money," Zoe said, hoping that was true. "She isn't a thief." Something dire would have to be happening for her to do something so drastic.

"Are you going to call the police?" Jessica wrung her hands. She already blamed herself for what had happened and if Zoe reached out to the authorities, no doubt the other woman would never forgive herself.

"No." That was the last thing Maggie needed. "I'll give her a call and hopefully we can figure out what's going on."

Zoe wasn't surprised when her attempt to reach Maggie ended in the phone being out of service. From their conversations, Zoe had learned that Maggie's ex had stalked her after she'd left and even gone so far as to damage her car. The way he'd isolated Maggie had triggered powerful emotions in Zoe and she recognized she'd retreated from Maggie when she should've stepped up and become her champion.

At three o'clock Jessica headed off to meet her children's school bus, leaving Zoe by herself. Fortunately a steady stream of customers entering the store kept Zoe from dwelling on her problems. But as five rolled around and she locked the front door, anxiety-raising thoughts swarmed her tired brain.

The business card Ryan had given her was on her desk in the back room. Given what was going on with her store, Zoe could've justified canceling that night's dinner with Ryan. But the man was a whole lot of distracting and, whether she liked it or not, the way he made her feel was exciting.

Zoe ruthlessly pushed aside her reaction to the man's charm and reminded herself that her real purpose in going out with him was to glean as much information as she could about his sister and her campaign. Bypassing an elegant sheath in her favorite shade of blue, Zoe chose a black-and-white-striped T-shirt dress, white sneakers and an oversize black cardigan. The outfit was similar to something she would've worn in her college days. Comfortable and down to earth, without a designer label in sight. Not exactly guaranteed to stop a man in his tracks.

Making herself forgettable was important if she was to get the goods on Susannah's campaign without calling attention to herself. If Ryan continued to pursue her, Zoe would be a topic of conversation among the staff. Yesterday, after Ryan had gone in to talk to his sister, Tonya had made it pretty clear that Zoe should maintain her distance from the candidate's twin brother. Tonya's reasoning had been a little muddy, but her irritation had come through crystal clear.

Zoe had made a point of declaring she wasn't interested in Ryan, but Tonya had obviously not believed her. The subtext being that no woman in her right mind could resist him. That question was front and center in Zoe's thoughts as she parked her car and spied Ryan waiting for her near the front door.

As she walked toward him, she gave herself several seconds to admire his lean, muscular form clad in worn jeans and a long-sleeved, black knit shirt with the cuffs pushed up to reveal his strong forearms. He appeared completely at ease in the modest surroundings.

Bertha's Kitchen was housed in a two-story building painted robin's-egg blue and trimmed in purple. Founded in 1979, the restaurant was a primer in Lowcountry soul food and one of Zoe's favorite places to stop whenever she made a trip to North Charleston to volunteer at the animal shelter.

"Hi," she said as she stepped within earshot. "Sorry I'm late. The traffic was worse than I expected."

"Not to worry," he said with a smoky half smile. "You are worth waiting for."

At a loss for a clever response, Zoe regarded him in silence. She was accustomed to a certain amount of flattery.

Tristan's friends had often commented on her beauty, but those remarks had always seemed to be for her husband's benefit, speaking to Tristan's potency that other men found his wife desirable.

Yet here she stood in her ordinary clothes and Ryan behaved as if she was the most well-dressed woman on the planet. Electricity sparked along her nerve endings, making her hyperaware that his skin radiated the wholesome scent of soap and his shampoo made her think of sunshine.

"Are you hungry?" she asked, grasping at the first safe subject that popped into her mind in an effort to keep the conversation rolling. "The food here is fantastic. Although probably not the sort of fare you're used to."

"On the contrary, I come here fairly often." He gestured for her to precede him into the restaurant. "More so now that Susannah's campaign headquarters is nearby."

Her lame attempt to point out their social differences and demonstrate that she wasn't the sort of highbrow date he was used to had failed miserably. Zoe reassessed her impression of Ryan as he grinned and flirted with the women dishing out plates of fried pork chops, fried chicken, stewed greens, dark roux okra soup and moist cornbread. It was pretty obvious he hadn't been exaggerating about being a regular because he knew several of the servers and kitchen staff by name and they all knew him.

By the time they carried their trays of food and sweet tea to a table, Zoe was feeling utterly defeated.

"Tell me about yourself," Ryan said, skipping small talk and jumping straight in. "I want to know everything."

She'd expected that he'd be like most successful men of her acquaintance and only interested in talking about himself. While she'd prepared a dull story that would ensure he'd lose interest quickly, something about his direct gaze warned her she'd better watch what she said.

"I'm pretty ordinary," she began, selling her claim with

a lackluster tone and cultivated casualness. The struggle to maintain her blasé façade while her pulse hammered away highlighted Ryan's powerful effect on her. "You're the one who's interesting. You run a successful engineering firm with projects all over the world."

Unfortunately, Ryan wasn't distracted by her attempt to deflect the attention away from herself. "Where did you grow up?"

"Greenville."

If Ryan was determined to mine her background, Zoe intended to keep her answers short and vague.

"What brought you to Charleston?"

"I came here after college."

She left out the part about being a brand-new bride bubbling with optimism about her new life with her handsome, wealthy husband. In the early days of her marriage she'd thought her life was going to be perfect.

"Where did you go to school?"

"University of South Carolina."

"Major?"

"I never graduated."

He cocked his head at her defensive tone. "You say that like you expect me to judge you."

"You're a brilliant engineer and a successful businessman," she said. "Your sister is a lawyer who's running for state senate." *I'm not in your league.*

"And because you didn't graduate college that somehow makes you less worthy?" He paused a beat before adding, "Or are you just passing judgment on me by assuming I think I'm better than everyone else? Is that why you wanted to come here? To point out that you're one of the people while I'm an entitled jerk?"

"No." But wasn't that exactly why she'd chosen Bertha's Kitchen?

"Then why make such a big deal about me being successful?" He asked like he was curious about her motivation. As if he was interested in getting to know her. Like he intended to uncover all her secrets. Her breath hitched at the danger this presented.

"I guess I've become accustomed to being judged for my choices."

"Are you happy with the decisions you made?"

"Is anyone?" The items in her poor judgment column definitely outweighed the accomplishments she was proud of.

"What would you go back and change if you could?"

Over the last few years Zoe had given the matter a great deal of thought. Her marriage to Tristan hadn't been all bad. He could be kind and funny and generous. At least, early on that had been the case. She'd been a naïve twenty when they'd gotten married and easy for him to control. She'd wanted to please Tristan and most of the time she had.

"That's a tough question to answer. The decisions I made helped me to become who I am today. I like that person. Other choices might have resulted in me becoming someone else."

"Do you wish you'd graduated?"

"Of course I wish I'd graduated." Yet was that completely true? She'd disliked the major she'd chosen and had struggled through her classes. When Tristan had insisted he couldn't wait to make her his wife, she'd happily forgone her senior year. It wasn't until she'd moved to Charleston that she'd realized her mistake.

The social circle Tristan moved in had been filled with beautiful former debutantes—with college degrees—who'd loved to talk about their alma maters. Zoe had always felt a little foolish for not completing her education.

"What did you major in?"

"Hospitality management." She made a face. "I went to college because everyone expected me to." At eighteen she'd been unable to visualize her future without that step. Unable or unwilling? Her family had expected her to go. Had she even considered what would be best for her? "I really didn't have a sense of what I wanted to do."

"Looking back, what do you wish you'd done instead?"

"Sociology or counseling." For a while she'd considered going back to school, but Tristan hadn't seen the purpose, pointing out that she didn't need a degree to be Mrs. Tristan Crosby. "I'd like to be able to help people."

"I'll bet you'd be good at it."

She wanted to point out that he didn't know her well enough to make that assessment, but the compelling light in his gray eyes left her wondering if maybe he saw deeper inside her than she realized. The thought unnerved her. And yet she was also flattered that he was making the effort to look beneath her surface.

No doubt about it. Ryan Dailey was a complicated guy who aroused complex emotions in her. That made him more dangerous than she might be able to handle.

"Can we talk about something else?" she asked. "I'm really not all that interesting."

"You don't give yourself enough credit," he teased, despite the somber feeling stealing over him.

His initial assessment that Zoe's edgy exterior protected a delicate core was proving true. Her insistence that there wasn't much he might find interesting about her intrigued him. Instead of convincing him she was ordinary, he grew even more curious about what she was hiding. And why.

"One last question," he insisted, ignoring her weary exhalation. "What do you do when you're not volunteering for my sister's campaign?"

"I work at a boutique store in downtown Charleston. Second Chance Treasures."

Her quick answer surprised him. As did the way her

spine straightened and her chin came up. Her whole manner brightened. She stopped avoiding his gaze and made eye contact. The beauty of her light brown eyes hit him full-force. For long seconds he lost his train of thought but finally shook himself free of her spell.

"What do you sell there?"

"We specialize in arts and crafts items made by women who are survivors of domestic abuse. Every sale helps them on their road to financial independence." There was pride in Zoe's voice.

From the beginning he'd thought her beautiful, but now, as she spoke about the store, her bright smile and fierce satisfaction captivated him. "Sounds less like a job and more like a calling for you."

As if realizing she might have given too much away, she dialed back her emotions. With a careless shrug, she murmured, "It feels good to help out."

He agreed but sensed she wouldn't accept any overture he might make. She obviously wasn't ready to trust him, but would she accept aid from a different quarter?

"It sounds like something my sister would be interested in helping with," he said. "Have you mentioned the store to her?"

Zoe shook her head. "She's busy with the campaign. I wouldn't want to bother her."

"You wouldn't be bothering her," he insisted, recognizing that the issue of domestic violence was something his sister could take up in her campaign. "In fact, having an event at your store might be good PR for both of you. It might be worth asking the owner about."

"I suppose I could do that."

Her vague answer left Ryan wondering if she actually would. Regardless, he decided to suggest Susannah check out the store. Even if an event couldn't be organized, Ryan knew his twin would do what she could to help out.

"You seem like the perfect person to be on Susannah's team," Ryan said, turning his attention to the onerous task of deciding if Zoe was in any way connected to Abernathy's campaign. "You have the sort of passion to effect social change that drew my sister to public office. Have you volunteered for any other campaigns?"

"No."

Zoe's short answer left Ryan regretting that he'd been too direct in his inquiry. Why not just come out and ask her if she was spying for Abernathy?

"Why now then?"

She became absorbed in pushing her uneaten lima beans into a neat line on her plate.

"I guess I realized that nothing is going to change unless people get involved."

"People?" he asked, nudging her to clarify.

A dry smile quickly passed across her lovely lips. "Unless I get involved."

"I think a lot of people are feeling that way," Ryan agreed. "Susannah said their volunteer list has doubled since Abernathy announced he was running."

"That isn't surprising. He's a terrible politician."

"You sound familiar with him."

She shook her head. "Not at all. It's just what I've heard."

While her denial didn't ring true, it was pretty obvious that her disgust was genuine. Maybe a little too obvious? Demonstrating an unfavorable opinion about Lyle Abernathy didn't exactly clear her of being a spy. Clearly she couldn't come right out and sing the guy's praises while volunteering for Susannah's campaign.

Ryan wished his gut wasn't warning him that her explanation for joining his sister's campaign wasn't the whole story. Clearing Zoe of suspicion would've opened the path to pursing her romantically. That Gil and his sister could be right to suspect her churned in Ryan's stomach like acid.

He'd hoped she'd ease his mind over dinner. Instead she'd awakened more questions.

Obviously he would have to continue investigating her.

"Thank you for dinner," she said as they exited the restaurant and headed for the parking lot.

"You're welcome," Ryan said, matching her slow pace. "Maybe next time you'll let me pick the place."

Zoe reached her car and turned to face Ryan. Every line of her body, her tense muscles and slight frown, screamed reluctance.

"Look," she began, obviously gearing up to blow him off. "You are a really nice guy, but this isn't going to work."

Ryan set his hands on his hips and wondered if she was as immune to him as she appeared. "Because?"

"We're way too different." She waved her hand between them as if to demonstrate her point.

"Being different is what makes things interesting," he countered, taking a step in her direction.

Her eyes widened as he invaded her space. "Being different is what leads to problems. You like champagne. I like beer."

"You like beer?" he echoed in surprise, unsure why he couldn't picture her with a bottle in her hand.

"Well, no," she admitted. "I usually drink vodka, but you get what I'm saying. You're South of Broad and I'm…" She trailed off as if her current address eluded her.

"Where do you live?"

"I'm crashing with a friend at the moment," she said, her whole manner evasive. "See, that's what I mean. You're rich and I can't afford to rent an apartment. It would never work."

"I disagree and frankly I'm a little insulted that you're judging me on my financial situation."

"You're insulted?" She crossed her arms over her chest and stuck her chin out.

"Yes. And I think you're lying about why you don't want to see me again."

"I'm not."

He ignored her denial and plowed on. "I think you're proud of your self-reliance to the point where you refuse to accept anyone's help no matter how dire your situation." From the way her eyes widened, Ryan saw that his point had struck home. "What are you afraid of?"

"I'm not afraid," she countered. "But you're right about my pride. It's important to me that I do it on my own."

Her fierceness fired his desire and forced him to shove his hands into his pockets to stop from snatching her into his arms and setting his lips to hers. Skittish and assertive in turns, she was a complex knot for him to unravel. The question remained whether or not he should.

"One more date," he declared. "We'll have dinner this weekend. Any place you want."

She shook her head. "You aren't going to take no for an answer, are you?"

"I like you. A lot. I think you like me, too." He paused, offering her the opportunity to disagree. When she didn't jump in, he had his answer. "Good. Saturday night at six. I'll be in touch to finalize the details."

"You're wasting your time," she declared, but her voice lacked conviction. "Good night, Ryan Dailey."

"Sweet dreams, Zoe Alston."

As she slid behind the wheel of her gray Subaru, Ryan headed to his own vehicle. He remained bothered that she'd listed a PO Box number as her home address and claimed to be staying with a friend. Why so vague about where she lived? What secrets was she trying to keep hidden?

Ryan was determined to find out and as she exited the parking lot, he let her get a little ahead of him before slipping into traffic behind her. He doubted his sister would approve of him tailing Zoe, but he wouldn't be able to rest unless he was satisfied that Zoe was telling the truth about her living situation.

From where they'd had dinner, it was a straight shot to downtown Charleston. As he tailed Zoe, Ryan wondered if he'd have done something like this before his troubles with Kelly Briggs. He'd never considered himself naïve when it came to women, but after the way he'd misread Kelly, Ryan's first impulse was to assume the worst. He wasn't proud of his newly cynical perspective or the way it warred with his innate desire to give people the benefit of the doubt. Being suspicious tainted him somehow.

When Highway 52 became King Street and Zoe's car continued straight on, Ryan suspected she wasn't heading home but rather to one of the downtown bars. This was where things could get dicey. He'd have to follow her in to see what she was up to, all the while staying out of sight.

But even as Ryan pondered how to accomplish this, Zoe turned onto a side street and parked behind a retail building. Ryan kept going, but slowed to read the name painted on the windows of the darkened store. Second Chance Treasures. The place where Zoe said she worked. What could she possibly be doing there so late?

Ryan circled the block and found a place down the street where he could observe the parking lot and keep track of who showed up. After an hour, all remained quiet and Ryan's curiosity morphed into frustration. The entire back of the building was windowless, offering no clue as to what could be going on inside. Additionally, Zoe's car was the only one in the parking lot. Unless someone had arrived on foot before he'd showed up, Ryan had to assume she was alone.

Frustrated by the lack of action, he put his car back in gear and cruised past the front again. Tapping his fingers on the steering wheel, he headed for his nineteenth-century Queen Anne house north of downtown.

He'd bought the home a couple of years ago after a major renovation had resulted in the replacement of the antiquated plumbing and electrical. Sitting on half an acre, the seven-thousand-square-foot home was way more space than he needed, but he loved the yard and the pair of one-bedroom apartments at the back of the property the previous owners had rented out. Ryan didn't need the hassle of tenants or the extra income, but he appreciated having additional space, separate from the main house, where he could put up out-of-town guests.

After parking in the three-car garage, Ryan made his way across the backyard and into his all-white, ultra-modern kitchen. Most people looking for a historical house would've been annoyed that the home's original character hadn't been maintained inside. Ryan appreciated the marble countertops, professional appliances and updated fixtures. The single nod to the home's age was the fireplace along one wall, painted white to blend in. For the rest of the home's styling, Ryan had chosen white for the walls to play up the original pine flooring and selected furniture pieces with clean lines and neutral tones and paired them with large abstract art pieces.

When visiting for the first time, people were struck by the contrast between the historic exterior and modern minimalist interior. Not everyone approved, but Ryan hadn't gotten to where he was by being swayed by other people's opinions.

He poured himself a drink and collapsed onto the couch in his living room with the TV remote in one hand and a crystal tumbler of bourbon in the other. He surfed the local news and stopped when he saw photos of his sister and Lyle Abernathy.

How long would it take for Abernathy to start stirring up trouble? His constituents had grown sick of his antics and he'd been facing a primary challenge in his home district that he was almost sure to lose. That's why he'd switched to Susannah's district. That he'd brought his dirty politics with him made Ryan grind his teeth.

He shut off the TV just as his cell rang.

"Nothing much came up during my initial search on Zoe Alston," Paul began, wasting little time on preliminaries.

"What does that mean?" Ryan asked, his suspicion intensifying at an equal pace with his disappointment. He'd counted on Zoe being as ordinary as she claimed.

"That she doesn't have any current social media presence or obvious electronic trail."

"So, she doesn't exist? Does that mean she gave us a false name?"

"Not false," Paul corrected. "She's recently divorced and back to using her maiden name."

"How recent?"

"A few days. The ink has barely had time to dry."

A powerful wave of relief blindsided Ryan, making him slightly light-headed. Her skittish behavior made a lot more sense. As did the reason why she'd been so reluctant to go out with him. She wasn't a spy, but someone who'd suffered a heartbreak. No doubt she wasn't ready to bare her soul to a stranger.

"Whom was she married to?" Ryan asked.

"Tristan Crosby."

"Sounds familiar." The name rang a faint bell, but Ryan couldn't recall where he'd heard it before.

"He runs Crosby Automotive. The family also owns Crosby Motorsports. The racing team."

A lightbulb went off in Ryan's mind. "Harrison Crosby drives for them."

"That's his younger brother."

So, Zoe's past was a lot more interesting than she'd admitted. And all her excuses about them being from vastly different worlds were a load of crap. Why not just explain that she wasn't ready to date and leave it at that? Why the fabrication?

The questions renewed Ryan's distrust.

"Can you do a background check on the owner of a store? Second Chance Treasures." Ryan gave Paul the address. "And maybe the person who owns the building, as well."

"Can I assume this is tied into your interest in Zoe Alston?"

"Yes. I can't explain why, but there's something up with her and I intend to get to the bottom of it."

"I'll see what I can find out." Paul paused a beat before adding, "You know not every woman has bad intentions."

Not every woman. But he wasn't about to drop his guards again unless he was sure he wouldn't get burned. If being overly suspicious kept his business, family and friends safe, then that's just the way it had to be.

"I…feel something for this one," he said, the confession coming from out of nowhere. "I just want to make sure she checks out."

"I get it." Paul's sober response mirrored Ryan's mood. "Give me a couple days to see what I can find out."

Stung by impatience, Ryan got to his feet. To hell with waiting a couple days for answers. No reason he couldn't do a little investigating of his own. He grabbed his keys and headed for his car. Too many questions swirled through his brain about Zoe Alston. There was no way he was getting any rest until he'd confronted her with what she'd not told him tonight.

Ryan noticed the uptick in his mood as he slid behind the wheel and recognized its origins. He was eager to see her again. Cursing, Ryan wondered if his sister had been right to warn him off. Obviously Zoe Alston was trouble. Perhaps not for Susannah's campaign, but definitely for his peace of mind.

Four

In the wake of her dinner with Ryan, Zoe had a hard time concentrating on the spreadsheet she'd created to chart her cash flow. Today's disastrous theft by Magnolia Fenton meant she had to figure out which bills she paid and which ones got pushed back a few weeks to a month. At the top of her priority list were the commission payments to the women who provided her inventory. They were counting on those dollars to feed and house their children.

Zoe rubbed her dry eyes and swallowed the bile that rose in her throat. She hated the wave of hopelessness that washed over her. Where could she possibly get more money? The obvious answer came from Ryan's suggestion that she talk to his sister. He was right that an event at the store would both benefit Susannah and bring awareness to Second Chance Treasures. She wished she knew how to overcome her reluctance to ask for help. Sure, she'd been burned in the past when she'd reached out, but Susannah wasn't at all like the women in her former social circle. She couldn't see Ryan's sister being nice to her face while stabbing her in the back.

When she picked up the cup of peppermint tea beside her laptop, Zoe noticed the black smudge of eye makeup on her hand and headed into the bathroom to wash her face. As she patted her skin dry, she scanned her features in the mirror, deciding without the dark makeup she looked younger than her twenty-nine years. At least until she met her reflected gaze and saw the weight of her experiences lingering in her eyes.

A knock sounded on the door that led from the stockroom to the parking lot, making Zoe's heart jump. A glance at her watch showed it was nearly ten at night. Who could possibly be stopping by at this late hour?

Many of the women she worked with knew Zoe's story and that she was living in the store's back room to save money. Opening up about her troubles hadn't been easy for Zoe. She'd spent nearly the whole of her marriage acting as if her life was perfect. But being authentic with these women was important for them and for her. As a result, Zoe was learning courage where she'd once feared. What she'd perceived as weakness and failure didn't have to define her.

With these thoughts lightening her steps, Zoe crossed to the door and opened it. The person standing outside wasn't at all whom she expected.

"What are you doing here?" Zoe asked, hoping her panic didn't show.

"I thought we should talk."

His gaze slid over her, rousing Zoe to the realization that her flowered loungewear and pink fuzzy slippers weren't in keeping with her badass chick persona.

"So you just show up here?" she demanded, outrage lending her the strength to stand her ground and glare at him when her instincts urged her to retreat. "And how did you know where to find me?"

"I followed you."

"You followed...?"

An overwhelming sense of anxiety pummeled her. Yet, even as she backed up a step and started to pull the door closed, she recognized that with his suspicions aroused, this man wouldn't trust her unless she gave him a chance to vent his doubts. Squashing her anxiety, she fell back and let him pass.

Ryan entered the back room, glancing around as he did so. Boxes filled with inventory occupied nearly a third of the wide room. A curtain divided the rest of the space into a staff break room and Zoe's office and living quarters. During the hours when the store was open, Zoe kept the curtain closed, but when she was alone, she tied it back. At the moment the cot she was sleeping on was visible.

"Are you sleeping here?" he asked, his hard gaze returning to her.

Shame sifted through her at her current circumstances. More than anything she'd like to be living like a normal person in a home with a proper kitchen and bathroom.

Instead of answering, she crossed her arms over her chest. "I have work to do. If you would quickly say whatever is on your mind, I can get back to it."

"Fine," he snapped, frowning. "Why didn't you tell me who you were?"

"I told you I'm—"

"Zoe Alston." He nodded. "What you didn't say is that you were formerly Zoe Crosby."

Zoe froze as horror filled her. He'd investigated her. The implications ricocheted through her mind, moving too fast for her to settle on any single reason to freak out. Did he know what she, Everly and London had been up to? Could he be there to threaten her? He hadn't hesitated to send Kelly Briggs to jail. What would he do to Zoe if he knew she'd intended to cause trouble for his sister?

"So I was married," she murmured, hating how exposed she felt at the moment. "It didn't work out." It got a little easier each time she admitted the failure. There was power in that. "What's the big deal?"

"The big deal is that you were acting odd."

"I wasn't." Or at least she'd been trying not to. The man made her nervous with his sharp mind and flagrant sex appeal.

"And you lied."

Lies of omission and of intent. Even so, she refused to apologize or to defend herself. Instead she let her stony expression speak for her.

When the silence stretched, Ryan continued. "You told Tonya you were crashing with a friend."

"Given everything that's happened to me in the last year, forgive me if I didn't feel much like bringing up all my dirty laundry."

"Did you really think anyone would care about your divorce?"

"In my experience, people are quick to judge. All I wanted to do was to help out someone I admired. Now you have to go and ruin that."

Bold words. She might have to follow through and quit the campaign to demonstrate her proclaimed level of outrage wasn't false. How was she supposed to mess up Susannah's campaign if that happened? Of course, there was always the possibility that Lyle Abernathy would succeed where Zoe failed and she could ride off into the sunset without the campaign's blood on her hands.

"Is that why you invited me to dinner?" she asked, feeling deflated. "So you could check me out?"

"No, I invited you out because I was attracted to you."

Pleasure short-circuited the steady rhythm of her breath. But she wondered if he still felt the same now that he'd seen her stripped of her makeup and the tough-girl clothes.

"I'm not your type," she said, returning to the same argument she'd used in the restaurant parking lot.

"How can you be so sure?" he asked, his eyes narrowing as he studied her.

"We might never have crossed paths at any of Charleston's social functions," she said, on safer ground now that they were talking about him, "but I've seen you out and about. Not to mention all the gossip surrounding the romantic intrigues of one of the city's most eligible bachelors." She gave him a cool smile. "I seem to recall you tend to favor leggy brunettes with blue eyes."

She had no idea if that was true, but enjoyed a stab of satisfaction when his brow wrinkled in surprise.

"I don't know if that's fully accurate." But obviously it was accurate enough.

To emphasize her point, Zoe ran her fingers through her short, spiky hair in a mocking salute. "I am neither brunette nor leggy. And my eyes are not blue."

"No, they are not. They remind me of autumn leaves."

To her dismay, he took a leisurely step in her direction, lowered his lashes and looked her over with predatory intent. Her pulse kicked into high gear when his gaze lingered on her lips and she had a hard time resisting the urge to nibble the lower one. The air in the room seemed suddenly supercharged with erotic energy and Zoe's nipples tightened in anticipation.

"I'm not interested in getting involved with you," she said, throwing up a warning hand even as she sensed that nothing she could do or say would stop the inevitability of their sexual chemistry.

"Then why did you agree to have dinner with me?"

Losing the battle against his magnetism, she replied, "My budget for dining out is extremely tight."

"Is that why you're living here?" Without taking his eyes from her, Ryan gestured with his head, indicating her cot.

She was abruptly bombarded by an image of them together on the narrow bed, his mouth on hers, his hands diving beneath her clothes, setting fire to her skin. As her blood pounded in her ears, she almost didn't hear Ryan's next question.

"Because you're out of money?"

"Not that it's any of your business," she began, irritated with herself for letting him get to her. "But between my extensive and contentious divorce and opening the boutique, I'm broke."

"You said you worked here," he reminded her. "But you actually own it?"

She nodded.

"That's why you spoke so passionately about the store during dinner."

She nodded again. "I've poured everything into Second Chance Treasures and we're starting to show a small profit, but not quite enough yet."

One dark eyebrow went up, but something akin to approval flickered in his gray eyes as he asked his next question.

"How long have you been living here?"

"Nearly six months. As my divorce dragged on, I gave up my apartment so I could pay the lease here." Zoe had no idea why she was pouring out her problems to Ryan, but it offered her some relief to share her troubles with someone.

"Are you waiting on a settlement?"

Zoe shook her head. "I barely received enough to pay my lawyer."

"Because you signed a prenuptial agreement?"

"That and according to Tristan's financial records, he's heavily mortgaged on every piece of property he owns. He maintains a lavish lifestyle." Her voice grew bitter. "Keeping his prize stable of polo ponies happy and healthy is very expensive."

"But—"

Zoe broke in. "Believe me, I hired the best lawyer I could afford and we looked at everything."

At least everything they knew to look at. Based on Tristan's spending, he had to have been hiding money somewhere. Yet tracing it had proved impossible.

Zoe's thoughts went back in time to that Beautiful Women Taking Charge event and the investigation London was doing on Zoe's behalf. A tiny portion of her held out hope that the event planner might just find something that Zoe could use to take Tristan back to court.

"Looks like you have a fair amount of money tied up in inventory." Ryan indicated the stacks of boxes before striding toward the door that led to the main part of the store.

"I mostly operate on a consignment basis." She trailed after Ryan, letting her fingers drift over the wall until they encountered the light switches. She flipped them on and the space was bathed in a soothing glow. "I buy outright from some of my artists because I want exclusive rights to their work, but most of what I sell I take a fifteen percent commission."

"Wouldn't you be better off owning the inventory?" he asked.

"Probably." Zoe straightened a rack of children's dresses made from organic cotton and nontoxic dyes. "But at first I couldn't afford to buy everything and the women make more by going the consignment route. Now, have I answered all your questions?"

"All but one."

"Fire away."

"Did you join Susannah's campaign on behalf of anyone connected to Lyle Abernathy?"

"What?" Surprise and relief flashed through her in rapid succession. "No. Of course not. Why would I work for Lyle Abernathy?" she asked, the truth coming easily. "I don't know the man. Or anyone connected to him."

Doubt was written all over Ryan's face.

"Look, I can see you don't believe me," she said. "And I will admit that I wasn't up front with you about my past. But if I'm guilty of concealing anything, it's who I am. Ending my marriage to Tristan caused a complete severing of every social tie I had. To the women I used to call friends, I am a pariah. Not one of them has reached out to me since I separated from Tristan."

Hurt gave her voice a quaver. She didn't try to control it. Appearing vulnerable would deflect Ryan's suspicions. Still, discovering that this bothered her surprised Zoe. Those women had never truly been her friends and she should be happy that she was free of their petty mischief.

"I was looking for a fresh start with people who wouldn't judge me based on a preconceived notion of who I was. So I changed my hair and bought some new clothes and joined your sister's campaign because I believe she's going to make a great state senator."

Through her tirade, Ryan remained silent, his expression unreadable.

"I won't apologize for following you here or checking you out," Ryan said. "This senate race is really important to my sister and I won't let anyone mess it up for her. So, if certain events have happened in the past year to make me suspicious as hell of people—"

"People?" she countered, interrupting him. "Or women?"

A muscle twitched in his cheek. "Look, I got burned because I didn't see certain signs," he admitted. But his candidness lasted no longer than a camera flash. "And I'll be damned if I let anything like that happen again."

"I can tell you exactly how to avoid any trouble with me." At his disgruntled snort, she set one hand on her hip and gestured with the other toward the back of the store. "You can walk right out of here and never bother me again."

* * *

After leaving Zoe, Ryan had headed home and spent several hours searching the internet for anything he could find on Zoe Crosby. There'd been less than he expected, but the few photos he'd found showed a slender woman with long, straight hair the color of caramel and a Mona Lisa smile. Tranquil and immediately forgettable, despite her beauty, she looked nothing like the spitfire standing before him in pastel floral pajamas and fuzzy slippers.

It struck him then that he didn't want to avoid the trouble she was likely to bring into his life. He wanted to wade right into danger and say to hell with consequences just so he could go on feeling the fierce emotions raging in him. He didn't trust her. He was convinced that much of what she'd told him tonight was grounded in truth, but not the entire story.

That his instincts continued to howl at him warned Ryan he should do as she suggested and never see her again. But his blood pulsed hot and fast through his veins, setting his entire body on fire. From their first encounter, he'd wanted her. Now that he had a better sense of who she was, the craving to slide his fingers over her naked skin was nearly painful in its intensity.

Ryan ground his teeth while his mind fought his body for control. Indulging his desire for her would be madness. Even if she hadn't joined the campaign as one of Abernathy's puppets, it was obvious that whatever she'd been through in the last year—maybe even her entire marriage— had left wounds that were far from healed.

He should just walk away. And in fact, he took several steps, intending to leave the store and never look back. But when he drew even with her, her tantalizing perfume tickled his nose, reminding him of the first time they'd met. With a sparkle of raspberry for sweetness and something peppery for heat and below it all a sensual layer of vanilla, her scent begged him to move in close and explore every inch of her skin.

"You're right. It would be better if I left and never came back," he said, cursing the insistent thrum of hunger that made him lean in. "But that doesn't stop me from wanting to do this."

He cupped her cheek, tilting her head and caught a flash of curiosity in her autumn-toned eyes before brushing his lips across her forehead. Her body went completely still and he was pretty sure she'd stopped breathing. His own breath grew unsteady as her hands came up and clutched at his shoulders, urging him ever so slightly closer. The sheer intensity of his need to kiss her messed with his head. What power did she possess that just holding her in his arms turned him on?

He dusted kisses over her cheeks, nose and jaw, testing his willpower. Tension vibrated in her muscles but she made no move to free herself. Ryan wrapped his arm a little tighter around her, drawing her slim curves more firmly into contact with his unyielding planes and, to his delight, her lips parted on a soft moan. This was his cue and he dipped his head, sealing his lips to hers.

Time didn't just slow. It stopped. Or maybe his heart had forgotten its primary responsibility was to keep him alive. Head spinning, he lost himself in the wet, delicious slide of their lips before flicking his tongue over a bit of peppermint toothpaste that she hadn't fully rinsed away at the corner of her lips. Setting his palm against her spine, he pulled her lower half into him, letting her feel the hard ridge of his growing erection.

Her lips parted on a luxurious sigh, granting him access to her sweet mouth while her body molded to his. Ryan sent his tongue questing forward, gliding over the ridge of her teeth, taking the time to learn every curve, every taste. Despite the increased tension in both their bodies, he concentrated on each new discovery. Rushing this first kiss would be a crime. Instead he intended to savor every slow, sexy second of it. To pay attention to each shiver that buffeted her slender form and learn what she liked.

Tunneling her fingers in his hair, she met the slow thrust of his tongue like a woman who hadn't been kissed in a long time. Like someone who craved tenderness and romance.

Ryan slid his hand over her hip and down her thigh, exploring muscle and sinew. Her thin frame had deceived him into thinking she was soft and delicate. Beneath her surface lurked power. The revelation excited him. And made him realize that once again he hadn't grasped the full story.

She looped her arms around his neck, pushed up on tiptoe. The move crushed her breasts against his chest and lightning stabbed through him. Ryan groaned, the carnal sound spurring her to nip at his lower lip with an impatient growl.

He needed no further encouragement. All thoughts of taking things slow vanished. Obviously she was feeling the same sort of insistent pressure. Running his fingers through her short hair, he cupped her head and tasted her a little more deeply. Hunger stormed his body as the kiss became harder, more intense. She wobbled and gave a little moan. He shifted his hold on her, taking a firmer grip, drawing her still tighter into the carnal interplay of lips and teeth and tongue.

Somewhere as if from a great distance came the buzz and trill that signaled he had a text message. Ryan's attention jerked toward the sound, making him aware of his surroundings, the danger inherent in his loss of control and the sheer joy of letting go.

He lifted his mouth from hers, marveling at the difficulty of such a simple task. He kept his lashes lowered as he listened to his erratic breathing and wondered how big a mistake kissing her had been. At long last he peered down at Zoe, grateful to note she was equally short of breath.

"You shouldn't have done that." Despite her words and her unhappy tone, she made no attempt to free herself from his embrace.

He had his own theories on why getting involved with her was a bad idea, but was curious about her opinion on the subject. "Why not?"

His question caused her to act.

She pulled his hands from her body and held them between them. Her fingers gripped his with surprising strength. "Have you forgotten why you showed up here tonight?" she countered.

"To accuse you of lying." Even as lust continued to rage through him, Ryan welcomed the cooling tenor of her words.

"And of being on Lyle Abernathy's team."

"So our relationship has gotten off to a rocky start," he teased.

"Relationship?" She released him and stepped back out of range. "Don't get ahead of yourself. My divorce was just finalized and the last thing I'm looking for is a new man in my life."

Despite what he'd learned about her tonight, his appetite for her remained strong. As long as he remained focused on the physical chemistry between them, he could see the benefit of pursing her sexually.

His lips slid into a half smile. "Haven't you heard about rebound relationships?"

"What makes you think I haven't already had one of those? I've been separated for nearly a year."

Ryan considered her for a long moment. "I don't think so."

"Why not?" She was frowning as she asked but curiosity flickered in her eyes.

"Because you're too uptight and at the same time a powder keg of unsatisfied desire." He reached out and brushed his knuckles across her cheek. To his delight, she tipped her head and pushed into the caress. Spying a softening of her resistance, he drove his point home. "I can help you with both."

Her eyes glowed with a dreamy light but her voice had a crisp edge as she asked, "So this is a simple offer of sex?"

"Not just sex. Great sex. Let me be the bridge between your past and future."

"My Mr. Right Now?" she murmured dryly.

He smirked. "Your Mr. Anytime You Want—Any Way You Want."

Hell, if she gave him the green light, he'd carry her to the cot in the back room and screw her brains out, probably breaking things in the process.

She spent a long time scrutinizing his expression. "Can I still work for your sister's campaign?"

Her shift in topic caught him off guard. "Ah —"

"You don't trust me." When he didn't immediately deny it, she shook her head. "I can't tell if you're trying to distract me with sex or if you're just horny and looking to hook up." She surveyed him for several long seconds. "Or maybe it's both. Did you seriously think I'd be so overwhelmed with lust for you that I'd toss aside things that are important to me?"

Ryan made sure not a trace of irony showed in his smirk. "It's happened before."

"No doubt." To her credit, she didn't seem all that outraged. With noticeable force she expelled the breath from her lungs. This seemed to bolster her already robust resolve. "I think it's great, the lengths you're willing to go for your sister, but I'm not sure she'd appreciate what you're trying to do here."

She made it sound like he was making a huge sacrifice.

"Do you think I only came here because I was worried for Susannah?" In truth, as excuses went, using concern for his sister's campaign to confront Zoe was as transparent as it got. "I'm interested in you. I have been since the moment we bumped into each other. Way before anyone was suspicious enough to wonder why you'd volunteered. Does it bother me that you withheld the truth? Yes. Do I trust you? No. But that isn't enough to keep me away."

Her eyes widened, but whether at his forthright admission or his intensity, Ryan couldn't tell. He saw doubt flash across her features and wanted badly to demonstrate once again the powerful attraction between them.

"Tell me you don't feel the sexual energy between us," he continued. "That we'd be tearing each other's clothes off and rolling around on the floor if we'd met under different circumstances."

She glanced down at the pine boards and frowned. "Look—"

"Be honest," he interrupted.

"Okay," she grumbled. "There's an attraction."

With her admission, something unraveled in his chest. Ryan recognized that, given his trust issues, he'd picked the absolute wrong woman to chase after, but at the moment it didn't matter as much as it should.

"But if I ran around sleeping with all the handsome single men in Charleston," Zoe continued, "my reputation would be worse than it is right now."

"Why do you care about your reputation?"

Her brown eyes took on a haunted look. "It's all I have left."

"You can say that even after what Tristan did to you during the divorce?" He'd just tipped his hand about how much he knew about her private life, but she didn't seem at all surprised.

"Now I see why it's your sister and not you who went

into politics." She turned aside and walked to the parking lot door. "Thank you for visiting. I hope you have a lovely rest of the evening."

Keeping her expression not just polite but sugar-sweet, she opened the door and the cool Charleston night air flooded the space, bringing with it the echo of distant church bells.

He moved toward her. She obviously expected him to do the gentlemanly thing and allow himself to be shown out without further protest, but what moved through Ryan whenever he was near her had no roots in Southern manners. Instead, as he drew even with her, he caught her wrist in a gentle but firm grip. Before she knew what he intended, he lifted her hand and deposited a sizzling kiss in her palm.

"Ryan," she murmured, but whether in protest or surrender he couldn't tell. She curved her fingers against his skin and sent a soft sigh winging into the night.

Her gaze lifted to his and the air around them contracted, encasing them in a bubble where no one else existed. Ryan wasn't sure how long they remained lost in each other before the sound of a car alarm several streets over brought them back to reality.

Reluctantly, Ryan let go of her hand. The instant he set her free, she set her fingers to her lips and tore her eyes from his.

"Sweet dreams, beautiful."

And with that, he stepped into the still night.

Five

With the insistent drumbeat of anger and frustration underlying every minute of every day, Everly Briggs had a hard time spending her free time having dinner with friends or reading the latest bestseller. How could she have fun when her sister sat in jail for something that wasn't her fault?

When Kelly had first been arrested, Everly had worked tirelessly to get her sister out of trouble. In the end, however, no amount of money or willpower could keep Kelly from going to jail. And as she'd been led off after being sentenced to serving two years, shocked devastation on her face, Everly understood that while she'd failed to save her baby sister, the real blame for what had happened belonged squarely on Ryan Dailey's shoulders.

Right then and there, as her sister's sobs filled the courtroom, Everly had determined she would do whatever it took to make him pay.

In the months following her sister's sentencing, Ryan Dailey had become her obsession. Everly had spent every free second plotting and planning. She'd researched every aspect of his life, including family and friends, spending long hours stalking him wherever he'd gone, learning his routines, contemplating all the ways she could ruin his life.

Almost immediately one thing became clear. As much as she hated to admit it, Ryan Dailey hadn't given her much to work with. Not only did his life appear impervious to meddling, his best friend was a cybersecurity specialist with friends in the Charleston PD and she didn't dare risk attacking him directly.

During the months between Kelly's arrest and her sentencing, Ryan had glimpsed Everly in the courtroom supporting her sister. Anything Everly might attempt that caused him or his sister harm would blow back in her face. That was when she'd come up with the idea of finding like-minded women with similar grievances to help her out.

Giving over control of Ryan Dailey's downfall to Zoe had been difficult, but necessary. Everly would not have chosen to partner with the former socialite. Zoe was too passive. Still, her pliancy made Zoe easy to manipulate and that was just as useful to Everly's drive for vengeance.

At the moment Everly was sitting in her car down the street from Second Chance Treasures, parked where she could see the door through which Ryan had entered the store. What was he doing visiting Zoe at this time of night? She'd been suspicious when they'd had dinner earlier, but from Zoe's tense body language as they'd said their goodbyes, the former socialite had looked uncomfortable with his interest.

Tonight when he'd showed up here, he'd been a man on a different sort of mission. His earlier flirtation had given way to anger. Everly wondered what had caused the change. Had Zoe somehow given their scheme away? If that was the case, Everly needed to formulate an alternate plan.

For days now she'd been following the political ramifications of Lyle Abernathy's entrance into the state senate race. It was well known that Abernathy was a snake. He'd stop at nothing to take down an opponent. Digging up dirt to throw Susannah Dailey-Kirby's campaign into chaos was something Everly had sent Zoe in to do. And if the pretty little former socialite couldn't handle her part? Maybe Everly could make do without her after all.

Everly was smiling over the variety of options available to her when the back door to Second Chance Treasures opened, silhouetting the couple and highlighting a disturbing tableau. Even from thirty feet away Everly recognized the chemistry that bubbled between the pair.

Rage clouded her vision for several thumping heartbeats. No. No. *No!* Ryan Dailey couldn't be allowed to seduce Zoe.

Zoe owed her allegiance to both Everly and London. Everly had ruined Linc's love life for London, who was close to securing Tristan's financial information for Zoe. Now it was up to Zoe to complete her part of the bargain.

It was imperative that Ryan Dailey be punished. Under no circumstances could he be allowed anything that might bring him joy. Especially not while Kelly was locked away because of him.

When a knock sounded on the back door less than five minutes after Ryan had left, Zoe almost didn't answer. In the wake of Ryan's kiss and the powerful emotions he'd roused in her, she was feeling shaky and raw. The idea that he might have returned for a second round of devastating kisses left Zoe filled with hope and dread.

From the moment she'd bumped into Ryan at Susannah's campaign headquarters, Zoe recognized that something about him called to her. Whether it was his knockout smile, powerful physique or the hint of wariness when he looked at her, the urge to take her clothes off and rub herself against his hard body couldn't be denied.

The knock turned to vigorous pounding and, with a

grudging sigh, she went to answer. With a *what now* expression firmly in place, she swung the door open. But to her surprise, her visitor wasn't Ryan. It was so much worse.

"Have you lost your mind?" Zoe demanded of Everly Briggs, dragging the woman into the store. Shutting the door, she rounded on her. "You aren't supposed to be here. We weren't ever supposed to communicate directly with each other again. Wasn't the whole point that we're strangers who can't be connected to each other?"

"Why was Ryan Dailey here? Are you sleeping with him?" From her narrowed eyes and accusatory tone, it was pretty obvious that Everly already believed it was the case. That she thought she had the right to demand answers fanned Zoe's temper.

"Am I sleeping with him?" After everything she'd been through tonight, this was the last straw. "What the hell are you talking about?"

"You two looked pretty cozy just now."

"What the hell, Everly?" Annoyance and apprehension battled for dominance as Zoe stared at the other woman. Not for the first time, Zoe wondered what sort of trouble she'd gotten herself into.

From their conversation at the Beautiful Women Taking Charge event Zoe had gathered that Everly had been distraught over what had happened to her sister. But they'd all been upset over their various problems. London's fiancé had given her no warning before breaking their engagement. Zoe was living through a nightmare divorce. And Everly's sister had recently gone to jail after destroying millions of dollars' worth of engineering plans.

But discovering that Everly was stalking her pushed all Zoe's buttons.

"Are you spying on me?" Zoe set her hands on her hips and gave Everly a disgusted look. "Because I really don't need to be dealing with that right now."

"No," Everly admitted. "I followed Ryan here."

With those four words Zoe recognized that Everly had issues that went far beyond her hurt and anger over what had happened to her sister.

"Why would you do that? He's not your problem, he's mine. Honestly, what is wrong with you?" Zoe exhaled harshly and started in again before Everly could answer any of Zoe's rapid-fire questions. "I've barely started to work on the campaign. Your presence here jeopardizes everything."

Zoe could see that Everly wasn't used to being on the receiving end of a scolding and that she didn't like it one bit. Well, that was too bad. What they were doing was delicate and risky. They'd come up with a plan and, if it was to work, each of them needed to follow protocol. That meant no direct contact.

"I'm here because I need to know what's going on," Everly explained.

"That may be what you *want*," Zoe fired back, "but it's not what you *need*." She had no patience for Everly's excuses. "What you *need* is for me to fulfill my part of the bargain. Whatever that takes. If it means joining Susannah's campaign or getting friendly with Ryan, then that's what I'll do." She was breathing hard as her anger rose. "Now here's what I need. I need for you to go and not come back. Ever."

While Everly's eyes never left Zoe, her expression made it clear she wasn't focused on Zoe's lecture. "Why did he kiss your hand?"

"Did you listen to what I just said to you?" Even if she thought Everly deserved an answer, Zoe refused to explain what had happened between her and Ryan when she hadn't yet made sense of it. "You need to leave my store. Now."

"Why are you in such a hurry to get rid of me?" Everly demanded. "Is he coming back?"

"Haven't you understood anything I've said?" Her righteous anger felt satisfying and powerful.

"I understand that you want me to go," Everly said, the fervent light in her eyes convincing Zoe that the woman was unbalanced. "But I'm not leaving until I'm satisfied with your answers."

"I don't owe you any explanations," Zoe responded even though she could see her words fell on deaf ears.

"That's where you're wrong. You do owe me. And you owe London. We're all in this together."

"Look, I didn't interfere with what you did to Linc or with London going after Tristan." That the latter scheme might still blow up terrified Zoe too much for her to risk showing any involvement. "You need to back off and let me handle this."

"Are you sleeping with him?"

"No."

"No not ever or no not yet?" Everly was a dog with a bone.

"Listen," Zoe said, nearing the end of her patience. "I'm playing him any way I can. Now I really need you to leave." She walked to the door and opened it.

When Everly didn't move, Zoe wondered if she'd have to get physical. As much as the idea of wrestling Everly out the door appealed to Zoe, neither one of them could afford the attention a catfight might attract.

"Fine," Everly snarled. "But I'm going to keep an eye on both of you. If for one second I think that you're betraying me, you're going to be sorry."

Zoe shivered at Everly's threat, recognizing the wisdom in treading carefully. Tristan had a temper like that. It burned slow and white-hot and, as she'd learned, with devastating results.

"I'm not going to betray you," Zoe said, "but you have to stay far away from me. Ryan knows who you are and if he sees us together, everything will be ruined."

"He won't see us together."

"You don't know that. He doesn't trust me," Zoe said in her most mild and reasonable tone. "That's why he came by tonight. To accuse me of lying to him and to find out if I'm a spy for Lyle Abernathy. It's possible that he's having me watched." Zoe doubted it was the case, but her words fed Everly's paranoia. Noting that Everly continued to hesitate, Zoe drove the point home. "After all, you're keeping tabs on him."

The wild light in Everly's eyes dimmed somewhat. "Okay, I see your point."

"Good. Now go home and get some sleep." Zoe gestured Everly out and, to her relief, the woman stepped into the parking lot. "I've got this handled."

Without answering, Everly marched toward the far side of the lot where a dark Audi sedan was parked.

Zoe sighed as she closed and locked the door.

For three days Ryan kept his distance from Zoe while he processed all he'd learned about her background. He avoided the campaign headquarters when he knew she was volunteering and resisted the temptation to stop into Second Chance Treasures to say hello.

But he couldn't stop his thoughts from lingering on the memory of their kiss or dwelling on the foolish longing to learn about her childhood and the sort of music she enjoyed.

Yesterday he'd sent her a text, reminding her about their Saturday night date. She'd tried to convince him to let her meet him at the restaurant where they were eating, but now that he knew where she lived, he intended to pick her up. If he told her they were eating at his place, he doubted she'd come. And she'd be right to resist. He intended to lull her with expensive wine and delicious food before encouraging her to spill all her secrets.

Ryan parked near the back door of Zoe's store and

glanced at the time. He was five minutes early. An uncomfortable anxiety gripped him as he exited the car and went to collect her. When was the last time going on a date with a woman had made him nervous? The answer disturbed him as much as the turmoil in his gut. Never. His reaction to Zoe was unique in his life.

Ryan knew part of his disquiet was based on a decision he'd made earlier that day. The wisdom of it utterly escaped him, but he was starting to realize that his behavior when it came to Zoe deviated from logic.

She answered the door casually dressed in a gray sweater and slim jeans. Her gaze roved over him; his jeans and white button-down shirt were similarly casual. She frowned.

"You look beautiful," he remarked, glad he'd shoved his hands into his pockets before she'd appeared. After being apart from her these last few days, the need to kiss her had grown stronger.

"Where are we headed?"

"It's a surprise."

"I don't like surprises."

"Not even good ones?"

She lapsed into silence and let him escort her to the passenger side of his car

The drive to his house took less than ten minutes. She looked relaxed and calm as he guided the car down King Street, but the minute he turned onto an obvious residential avenue, she sat straighter.

"Where are we going?"

"Dinner."

"Yes, but where?"

"My house." He glanced in her direction as he slowed and parked beside the curb. "A friend of mine planned a wonderful menu especially for us."

"This is yours?" She stared at the house. "Funny, you don't strike me as a Queen Anne."

"The inside is more modern." Suddenly he was eager to show it off.

She looked concerned. "Not too modern, I hope."

"You'll see."

The full tour took them nearly thirty minutes. Ryan paid careful attention to her every expression as she strolled through the rooms, missing none of the crown moldings or the wood inlays in the living-and dining-room floors. Her eyebrows rose as she assessed his minimalist styling, modern light fixtures and enormous upstairs bedrooms.

"Come outside and see the pool," he coaxed, drawing her onto the back porch.

"This is really beautiful back here. How big is the lot?"

"A quarter acre."

"That's big for downtown Charleston."

"Come this way. I have something else to show you." He led the way along the porch to the first of his guest apartments. "The previous owners created two one-bedroom units back here that they leased out. I use them when family or friends come from out of town." He opened the first door and gestured her inside.

"This is nice," Zoe commented, her gaze sweeping over the open galley kitchen, cozy navy sofa and high ceilings. "I imagine your guests enjoy the separate space."

"It's yours for as long as you need it."

"What?" She gaped at him.

"Most of the time the apartment is empty. I'd like for you to stay here until you can get back on your feet."

She made a series of faces as she thought it over but it was obvious she was tempted. At long last she sighed. "I can't."

"Why not?"

"Whatever you're charging, I can't afford it."

"I'm not charging you anything."

"But you don't know me. And may I remind you that

earlier this week you were accusing me of working for the opposition."

"I talked to Susannah and told her I believed you could be trusted."

The morning following their dinner at Bertha's Kitchen, he'd met with his sister and Gil, passing on everything that he'd learned. Susannah had been satisfied, but Gil hadn't been ready to give up so easily. Several run-ins with Abernathy over the years had left him very suspicious.

"What if I move in and get so comfortable I never move out?" Zoe continued, her arguments growing more desperate.

"I doubt you're going to do that."

"You don't know me," she repeated, but with less vigor this time.

"So, let's go have dinner and you can fill me in."

Ryan had no idea if she was giving his offer serious consideration as they settled in the dining room. His table was large enough to accommodate ten, but Ryan wanted a more intimate meal so he had set two places on one end. With the lights of his modern chandelier dimmed to romantic levels and candles flickering, the mood was intimate and relaxed.

"This is quite nice," Zoe commented vaguely, her expression unreadable as she sipped a chilled glass of crisp white wine and glanced around.

"Do I make you nervous?" he asked, sensing the ambience wasn't having its desired effect.

"Yes."

As much as he wanted to grill her, Ryan held silent, hoping she'd fill the emptiness with explanations.

"It's all a bit much, don't you think?"

He shook his head. "I'm not sure I understand what you mean."

"The offer to move into your house. The romantic dinner." She leaned back in her chair and regarded him. "I feel as if you're an advancing hurricane and I waited too long to evacuate."

"You need a place to stay. I have one. I like helping people."

"So your sister mentioned a few days ago." Zoe cocked her head. "She said you tried to help someone last year and it led to the trouble at your company."

Ryan's gut clenched and he gave a tight nod. "Kelly Briggs was a disturbed young woman."

"She cost you millions."

"Yes."

"And yet you don't know me at all and you're willing to help me out." Her eyes drilled into him as she searched for answers. "What if the same thing happens again?"

"Will it?"

Before she could answer, they were interrupted by the arrival of the first course delivered by Paul's cousin. Dallas Shaw had worked for several upscale Charleston restaurants over the years. She was currently a private chef looking for investors so she could open her own restaurant.

The redhead smiled as she set the plates down and began her presentation. "What I have for you to start is smoked salmon toast with petite arugula and cucumber salad. Enjoy."

"This looks wonderful," Zoe murmured, taking a bite, her eyes going wide with pleasure.

As he watched her savor the appetizer one delicate bite at a time, Ryan realized how much he wanted to make her happy. She'd obviously had a hard time in the last year, but instead of whining about it, she'd dug in and tried to improve her situation. His family valued hard work.

"Earlier you said you want to know more about me," Zoe said, her grim tone making her sound like a suspect sitting in an interrogation room. "Where should I start?"

"Wherever you wish."

Zoe waited until Dallas replaced the appetizer plates with a beet and pistachio salad before declaring, "Tristan accused me of infidelity as the reason he wanted a divorce."

Shock stabbed Ryan. "You cheated on your husband?"

Her lips twitched in amusement at his sharp reaction. "No, but Tristan made it look as if I had."

"How did he do that?"

"He paid someone to falsify a paper trail and doctor photos. You can make anything look real if you throw enough resources at it."

It struck Ryan then how cynical she was. And damaged. Her ex had done a number on her. Red flags began to flutter in his mind and he decided to ask Paul what he knew about Tristan Crosby.

"But in your case the truth won out," Ryan said.

Zoe's eyes reflected a deep and profound sadness as she said, "Sure, but this town is all about appearances and doubts will linger long after the real story comes out."

She wasn't wrong, and it irritated Ryan how often gossip trumped truth. His parents had emphasized fair play would take the twins farther than cutting corners or cheating. Because not everyone subscribed to the same lofty values, sometimes doing the right thing didn't mean you were going to win.

"A week from today there's a fund-raising dinner for Susannah at the Whitney Plantation," Ryan said. "I agreed to go, but I don't have a date."

"Do you need one?"

Ryan wondered if she was being deliberately obtuse. Didn't the woman realize he'd brought it up because he wanted her to accompany him?

"It gets old always being the third wheel around my sister and her husband," Ryan said. "They are the perfect couple."

"It must be terrible for you being the eligible bachelor all the time."

"You have no idea," Ryan told her. "Will you be my date for the evening?"

She gnawed on her lower lip as she gave the invitation some thought. "I haven't gone to any events where I might run into...people from my former life," she murmured, taking a sip of wine.

"It would be a great opportunity to promote your store," he said, hoping that would be enough to entice her. "And I'll be there to look out for you."

"It seems like I should say yes then," she replied with a slow smile.

"Good."

For the rest of the meal they stuck to easy topics like tourist attractions around Charleston neither one had visited and favorite area beaches. Ryan spoke about growing up as a twin and discovered Zoe had three older sisters who lived all over the country. Two were married with children and one worked on Wall Street.

He was finishing the last bit of chocolate hazelnut mousse when Zoe gave a huge sigh. Unsure what had prompted such a dramatic sound, Ryan glanced her way. To his surprise, her eyes were filled with tears.

"I'm really tired of sleeping in the back room of the store," she announced in a shaky voice.

"I imagine you are," he said, his heartbeat a hard thump against his ribs as he watched her dab at the corners of her eyes with her napkin. "Let's finish our wine and go get your stuff."

The limited number of things Zoe owned was brought home in a big way as Ryan regarded the two suitcases she rolled toward the back door of the shop.

"Is that everything?" he asked, making no effort to hide his surprise.

She hiked a large tote onto her shoulder and nodded. "I didn't take much when Tristan evicted me from our house on Daniel Island. If I'd been less shell-shocked, I might've grabbed more than just some essentials, two suitcases full of clothes and the few pieces of jewelry he let me take." As she spoke, her expression twisted with embarrassment and regret. "Everything was in his name. The cars. The house. My credit cards. I left the house the same way I'd arrived, owning nothing except what he'd given me." She paused a beat before finishing, "And what he gave, he could also take away."

That she continued to open up about things that had bothered her a great deal gave Ryan hope that she was feeling more comfortable with him by the moment. Hearing the pain in her voice helped him understand why she'd been so cagey about her past.

Moving her into the guest apartment took less than ten minutes. Sensing that she still needed some time to adjust to her new situation and surroundings, he left her to explore the space and returned to the main house.

As he was heading upstairs, Ryan noticed that Paul had tried to reach him while they'd been at the store and he called him back. "Hey," he said when his friend picked up. "What's up?"

He moved to the double window in the master bedroom that overlooked the backyard. The pool glowed a bright turquoise below.

"Sorry I haven't gotten back to you sooner about that store you wanted me to look into, but one of my cases heated up in the last few days."

"No problem," Ryan said, figuring he already knew what Paul had learned. "Were you able to find out anything interesting?"

"Zoe Alston owns Second Chance Treasures," Paul said, confirming what she'd already admitted. "The building is owned by Dillworth Properties."

"Dillworth Properties," Ryan repeated, the name a faint whisper in his memory. Something about it made him uneasy, but he couldn't place the reason. "Why does that sound familiar?"

"Because it's owned by George Dillworth."

Ryan cursed. "As in Lyle Abernathy's oldest and dearest friend."

"That's it. Also, I did a little checking. She's three months behind on her lease, but so far they haven't shown any signs of evicting her."

She'd mentioned having financial difficulties, but three months was a long time to go without paying rent.

"How much does she owe?" Ryan asked.

"Fifteen thousand."

He rubbed at his temples as a dull ache began to throb there. "That might be enough to make her desperate. It wouldn't surprise me if Abernathy took advantage of her situation."

"I was thinking the same thing."

Neither man spoke for a long moment, giving Ryan an opportunity to ponder how to handle this new revelation.

At last Paul spoke again. "What are you going to do?"

"I can't confront her about it. She won't appreciate that I'm still having her investigated."

"So what's left?"

Ryan hesitated a beat. "I'd already decided the best way to keep an eye on her was to stick as close as possible."

"How close is that?" Paul asked, his voice a blend of curiosity and amusement.

"I moved her into one of my guest apartments."

"That's awfully close. Are you sure it's a good idea?"

"Probably not, but she was sleeping in the back of her

store because she ran out of money." And Ryan was banking on proximity fanning the sparks between them into flame. "You know, if Abernathy is using her financial problems to put pressure on her to dig up dirt on Susannah, then maybe I can take away his leverage."

"And how do you plan to do that?"

"By making an anonymous payment to Dillworth Properties on behalf of her store."

"You know this is all speculation and there might not be anything going on," Paul pointed out, his level tone giving no hint of his opinion. "You could be throwing money away for no good reason."

Ryan considered that, but whatever Zoe was mixed up in, he had faith that when it came to the women she was trying to help, her heart was pure.

"I give to charity all the time," Ryan pointed out. "This is no different."

Except that this cause was acutely personal to him.

"And," he added, "we still don't know if she's at all connected to Abernathy."

"Do you want me to keep digging?"

"Thanks for the offer, but I think you've spent more than enough time indulging my paranoia."

Ryan hung up and considered what he'd just learned. Although the news brought back the demons of distrust, he realized that even though he still had questions about her motivations, his suspicions, potent though they might be, weren't enough to stop him from wanting her.

A voice in his head reminded him that he'd known Zoe for little more than a week, but a drumbeat of lust and longing held more sway. He felt a connection with her that outstripped anything he'd ever experienced before. He simply couldn't let her go until she'd worked her way out of his system. Whatever that took.

Six

For the last week, Zoe had been staying in Ryan's guest apartment. Each morning that she woke up in the king-size bed and shuffled into the open-concept kitchen, dining and living space with its high ceilings and heart-pine floors, the hardships of the last year faded a little more. And it wasn't just her new environment having a positive effect on her psyche, but also the amount of time she'd been spending with her handsome landlord that lent her optimism a gigantic boost.

The night after she'd moved in, he'd appeared at her door at six.

"Hungry?" he'd asked.

She'd gone out earlier and stocked her refrigerator, but hadn't decided on what to make for dinner. "I guess."

"I'm about to throw something on the barbecue," he said, not seeming at all put off by her ambivalence. "And I hate eating alone."

"Me, too."

Though she'd gotten used to it, being married to Tristan. He often worked late. Or at least that was the excuse he'd given on the nights he'd come home late smelling of perfume and red wine.

"I'll throw together a salad and come over."

That dinner became the first of many. Every night Ryan would stop by her door with an invite, sometimes still dressed in his tailored suits, other times in jeans and a T-shirt. Every night she said yes because being with him was so much fun. With Ryan she laughed and argued and felt utterly normal.

He possessed exactly what she needed to make the world go away. Or at least to enable her to forget all about it for a while. His smile kindled a glow in her chest. The glancing contact with his body as they worked side by side left her giddy and breathless. His fingers tantalized her skin as he caressed her cheek or held her hand. And when his lips closed over hers at the end of the evening, stealing her sighs and setting her blood on fire, she couldn't imagine being happier.

Tonight's dinner was different from the last few. Instead of fixing a meal together in Ryan's big, white kitchen, he was taking her on a double date with Susannah and Jefferson. Everything in her rebelled against getting in deeper with the Dailey siblings because the more time she spent with them, the harder it would be to do them harm. And she was starting to wonder if there was anything to dig up concerning Susannah or her campaign.

What if it was impossible to come up with something? That sure wouldn't make Everly happy and her erratic behavior the night Ryan had come by the store left Zoe convinced the woman might do something disastrous.

Pushing aside the problem of Everly's unwanted intervention for the moment, Zoe turned her attention to another bit of trouble. She picked up the envelope that had arrived in the mail today. For weeks now she'd been expecting something from the property management company telling her that she had to vacate. She was three months behind on the rent and it was only a matter of time before they kicked her out.

With a heavy sigh, Zoe slit open the envelope and pulled out the invoice from Dillworth Properties. She smoothed the sheet of paper and braced herself for the total at the bottom.

The number was zero.

How was that possible? She owed fifteen thousand dollars.

Zoe pulled out her phone and dialed the number of the management company. When the receptionist answered, she asked to speak to Tom Gossett.

"Tom, it's Zoe Alston," she began, her voice vibrating with anxiety. "I just received my monthly invoice and it looks like there's been a mistake."

"Oh?" Tom was in his midfifties and had a calm, methodical way about him. "How so?"

"It shows that I don't owe you any money when I'm sure that I'm three months behind."

"Well," he said, chuckling. "I'm pretty sure I've never had a tenant call to complain that they didn't owe us any money."

Zoe bit her lip, not finding the situation at all funny. "I don't understand what's going on. I know I haven't sent you any money."

"Well, someone did." The sound of computer keys clicking came over the phone. "I show a payment coming into our office two days ago."

"Are you sure it was for my store?"

"I have a copy of the cashier's check in your file. It says Second Chance Treasures on it. That's your store, right?"

"Yes." Zoe felt light-headed. Who could possibly have done something like that? "I can't believe this happened."

"Believe it. Is there anything else?"

"No. Thank you."

Zoe hung up the phone and clasped her shaking hands together. She didn't know whether to laugh or cry. On the one hand, the incredible gesture relieved a huge burden and left her feeling as if someone in this world cared about her well-being. It also meant she could move forward with a nearly clean slate. The store could stay open. She could continue her crusade to help victims of domestic violence. On the other hand, the fact that she'd needed to be bailed out filled her with shame and anger.

And the fact that the payment's origin was a mystery bothered her. Who knew exactly how much she owed? The answer struck her a second later. She'd mentioned to Ryan that she was behind on the rent, not so that he'd help, but because she'd grown comfortable enough with him that she'd begun to share some of her fears as well as her hopes.

Had Ryan made the anonymous payment? He'd already demonstrated his helpfulness when he'd given her a place to live rent-free. But offering an empty apartment was different from shelling money out of his pocket. And why hadn't he been upfront and offered her a loan? Because he knew she wouldn't have taken the money?

Instead he'd snuck around behind her back?

And done something incredibly nice.

Meanwhile she was plotting to destroy his sister. How could she blithely accept his help while actively working to cause him harm?

Ryan had texted to say he was running a bit late, giving Zoe even more time to stew and fret about confronting him. As the afternoon had worn on, she'd changed her mind a dozen times about how to approach the subject. Outrage and appreciation went hand in hand as she'd reimagined her budget, finding ways to economize so she could repay him.

But all her judicious statements vanished as she opened

her front door and spied him standing on the side porch, looking confident and authoritative in a blue-plaid blazer, gray slacks and white dress shirt. He looked relaxed, elegant and so happy to see her.

Zoe's heart clenched, driving tears of frustration to her eyes.

"Damn it, Ryan," she protested, wanting badly to feel either one way or another about him.

Angry. Happy. Hate. Love. Desire. Disgust.

Emotions swirled through her in a complicated tornado, moving too fast for her to latch onto just one.

"What's the matter?" He frowned in confusion. "I texted and told you I was going to be late."

"That's not the problem," she muttered, flashing the invoice she'd received from Dillworth Properties. "This is the problem. Did you do this?"

He took the paper from her and scanned it. "Looks like your rent is current. Congratulations."

"It's current because someone paid my rent for me. Was it you?"

For several heartbeats he looked as if he wasn't going to answer truthfully, but he must have recognized she'd already decided he was responsible and wouldn't let the matter drop.

"I know how worried you were about losing your lease and having to close the store."

Although she'd expected his confession, she was stunned. What was he thinking? Days earlier he'd regarded her with suspicion. Now he was bailing out her store?

She didn't ask him why he'd done it. His sympathetic expression illuminated his motives. He'd been trying to help her out. But the way he'd gone about it made her failure so much more acute. And how could she accept money from him when her purpose in getting close to him was to cause him and his sister harm? Contradictory forces tore at Zoe, making it hard for her to breathe.

"I'm going to pay you back every penny," she said, fighting to lift her voice above a whisper. "It's going to take me a while, but the store's doing better every single month."

"You don't have to pay me back," he replied, returning the invoice. "Consider it a donation to your cause."

Zoe's hands balled into fists. Admitting she couldn't afford to turn enough of a profit to support her dream roused her shame. Through their entire marriage, every time Tristan had given her money, she'd surrendered her independence and damaged her self-worth.

"Second Chance Treasures isn't a charity," she shot back, her pride rallying. "And neither am I."

"That's not at all what I thought." He caught her hand and gave a reassuring squeeze. "I just wanted to help out a friend."

Zoe fought the calm that filled her whenever he was around. She couldn't just let him soothe her concerns. "But you did it anonymously."

"So you didn't have to worry about paying me back."

"I can't just take your money," she countered, recognizing as much as she wanted to make it on her own, the awful truth was that she would've eventually been out on the street without his help.

"Are you really going to be this stubborn? If one of your friends had given you the money with no expectations of getting it back, would you be digging your heels in?"

What friends? The sardonic question was on the tip of her tongue, but she held it back.

"Please understand that being able to make it on my own is very important to me," she said quietly. "I appreciate your help, but I wish you'd offered me a loan or told me what you were going to do."

"My actions might have been a little heavy-handed. Susannah is often telling me that I run roughshod over people when I try to help." He pulled her forward and wrapped his arms around her. "What can I do to fix it? If you want, I can call Dillworth Properties and get my money back."

At his mocking tone, Zoe jabbed her knuckles into his ribs hard enough that he winced. "I spent some time looking at my books today and I think I can pay you back over the next six months."

Ryan stepped back and cupped her face in his hands. He lowered his lips to hers and kissed her with great energy, snatching her breath away and making her head spin. Lust surged and she gave herself over to it, even as he backed off before things heated up too much. Once again his control awakened her anxiety. Didn't he want to have sex with her?

Even as the question popped into her head, Zoe cringed. Not only had they only known each other a week, but there was this little matter of her role in the revenge bargain she'd made with Everly and London. But every moment in his company drove her libido into the red zone. She craved his hands on her and took every opportunity to bring her body into contact with his. Although she could see he recognized her not-so-subtle signals, he had yet to act.

She told herself to be grateful for his restraint even as she swooned against him, surrendering her mouth to the masterful pressure of his lips and sweep of his tongue. Moving forward into deeper intimacy with Ryan would only intensify her already complicated battle between what she wanted and what she'd promised to do.

Oblivious to her inner struggles, Ryan kissed his way toward her cheek to whisper in her ear. "Take a year if you need it." His statement ended in a grunt as her knuckles connected with his ribs a second time. "Okay. Okay. Six months is perfect," he amended, his tone teasing. "And I think ten percent interest should be just about right." He caught her hand before she could strike again and dusted a kiss across her knuckles. "You know I'm kidding about the interest, right?"

She nodded, her throat tight with overwhelming gratitude at the easing of her immediate financial concerns.

"Good." He smiled down at her. "Now, we're going to be late for our reservation if we don't get going."

"Enough stories about my ill-spent youth," Ryan groused fondly, interrupting his sister and Zoe, who were laughing at his expense. "Talk to Susannah about your store and all the women you're helping."

With a glance his way, Susannah sobered. "Ryan mentioned you had a boutique in downtown Charleston that is doing great work with victims of domestic violence. He said they make things that you sell."

Zoe's eyes glowed as she launched into her story. Watching her friendship with his sister develop over cocktails and crab cakes was exactly what Ryan had hoped for this evening. Susannah was such a huge part of his life and her approval was more than important. It was imperative.

His perspective had shifted over the last week while he'd gotten to know Zoe better. Moving her into his guest apartment meant that he was no longer thinking of her in terms of someone he intended to hook up with and move on. He enjoyed having her around. The more time they spent together, the more she opened up, and he was discovering she suited him quite well.

Standing in the way of that were his seesawing concerns whether or not she was a spy for Lyle Abernathy. Which demonstrated that he didn't fully trust her. Nor was he sure what it would take until she was completely above suspicion. It frustrated him that he couldn't move their relationship forward while his first thought was to question her motives.

When they'd arrived at the table, they'd settled in with

the women on one side and the men on the other. The seating arrangement and the way the women took to each other had made it challenging for the men to stay engaged in their conversation. Now, with Zoe and Susannah engrossed in a discussion about Second Chance Treasures, Ryan glanced toward his brother-in-law and found him texting.

"So, Jefferson, how're things going with you?"

The innocuous question startled his brother-in-law into slamming his phone facedown on the table and snatching up his drink. A flush crept up his neck as he answered.

"You know. Business is good. Family is fine."

Ryan eyed Jefferson and wondered why the guy was so jumpy. "How is it with Susannah on the campaign trail? I suppose you're busier than ever with the kids' activities."

"That's for sure." From beside his plate came a buzzing sound and Jefferson's gaze shot to his phone. "Between Violet's dance lessons and Casey's soccer games, it feels like all we do is run."

The buzz came again. And a muscle in Jefferson's jaw worked.

"Sounds like someone is eager to get hold of you," Ryan commented, wondering why his brother-in-law seemed so on edge. "Go ahead and answer if you need to."

"It's fine."

A third buzz sounded and a thin layer of sweat formed on Jefferson's brow. "Ah, maybe I'll just step outside and see what's going on. My mom's trying to coordinate Thanksgiving dinner with my sister and her family…" Trailing off, he snagged his phone and got to his feet. "I'll be back in a couple minutes."

Ryan watched him go with a sense of uneasiness before his attention was caught by the women's conversation across the table.

"I'll talk to Gil to make sure we can fit it in the schedule, but I think it would be a great idea," Susannah said.

"What would?" Ryan interjected.

"Susannah is going to come talk at one of our Wednesday night events at the store."

"See," Ryan said to Zoe, "I knew my sister would be interested in helping you out."

"We're helping out each other," his sister corrected, her gaze lingering on Jefferson's empty seat. "Does anyone want this last shrimp? Otherwise I'm going to eat it."

After dinner the two couples parted ways with Susannah insisting they needed to head home to relieve the babysitter. Ryan was happy to cut the evening short. He was interested in some alone time with Zoe.

"That was more fun than I expected," she said on the way to his house. "Your sister is very different away from the campaign."

"Susannah has two personalities. Private and public. It's grown even more pronounced since she decided to run for office. Tonight you saw little of the mischief-maker I grew up with. She can be pretty unrestrained at home."

"I enjoyed hearing stories about you growing up."

"I assure you only ten percent of what she told you was true."

"Only ten percent?" Doubt salted Zoe's voice. "I'd guess more like fifty or sixty percent."

"Notice I didn't return the favor," Ryan muttered as he pulled into his garage. "I have stories about my sister that would change your opinion of her."

"You showed great restraint," Zoe replied.

"Do you want to come in for a while?" Ryan reached out and ran his fingers lightly over her knee. "It's too early to call it a night."

Her voice was a little breathless as she answered. "Sure."

As they walked hand-in-hand along the side porch, Ryan's anticipation reached a feverish point. He barely managed to close the back door before he backed her up against his kitchen wall.

"I can't wait any longer," he murmured, bracing his arm beside her head so he could lean in. "I have to kiss you."

"Just kiss?" she murmured, peering at him from beneath her long lashes.

When surprise made him slow to respond, hot color flooded her cheeks.

"Do you want to do more?" he asked, his voice thick and dark with hunger.

Her hands coasted around his waist and up his back. "That's been my hope for days now."

"How much more?"

She lifted on tiptoe and pressed her lips to his ear. "I want to get naked with you," she whispered, her breath sliding over his skin.

He groaned. "Baby, you have no idea how good it is to hear you say that."

She gasped in surprise when he scooped her off her feet and carried her into the living room. He lowered her to the couch before settling his weight onto her. She stretched beneath him and gave a sexy little murmur that lit up his body like a fireworks finale.

Cupping her cheek, he brushed his thumb over her full lower lip. He wanted to make what came next good for her. That meant taking things slow and making sure their love-making offered mutual combustion.

"Zoe," he whispered, his heart racing as she clutched his shoulders.

"Yes, Ryan?"

"I'm gonna make this really good for you."

Her smile was like dawn breaking over Charleston Harbor. "You know you don't need to worry about me."

He blinked. Had she actually just said that? "Baby, you can't stop me from putting your needs first."

At his declaration, she glanced away, but not before he spied a glint of moisture in her eyes.

"Thank you."

His chest tightened. Such simple words, but her tone was poignant with surprise and relief. The urge to find her ex-husband and punch the living crap out of him burned in his gut.

Ryan drew in a long, slow, steady breath and pushed all thoughts of anger or violence to the back of his mind.

Her fingers slid into his hair as he dropped his head and lowered his lips to hers. He wanted to start slow and let the passion build at a measured pace, but her hands skimmed over his shoulder and ribs, fingers digging into his skin as her lips parted and a hungry moan erupted from her throat.

Suddenly, holding back was beyond his control. His desire for her had been building since the moment she'd bumped into him at Susannah's campaign office.

Ryan swept his tongue around hers, deepening the kiss, reveling in the raw hunger with which she kissed him back. In that moment he knew he could never get enough of her. Of the give-and-take between them. Of her passion. Her taste. The way her nails dug into his back and her teeth nipped at his lower lip.

For several seconds her ferocity surprised him. There was always something so reserved and guarded about the way she spoke and moved. Who would've guessed all this unruliness bubbled beneath her watchful eyes and careful expressions?

"Tell me what you like," she whispered.

"How about I show you instead."

Seven

Ryan's words sent a cascade of happiness through Zoe. For days she'd been imagining this moment, but nothing she'd dreamed up had come close to the thrill of Ryan's hard body pressing her into the cushions. She bent her knee and the fabric of his slacks scraped against her sensitive inner thigh. Every nerve ending cried out for the touch of his skin on hers.

She'd worn her sexiest underwear tonight and a wrap dress that came undone with a simple tug. She hadn't wanted buttons or zippers to get in the way of his hands finding her naked flesh. Unfortunately, with his weight bearing down on her, she couldn't get free of her clothes. The frustration made her groan.

"You smell delicious," he murmured, trailing soft kisses down her neck. "It was the second thing I noticed about you."

"What was the first?" she asked.

"Your eyes," he told her. "They were the most amazing color I'd ever seen."

"I noticed that your hands were strong and also gentle.

It made me wonder what it would be like to have them all over my body."

Setting her foot on the couch, she shifted her position until he slid into the V between her thighs. He was now in a much better position for her to get some relief from the ache pulsing between her legs.

She bumped her hips against his, rocking the most sensitive part of her against the hard ridge straining his zipper. The move caused him to release a husky groan. He slid his hand over her butt, pulling her hard against him.

"Do that again," he commanded, his fingertip skimming beneath her silk panties.

This time when she repeated the move, she gave her hips a little twist and his fingers grazed close enough to where she so desperately craved his touch that she whimpered.

She slid her fingers into his hair and imagined all the sexy, dirty things she was going to do to him. Sex with Tristan hadn't always been about romance or even passion. Sometimes she'd felt anonymous beneath him. Especially when he'd flip her onto her stomach and take her from behind. At that moment she could've been anyone to him. It hadn't occurred to her at first. She'd been a virgin on her wedding night, having never experimented with boys her own age. Which meant that a man who was eleven years her senior, with a lot more life experience, could convince her that whatever he told her was the truth.

And it wasn't as if she had friends she could reach out to about the subject. She'd run with a similarly sheltered group of women who'd pledged virginity until marriage. Nor could she speak to her mother about such a subject. Helena Alston was a soft-spoken, Southern gentlewoman who would be scandalized to discuss such private bedroom matters.

Later, when Zoe had established herself in society and gained some confidence, she'd realized that asking questions of her peers about their intimate moments would only point out her naïveté and open her up to ridicule. Since maintaining appearances was so important to Tristan, she'd hesitated to say or to do anything that might leave anyone questioning his ability to satisfy a woman in bed.

One thing he had done was teach her how to please a man, something she was about to demonstrate to Ryan. Even more, possibly for the first time ever, she wanted to give pleasure. And Ryan was the target of all those persistent impulses.

Her heart was pattering way too fast and none too steadily. What if she couldn't please him? Almost as soon as the thought speared her mind, she felt strong fear dig in.

"Look," Ryan began, obviously reading uncertainty in her hesitation. He ran his thumb over her cheek. "We don't have to do this."

Oh, hell no. He wasn't getting away that easily.

"I need to do this," she explained, her focus centered on the hard bulge pressed against her.

"'Need'?" he repeated, his voice reflecting concern. "You don't need to do anything. Let me take care of you."

He lifted his hand and ran the tips of his fingers over her cheek. The tender gesture made tears spring to her eyes. Talk about a mood killer. Crying a bucket of tears onto a man's erection wasn't exactly sexy.

"I...*want* to do this." She stressed the second word, making herself sound powerful and confident. And it was the truth. "Kiss me," she begged, loving that he knew exactly what she liked best. Hard and soft. Tender and hungry. In his arms her senses came alive and she adored every second.

"My pleasure."

As his mouth settled over hers, she crushed her lips to his. This man turned her on and she wanted him to know it. A deep, sexy rumble of pleasure sounded from his throat.

He curved his fingers over her waist and rode the bumps of her ribs to her breast. As his palm covered her, she whimpered with joy.

"You are so beautiful," he murmured against her neck, his teeth raking across her throat. "I can't get enough of you."

Zoe gripped his hair and gave a sharp yelp as he tweaked her nipple through her clothing. She saw his half smile as he lowered his mouth to her breast. As her blood pounded in her ears, she almost missed his appreciative groan when her nipple tightened against his tongue.

A curse slipped from her lips. The sensation of his mouth on her breast was blunted by the fabric that separated them.

"This isn't working," she protested, tugging at his hair.

He lifted his head and gave her a wicked smile. "Could've fooled me."

"We're both wearing too many clothes."

"I know." But he didn't seem immediately inclined to tear her clothes off.

His mouth drifted across her chest to her other breast and her thoughts turned to ash as a jolt of pure lust blasted through her. He hooked his fingers in her neckline and pulled both her dress and bra aside so he could flick his tongue over her nipple.

"Oh, yes," she murmured, a cry lodging in her throat as fire swept through her. "So good."

She held him against her as he plied her with lips, teeth and tongue. Meanwhile the insistent drumbeat of hunger grew louder and faster. She was burning up and gyrating beneath him on the couch wasn't getting her anywhere near where she wanted to go.

"Take me upstairs," she demanded, pushing her hips into his hand as he eased his way down her body until his shoulders shifted between her knees, pushing them wider.

He dragged his finger over her panties and cursed. "You're so wet."

She squeaked something incoherent as he pressed a kiss over her clit. White-hot lightning shot through her, leaving Zoe panting and trembling.

"And so gorgeous," Ryan continued. "I love the way you smell and can't wait to find out how you taste."

His words were almost as arousing as the firm grip he took on her panties. With a sudden tug, he shifted them off her hips and down her legs. The damp fabric hadn't done much to shield her most intimate self, but as he stripped away the silk underwear, Zoe's sudden exposure made her tremble.

With her underwear no longer a barrier between them, Ryan lay between her thighs and slid a finger along the landing strip that led to the heart of her. While her body vibrated with sharp longing, he seemed content to slow down and take his time.

Zoe closed her eyes as he grazed his fingers along the folds that hid her sex from him. As he dipped ever so delicately into her slick heat, she arched into his touch. Was he toying with her? Did he want her to beg? Because she was ready to say whatever he wanted to hear if only he would make the ache go away.

"Please," she pleaded, nearly incoherent as he continued his gentle exploration. "I need more."

"My tongue?"

Now he was understanding her. "Yes," she breathed, light-headed with relief. "I need your mouth on me. Now!"

"Like this?"

He flicked his tongue against her swollen clit and the noise that erupted out of her was like a mad keen. The pleasure felt so intense and perfect.

"Oh, yes! More like that."

His deep chuckle echoed through her body, intensifying

the hum of anticipation flowing through her. He sounded so pleased with her answer that despite the tension locked in her muscles, she felt a sudden rush of joy. In that instant she knew it was going to be good between them. Better than she'd ever known. Ryan was going to take care of her.

Gratitude made her heart clench, but she barely had a chance to register the emotion because a second later the only thing she knew was a white-hot blaze of desire as Ryan spread her legs wider and sent his tongue into her heat.

In an instant she was lost. In the man. In her need. In their desire as she rocked her hips and groaned his name. Distantly she heard her name as well as some deliciously erotic murmurings from Ryan's lips.

He made her feel sexy. Letting go during sex was about trusting her partner enough to be vulnerable and for most of her marriage Zoe hadn't known what to expect from her husband. Ryan was a completely different story and her body reacted accordingly. Pleasure coiled tighter and tighter inside her so fast she barely recognized what was happening until she felt herself start to unravel.

"Ryan. Oh, Ryan." Then she made incoherent noises as a million tiny stars burst into life behind her eyelids.

Shockwaves rolled over her, each one smashing her safe-guards and leaving her trembling and overwhelmed. It was all too good. Too perfect. Too much. Tears poured down her cheeks and she threw her arm across her eyes to hide them. Surely no man who'd just given a woman such an explosive orgasm would want to see her bawling in the aftermath.

"That was incredible," she told him, the hitch in her voice betraying her emotion.

"I'll say." Ryan eased up her body and trailed kisses along her neck. "I've never known anyone who comes the way you do. I'm going to take you upstairs and get you naked. Then you're going to do that all over again. And again."

Zoe lifted her arm off her face and looked at Ryan. His gray eyes had an earnest glow that made her heart skip a beat.

"Sound good?" he prompted.

She nodded. "Really good."

Laughter and panting bounced off the walls of the wide staircase as they raced to his second-floor master suite. Usually, Ryan would've had the advantage with his longer legs, but they were stripping off their clothes as they ascended and Zoe's dress and bra seemed to fall off her body with very little effort while Ryan fumbled with his clothes.

Then, too, he was slowed by the glorious sight of her nakedness as she crooked her finger and lured him after her. After shedding his shirt and tie, he wrestled off his socks and nearly tripped over his pants. Sucking in a giant breath, he turned the corner and entered his bedroom.

Ryan came to a dead stop at the sight of Zoe standing near the window overlooking the garden. She'd draped herself in the curtain and the challenge on her face told him she expected to be unwrapped in spectacular fashion. Putting on a mock scowl, he stalked toward her.

"You said you wanted to get me naked," she reminded him, clinging to the fabric. "I got you partway there."

Grinning, Ryan plucked the curtain from her grip. "Thank you for that," he said. "But now I want to see all of you."

He took her by the hand and twirled her. Zoe was all lean, hard muscle and athletic curves. Her breasts were small, but the round shape was perfect and he couldn't wait to get his mouth on them again.

"You are gorgeous," he declared, lifting her into his arms and carrying her to his bed.

"So are you," she murmured, her fingers tunneling into his hair.

He followed her onto the mattress, taking her nipple into his mouth and rolling his tongue around the plump tip until it became a hard bud. Zoe's husky moan filled his ears, making him smile as he repeated the move with her other breast. He kept his fingers skimming over her face, her torso, her thighs, wanting to return her to the keen state of arousal that had led to her explosive climax earlier.

He trailed his lips over her shoulder and breasts one last time before reclaiming her mouth in a kiss. Curving his fingers around the back of her head, he drove his mouth against hers, devouring her while encouraging noises erupted from her throat, urging him on.

She spread her legs and slid her hands over his hips, urging him between her thighs. He hooked his fingers behind her knee and lifted it toward his waist, opening her. The move allowed him to settle his erection against her wet heat. He groaned as the pressure drove his lust higher, and then he was grinding against her and she rocked in frenzied movements, moaning and arching her back.

Incoherent thoughts swam through Ryan's head as his mouth fell to her throat and his teeth sought for purchase against her skin. The light nip he gave her caused her hips to buck. He met the move with a deep thrust, letting her incredible wetness soak the fly of his boxers.

"I promised myself I'd take it slow," he growled, warning her that he was more than a little out of control. "But I just can't wait to be inside you."

"I need that, too."

"It's going to be amazing. I promise—"

She sent both hands diving under the waistband of his boxers and dug her nails into his butt muscles just as he thrust into her again. His hips jerked forward, bumping him against her with more force than he intended. To his surprise she matched his fierce charge with a roughness that send an electric surge of pleasure down his spine.

It took him a second to realize she'd tugged his underwear down. But when the fabric hooked on his erection and she began to tug frantically, he came to his senses and eased her hands away before she damaged him beyond saving.

"Wait," he murmured. "I need to get a condom."

"Hurry."

If every atom in his body wasn't focused on what was to come, he might have smiled at her eagerness. Instead he concentrated all his energy on digging a foil packet out of his nightstand, tearing it open and rolling the condom onto his erection with hands that shook.

While he'd been so occupied, she hadn't been idle. She'd thrown off the comforter and top sheet, leaving nothing on the bed to interfere with their lovemaking. Now, as he stood beside the bed, his shaft pointing directly at her, she reclined on her elbows. Offering him a small, satisfied smile, she parted her legs and let him drink his fill of the lush, rosy perfection that awaited him between her thighs.

With a shaky exhale, Ryan moved over her and rubbed the tip of his erection against her. Her head fell back and she moaned greedily. The glorious sound made him smile. He pushed a little way in and the wet slide into her tight heat made him shudder with pleasure.

"That's it," she moaned, her entire body vibrating as he slid deeper.

Her fingers curved into his back, nails digging. The sharp pain zinged along his already overwhelmed nerve endings as he pulled back and drove forward again.

"Like that?" he asked.

"Perfect." She purred the word, her eyes slipping shut.

"This is just the beginning," he promised her. "Don't hold back."

"Never."

And she didn't. She cried out at every thrust, giving herself over to him. It was a beautiful thing to watch as her earlier wildness became fierce demand. She rode her desire for dear life, claiming her pleasure without reservation. Equal parts awe and pride suffused him at the exquisite focus on her face.

Ryan slid his hand over her hip and drove into her harder. She moaned his name and he tried to form words to convey how he felt about her. What being inside her did to him.

"I need to come with you inside me," she moaned, her husky voice rasping pleasantly against his raw nerve endings. "Make me come, Ryan."

Her command echoed his need. Although he'd already given her one orgasm tonight, sharing a second one with her became his top priority. But already he was closer to finishing than he wanted to be. Being inside her short-circuited his willpower. He was too close to the edge. And he needed her to be there with him.

He shifted his hips and thrust into her at a different angle. She clutched him hard and the noises she'd been making morphed into something eager and frantic. Cracks appeared in the dam holding back his pleasure. He clenched his teeth, unsure how much longer he could keep his release at bay.

The need to connect with her overwhelmed him. He opened his eyes and looked down at her. Lust blasted through him when he realized she was watching him. Their gazes tangled and locked. Something tore loose in Ryan's chest as he realized he was exactly where he wanted to be. Not just buried deep in Zoe. But with her in this moment, watching her slowly shatter beneath him.

An electric, dangerous emotion sizzled down his spine and tightened his gut, then he felt nothing but searing heat and pounding heart and endless desire.

"Come with me, baby," he urged while all the stars in the sky blazed to life in his mind. "Please. Come with me."

But she needed no urging. She moaned his name, shock

plain on her features. A shudder racked her torso as her breath came in ragged pants. They tumbled over the edge together and for what seemed like minutes Ryan shook with pleasure as his orgasm shocked his system over and over.

His muscles failed him and Ryan dropped onto his elbows, somehow managing at the last second to spare Zoe the full crush of his weight.

A curse rattled through his unsettled thoughts. What the hell had just happened?

"That was absolutely amazing," she declared unsteadily, her fingers gliding over his shoulder. "You are a wonder."

He was a wonder? Did she have any idea what she had just done to him?

Ryan rolled them across the mattress until she lay sprawled in languorous repose atop his chest. Tangling his fingers in her hair, he tugged until she met his gaze. The contact was brief and unsatisfying.

"You're magnificent."

Even as he spoke, the description struck him as less than satisfactory after what had just happened between them, and he was surprised when she winced away from the compliment.

"I've never known…" She trailed off without finishing her thought. "I didn't know."

"Didn't know what?"

Her fingertips created swirls on his sweat-dampened shoulders. He watched her face, trying to read her expression and guess at her thoughts. It turned out he didn't yet know her as well as he hoped because he had no idea what was behind her pensiveness.

"Until now I've only ever been with one man."

That one man being her husband. Ryan didn't respond and shifted his gaze to the ceiling, giving her space to share and work through what was on her mind.

"I suppose in this day and age that seems very backward," she continued in a rueful tone.

Once again she was making assumptions about his opinions. Why did she always believe that her choices were the wrong ones?

"Not necessarily." Ryan dusted his fingers down her spine. "You were young when you got married."

"Not that young. I was twenty. Lots of girls have sex in high school."

"Not everyone is ready to take that step so early."

"I don't know if I was or wasn't. Boys didn't notice me. I was too quiet. Utterly forgettable."

"Now *that* I don't believe."

If he'd met her at seventeen would he have been equally blind? Probably. Only a mature man could appreciate a woman with complex layers. Had that been the case with her ex-husband? There had been a ten-year age gap between them. Yet from everything Zoe had—and hadn't—said about her ex, it didn't sound like the man had wanted to cherish, only to control.

"It's true. I was pretty socially awkward. I still am. As Tristan's wife I learned to handle myself in public, saying all the right things, joining the right groups, making the right friends." Bitterness gave her voice a sharp edge. "I lost sight of who I was."

"I think most people wear some sort of façade in public," he said. "We want to fit in and be liked."

"You don't do that."

His tone was firm as he said, "We all do it."

"Until I met you I'd forgotten how nice it was to speak my mind and not worry about the consequences."

Consequences? Ryan frowned. What sort of cost had she endured just because she'd voice her opinion? His chest tight with emotion, Ryan wrapped his arms around her and buried his face in her neck.

Playing the part of Zoe's hero might lead him down a dangerous road. The last time he'd tried to rescue a damsel in distress it had backfired spectacularly. Yet tonight he'd embarked on a journey. A first step back to trust. And Ryan couldn't bring himself to slow down.

Eight

Zoe caught herself humming as she worked on the books in her "office" in the back room of Second Chance Treasures. For the first time since she'd signed the lease, Zoe glimpsed light at the end of the tunnel and knew they were going to be okay. The relief made her feel lighter than air.

Or maybe her positive outlook had more to do with Ryan

After being married to Tristan for eight years, she was cynical enough to attribute her happy glow to all the fantastic sex she and Ryan were having, but deep down she acknowledged there was more to it. She enjoyed hanging out and talking with Ryan. And the man actually listened while she went on and on about her hopes for the store and the challenges of helping victims of domestic abuse. He didn't shy away from her need to vent and Zoe valued that as much as she did his glorious kisses.

"Here's the mail," Jessica said, setting a stack of envelopes on the desk and startling Zoe out of her musing. "Is it okay if I head to lunch in ten minutes?"

"Sure." She realized it was nearly noon. She saved the

spreadsheet she'd been working on and closed her laptop. "I'll just go through the mail real quick, and then come up front."

"No hurry. The morning rush has mostly cleared out and Eva mastered the register really fast."

With the store's desperate and immediate financial pressures eased somewhat, Zoe had hired Eva to replace Magnolia. Like Jessica, Eva had a school-age child, a daughter with her mother's blond hair and big brown eyes. She had a neighbor who could watch the little girl on Saturdays so Eva could pick up some extra hours at the store.

In the wake of the theft, Zoe had pondered what to do about reporting the stolen money. After much soul searching, she'd chosen not to pursue legal action. Magnolia had never struck her as a thief. If she needed the money that badly, her situation must have been desperate. And Zoe was all too familiar with how that felt.

Besides, the way traffic continued to increase over the last couple of weeks, the store was in a much better situation. She might be able to bring on even more help. The irony wasn't lost on Zoe. None of this would be possible without Ryan and Susannah's support. Zoe had wormed her way into the candidate's orbit so she could dig up dirt. Instead she'd been helped by Susannah working her connections to bring Second Chance Treasures to the attention of other well-meaning socialites. The word-of-mouth advertising had brought women in, but it was the quality of the inventory that encouraged them to pull out their wallets.

It seemed as if ever since she'd set foot in Susannah's campaign headquarters, her financial and emotional situations had taken a positive turn thanks to the Dailey siblings. And how was she responding to their kindness? With betrayal and lies.

Hundreds of times a day she sought a way out of her pledge to harm Susannah, knowing that Everly wouldn't listen to any of Zoe's pleas to escape their revenge bargain. Everly was determined to have her pound of flesh and expected Zoe to serve it up on a silver platter.

Plagued by gut-churning anxiety, Zoe made quick work of sorting the mail. Most of it was advertising and catalogs. She set the phone bill on the pile of invoices she needed to write checks for and reached for the final envelope. It was large and plain with only her name and the store's address neatly printed on the front. Expecting it was one of those tricks companies used to pique someone's curiosity so they'll open the envelope instead of sending it straight to the trash, Zoe slit it open and pulled out the contents.

At first she had trouble registering what she held. Quickly, however, uneasiness spread through her as she realized it was pages and pages of legal documents and bank statements belonging to a series of limited liability companies. There were five companies in all, each owned by a different LLC entity. The exact meaning of what she was staring at escaped her, until she scanned the paperwork for the last company and noted her ex-husband's name.

An electric shock blasted through her. She matched up the legal documents with the bank statements. Here was the money Tristan had hidden from her. He'd created a series of foreign shell companies to conceal his funds, but the banks he'd used were all located in the United States. How could he do something like that and get away with it?

That was a question for someone knowledgeable in such matters. Zoe considered if she should take this to her divorce lawyer. The idea of going up against Tristan in court a second time with Sherman Sutter at her side gave her pause. He'd been badly outmatched by Tristan's team of sharks. It almost wasn't fair to put him through what would likely be an even more contentious fight.

The bell on the store's front door tinkled merrily, reminding Zoe that Eva was alone out front. She tucked the papers back in their envelope and slid them into the desk drawer. Then, feeling as if she'd just been handed a ticking time bomb, Zoe headed into the store.

Not even a steady stream of customers could keep Zoe's thoughts off the implications of the documents in her possession. Once the shock had worn off, it had occurred to her that they'd probably come from London. How she'd managed such a daring feat, Zoe had no idea, but it drove home a painful truth.

Everly and London had completed their part of the bargain. Now it was up to Zoe to either find or fabricate something that would damage Susannah's campaign. The thought of hurting Ryan or his sister made her ill, but she couldn't back out of the plan. Everly was too invested in avenging her sister to ever let Zoe walk away.

Ryan flopped onto his back, chest heaving. On the living room rug beside him, Zoe was equally winded. As they panted in unison, he found that he was grinning. Once again they'd been unable to make it upstairs to his bedroom. They hadn't even managed to get fully undressed before lust had overpowered them.

Since finding out Zoe was on birth control and they'd agreed condoms weren't necessary, every room on the first floor had seen some sort of action. Ryan couldn't seem to keep his hands off her and Zoe had proved an eager and willing partner.

"Damn," he murmured in appreciation. "We did it again."

"Third time this week," Zoe agreed, sounding somewhat bemused. "I've never been like this before."

Ryan turned his head and gazed at her profile. "Like what?"

"Horny all the time." She heaved a long-suffering sigh.

"It's really distracting. And annoying. I'm half as productive as I used to be."

"I like this new side of you." In fact, he liked all sides of her.

Without moving her head, she shifted her gaze from the ceiling to him. "What new side of me?"

"The one where you're a lot more open."

"How do you figure I'm more open?"

"When we first met you were a closed book. Now you speak your mind."

"It's not always polite to do so."

"Maybe not," Ryan said, "but it's real." He ran his lips across her shoulder, sending a shiver down her arms. "I can work with real."

"What does that mean?"

Zoe sat up and started to pull her clothes back into place, signaling the end of their intimacy. She was often skittish after they made love, as if she regretted letting go. Her defensive behavior left Ryan wondering what had gone on during her marriage. So far he hadn't pried, but his curiosity was getting the best of him.

He'd already concluded that she was a survivor. Not that she'd confided any such thing, but her passionate stand against domestic violence hinted that she'd been a victim herself.

"I hope you realize that this has grown past a casual fling for me," Ryan said, deciding to put his cards on the table in a show of good faith. "I want you to be able to trust me."

"I do."

Her quick answer didn't satisfy him. "Sometimes I feel like I barely scratch the surface with you."

She drew her knees to her chest and faced him. "I've spent a lot of years hiding my true feelings."

"You don't have to do that with me."

"Opening up scares me." She set her chin on her knees and avoided his gaze. "I feel vulnerable and exposed."

"What do you expect me to say or do to hurt you?"

"Nothing." Yet her flat expression and closed body language said otherwise. "I don't think you're the sort of person who would judge or ridicule me."

Meaning others had come before him who had. "Did your ex-husband do those things?"

"I don't want to rehash my marriage."

"I'll take that as a yes."

She scowled. "You are so annoying."

"So you've mentioned." He grinned at her, preferring insults to carefully worded statements that hid her true emotions. "You know I'll eventually get the truth out of you, so why not just come clean now?"

"Ugh." Zoe pushed to her feet and stalked to the dining table where they'd abandoned plates of chocolate cake to feast on each other. She returned with one of the decadent desserts and plopped down beside him. "Why would you want me to talk about my relationship with Tristan?"

"Because I want to know more about you and I think you're holding on to a lot of pain and anxiety about your marriage."

She popped a bite of cake into her mouth and took her time savoring the flavors. "He was very controlling and highly critical of my appearance." As she spoke, she offered him a forkful of cake.

"You're a stunningly beautiful woman," he told her, his tongue flicking out to catch a bit of chocolate off his lip. "What is there to be critical of?"

"He wanted me to look a certain way. I was expected to be thin, but without muscle definition. He demanded my hair be a certain length and color. He preferred me in pastels, pink, peach or blues, and hated any shades of yellow or green. No bright colors and no black." Her hand shook as she speared into the cake once more. "I learned early on not to voice my opinion or to offer suggestions."

"Why did you marry him?" The question came out more bluntly than Ryan would've wished, but he couldn't reconcile the Zoe he'd come to know with the woman she was describing and needed to understand.

"I was young and naïve and I didn't have a clear sense of what I wanted to do with my life. My mother was thrilled that I'd caught the interest of a handsome, wealthy businessman and pushed me to 'be smart' every time I doubted if he was the right man for me." While she talked, Zoe devoured the rest of the cake as if the sugary dessert eased her discomfort.

"So your new look..." Ryan indicated her short hair and the long graphic tank she wore like a minidress that bared the strong, sexy muscles in her arms and legs. Her over-the-knee boots lay a little distance off. "Is it a complete rejection of everything your ex demanded or the real you?"

A fleeting smile crossed Zoe's lips. "There's no question I'm rebelling. When I first cut my hair, I felt empowered and revolutionary."

"Now?"

She shrugged. "I'm a work in progress." Her gaze caught his. "Does that bother you?"

"Why should it?" He had no intention of judging her. "I like to think we're all evolving."

"Even you?"

He'd asked her to talk about herself, so it was only fair that he share a bit of his own inner struggles. "After what happened with Kelly Briggs, I've had a hard time trusting people I don't know well."

"Like me?"

"Yes." He wondered if he should come clean about his ongoing suspicions. If he kept silent and the truth came out later, it might damage their intimacy during a period when their relationship was heating up. "When you first volunteered for Susannah's campaign, we all thought you were working for Abernathy."

"And now you believe otherwise."

Ryan paused a beat before answering. "The reason I caught your lease up was because your landlord is a friend of Abernathy's and I wondered if they were using your financial problems as a way to get you to spy."

Zoe's eyes widened. "But that was only little over a week ago. You still thought I might be working for Abernathy when we…" She shook her head. "And now?"

"Now, I—"

"Wait," she said, interrupting him. "I understand if you still don't trust me. I haven't exactly been an open book. And after what happened with your company, you have every reason to be suspicious."

Taking the empty plate from her, Ryan set it aside and slid his fingers around the back of her neck, drawing her in for a kiss. "But I don't want to be," he told her, his lips drifting against hers. "I think there's something really great happening between us and I don't want our past experiences to mess up what's going on now or what could develop in the future."

As he finished speaking he noticed how Zoe's muscles had gone still. He glanced down at her expression and noticed her frown. Was he moving too fast? She'd only recently finalized her bitter, contentious divorce. Maybe she wasn't ready to think about a future with him.

Just as Ryan was wondering whether he should walk back his declaration, Zoe scooted closer and put her hand on his knee and said, "That's exactly how I feel."

As she pushed her lips hard against his, stirring the explosive chemistry between them to life once more, hazy suspicion lingered in the wake of her declaration. However, before he could pursue the questions that infiltrated his thoughts, they were incinerated by a fiery rush of passion.

On the Saturday of Susannah's fund-raiser, Zoe regarded her reflection while a familiar anxiety created a lump in her stomach. As she'd applied her smoky makeup and slipped into the strapless navy gown embellished with gold sequins, she'd been imagining the shocked disapproval of her former acquaintances as they took in her short blond hair and celestial-themed dress.

One purpose in changing her look had been to reinvent herself postdivorce. But had she gone too far?

It frustrated Zoe that she cared what anyone from her previous life thought. Maybe the resilience she'd gained in the wake of her divorce was proving to be more fragile than she'd hoped.

Had it been a mistake to attend an event where she ran the risk of crossing paths with people from her past? Only time would tell. At least she wouldn't have to face them alone. She'd be on Ryan's arm and that was a huge confidence booster.

A knock sounded on her front door, jolting her out of her reverie. Mouth dry, palms clammy, she rushed to it, hoping to see Ryan's eyes light up when he saw her. Swinging the door open, she stared at the man standing before her. His broad shoulders looked even more imposing clad in a flawlessly tailored tuxedo jacket. Instead of the traditional black bow tie, he'd chosen to accent his crisp white shirt with a dark gray tie dotted with white. She loved his unconventional approach to formal wear.

"Wow," she murmured, leaning against the door while she took him in. "You look great."

His slow smile sent heat rushing through her. "You look pretty wonderful yourself. Let me get a better look at you." He captured her hand and spun her slowly. "Gorgeous."

The approval glowing in his gray eyes unraveled the knot of worry in her chest. If she'd believed herself past the point where she required a man's praise, she'd been completely wrong. But Ryan was different in that he would have appreciated anything she'd chosen to wear. Not once had he passed judgment on her appearance.

When she'd left Tristan's house, she'd abandoned most of her formal wardrobe, except this one dress that she'd bought, knowing Tristan would never let her wear it. The mermaid-style gown showed off her toned arms and clung to her lean curves, accentuating her sensuality. In it she felt sophisticated and strong, two things she'd never known during the years she'd been married to Tristan.

"I'm going to be the luckiest guy there tonight with you as my date."

"And I'm the luckiest girl," she murmured, for the moment letting herself bask in the glow of his admiration.

For several heartbeats they stood grinning at each other and then Ryan tugged at her hand. "Let's get going. The sooner we put in an appearance, the quicker I can get you home and out of that dress."

"And here I thought you liked it," Zoe teased, pulling the door shut behind her.

"I love it." He wrapped his arm around her waist and bent his lips to her ear. "It's just that I love your beautiful soft skin so much more."

She felt goose bumps at his words. He had a knack for turning her on with a look or a compliment. She became aware of the pulse throbbing between her thighs as she anticipated his hands coasting over her body, stripping the gown away, baring her to his gaze and touch. A groan built in her chest as desire bloomed, but she held it in and savored the rush of longing that flowed through her veins.

Being around Ryan made her happier than anything she'd known before. On the heels of this realization came a bitter reality check. The purpose behind why she'd met him in the first place. The reason she'd moved into his spare apartment and had cultivated his friendship was to cause him harm.

Despair struck at her, ruining her mood. Her smile faded as they neared Ryan's car. He noticed the sudden change and pulled her into his arms before opening the car door.

His thumb caressed her cheek. "What's wrong?"

"Nothing." The lie came easily to her lips. So did the reassuring smile.

She'd spent most of her married life pretending to be something she wasn't. Lately she'd felt safe enough to display her true emotions. Ryan was a rock that she could batter with sarcasm, anger and tears. Nothing she said or did seemed to faze him. He absorbed everything and gave back understanding and acceptance.

"Are you worried about seeing your ex?"

"It's not just him. Everyone I used to know will be there tonight. They're all going to be judging me." Perhaps it wasn't the whole truth, but it was true enough to justify her sudden bout of melancholy.

"You don't have to let their opinions matter," he reminded her. "They can't hurt you unless you let them."

"You're right." She heaved a sigh. "It's just really hard to stop caring that they disapprove."

The admission wasn't one she'd confided to anyone before Ryan. She trusted him not to dismiss her concerns. Somehow he recognized how determined she was to face up to the challenges she'd once avoided.

"You'll get there." He kissed the top of her head. "In the meantime, you can count on me to play guard dog for you. I'll bare my teeth at anyone who makes you uncomfortable."

She smiled as no doubt he'd hoped she would. Grinning at him released more of her tension. She captured his face between her palms and kissed him firmly on the lips.

"Thank you," she said, feeling her heart expanding as she gazed at him.

"I'm serious."

"I know." She released him and stepped back. "And you're a wonderful champion." *I don't deserve you.*

The thought continued to ring in her mind as Ryan drove them to the venue, and even when he tucked her hand into the crook of his arm and led the way into the party. Her agitation grew with each stride into the historic downtown Charleston plantation home overlooking the Ashley River. Who would she run into at tonight's thousand-dollar-a-plate fund-raiser for Susannah's state senate campaign?

"Zoe Crosby." A beautiful brunette stepped into her path. "I almost didn't recognize you. You cut all your hair off." Before Zoe could update Polly Matson with her post-divorce surname, the woman's keen blue eyes shifted in Ryan's direction and lingered. "Obviously divorce agrees with you." She stuck out a slender hand tipped with blush-tinted fingernails. "You're Susannah's brother, aren't you? I'm Polly Matson."

"Ryan Dailey." He shook her hand and gave her a polite smile.

"Susannah's brother. You must be so proud of her," Polly gushed, her entire focus coming to bear on Ryan.

"Of course." Ryan nodded. "If you'll excuse us, we were on our way to find her."

"Don't let me hold you up," Polly said as Ryan guided Zoe away.

Zoe didn't need to look back to know that Polly would make a beeline for Callie Hill and Azalea Stocks. The trio had never been all that fond of Zoe before her divorce. No doubt they'd been gleeful when the rumor of Zoe's supposed infidelity had begun to spread. Charleston's elite loved a juicy scandal and of course everyone had come down on Tristan's side. He'd been the model husband, after all. The darker elements of his controlling nature had never made a public appearance. And those pesky rumors surrounding his supposed infidelity? No one cared. Yet Zoe had been shunned after the same allegations had been lodged against her.

"I take it she's not a friend of yours," Ryan said.

"I didn't really have any friends." That sounded overly dramatic so she quickly clarified, "Not true friends anyway. Not the sort you can trust with your darkest secrets and deepest fears."

"Did you have a lot of those? Secrets and fears, I mean."

"Doesn't everyone?"

For several seconds Ryan regarded her somberly. She knew he hated it when she deflected his attempts to understand her better, but she'd spent so long guarding her true feelings that it was second nature to hide behind flippant remarks and bravado.

Zoe gave a huge sigh. "I'm sorry. It's been a while since I felt this exposed."

"I understand."

And she knew he did. He'd proved to be more sensitive to nuance than any man she'd ever known. Was it because his twin was female? Whatever the cause, he knew how to listen.

"Shall we go find Susannah?" she suggested, taking his arm.

The steely muscles beneath the elegant tuxedo jacket reminded her that he'd promised to be her champion tonight and she relaxed slightly. Unfortunately her calm lasted for only a few steps because across the room she spied her ex-husband.

Tristan was deep in conversation with a slender brunette. Although she wanted to tear her attention away, something about the woman struck a chord. The elusive familiarity nagged at her while Ryan paused to chat with a friend. It wasn't until the woman glanced over her shoulder and made direct eye contact that Zoe realized that the brunette was Everly in disguise.

What the hell?

Her anxiety spiked into the red zone as she was swamped by a barrage of questions. What was Everly doing at Susannah's fund-raiser? Why was Everly talking to Tristan? What could possibly be going on? Panic roared through Zoe as she noted their ease with each other. Not once had Everly indicated she'd known Tristan. Was their association a recent development? If so, had she sought him out? Zoe wouldn't put it past her. Damn the woman for stepping over the line again.

Zoe couldn't tear her attention from the pair and when she saw them part ways, she excused herself from Ryan and headed after Everly. With the other woman demonstrating she had no intention of sticking to their original agreement of no interference, Zoe decided that gave her grounds to back out of the revenge bargain. And it wasn't as if she'd done anything with the documents London had given her about Tristan's financial dealings. If Zoe never went after her ex-husband's offshore accounts technically she'd never get her revenge on him.

Hope bloomed. Maybe there was a way she and Ryan could be together. But first, she intended to get some answers.

She caught up to Everly near the bar and nudged her away from the guests and toward a quiet corner on the far side of the party. Once isolated, she let her irritation show. "What the hell are you doing here and what were you and Tristan talking about?"

"I was just saying hello."

"You were saying hello?" Zoe echoed in disbelief, dumbstruck that Everly could be so flippant about approaching Tristan. "I don't believe you."

"Fine," Everly said, all glibness leaving her manner. "I came to remind you to keep your eye on the ball."

"What's that supposed to mean?"

"It means you've forgotten why you were supposed to get to know Ryan in the first place. We had a bargain, you, London and I. We did our part. Now it's your turn."

"I don't need you riding me all the time. And now I see you talking to Tristan. That's taking things too far." Zoe's hands shook and she gripped her evening bag to keep her anxiety from showing. "In fact, this whole thing is making me uncomfortable." Suddenly Zoe saw a light at the end of the tunnel. A way out of this mess. "I'm done."

Her giddy sense of relief lasted barely a second.

"Excuse me?" Everly's lips tightened and when she spoke next, her words were barely audible. "You can't just quit."

"I can and I am." Zoe's stomach gave a sharp lurch as fury exploded in Everly's bright green eyes. "Because here's the issue. I don't trust you."

With the dinner portion of Susannah's fund-raiser over, Ryan had no interest in lingering. While three of his sister's friends were asking Zoe questions about her store, Ryan went in search of his twin to say goodbye. Seeing that she was deep in conversation with one of her biggest donors, he decided not to interrupt and was about to reverse direction and head back to Zoe when a man spoke from behind him.

"You really should watch yourself with Zoe."

Ryan turned to confront Tristan Crosby, anger lancing through him at the man's warning. "I don't think that's any of your business."

"She's going to cause you nothing but trouble," Crosby continued smoothly, as if Ryan hadn't spoken.

"Seems to me you're the one looking to create problems," Ryan responded, his tone hard and cold. "Why don't you mind your own business and let Zoe get on with her life?"

"You know, my ex-wife is full of sob stories," Tristan said, undaunted by Ryan's warning. "The last thing you want to do is believe everything she says."

Although he regretted engaging the man, Ryan had promised to defend Zoe. "I have no reason to doubt anything she says." Yet at one point in time hadn't he done exactly that? Of course, that was before they'd started sleeping together.

The explosive chemistry Ryan enjoyed with Zoe had blunted his initial reservations about her.

As if Zoe's ex could read Ryan's mind, a cruel smirk formed on his lips. "She's good at keeping secrets, but I think you'll find that out soon enough."

When Ryan refused to respond, Crosby offered a mocking salute before walking away. The exchange had been both brief and unpleasant, yet its disturbing aftertaste lingered in Ryan's mind. Obviously, Crosby wasn't satisfied with all the damage he'd done to Zoe during the divorce proceedings. He intended to pursue his grudge even further.

"Why were you talking to Tristan?" Zoe demanded as she approached him, her frightened expression startling Ryan.

"He was just trying to cause trouble between us."

Zoe frowned. "What did he say?"

Ryan cursed the distrust Tristan Crosby had stirred in him. Thanks to all the fantastic sex Ryan had been having with Zoe, he'd stopped suspecting her.

"He made some vague warnings about you being trouble," Ryan replied, his tone dismissive. At the horror reflected in her expression, he added, "I set him straight, and then told him to back off and leave you alone."

"Thank you for standing up for me." She reached out

and took his hand in a fierce grip. "It's not something I'm use to."

Her appreciation left him feeling guilty for his earlier doubts. Suddenly he was remembering what had happened with Kelly Briggs. When he'd discovered her boyfriend had locked her out of the apartment they'd been sharing and wouldn't give her back her stuff, Ryan had found her a new place to live and persuaded the ex to turn over her things as well as to give up several expensive items Kelly had purchased while they'd been living together.

While Ryan had never crossed a line with Kelly because she'd been his employee and he hadn't been attracted to her in the least, he missed how emotionally vulnerable she was. To his dismay, she'd misinterpreted his motivation behind aiding her and created a fantasy where he'd felt something for her beyond friendship. When he'd set her straight, she'd overreacted to his rejection and retaliated by deleting his company's important engineering schematics.

Ryan recognized that he'd made a huge mistake with Kelly Briggs. Had he repeated the error with Zoe? Would his actions once again come back to bite him in the ass?

His choice to invite her to stay in one of his guest apartments had been far from prudent, but lust had proved stronger than curiosity or suspicion. He might have overpowered his desire to take her to bed if their chemistry had been less explosive.

The speed with which things had been moving between them coupled with Crosby's warning awakened Ryan to just how fast Zoe had slid beneath his skin. Should he tap on the brakes? Her financial situation wasn't the best. Did his wealth make him more attractive to her? She hadn't asked him for help, yet she'd made it clear that her situation was desperate.

Ryan believed he'd resolved the questions surrounding Zoe joining Susannah's campaign. He'd been lulled by their deepening connection to invite her into his inner circle. Now, Crosby's ambiguous threats reminded Ryan that in many ways she remained an unknown entity. If things fell apart with their fledgling relationship, would she act out the way Kelly had? What sort of fallout should he brace for?

Her fingers tightened around his. "What are you thinking about?" she asked, peering at him in concern and leaving him to wonder if his expression had revealed his inner turmoil.

"Let's get out of here," he said, pushing aside his doubts about what was or wasn't real about their relationship. "I think I've supported my sister long enough."

"Sure." The smile she gave him would've appeared perfectly natural if it had reached her eyes. "I'm dying to be alone with you."

Her response was perfect. Too perfect? Disgusted with himself, Ryan led her toward the exit. "Do you want to grab a drink somewhere or head straight home?"

"Let's go back to your place," she said, leaning into him. "I want to get naked with you."

Her whispered words sent lust raging through him, but Ryan couldn't stop himself from wondering if she was saying what she knew he wanted to hear or if sex was truly on her mind. It would be so easy to take her at face value. He could just consider himself incredibly lucky to be involved with a woman whose passion matched his own.

"Keep talking like that and I'll get pulled over for speeding," he teased, shoving aside his doubts for the rest of the evening.

Everly sat in her car outside Susannah Dailey-Kirby's campaign headquarters, replaying her latest conversation with Devon Connor and wondering how long her business would survive if she lost her biggest client. The golf resort magnate was far from happy at her latest ideas to brand the new property he'd purchased and had given her a week to come up with a fresh concept.

Which was why she should be brainstorming at her office instead of watching the campaign staff file out one by one until only the deputy campaign manager remained. In the past, when Everly cruised by at this time of night, she'd noticed Patty Joyce working late, putting in ridiculous hours to make sure everything ran smoothly.

Everly expelled a frustrated breath. Sitting here while nothing was happening was a huge waste of time, but since Zoe had decided to renege on her part of the bargain, it wasn't like Everly had any choice. From the start it was obvious that Zoe lacked commitment. Everly's fury with the former socialite had grown in the days following the fund-raiser and she'd added Zoe to her growing to-do list. As soon as Everly dealt Susannah's campaign a death blow, she would make Zoe pay for turning her back on all Everly's careful planning.

Deciding tonight's surveillance was a bust, Everly took a hold of the keys in her ignition, but before she could fire the engine, she spied a man approaching Joyce. The late hour and darkened storefronts he passed prevented her from seeing his features, but she assumed it was Gil Moore, the campaign manager. Nothing new there. Moore worked as hard as his deputy.

Only as she watched the man approach Patty Joyce, Everly realized she'd guessed wrong. Crowing with delight, Everly lifted her cell phone and zoomed in on Jefferson Kirby as he pulled his wife's deputy campaign manager into his arms and kissed her.

In seconds Everly had captured a dozen images of the couple's passionate embrace. While she waited for them to leave, Everly studied the fuzzy pictures, wishing the faces were clearer. From their body language this wasn't a first-time event.

Moments later the lights went dark and Everly tracked the pair as they headed for Patty Joyce's car. Disappointed that she hadn't done a better job documenting Jefferson Kirby's infidelity, Everly started her car and put it in gear, following the couple.

Their destination turned out to be a motel a mere ten-minute drive from the campaign office with access to the room off the parking lot. With no hallway to walk, they ran less of a chance of being seen. Only, they hadn't counted on Everly.

Thanks to the couple's preoccupation with each other, neither one noticed as Everly parked close enough to capture the whole sordid scene as they kissed their way to the door. The entire spectacle lasted less than thirty seconds, but Everly recorded every instant.

She'd been hoping for dirt on Susannah Dailey-Kirby but, like her brother, the candidate had proved squeaky-clean. Never had Everly expected anything like Jefferson Kirby's affair to fall into her lap, but now that it had, she needed to figure out the best way to capitalize on what she'd uncovered.

Nine

Zoe was picking up lunch for Eva and Jessica at the coffee shop down the street when her phone chimed, indicating an incoming email. With two people ahead of her in line, she'd been scrolling through her social media feed liking cute pictures of cats and sharing photos of the store's newest inventory. The number of people who followed Second Chance Treasures on social media had tripled in the weeks since Susannah had thrown her support behind the store and Zoe was humbled and grateful. If not for Ryan and his sister, Zoe would've had to close the boutique. She owed them an incredible debt.

With so many things going her way, Zoe should've been floating, but she couldn't stop looking over her shoulder at odd moments, expecting to see Everly lurking around every corner. That the other woman hadn't been in contact brought Zoe no peace. Everly's fanatic determination to get revenge on Ryan wasn't going to just vanish because Zoe was no longer participating in the plot and it troubled her that she might now be a target of Everly's vindictiveness.

Zoe glanced at the email that had popped into her

inbox, noting the unfamiliar address before the subject line snagged her attention. She read the single word several times while her heart rate skyrocketed.

Busted.

What did that mean? Apprehension surged through her. The only way for her to know for sure was to open the email.

A video file waited below the message Watch this—E. What could Everly possibly be up to now? Bracing herself, Zoe clicked on the attachment and watched in horror as Jefferson Kirby entered a hotel room with his wife's deputy campaign manager, Patty Joyce.

This was the exact sort of dirt that could take down a campaign. Worse, it could destroy two marriages and ruin the lives of both families. The pain that would be unleashed on innocents if this got out would last for years, maybe decades, to come.

She'd volunteered in the hope of finding something exactly this scandalous. That Everly had been the one to uncover the affair instead was unsurprising. The other woman's interference was out of control.

At the end of the short video, Zoe placed her hands against her roiling stomach, contemplating the devastation if this got out. Susannah's campaign might survive the blow, but what about the couple's children? They didn't deserve to be harmed by the vicious gossip the revelation would stir.

Zoe's finger hovered over the delete button. She wouldn't have wished such a difficult situation on her worst enemy, much less someone she admired. But although she longed to erase the email and forget she'd ever seen the video, that wouldn't stop Everly from using it to hurt Susannah. All Everly had to do was to leak the recording to the media or to Lyle Abernathy. He'd make hay with it, gleefully twisting the knife deep into Susannah's heart. He wouldn't care that her husband's affair had nothing to do with the issues or Susannah's ability to represent the people of her district. Instead he would make sure no one could focus on the fact that Susannah was the better candidate.

A familiar rush of helplessness swept over Zoe followed closely by sharp regret. She never should've fallen in with Everly and London. The mad scheme they'd concocted had reached far beyond anything Zoe had imagined and the results hadn't brought her the satisfaction or the peace of mind she'd anticipated. Quite the opposite. Relentless waves of guilt and remorse had torn at her, disturbing her sleep and ruining her appetite. She grappled with how to disengage herself from the revenge bargain and rid herself of Everly. Today's email demonstrated how impossible that would be.

Fifteen minutes later Zoe exited the coffee shop with the lunch order and retraced her steps to the store. With her thoughts racing, she didn't register the tall man approaching her until he spoke.

"Zoe Alston?"

Her attention snapped back to her surroundings and she sized up the bald man in his ill-fitting suit. Was this another of Everly's tricks or the abusive spouse of one of her artisans?

"Can I help you?"

"This is for you." He extended an envelope.

Zoe took it automatically and the man walked away without another word. Besieged by dread, she entered the store and set the lunches on the counter.

"Bianca brought these by a little while ago. Aren't they incredible?" Jessica indicated a stack of watercolor paintings she was recording in the computer. Then, she caught sight of Zoe's face. "Is everything okay?"

"I don't know. A man just handed me this envelope."

Zoe held it up, noting the lack of identifying marks. "This just feels wrong."

"You won't know until you open it," Jessica said, displaying the pragmatic nature that had prompted Zoe to hire her.

With a nod, Zoe tore open the flap and pulled out a letter. Anxiety shifted to sorrow as she scanned the lawyer's name before skimming to the meat of the message.

"Looks like the building has been sold and we have thirty days to vacate." Zoe was surprised she managed to maintain a calm tone when everything inside her howled in protest.

"That's terrible. Who would do something like that?"

Zoe reread the letter, paying closer attention to the details. This time the new owner's name jumped out at her. TA Charleston Holdings, LLC. "TA" as in Tristan Anthony? Zoe reached into her purse for the financial documents belonging to Tristan's shell companies. She'd spent several hours studying the legal paperwork in an effort to make sense of what he'd been up to. She pulled out the sheet containing her notes. There, halfway down the list of names was the one the letter referenced.

Tristan had bought the building containing her store with the sole purpose of kicking her out.

The floor shifted beneath Zoe's feet as the implication struck her and she braced her hand on the counter to steady herself. "Damn it."

She'd foolishly thought there was nothing left for him to take away. Her money was gone. As was her position in the community. Now she was going to lose her store.

"Zoe? Are you okay?"

"It's my ex." She brandished the letter. "He's the one behind this."

Jessica knew all about Zoe's nasty divorce and came

around the counter to give Zoe a hug. "We'll get through this," she whispered. "It's going to be okay."

Although Zoe nodded, in her mind she had already started to pack up her inventory. She didn't have the money or the strength to start over a second time.

"I need to clear my head," Zoe said, offering up a wan smile. "Can you and Eva handle things for a little while?"

"We've got this," Jessica said. "Don't worry about anything."

Unsure where she was going, Zoe headed out the back and got into her car. Her initial instinct had been to call Ryan and spill the news, but then she remembered the video she'd received while at the coffee shop and knew she couldn't dump her problems on him with the threat of the video hanging out there.

No, this was something she had to handle herself. When she reached Crosby Automotive, she parked in an empty visitor spot before marching into the lobby. Pretending to be deaf and blind to the receptionist's greeting, Zoe barreled through the lobby and headed down a series of familiar hallways.

Tristan had a large corner office in the back of the building with floor-to-ceiling windows that overlooked a landscaped stretch of grass and trees. As she neared his assistant's desk, she noticed his door was closed. Usually that meant he was in a meeting. For an instant her rash determination faded. What was she doing? Anything she said or did in the next few minutes was guaranteed to blow back in her face. Tristan was a master at deflection. No matter how badly he behaved, in the end he was never at fault.

"You can't go in there," Ginny Anderson cried as Zoe sailed past and grabbed the doorknob to Tristan's office. "He's in a meeting."

Zoe ignored her and opened the door. Tristan was on

the phone. His eyes widened when she stepped in and shut the door behind her.

"Someone just came in," he said to whoever was on the other end of the call. "I have to go. I'll call you later." Hanging up, he got to his feet and came around the desk. "What the hell do you think you're doing bursting in on me like that?"

Once his anger would've cowed her, but she was no longer the woman he'd dominated. She stared her ex-husband down as he approached, refusing to back down as he came to tower over her.

"You bought my building so you can evict me?" She brandished the letter. "That's low even for you."

His eyes narrowed. "How'd you know it was me?"

She immediately saw her mistake. Without the documents she'd received about his shell companies she'd have no idea he was behind her eviction. Zoe hiked her purse higher on her shoulder, the weight of Tristan's secrets a burden she should've left in the car.

"Who else could it be?" she retorted, bluffing like her life depended on it. "You've done your best to ruin me. This is just another in a long list of dirty tricks."

"You seem pretty certain it was me," he replied smoothly. "You must have some sort of proof."

His absolute confidence suggested he knew exactly what had been sent to her.

Inwardly cursing that she hadn't thought her accusation through, she said, "I have no idea what you're talking about."

"I know what you've been up to." He leaned into her space, his manner growing even more menacing.

"I haven't been up to anything." Zoe took a firmer grip on her purse.

"You're a liar." Without warning, Tristan whipped his

hand forward, latched onto her handbag and yanked it off her shoulder. "Do you have it with you?"

"Stop that!" Zoe snagged the strap and held on. "Let go! What are you doing?"

With a sharp sideways jerk, Tristan stripped the purse from her hands. Pulled off-balance, she stumbled and nearly fell. By the time she straightened, Tristan had freed the envelope. He threw the bag at her feet. Fighting helpless tears, Zoe scooped up her purse and held it against her chest.

"You have no right," she cried, wondering why she thought this encounter would go in her favor when none had before.

"I have every right." He scanned the contents of the envelope, mouth tightening at what he found. "You were stupid to bring this with you today." While Zoe watched in helpless dismay, Tristan tossed the envelope onto his desk and straightened his tie. "But then you've never been all that smart."

Zoe barely registered the insult. Her throat tightened as she fought overwhelming despair. Because of her rashness, she'd lost the only leverage she'd had against him.

"That boyfriend of yours has no idea about you," Tristan continued, more relaxed now that he'd regained the upper hand. "Or what you've been up to."

"What are you talking about?" she demanded, cursing the impulse to engage him.

Her stomach clenched in fear as a sly smile appeared on his face, making it clear he knew every sordid detail of what she'd been doing.

"You know," he said. "The little revenge pact you made where you receive dirt on me in exchange for you getting dirt on Dailey's sister. I had no idea you had it in you."

"How...?"

Only three people knew about that. London would never

risk her reputation by telling anyone. And unless she'd started talking in her sleep, Zoe hadn't spilled the beans.

"Your friend Everly told me," Tristan said, confirming Zoe's conclusion.

"Who?" she asked breathlessly, hearing the lie.

"Everly Briggs." Tristan smirked. "I guess she's not as good a friend as you thought."

"She's not my friend. She's barely even an acquaintance." At least that much was true.

"Don't bother denying it," he countered. "She told me you had someone steal information from my computer."

Zoe was sure Everly hadn't sent the documents, so how had she known? "Sounds like a pretty fantastic story."

"It's not a story. It's the truth."

"Like when you accused me of having an affair?" Zoe congratulated herself on her sarcasm. "Those lies didn't work then and they won't work now."

"Really?" He sneered. "How long before Dailey dumps you after he finds out you joined his sister's campaign to gather dirt on her?"

"Stay away from Ryan."

"Or what?"

Yes, or what? Tristan had reclaimed the proof of his illegal activities.

"It's your word against mine," she blustered. "And he already knows better than to trust you."

"Maybe, but he's been burned before," Tristan said, spilling just how thoroughly Everly had betrayed their pact. "I'm going to guess that he's not going to make the same mistake twice. And that means all I have to do is make one little phone call and you two are done."

With grief rising to nearly intolerable levels, Zoe pivoted on her heel and walked out of Tristan's office. Although she'd closed her eyes to the inevitable, she'd known her relationship with Ryan would eventually end in heartbreak.

But she would be damned if either Everly or Tristan dealt the killing blow. If she and Ryan were over, Zoe would be the one to shatter the connection.

Suspecting that Tristan would hold off calling Ryan to torment her as long as possible, Zoe pulled out her phone and dialed Ryan's number.

"Something has come up," she said after he picked up. "We need to talk…"

After Zoe's dire "we need to talk" declaration and her unwillingness to get into anything more over the phone, Ryan spent several minutes wondering if he was facing the abrupt end of their relationship and disturbed at the idea of losing her. Luckily, the rest of his day was taken up by a series of meetings that left him too busy to dwell on what she had on her mind.

Now, however, as he stood in his kitchen, pondering what to do for dinner, Ryan considered how fast he'd gotten used to having Zoe around all the time. They ate together most nights, either at his house or at one of downtown Charleston's numerous restaurants. Those dinners often segued into passionate lovemaking and he'd lost count how many times she'd spent the night. Waking up with her in the morning had become his favorite way to start his days.

When a knock sounded on his back door, his heart gave a joyful leap. Many days had passed since he'd given up claiming that he wasn't emotionally engaged. At first he'd told himself such reactions were a predictable chemical response to someone he lusted after. After all, he'd enjoyed the best sex of his life with her.

But it wasn't only physical for him. He'd made an effort to get to know her. Drawn out her fears. Learned about her dreams for the future. Discovered they shared a passion for helping people and a flaw that kept them from spotting trouble before it was too late. And he'd shared parts of himself with her that only his twin had seen.

He went to answer the door and his mood crashed at the somber expression on her face.

"What's wrong?" he asked as she strode past him.

"Everything's messed up," she replied, dumping her purse on the kitchen counter and heading straight to the cabinet in the living room where he kept his liquor. Setting her cell phone down, she indicated the bottles. "Do you mind?"

"Help yourself."

While she poured a healthy shot of vodka into a crystal tumbler, Ryan surveyed her appearance, noting her paleness and smudged eye makeup. She looked as if she'd been crying. What had happened to upset her between their early morning romp and now?

"Feel like talking about it?" he prompted.

"That's why I came by. I need to tell you some things." She finished her drink and poured a second shot. This time, instead of drinking, she rolled the glass between her palms and watched the liquid swirl. "Things you're not gonna be happy to hear."

Her ominous words rousted the doubts he'd put to rest after his encounter with her ex-husband at Susannah's fundraiser.

"Okay."

But before that happened, he needed to connect with her. Crossing to where she stood, Ryan plucked the glass from her hands. Before she could protest, he pulled her into his arms and kissed her hard. She immediately melted into his embrace. All the tension fled her muscles as she looped her arms around his neck and pressed her body into his. The kiss grew ravenous as frantic, impassioned noises tore from her throat.

Ryan sent his fingertips diving beneath the hem of her

sweater dress, eager for the silky warmth of her skin and the tantalizing heat of her arousal. She groaned and sucked his lower lip into her mouth, setting her teeth against the tender flesh as he slid his finger through the wetness between her thighs.

"Oh, Ryan." She gasped when he freed her mouth so he could trail his tongue down her neck and nip at the sensitive cord in her throat.

"I need to taste you," he growled, stripping her thong down her thighs.

Together they sank to the floor. She lay back and Ryan pushed her dress up. Setting his hands on her knees, he pushed them apart, opening her to him.

The noises she made as he drew his tongue along the most sensitive part of her fanned his lust to white-hot brilliance. He ignored the tight ache below his belt and focused on driving her pleasure higher. By now he knew both a fast and slow way to make her crazy, but she'd learned a thing or two about him, as well.

"I want to come with you inside me," she panted, tugging on his hair as her climax drew close. "Please, Ryan."

He had no reason to deny her request and swiftly stripped out of his clothes. She did the same, yanking the Aztec-patterned dress over her head and shimmying out of the tank she wore beneath it. He took a second to admire her lithe, toned body as she set her hand to the zipper of her favorite boots.

With a slow smile, Ryan shook his head. "Leave them on."

This command gifted him with her first smile of the night. She held out her arms and he moved between her thighs. Her gaze locked on his as he slid inside her.

"I love you," she murmured, so quietly that he thought he'd misheard.

His heart gave his ribs a painful kick. An instant later

she squeezed her eyes shut and began rocking her hips in the way she knew he adored. Ryan began to move in response and the raw, frenzied lovemaking that followed left him reeling. They climaxed together, Ryan making sure Zoe came hard before surrendering to his own pleasure.

In the aftermath, he lay beside her on the carpet. Completely wrung out, Ryan rolled his head in her direction. She lay with her forearm flung over her eyes, lips parted as her chest rose and fell, lungs laboring. Her skin wore a sheen of sweat, inviting his touch, but she spoke before he could summon the strength to move.

"I need to tell you something," she announced, her tone grim.

"I'm listening."

"Something bad is going to happen to your sister."

His lethargy vanished as a jolt of adrenaline flooded his muscles. Ryan sat up and grabbed her wrist, pulling her arm away from her face so he could see her expression.

"What sort of something?" He heard the suspicion chilling his voice and wasn't surprised when she shivered.

She sat up and pulled free, rubbing her wrist before she tucked her knees against her chest and wrapped her arms around her legs. Her self-protective pose added to his irritation. She had no reason to be afraid of him.

Sorrow filled her eyes. "Jefferson is having an affair with Patty."

For a second he couldn't process her words. Of all the things Ryan was prepared for her to say, hearing that his brother-in-law was cheating wasn't even on the list.

"Susannah's deputy campaign manager?" Ryan shook his head, unable to wrap his mind around Zoe's story. "I don't believe you."

Jefferson would never cheat on Susannah. He adored her. He loved their life and would never do something like that to their children.

"It's true," she insisted. "And there's proof."

"What sort of proof?" he asked, his skepticism raging.

"There's a video."

Damn it all to hell.

"Of what exactly?" he challenged, hoping like hell that she didn't have the goods. That it was all an ill-conceived lie to stir up trouble. Yet what could she possibly hope to achieve by spinning such a tale?

"It's a video of the two of them going into a hotel room."

In this age of technology, things like that could be doctored. And it sounded exactly like something Lyle Abernathy would be behind. Ryan ground his teeth together.

"Have you seen it?" He couldn't just accept her word. Unless he saw it with his own eyes, he'd never accept that Jeff could betray Susannah.

She nodded.

"How? Where?"

Zoe got to her feet and grabbed her cell. She manipulated the phone for a few seconds and then handed it to him.

The video was shot at night and from a distance, but there was no question it was Jefferson Kirby and Patty Joyce and they were romantically involved. The segment was no longer than twenty seconds, but it was more than enough to damn Jeff's actions. Ryan badly wanted to punch something long before the hotel room door shut behind the couple.

"Did you follow them?" He slashed a glance in Zoe's direction and discovered she'd taken the moments of his distraction to put her clothes back on.

Part of his brain mourned that she'd covered up all her beautiful skin, but he recognized that the last thing he needed right now was to be distracted by her nakedness.

"No," Zoe said, retreating to one of the chairs in his living room. "Someone sent the video to me."

"Someone?" he snapped, frustrated by her vagueness. "You mean Abernathy?"

Overwhelmed by fury at Zoe's betrayal, Ryan kicked himself for all the times he'd let lust override common sense when it came to her. From the first he'd suspected something was off about Zoe, but he'd let his hunger for her lead him to stop questioning her abrupt appearance in Susannah's campaign.

"No." Zoe shook her head. "Not Abernathy. He doesn't have anything to do with this."

Not yet.

The unspoken words hung in his thoughts like a deadly virus. There was no doubt that the video would end up in Abernathy's hands eventually. No matter how many assurances Zoe made, the fact that it existed at all meant it would be leaked.

"Who else knows?"

Her gaze pleaded with him for mercy. "I don't know."

"Help me to understand what's going on," Ryan said. "Why did such a damning video come to you?"

The distant rumble of a truck along King Street a few blocks away was the only sound in the room for a long minute until Zoe heaved a weary sigh.

"Because of something I came here to do," she murmured, forcing Ryan to strain to hear her.

"And what is that exactly?"

She wrapped her arms around her waist. If her slumped posture and forlorn expression was supposed to invoke his sympathy, it wasn't working. His blood turned to ice in his veins as he waited for her to speak.

"To mess up your sister's campaign as a way of getting revenge on you."

Ten

Ryan's expression went cold at her words, but Zoe experienced none of the gut-wrenching panic that used to besiege her whenever she'd done something to upset Tristan. No matter how angry he became at her, Zoe trusted Ryan would fight fair.

"Revenge?" Gravel filled his deep voice. "On me? Why? What did I ever do to you?"

"Nothing. It's not me who wants revenge," she explained. "It's Everly Briggs. Because of what happened to her sister Kelly."

"Why would you get involved? Who is Everly to you?"

Ryan pushed to his feet and retrieved his clothes. After slipping back into his boxer briefs and jeans, he thrust his arms into his white button-down shirt and came to stand over her, hands planted on his narrow hips, irritation pulling his brows together.

Although her chest ached, tears hadn't yet made an appearance. For that she should be grateful. Her story would be much harder to tell if she was blubbering incoherently.

"Earlier this fall I went to a networking event and met

two women. Everly Briggs and London McCaffrey. I was near the end of my divorce and feeling bitter and helpless. Out of money, beaten up by Tristan's lawyers, I wasn't in my right mind. We were all in a similar state. London was angry at being dumped by Linc Thurston and Everly was devastated that Kelly was in jail. We were all feeling wronged and helpless and vindictive." She stared at her hands, trying to avoid the outrage blazing in Ryan's gray eyes.

"So you decided to get back at us?" Ryan demanded.

Zoe nodded. "We started talking about how great it would be to make you all pay, but knew anything we did would only come back to bite us."

Ryan's expression reflected horrified amazement. "So what did you do?"

"We decided to each go after one of you. We were strangers at a cocktail party. The idea being that whatever bad thing we made happen, it couldn't be traced back to the one who bore a grudge against you. Everly broke up Linc and his housekeeper for London. London secured some documents from Tristan that proved he has money hidden offshore for me."

"And you were supposed to come after me for Everly," Ryan said. "Only you didn't. You went after Susannah."

Zoe wanted to remind him that she hadn't actually done anything to harm his sister, but recognized it was pointless to defend herself.

"Everly suggested that since you'd hurt her sister," Zoe said. "I should hurt yours."

Ryan stared at her in silence for so long Zoe wondered if he ever intended to speak. His eyes were chips of gray ice, reflecting his mood, and when he next spoke, his tone chilled her to the bone.

"What are you planning to do with the video?"

Zoe gave her head an emphatic shake. "Nothing. Don't

you get it? I didn't shoot this. I couldn't do anything to hurt Susannah or you. I lov—" She bit her lip as Ryan threw up a hand, preventing her from finishing. "No," she cried. "I'm going to say it. I love you and I'm sorry about everything. My involvement in this has been eating me up."

"You love me?" he demanded, voice rising in outrage. "I'm supposed to believe that when this whole time you've been lying to me?"

"Only about why I volunteered for Susannah's campaign. You have to believe me." Zoe put her hand on his arm and flinched when he jerked away. "I've been honest about everything else."

"Honest." He growled the word. "Why tell me any of this? You could've just kept quiet and I'd never have known you were involved."

"Everly told Tristan the truth," Zoe admitted, knowing this was the thing that would sink any chance of saving their relationship. If she'd told him the truth before circumstances forced her hand, she might've been able to make him understand. Instead she'd pledged her loyalty to the wrong cause. "He's threatened to tell you."

Ryan rubbed his hands over his face. "That's what he meant at the fund-raiser."

"I did try to back out," Zoe said, doubting he'd believe her. "After getting to know you and Susannah, I couldn't go through with what we'd planned. But Everly was determined to make you pay and she wouldn't listen to reason."

"Do you know what your scheme is going to do to my sister?" Pain filled his voice. "Forget her campaign for state senate, this video will ruin her marriage. Did you stop for one second to think about the potential damage to her family when you started your little game?"

"I'm sorry," she whispered, recognizing mere words could not atone for her mistakes.

Ryan cursed. "I have to warn Susannah." He took several steps in the direction of the hallway before pausing. Without turning around, he delivered his final words. "You need to be gone before I get back."

Ryan grabbed his keys on the way out the back door and headed for the garage. A volatile mix of emotions raged in him, from fury at his brother-in-law's betrayal to despair over the devastation this would cause his sister. Anything related to Zoe he banished to the furthest reaches of his mind.

I love you.

Damn her.

His chest tightened as her declaration reverberated in his mind. Pain and longing battled for dominance. How was it possible that only an hour earlier he'd been reflecting on the mind-blowing sex he'd been having with her and worried that she might want to end things? Ryan bottled up all emotion related to Zoe. She was a distraction he couldn't afford.

He needed to focus his energy on Susannah and to support her as she learned what her husband had been up to.

Before heading to his sister's campaign headquarters, Ryan sent a copy of the video to Paul. He'd forwarded it to himself from Zoe's phone once he'd finished watching it. Now, as he threw his car into reverse and started backing out of the garage, his phone rang.

"What the hell is up with this video you sent me?" Paul demanded, his ferocity feeding Ryan's own ire. "Has Susannah seen it?"

"Not yet. I'm on my way to tell her about it right now."

Paul swore. "Where did it come from?"

"Zoe showed it to me." Ryan clenched the steering wheel until his fingers cramped, but it wasn't enough to overpower the ache in his chest. "It was taken by Everly Briggs."

"Kelly's sister?" Paul sounded as confused as Ryan had been moments earlier. "Why? What's going on?"

"It's a long story."

Ryan went on to repeat what Zoe had told him, keeping the focus on the facts even when his friend's tone grew sympathetic.

"Oh, hell," Paul said. "Susannah doesn't deserve any of this."

"I know. I just wish there was something we could do to mitigate the fallout, but even if we could somehow keep the video from coming out, I don't think that will stop Everly Briggs from further mischief in the future."

"Legally she hasn't done anything wrong," Paul agreed. "How did you leave things with Zoe?"

Ryan was surprised his friend had to ask. "Obviously we're done. I told her to move out."

"Sure, that makes sense." But his tone indicated otherwise.

"She's been lying to me this whole time," Ryan reminded his friend. "Since the day we met."

"Well, to be fair, you suspected her motives for joining the campaign. Turns out you were right. Just the players were different."

"So that somehow makes it okay?" Ryan fumed.

"Not okay, but what exactly is it she did that was so bad besides not tell you what she'd gotten involved in?" Paul asked. "Granted, she started out conspiring against you, but she didn't take any action. And she brought the video to you before it got leaked."

"I can't believe you're taking her side."

"Look," Paul said soothingly, "I get that you're hurt because she wasn't completely honest with you, but it sounds like she got in over her head. It's pretty obvious that Everly Briggs took advantage of her. And, from the sound of things, London McCaffrey as well. I've seen you two together and it's pretty obvious how you feel about each other. Don't let one mistake ruin what you two could have."

I love you.

"You don't get it..." Further protests lodged in his throat. She loved him? How was that possible when she'd lied to and betrayed him?

The video of Jefferson and Patty Joyce played in his mind. His pain was nothing compared to what Susannah was about to feel.

"Ryan?"

He realized Paul had continued talking. "What?"

"I asked if it was okay if I called Zoe about the documents she got from London McCaffrey."

"Sure. Fine."

If Paul was interested, did that mean something illegal had taken place? Would Ryan be responsible for sending two more women to jail? The thought of Zoe behind bars turned his blood to ice.

"Paul, wait a second," Ryan said. "I don't want anything to happen to these women because of me."

"Not even after they conspired to get revenge on you?"

Ryan ignored his friend's amused tone. "Just go at this as my friend, okay? Not as a former cop and cybersecurity specialist."

"Whatever you say. Call me after you talk to Susannah."

"Will do."

Ten minutes after hanging up with Paul, Ryan parked outside the campaign headquarters and headed in. Over half the desks were full of volunteers and campaign staff, most of whom were on the phone. Ryan made a beeline for Susannah's office, unsurprised to find her talking with Gil.

"I need to talk with my sister in private," Ryan said after exchanging a brief greeting with her campaign manager.

"Sure."

Ryan shut the door after the man departed and then lowered all the blinds to ensure complete privacy. Susannah watched him in silence, her eyebrows raised.

"Well, this is dramatic," she said as he sat across from her. "What's going on?"

"I found out something about Zoe today that proves I was right about her motives for coming to work for the campaign."

Susannah's amused expression faded. "Ryan, I'm sorry. I know how much you care about her."

That his sister's first reaction to his news was concern for him was a poignant reminder of why he loved her so much. His heart ached at the blow he was about to deliver.

"It's bad, SuSu." He pulled out his phone and queued up the video. "She's been working with Everly Briggs to mess up your campaign. Today, she showed me this."

He started the video and handed Susannah his phone. Susannah's expression went from confusion to shock and finally horror as she watched her husband head into a hotel room with her deputy campaign manager.

"Zoe took this?" Susannah's neutral tone was at odds with her shaken appearance.

"No. Everly did. I think we can expect this will be leaked to the press or possibly sent to Abernathy at some point in the near future."

"Can you send this to Gil?" Susannah's hands were shaking as she handed the phone back to Ryan. "He'll want to start strategizing damage control as soon as possible." Before she finished speaking, she got to her feet and pulled her purse out of a drawer. "Tell him if he needs to get hold of me later, I'll be at home discussing the situation with Jefferson."

"Is there anything else you need for me to do?" Ryan asked. "Do you want me to come with you and maybe take the kids out for ice cream so you can have the conversation in private?"

"Thanks for the offer, but Candi will be there," Susannah said, referring to her housekeeper. "I'll get her to take them."

Ryan wasn't fooled by his sister's appearance of calm. She was passionate about fair play and justice, and he knew firsthand the painful penalty she dealt when crossed.

"Don't worry about anything here," he told her, catching Gil's eye and motioning him over. "Gil and I will handle everything."

Eleven

It had taken Zoe less than an hour to pack up and vacate Ryan's guest apartment. He'd installed electronic door locks so she had no keys to drop off. In no time at all she was settled back into her storeroom almost as if staying with Ryan had been a wonderful dream she'd awakened from.

In the aftermath of her tempestuous day, Zoe was too overwhelmed to process all that had happened. Thinking about any of it made her chest tight and sent black dots swimming across her vision. She longed for someone to confide in, but couldn't imagine burdening anyone with her story who wasn't already involved. She couldn't contact London…

And yet, why not?

Everly had shattered their pact by telling Tristan that Zoe had his legal and financial documents. Maybe she'd also divulged that London had been the person responsible for securing the information. In which case, she needed to be warned.

Zoe looked up the address for London's ExcelEvent company. To her surprise, the office was three blocks away from Second Chance Treasures. Impulsively she dialed the phone number. Since it was nearly eight, she didn't really expect anyone would answer.

"ExcelEvent, London McCaffrey speaking."

For several heartbeats, Zoe was too stunned to speak. She hadn't expected getting hold of London would be this easy and had not planned what to say.

"Hello?" London sounded anxious. "Is anyone there?"

"It's Zoe." The words came out of her in a hoarse whisper.

"Zoe, oh my goodness. You scared me. I thought it was Everly. Are you okay?"

Relief swept through Zoe that she wasn't the only one suffering at Everly's hands. "It's all coming apart. I think we should meet and talk."

"I'm at my office. Can you come by now? I don't think we should be seen together in public."

"I'm at my store. Turns out we're just a few blocks apart." She sounded a little hysterical as she relayed that detail. "I'll be by in ten minutes."

The walk helped calm Zoe down and by the time she arrived at ExcelEvent, she was ready to have a productive conversation.

London had been watching for her because before Zoe could knock, the door opened and the beautiful blonde gestured her inside. Although the two women hadn't been in contact since the Beautiful Women Taking Charge event, they hugged like old friends.

"I love your new look," London told her as they drew apart. "The cut really shows off your bone structure."

"I needed a change," Zoe murmured, feeling no less intimidated by the successful entrepreneur than she had at their last meeting.

"Come into my office."

While London led the way through the reception area

and down a hallway, Zoe couldn't help but absorb the chic, elegant offices of ExcelEvent and find them far superior to the casual, eclectic styling of Second Chance Treasures.

"I think we both have a lot to tell each other," London said as the two women settled onto the sofa in her large office.

"First, let me start by thanking you for getting the legal and banking documents from Tristan."

"I didn't," London admitted. "I couldn't. Harrison got them for me."

"Harrison?" Although she liked her former brother-in-law, they hadn't been close and she couldn't imagine why he'd take such a big risk to help her. "Why? How?"

"I told him the truth. All of it. He knows what you've been through and decided to help you out."

That's where London had it wrong. He'd acted to help London. She knew London and Harrison had been seen out together. Until now she hadn't realized they'd become involved.

"But this means he sided against his brother," Zoe said. "Tristan isn't gonna like that."

Pride glowed in London's eyes. "Harrison doesn't care."

"You're in love with him." Sympathy rushed through her. She knew firsthand how difficult it was to find yourself falling for someone you were working against.

"I'm crazy about him."

"How does he feel about you?"

"The same."

Envy speared Zoe straight through the heart. She wanted to be happy like London, forgiven, loved, eagerly looking to the future. Instead the man she loved despised her. Add to that her guilt over the damage she'd done to Ryan and his family, her financial challenges and the loss of her store. Her will to fight was gone. She might as well give up and return to Greenville.

"I'm happy for you both," Zoe said. "Harrison is a great guy and he deserves to be with someone wonderful."

"I don't know that I necessarily fit the bill." London's expression twisted with remorse. "We've done a terrible thing."

"I know," Zoe admitted. "I really regret meeting Everly and agreeing to go after Ryan."

"So do I." London's voice dipped into ominous tones. "I think she's crazy."

Zoe nodded. "And dangerous. She told Tristan what we're up to."

London looked more annoyed than surprised. "She sent Harrison a recording of me saying that I'd used Harrison as a way to get to Tristan and that Harrison meant nothing to me. I was trying to conceal from her that I'd fallen in love with him and he took my words at face value."

The video of Jefferson and Patty Joyce flashed in Zoe's mind. "What happened?"

"I told him everything and miraculously we're still together."

"I'm glad," Zoe said, recalling her own stab at telling Ryan the truth.

"I'm really lucky he did. When trust leaves a relationship, it's a hard thing to regain."

"And sometimes you never can."

Despair consumed Zoe without warning. The pain of it struck fast and hard, doubling her over. She buried her face in her hands as hot tears filled her eyes. A gentle hand rubbed her back, soothing her.

"It's going to be okay," London murmured. "Whatever you need, Harrison and I will help you."

"No one can help. Everly…" She gulped air into her lungs, shuddering at the effort it took to breathe.

"Let me get you some tea and then you can tell me all about it."

London set a box of tissues on the coffee table within Zoe's reach and headed out of the room. With her bout of hysteria fading, Zoe wiped her eyes and blew her nose.

"Here you go," London said, setting down a tray containing two steaming bone-china cups, crystal sugar and creamer containers, and cloth napkins. "It's Lavender Earl Grey."

While Zoe added a splash of cream to her cup, London departed, returning a minute later with a plate of cookies and several strawberries.

The impromptu feast made Zoe smile. "You sure know how to throw a party," she murmured, nibbling on a shortbread cookie.

"It is what I do for a living, after all," London pointed out. "Are you feeling better?"

"Much. Tea and sugar helps," Zoe said. "Thank you." To her dismay a fresh wash of tears filled her eyes. "Oh, damn." She dabbed at her eyes with a tissue. "I'm not usually like this, but it's just been a terrible day."

"Earlier you said it's so much worse than I knew," London said. "What has been going on?"

Zoe went into detail about her financial difficulties because of the divorce and how they'd affected her store. How Ryan and Susannah had helped. She explained about the video and that Ryan was on his way to break the news to his sister.

"Susannah was so wonderful," Zoe finished. "I couldn't bring myself to do anything bad to her or the campaign, but in the long run it didn't matter. Everly took matters into her own hands."

"I know it seems bad," London said, "but I can't imagine that if the affair gets out it's going to cause Susannah any lasting damage. It's not as if she was the one caught cheating. In fact, people might feel bad for her."

"I hope that's the case, but she's still going to be devastated."

"I agree, but it's not because of anything you've done. Or even what Everly did. Her husband is the one who betrayed her."

"I'm not sure either Ryan or Susannah will see it that way. He's fully blaming me for the mess."

"That's ridiculous."

Whatever else London intended to say was interrupted by a call coming in on Zoe's cell. She frowned at the unfamiliar number.

"Are you going to answer it?" London asked.

"What if it's Everly?" Zoe let the call roll to voice mail and then listened to the message on speaker.

"Zoe, this is Paul Watts. Ryan told me what's going on and I'd like to talk to you about the documents you received from London McCaffrey."

Both women looked up from the phone at the same time and their gazes locked. In London's gaze she saw the same anxiety fluttering in her chest.

"Who is Paul Watts and why is he asking about the documents?"

"He owns a company that specializes in cybersecurity, and is Ryan's best friend."

A very unladylike curse slipped from London's lips, but her expression grew resolute. "Call him back. See if he can come here tonight."

"Are you sure?"

"I think we both need to face up to what we've done," London said. "And if we can take Everly down with us, all the better."

In the three days since Ryan had broken the news to his sister about her husband's infidelity, Susannah had been square in the middle of a media storm. She and Gil had decided to go on the offensive about Jefferson's affair before the video could be leaked and effectively turned the court of public opinion in her favor.

Susannah's campaign had picked up dozens of volunteers and the inflow of donations had skyrocketed. As far as her run for state senate went, Zoe and her friends had actually helped his sister. Personally, however, Susannah had been dealt a significant blow.

Ryan trotted up the stairs to his sister's house, noting the darkness lurking behind the French doors that opened up onto the wraparound deck. The air of emptiness was unusual for a house that was usually blazing with light. With his uneasiness increasing, he rang the bell and barely heard the chime ring over the cacophony of insect noises.

The home sat on two acres and backed up to deep-water access just minutes from Charleston Harbor. Jefferson was an avid boater and loved to spend the weekends on the water with his kids. Susannah preferred to keep her feet on solid ground and didn't usually accompany them on their adventures.

On the other side of the glass door a figure came toward him through the darkness. Ryan recognized Susannah's housekeeper by her petite frame.

Candi opened the door and scowled at him. "It's late."

Ryan ignored the rebuff. "How is she doing?"

"How do you think she's doing?" Candi had been with the Kirby family since Susannah and Jeff had married. She was an integral part of the household and fiercely loyal to Susannah.

"Can I come in and talk to her?"

With a disgusted snort, Candi stepped back and gestured him inside. "She's on the dock."

That caught Ryan by surprise. He would've expected to find his twin in the place she was most comfortable: her home office. "What is she doing out there?"

Candi glared at him. "She's a grown woman, not a child for me to check on."

Throwing up his hands in surrender, Ryan cruised into the kitchen for a beer before heading out the French doors leading from the kitchen to a set of stairs down to the yard. From the back steps to the end of the dock, it was the length of a city block. With each stride Ryan's heart hammered harder and harder as he contemplated what sort of state his sister was in.

Although she had to hear his footsteps on the wood dock, she didn't shift her gaze away from the moonlit water as he slid onto the Adirondack chair beside hers. A half-empty bottle of bourbon sat near her feet and she was swirling liquid in a crystal tumbler.

Ryan sipped his beer and filled his lungs with the night air while he waited for whatever Susannah felt like sharing.

"Jeff's gone," she said at last. "Just packed a bag and walked out on ten years of marriage."

"Ah, hell, SuSu, I'm sorry."

"You should be," she said dully. "It's all your fault."

The accusation didn't surprise him, but her defeated tone did. It wasn't like his sister to give up.

"If it wasn't for you, my campaign wouldn't be under attack."

Even though Zoe and her friends had caused Susannah's current situation, Ryan recognized his actions had created the problem.

"I'm sorry," he said. "If I hadn't tried to help Kelly Briggs—"

Susannah seemed oblivious to the tears pouring from her eyes and soaking her cheeks. "What am I going to do without him?"

The raw despair in his twin's voice savaged Ryan's heart. He'd never heard anything like this from Susannah. She was the strong, steady one. Now, to hear her sound so despondent, it was as if some fundamental part of her had shattered, never to be repaired.

Ryan reached for her hand and wrapped his fingers around hers. "You can do anything you set your mind to," he told her, squeezing gently. "Fix your marriage. Go on without Jeff. You are our family's greatest success story."

Susannah dashed the back of her free hand across her cheek. Her breath flowed out of her in a ragged hiss. She looked no less beaten, but her fingers pulsed weakly in Ryan's grip.

"My husband cheated. And even though Abernathy didn't get to leak the video, he will use it to attack my worthiness as a state senate candidate. I think most people would point to me as a blistering example of what not to do." She picked up her glass and swallowed the remaining contents in a single gulp. For a long moment she stared out over the water. "Maybe I took too much for granted. My marriage. My career. It was always about what I wanted. What was good for me."

"Don't start blaming yourself. Jefferson had the affair."

"Sure, but did I drive him to it?"

"'Drive him'?" Ryan echoed with a heavy dose of skepticism. "Why? Because you were focused on your career and your family? Because he wasn't your first priority? Don't be ridiculous."

"Nothing this bad has happened to me before." She turned her gaze on him. "I wasn't there for you enough during the Kelly Briggs incident," she said, her fingers tightening fiercely over his. "I'm sorry."

"Don't be." Ryan hated seeing his sister like this. "What can I do to help you? Name it. Anything goes. I can beat the crap out of Jefferson if it would make you feel better. Just say the word."

"I think there's been more than enough payback going

on, don't you?" Susannah sighed. "Have you spoken with Zoe?"

"No. Why would I do that?"

"To see how she's handling things."

"Can you really be worried about her after what she did to you?"

"She didn't do anything to me." Susannah frowned at him. "This wasn't her fault. Jefferson cheated. Your actions brought Everly Briggs into our lives."

"Zoe lied to us."

"Not about who she is or how much she cares about you."

Ryan shook his head, vigorously denying Susannah's claim. "She used me to get to you. That's all there is to it."

"Oh, don't say that. I don't want both of us to lose the people we love over this."

"I don't love her."

"Really? Because you've been acting as if you do." Before he could dispute that, she continued. "I've never seen you this miserable over a breakup before. She hurt you badly and you're busy beating yourself up about how you should've seen it coming."

"Whatever." Ryan hated how well Susannah knew him. "The fact is she lied to me and I can't ever trust her again."

"People make mistakes all the time," his sister said. "The key is to learn from them. I think Zoe has done that. She must feel terrible for what she did to you. Forgive her."

"Are you going to forgive Jefferson?" Ryan countered. "Can you ever trust him again?"

"I don't know yet, but I'm not giving up without trying and neither should you."

Ever since she'd first started Second Chance Treasures, Zoe had kept the store open on Wednesday nights until nine. Labeling the event Girls Night Out, she served glasses of wine and treats to draw in customers and offered crafting or art demonstrations. Some weeks they made as much money in those few hours as they did the balance of the week. Tonight had been no exception.

Too bad it wasn't enough to save the store.

Earlier that day, Zoe had contacted her artists with the terrible news that Second Chance Treasures was closing in less than a month. She'd received responses of sorrow and sympathy with some anger mixed in. Zoe weathered it all with ever-sinking spirits, knowing that she'd failed these women who'd counted on the money they made from selling items in her store.

All through the evening, Zoe had called on reserves she'd never plumbed before and maintained a bright smile. As much fun as the event could be, the long day was draining and with her emotions running high, Zoe was glad when at a little after nine, she headed to the front door to throw the lock.

As she reached the glass door, a figure stepped into the glow of light spilling onto the sidewalk. Zoe's heart plunged as she recognized Ryan's sister, but dreading what Susannah had to say didn't stop Zoe from welcoming her inside.

"Can we talk?" Susannah asked, showing none of the hostility Zoe would've expected.

"Talk?" she countered, locking the door and sealing them in like two combatants in a cage fight. "Or are you here to yell at me for everything that's happened?"

"I don't yell," Susannah replied tartly.

"No, you just shred people with your rhetoric."

The corner of Susannah's mouth kicked up. "While that's more accurate, I'm not here to accuse you of anything. I want to understand."

And Zoe wanted to explain.

"Come into the back," Zoe said, flipping off the light at the front of the store and gesturing for Susannah to follow her.

Susannah's keen gaze swept over the cot and packing boxes that held her extra inventory. Zoe had shopped at several thrift stores to find furniture pieces, lamps and decorative things to make the space more comfortable, but it was still a storage area in a retail space.

"Are you living here?"

"For another couple weeks and then I'm closing the store and moving to Greenville." Zoe offered no more explanation and Susannah didn't ask any follow-up questions. "Would you like some tea?"

"Do you have anything stronger?"

Zoe shot a glance at Ryan's sister, trying to determine if she was being serious. How much stronger?

"There's lemon vodka in the freezer for emergencies."

"Perfect." Susannah nodded. "Break it out. This is definitely an emergency."

Unsure what the other woman meant, Zoe nevertheless poured shots of vodka over ice and gestured at the small table the staff used for breaks. Since Susannah had been the one who'd initiated the encounter, Zoe decided to let her speak first.

"Tell me about your relationship with Everly Briggs."

Zoe winced. "Relationship is the wrong word. It started with a random encounter at a networking event."

She then went on to lay out their conversation and how they'd arrived at the scheme to take down the three men who'd hurt them. Susannah listened in silence, asking no questions, but her eyes glowed with keen interest.

"It sounds like she played both you and London to get what she wanted," Susannah remarked over an hour later as Zoe's tale wound down.

"You're probably right. We were stupid to get involved with her, but in our defense, we were both in a pretty bad place emotionally and mentally."

During her narrative, Zoe hadn't taken a sip of her drink,

but now she swallowed nearly half the shot, closing her eyes as the watered-down liquor burned her throat and warmed her chest enough that the ache around her heart eased somewhat.

Regardless of whether Susannah remained angry, the confession had brought Zoe a modicum of peace. For so long she'd held on to fear, unhappiness, anger and remorse. Being filled with so many negative emotions had kept her from embracing the brighter, lighter feelings from all the good in her life.

Opening the store had inspired a sense of accomplishment and given her a community of women she could trust. Meeting Ryan had awakened hope and given rise to her sexuality in a way she'd never known. Yet full happiness had eluded her because she remained tethered to the revenge bargain she and London had made with Everly.

"I'm really sorry for everything that happened between you and your husband. I had no business going after you as a way to hurt Ryan. It was wrong and I have no way to make any of it up to you."

"I've spent a great deal of time thinking about you these last few days," Susannah said, her gray eyes—so like her twin's—drilling into Zoe with all the force of her significant resolve. "As well as reflecting on my marriage and the choices I've made."

Zoe resisted the urge to squirm as she awaited whatever hell Susannah decided to rain down on her, knowing she deserved everything the lawyer had to say.

"If you'd never showed up in my life, Jefferson would still be cheating. No doubt Abernathy and his dirty tactics would've broken the scandal as a way to muck up the race."

"That's not necessarily true," Zoe said, but she didn't fully believe it.

Susannah shrugged. "Regardless, Everly Briggs would've come after Ryan via my campaign if you'd never been in the picture. From what you've told me, she interfered between London and Harrison Crosby the same way she did by telling your ex-husband what you were up to."

"I suppose you're right." Zoe wasn't sure if she should let herself feel relieved that Susannah was showing mercy.

Since getting to know Susannah, it had bothered Zoe more and more that by betraying Ryan's sister, Zoe had behaved like some of the women in her former social circle.

"If I asked you stay away from my brother, would you?" Susannah's abrupt question wasn't one Zoe had expected, but she should have.

"You don't need to ask." The tightness in Zoe's chest made breathing difficult so the words came out in a wheezy rush. "He made it clear that he doesn't want to have anything more to do with me."

"He's hurt."

A lump formed in Zoe's throat. "I hurt him."

Susannah waggled her glass, setting the ice cubes to tinkling. "I think I could use a refill."

Zoe fetched the bottle and more ice, setting both on the table within Susannah's reach.

"You didn't answer my question," Susannah said. "Would you stay away from my brother?"

Susannah's request wasn't particularly difficult to agree to given Zoe's last conversation with Ryan. "Yes."

"Because I asked or because you're not in love with him?"

"I don't see why it matters. Your brother made it clear how he feels about me."

"It matters because I'm trying to decide whether or not to fight for my marriage and I really need to believe that love can conquer all right now."

"Love…" Zoe mused. "Before Ryan came along, I'd never believed in it. I think you know that my own marriage wasn't based on anything romantic or grounded in respect and trust."

"And now?"

"I love Ryan with all my heart. It's why I couldn't go through with damaging your campaign. You are so important to him that by harming you, I'd be hurting him." Zoe blew out her breath. "I just wish I'd been truthful earlier. Maybe I could've saved all of us a lot of pain."

"Not me," Susannah said, her dry smile one of sorrow but also strength. "I created my heartbreak all by myself."

Silence filled the room for several minutes while Susannah stared off into space, giving Zoe time to contemplate all that had been said. Did Susannah want Zoe to stay away from Ryan? Why not just say that instead of asking if she would?

Could Susannah be okay with Zoe and Ryan being together? More importantly, was it possible that Ryan could someday forgive her? And was she strong enough to fight for his love?

"Why are you closing Second Chance Treasures?" Susannah said, breaking into Zoe's thoughts. "Ryan told me you'd gotten a handle on your financial troubles and that the store was doing better."

"My ex-husband bought the building so he could evict me."

"You could move somewhere else and start over."

"I don't have enough money." Grief welled up in Zoe. She blinked back tears. "And even if there was, I don't have enough fight in me to pick up the pieces."

"So what are you going to do instead?"

"Go back to Greenville and get a job."

"What about all the women you help with the store? If you aren't able to fight for yourself, what about them?"

Zoe's heart gave a painful wrench at Susannah's question, but she set her chin and gestured around the space. "This is all I have. Once I lose it…"

"Let me help you."

Even as Zoe shook her head, she realized she'd under-estimated the strength of Susannah's will.

"You can and you will." Susannah's eyes burned with feverish intensity. "Now, why don't you pull out the docu-ments London got from Tristan and let's see what we can do to get you a better settlement."

"I gave everything back to Tristan."

For several seconds Susannah regarded her in surprise. "Can you go after the company who bought the building? Tristan is the owner, correct?"

Zoe brightened. Here was a question she could answer. "TA Charleston Holdings, LLC. But it won't do you any good. It's an offshore company that isn't subject to US laws." She'd done some research.

"Don't be so cynical. I know several very good attor-neys who are quite familiar with the ins and outs of off-shore tax shelters."

"I don't know if it's worth pursuing," Zoe hedged. While the idea of hitting Tristan where it hurt appealed to her, her instincts cautioned against trying. "You don't know what Tristan is like."

"You're afraid of him."

Zoe nodded. "He scares me more than Everly does."

"Well, neither one of them scares me," Susannah de-clared and Zoe hoped that wasn't the vodka talking. "You deserve to be treated fairly and I'm willing to play dirty to make that happen."

Twelve

"What brings you by?" Ryan asked, gesturing his sister inside.

"I wanted to talk to you about Zoe."

Ryan's first impulse was to snap at his twin about staying out of his personal life, but he swallowed it. Susannah's concerned expression told him she was trying to help.

"What about Zoe?"

"I went by the store to see her."

He led the way into his living room and turned off the TV. As silence pressed down on the space, he exhaled heavily.

"Why did you do that?"

Susannah sat on his couch, looking unruffled at his grouchy attitude. "I wanted to hear her version of what happened with Everly Briggs."

"And now that you have?"

"She regrets ever meeting the woman and wishes she could change the decisions she made."

"Don't we all." Ryan flopped onto the couch and leaned

his head back against the cushion beside his sister. "Have you spoken with Jefferson?"

"Of course." Susannah sounded surprised at his question.

"And?"

"And what?"

"Are you getting a divorce?"

"It's far too early to make such a decision. He's ended the thing with Patty." Susannah's even tone gave no indication how she felt about that.

Ryan's heart ached for his sister. "I guess that's a start? So, what's next?"

A faint line appeared between Susannah's brows. "I'd like to keep my family intact. We've decided to seek counseling." With a fond smile, Susannah reached out and squeezed his hand. "But what I really wanted to talk about tonight is you and Zoe."

"There is no me and Zoe."

"She's planning to leave Charleston," Susannah said.

This news was a blow Ryan wasn't ready for. "When?"

"As soon as she gets everything settled with the store. She's being evicted."

"Why?"

"Seems her ex-husband bought the property so he could continue to mess up her life." Sympathy glinted in Susannah's eyes.

The news roused his protective instinct. "Why didn't she tell me?"

"She found out the same day she received the video," his sister explained. "Maybe she thought my problem was more important than her own."

Ryan closed his eyes against the sharp pain in his chest. "You can't possibly be taking her side in this, too."

Susannah waved away his accusation. "I'm not taking sides. What do you mean 'too'?"

"Paul thinks I'm crazy to let her go."

"I've always liked Paul. He's very sensible."

"You only like him when he agrees with you."

"That's not true." Susannah grinned. "I had a huge crush on him in high school. We even dated for a month."

"You what?" Ryan couldn't believe what he was hearing. "When?"

"Spring of senior year." Susannah's eyes twinkled. Actually twinkled. "We decided you wouldn't like it so we kept our relationship a secret from you." While Ryan tried to wrap his head around his sister and best friend dating, Susannah continued. "Do you hate me? Or Paul? Are we less trustworthy because we kept something from you all these years?"

Ryan saw right away where she was going. "Of course not," he snapped, but couldn't ignore a tiny blip of discomfort. The feeling faded quickly, but there was no denying that his perception of Susannah and Paul had altered minutely. "And what Zoe did was so much worse."

"Was it? She planned to do something and didn't. In high school Paul and I actively spent a month lying to you and have kept you in the dark ever since." Susannah paused, giving him a moment to absorb her point. "Your relationship with Zoe progressed faster and farther than any before it. You've probably been feeling a bit exposed and insecure, but latching onto her mistake as an excuse to dump her so you avoid getting hurt?" Susannah shook her head. "Not cool, brother."

"I need to think about it."

"Don't think too long. She needs a hero to rescue her from that wretched ex-husband of hers."

"How am I supposed to do that?"

"Paul and I have some ideas how to make that happen." Susannah's expression was positively devilish. "And to put an end to Everly's revenge plot once and for all."

* * *

Zoe started as a knock sounded on the back door leading out to the parking lot. She wasn't expecting any of her artists to stop by to pick up their inventory and the next person who popped into her mind was Everly. Although she was tempted to ignore the summons, curiosity poked at her and she went to open the door.

"Ryan?" Her lungs seized as she stared at him, buffeted by longing and regret. "What are you doing here?"

"Susannah told me you were closing the store and leaving Charleston."

A lump formed in her throat, preventing her from speaking, so she nodded. He looked so wonderful standing there with his dark hair tousled and his gray eyes somber and concerned. She clenched her hands into fists to keep from throwing herself against his wide chest, wrapping her arms around his neck and sobbing her misery on his strong shoulders.

"Do you want to come in?"

"Thanks."

The instant he stepped across the threshold, she knew she'd made a mistake. Overwhelming despair swamped her, bringing tears to her eyes.

"I'm so sorry," she murmured, turning away. She dashed moisture from her cheeks, but it was just as swiftly replaced with new tears.

"Zoe."

It was just her name, but the throb of emotion in Ryan's voice sent her anguish spiraling ever deeper. Over the last year she'd spent way too much time pondering all the poor choices she'd made. Yet, the entire list of regrets didn't equal her remorse over what she'd done to lose Ryan's trust.

When his hands closed over her upper arms, she covered her face with her hands and nearly doubled over as raw pain bloomed in her chest. She wished he wasn't being so kind. His anger she could face without breaking down, but his compassion twisted her inside out.

"Ah, sweetheart, don't cry." He pulled her back against his chest and wrapped his arms around her. "I'm sorry."

His apology shocked her into laughter. "Why?"

Ryan spun her around and wiped her tears away with his thumbs. "Because I overreacted when you told me what you'd been up to."

She gulped in several ragged breaths before she could speak. "You didn't."

"Everyone disagrees with you." He pulled her back into his arms and set his cheek against the top of her head.

Zoe resisted his warm embrace. She couldn't reconcile how angry he'd been at their last meeting with this loving, forgiving man. What had transformed his attitude in the days since she'd shown him the video? Zoe knew Susannah had gone public with Jefferson's affair, and that must've taken a toll on the entire family. Yet Ryan's twin had graciously reached out to Zoe. And forgiven her. Why did she believe Ryan would do anything less?

Because her perceptions of Ryan had been poisoned by Everly describing him as vindictive when crossed.

"I'm so sorry," she repeated again. Surrendering to her heart's desire Zoe wrapped her arms around his waist and held on tight.

"Let's be done with all the apologizing. I forgive you. If you can forgive me, then we can get past this and move forward with our lives."

She wasn't surprised he wanted closure on their relationship. He wasn't the sort who left things undone.

"Okay."

Relief mixed with disappointment as Zoe pressed her cheek against his thudding heart. If they weren't meant to be together, at least she could find peace in a warm parting, released from guilt and able to recall their time together free from shadows.

"Good." Ryan's gave her a squeeze before easing away. "Now, I have something for you."

While Zoe wiped away the last trace of tears, Ryan pulled an envelope out of his jacket pocket.

"What is that?"

"Open it and see."

Unsure what to make of his eager expression, Zoe opened the flap and peered inside. She glimpsed some sort of legal documents and frowned.

"Are you suing me?"

Ryan's eyes went wide and for a long moment he appeared too stunned to speak. Then his breath hissed out and he shook his head.

"Damn, you've really been through the wringer, haven't you?" He took the envelope back and pulled out the pages, turning them so she could read what was written. "You are now the proud owner of this building."

Unable to process what she was hearing, Zoe stared at the document. "But Tristan owns the building."

"Not anymore. For the sum of ten dollars, he sold it to you."

The news jolted her, giving rise to hope. "Why would he do that?"

"Let's just say that Paul, Susannah and I can be very persuasive when we combine our talents."

"You did this?" Zoe shifted her gaze to Ryan. "Why would you help me after everything…?"

"I needed a way to keep you around." He put the papers back in the envelope and dropped them on a nearby box before taking her hands in his.

"You do?" Zoe's heart began to race at the expression on his face. "But you said we should move forward with our lives."

"Damn it, Zoe." He dropped his chin to his chest and shook his head. "I meant together."

A strange buzzing filled her ears as she gazed up into Ryan's gray eyes and drank in the open affection with which he stared down at her. Her mind was slow to accept what she was seeing. Could he really want to be with her after everything she'd done?

"Oh."

"'Oh'?" he echoed, his tone wry. "Is that a yes?"

Yes. Yes. Yes! The word blasted through her mind, but she'd been through so much in the last year. It seemed impossible that everything had worked out so perfectly for her.

"Are you sure?" she asked, wanting so desperately for him to reassure her, but terrified that he might change his mind after further thought.

His eyebrow rose. "Do you still love me?"

"Of course," she shot back, a smile trembling on her lips even as her throat tightened. "Always and forever."

"That's exactly how I feel about you." His smile lit up her entire world. "I love you so much. You're the best thing that's ever happened to me and I want to spend the rest of my life with you."

This perfect moment seemed too fragile to last. Zoe needed a few seconds to linger in the perfect bliss of Ryan's declaration. While her gaze toured his handsome face, she let her past hurts and failures fall away. Those things no longer had power over the Zoe Alston reflected in Ryan's eyes.

He saw her as good and strong and worthy. Basking in his admiration, she felt beautiful both inside and out.

"I want that, too," she whispered, her confidence skyrocketing.

This man had seen her at her worst and found a way to love her despite all her flaws. He'd accepted that she wasn't perfect and had never required her to be anything other than who she was. They'd weathered her mistakes and she trusted that their love would carry them through any crisis.

That was more than enough to build a future on and Zoe couldn't wait to begin.

Epilogue

At a little after three thirty in the afternoon, Everly entered Connor Properties and stepped up to the receptionist desk. "Everly Briggs to see Devon Connor."

The pretty brunette smiled and said, "Have a seat. I'll let Gregg know you've arrived."

Ten minutes later, a slender man in his midtwenties entered the lobby and headed in her direction.

Gregg's smile was cool as he approached. "Hello, Everly. How nice to see you're early." No doubt Devon's assistant was referring to a meeting a couple of weeks earlier when she'd stood Devon up. "I'll take you to the conference room so you can get set up."

"Thank you," she said, scowling at Gregg's back as she followed him down the hall.

She'd been to Connor Properties several times since she'd pitched her branding approach to Devon three years earlier. Since then he'd doubled the number of resorts he owned and his account had grown to the point where it was over two-thirds of her business.

"Right in here." Gregg ushered her into a conference

room. "Can I get you anything? A cup of coffee? Some bottled water?"

"I'm fine."

After showing her how to connect her laptop to the projector, Gregg left Everly to set up her presentation. In addition to the new design for the website, she had mocked up some brochures and promotional materials. Everly hoped Devon liked this version. He'd been very disappointed with the last two concepts she'd presented and if this round went badly, she might lose all his business.

The conference room door opened and Everly looked up. Delight coursed along her nerve endings as Devon Connor entered the room. Not only was he a brilliant businessman, but also one of Charleston's most eligible bachelors and Everly had long wished they had more than a professional relationship. However, her heart stopped a second later as she spied the pair who came into the room behind him.

"Good afternoon, Everly," Devon said.

Usually his deep voice gave her butterflies. Today all she felt was nauseated.

"Hello, Devon." Although she greeted him, her eyes were drawn to his companions. "What's going on?"

"These two were interested in speaking with you before our meeting." He arched one dark eyebrow at her. "That's not a problem, is it?"

"No, of course not." She swallowed hard and forced a smile.

"Wonderful. I'll be back in fifteen minutes." With that, he exited the room, abandoning Everly to her fate.

"What the hell are you doing here?"

London raised her eyebrows at Everly's tone. "Being blindsided isn't a lot of fun, is it?"

"We regret our part in plotting against Linc, Tristan and Ryan," Zoe piped up. "It was wrong."

"People were hurt." The event planner looked cool and composed in an exquisite sky-blue suit and triple string of pearls. "Ourselves included, and we want you to stop."

"Stop? Why would I do that? You both betrayed me." Everly glared from London to Zoe. "You two deserve everything that happened to you and so much more."

"You have to stop," Zoe exclaimed, glancing to London for support.

From the start Everly had pegged her as the weak link and sent her next words into the heart of Zoe's fears. "I don't have to do anything of the sort. And you forget I have an ally in this little game we've all been playing. Have you forgotten what you tried to do to Tristan?"

"What she tried to do?" London countered. "You disclosed that Zoe had targeted him. He went after her store."

Everly hadn't heard that. She smiled in satisfaction. "Good."

"No," Zoe shot back. "It's not good. All the revenge and payback has to stop."

"We're going to stop you."

There was no way Everly was going to let these two tell her what she had to do. "And how do you plan to do that?"

As she spoke, the conference room door opened again. Everly composed her face, expecting to see Devon Connor, but the four people who walked in shocked her to her toes.

Susannah Dailey-Kirby entered first, her beautiful face lit with satisfaction at Everly's surprise. She was followed by her brother, who stopped behind Zoe. From their body language, Everly guessed the break-up rumors were wrong. Harrison Crosby was there, as well, lending London his support.

Rounding out the quartet was Paul Watts, Ryan's best friend. Everly wasn't sure whether he or Susannah presented the most danger, but suddenly she wasn't feeling all that steady.

"I don't know what you all think you're doing here," she declared, deciding to go on the offensive. "But I won't be intimidated."

"Oh, I think you will," Susannah Dailey-Kirby replied smoothly.

"Your little vengeance plot stops here and now," her brother put in, his expression like granite.

Everly crossed her arms over her chest. "Or what?"

Ryan Dailey scowled. "Or we'll ruin you."

There was a reason they'd chosen to confront her at Connor Properties. Meeting here delivered a strong message. If she didn't agree to their terms, they would mess with her business. Well, she wouldn't be strong-armed like that.

"I'll take you all down with me."

"And who do you think the world will believe?" Zoe demanded, showing more backbone than she ever had before. "All of us or you?"

"In addition, I have a statement from the hacker you hired to get into Tristan Crosby's computer," Paul Watts said.

"But I didn't use the flash drive," Everly protested, pointing at London. "You did."

The event planner shook her head. "Wrong again."

Everly did not like how this was going. She hadn't been able to get justice or revenge for Kelly. Neither Linc nor Ryan had been punished. And London had fallen in love with Harrison. Nothing had gone according to plan and she seemed to be the only one paying a price.

"So are you going to give up and leave us in peace?" Zoe asked, her voice softening.

The sympathy in her gaze was almost more than Everly could bear. "I hate all of you," she snarled.

"But you'll leave us alone," London persisted.

"We don't want to hurt you," Zoe said. "We just want all this to end."

A coalition of six determined people stared at her, awaiting her answer. Everly was out of trump cards and dirty moves. Despite what Zoe had said about not wanting to hurt her, Everly knew if she persisted, they would do whatever it took to make her pay.

Still, seeing London and Zoe so happy, while her sister rotted in jail, made her more resolved than ever to fight. At least that was her plan until the door opened and Devon Connor appeared. His attention went straight to her and something in his unrelenting stare warned her he knew more than he'd let on.

"Have you settled everything?" he asked.

"Not quite," Susannah said. "But I think Everly was just about to agree to our terms."

Rage rose in her. She didn't want to give up or to give in, but with Devon's keen blue eyes watching her intently, Everly recognized she had to stop her vendetta or risk losing her business.

"Fine," she snapped, unsure whom she hated more, the six of them or herself for failing. "Negotiations are over. You win."

"Whew." Zoe blew out her breath as they exited Connor Properties, giddy at being free of Everly and her stupid revenge plot. "That was intense."

The late November sun warmed her face and a light breeze brought the distant chime of a church bell. She linked arms with London, basking in their camaraderie.

"You know," London said, "I almost feel sorry for her."

"Don't you dare," Susannah scolded, coming up on Zoe's other side. "She's responsible for so much heartache. Frankly, I think we let her off too lightly."

Over the last few days Zoe's life had changed in ways she'd never imagined. Not only had she and Ryan made their way back to each other, but now she also had a group of friends she trusted. Starting today, she could stop fretting about what Tristan or Everly might be plotting to do next and start to focus on all the wonderful possibilities her future held.

"Where are we going to celebrate?" Harrison asked as the six of them reached the parking lot.

Paul was the first to shake his head. "Rain check. I'm in the middle of several investigations."

Ryan rolled his eyes at his friend. "When aren't you?"

With a shrug and a wave, Paul headed for his Land Rover.

Zoe watched him go before turning to Susannah. "What about you?"

"Jefferson and I have a counseling session in an hour. I want to swing by the campaign office and let Gil know how this went today." She gave Zoe a quick, hard hug. "You four have fun."

Zoe suggested the rooftop bar at the Vendue and fifteen minutes later they were seated at a table with great views of historic downtown Charleston and the Cooper River. They'd just finished ordering a round of cocktails when Zoe noticed the large diamond sparkling on London's left hand.

"Are you two engaged?" Zoe asked, grabbing her friend's hand and inspecting the engagement ring.

"It must seem fast," London said even as she beamed at Harrison.

"I'm a race car driver," Harrison countered. "Fast is what I do."

"What about you two?" London countered slyly.

Ryan grinned. "I haven't asked her yet."

Yet?

The ink was barely dry on her divorce. It was too soon to think about getting married again. Wasn't it? Zoe's heart skipped at the way Ryan was gazing at her.

"It's been less than a month," Zoe protested but her objection lacked strength.

"Well, what are you waiting for?" Harrison asked.

Ryan pulled something out of his pocket. "I wanted the whole revenge plot problem behind us." He scowled at their companions. "And a little privacy. But after what we've all been through together, maybe it's right that you two are here."

"What are you talking about?" Zoe clapped her hands over her mouth as Ryan slipped from his chair and knelt beside her. "Ryan..." His name escaped her on a low moan.

"Zoe Alston, woman that I love." He paused to grin at her and then, with a dramatic flourish, he popped open the box in his hand. "Will you marry me?"

Zoe's gaze remained locked on Ryan's face as she nodded. Her heart was pounding so hard she thought it might break out of her chest. Never had she imagined it was possible to be this happy.

"Yes. Oh, yes." She leaned forward and wrapped her arms around his neck. "I love you so much."

And then they were kissing and Ryan was sliding the ring on her finger while London and Harrison showered them with congratulations. A bottle of champagne appeared at their table with four glasses so they could toast to love, engagements and the future.

While the men talked football and car racing, Zoe held Ryan's hand and noticed London's fingers were also linked with Harrison's. Luck, fate or some sort of miracle had transformed something that had started so wrong to end so right.

Catching her eye, London leaned in and surprised Zoe by whispering, "I never imagined I could be this happy."

Zoe's throat tightened at the catch in London's voice and she nodded her agreement. "It's pretty amazing how wonderful I feel right now, too."

As she spoke, Zoe caught London's hand, connecting the two couples while the sky darkened above the rooftops of historic Charleston.

* * * * *

A CONVENIENT
SCANDAL

KIMBERLEY TROUTTE

Dedicated to the strong women I call my friends.

History of Plunder Cove

For centuries, the Harpers have masterminded shrewd business deals.

In the 1830s, cattle baron Jonas Harper purchased the twelve-thousand-acre land grant of Plunder Cove on the now affluent California coast. It's been said that the king of Spain dumped the rich land on the American because pirates ruthlessly raided the cove. It is also said no one saw a pirate ship after Jonas bought the land for a rock-bottom price.

Harpers pass this tale on to each generation to remind their heirs that there is a pirate in each of them. Every generation is expected to increase the Harper legacy, usually through great sacrifice, as with oil tycoon, RW Harper, who sent his children away ten years ago.

Now RW has asked his children to return to Plunder Cove—with conditions. He is not above bribing them to get what he wants.

Harpers don't love, they pillage. But if RW's wily plans succeed, all four Harpers, including RW, might finally find love in Plunder Cove.

One

Jeff Harper pressed his forehead to the glass pane of his floor-to-ceiling living room window and watched the mass of reporters swarming below.

They couldn't get a good shot of him at this height, since he was twenty-two floors above Central Park, but once he stepped outside his building they'd attack. Every word he said, or didn't say, would be used to bury him—shovel after shovel piled on top of his rotting career.

Dammit, he hated to fail.

Before this week, Jeff had been able to live with the invasion of his privacy and had learned to use the cameras to his advantage. The press followed him around New York because he was the last unmarried prince of Harper Industries and a hotel critic on the show *Secrets and Sheets*. Paparazzi photographed his dinner dates as if each one was a passionate love match. His name had appeared on the list of America's Most Eligible Bachelors for the last three years running. When pressed during interviews, he always said there was no special woman in his life and he was never getting married. The author of the article inevitably wrapped up with some bogus statement about "Jeffrey Harper just needs to find the right woman to settle him down." Which was a big *hell no*.

Why end up like his parents?

He'd mostly put up with the press until he'd seen his own

backside plastered across tabloid front pages with the head-line "Hotel Critic Caught in Sex Scandal."

Sex scandal. He wished.

He'd been set up.

And the incriminating video had gone viral.

The show he'd created and nurtured was canceled. Everything he'd built—his career, his reputation, his lifelong passion for the hotel industry—had exploded.

Just like that, Jeff was done.

If he didn't fix this, he'd never regain what he'd lost.

Only one person might hire him at this point. Of course, he was the one person Jeff had vowed never to beg.

Grimacing, he dialed the number.

The phone rang once. "Jeffrey, I've been waiting for your call."

Not a good sign since Jeff never called.

"Hey, Dad. I was wondering…" He swallowed hard. This was going to be painful. "Is the family hotel project still on the table?"

A year ago, when Jeff's brother had returned home to Plunder Cove, their father had offered to put Jeff in charge of converting the Spanish mansion into an exclusive five-star resort. He liked the idea more than he'd dared admit. Hotel design, development and management had been his dream career since he was old enough to put blocks together, and he'd steadily worked to become an international expert in the field. But it was more than that. He couldn't put into words why turning his childhood home into a safe place was important. No one would know why using his own hands to reshape the past meant everything to Jeff. Yet…he'd declined his father's offer because RW was a mean, selfish, poor excuse for a father, and he'd never respected Jeff.

But beggars couldn't be choosers, and all that.

"You've reconsidered." RW stated it as fact.

Did he have a choice? "The network pulled my show. I've got time on my hands."

"Wonderful."

Strange word to use under the circumstances, but his father sounded pleased. The tightness in Jeff's chest loosened a bit when he realized he didn't have to beg for the job. He'd half-expected his father would make him grovel. "I'll be there tomorrow."

"There's one condition."

He should have guessed that. Those three words lifted the hairs on the back of Jeff's neck. "Yeah? What?"

"You've got to improve your image. I've seen the video, son."

Jeff paced his living room. "It's not what it looks like."

"That's a relief because it looks like you had a quickie in the elevator at Xander Finn's hotel with a hotel maid. Low-class, son. Harpers pay for suites."

Jeff ground his molars together. "I paid for a suite."

He just hadn't had time to use it while he was undercover exposing a social injustice.

Jeff cared about people and used the power of his name and his show to set things right. The great RW would never understand why Jeff went out of his way to expose the mega-rich like Xander Finn.

Weeks earlier, Finn had threatened bodily harm to the *Secrets and Sheets* crew if they stepped inside the gilded doors of his most expensive Manhattan hotel. The threat had made Jeff wonder what the man had to hide. He'd filmed the episode himself, and the dirt he uncovered would show viewers how badly customers were being ripped off by one of the richest men in New York.

Little did Jeff know that *he* was about to become the one to "break the internet," with ridiculous GIFs and memes.

The latest one said, "Those who can, run a hotel; those who can't, become sex-crazed critics."

"Success is all about image," RW was still talking over the phone. "Yours needs an overhaul, Jeffrey. Didn't you know hotels have video cameras in the elevators?"

"Of course, I do. I was set up!" Jeff slammed his teeth together to keep from blurting out what really happened in the elevator. His father hadn't shielded him from abuse when he was six; why would he shield him now?

No, except for this job offer—with conditions—Jeff was on his own. Always had been.

"Wait." A flicker of foreboding licked up Jeff's spine. "How did you know I was in Finn's elevator? Did he send you the entire video?"

"Xander and I go way back. He's always been a pain in the ass. No, I haven't seen it all, but he promises me it gets worse. I get the sense you don't want the public to see what happens next. Am I correct?"

Jeff let out a slow breath. The small digital slice encircling the internet was bad enough. If the rest went public, there would be no coming back. "What does he want?"

"I bet you can guess."

Jeff rubbed the back of his neck. "The recording I made of his hotel."

"Bingo. And a televised statement that his hotel is above reproach. The best damned hotel you've ever seen." RW paused. "Xander wants you to grovel."

"I'm not doing that. It was one of the worst I've ever seen. Think about the people who save for years to vacation at his fancy hotel. No. It's unacceptable. No one can bully me anymore, Dad."

"Then we have a problem," RW said.

"We?"

"Harper Industries has a reputation to uphold and stockholders to please. We can't go around hiring a sex-crazed—"

"Dad! I was set up."

"Blackmail only works because you were caught on tape. You screwed up." There. That was the father he'd expected when he picked up the phone. The superior tone and words dripping with condemnation were signature RW Harper.

"Blackmail only works if I roll over. I won't do that," Jeff snapped.

"Think carefully," RW said. "He's threatening to release bits and pieces of your damned sex video for eternity unless you agree to his terms. With a constant stream of bad press, you'll never work in New York's hotel industry again. Or anywhere else for that matter. Not even for me."

Jeff pinched the bridge of his nose. "Then he's got me."

"Not if we stop him with good PR. It must be done quickly to keep your train wreck from derailing the entire Plunder Cove project. I promised the townspeople their percentage of resort profits and I intend to keep my word."

"The people in Pueblicito not getting their share. *That's* what bothers you the most about what happened to me?"

"The Harpers owe them, son."

Jeff shook his head. Harpers were pirates—takers, and users. The family tree included buccaneers and land barons who'd once owned the people in Pueblicito. RW was just as bad as past generations because he only cared about increasing profits for Harper Industries.

Greed had destroyed his family.

And now Dad wants to donate profit to strangers? What's the catch?

Jeff didn't believe the mean oil tycoon had grown a charitable heart. It wasn't possible.

"Why now?" Jeff pressed.

"I have my reasons. They're none of your concern."

Deflection. Secrets. Now *that* was more like the father Jeff remembered, which probably meant the old man was stringing the townspeople along in an elaborate con. The RW Jeff knew was a master schemer who fought dirty and stole what he wanted.

"You have a choice. Agree to Xander's terms or agree to mine." RW paused for effect. "Together we can beat him at his own game."

"I'm listening."

"We offer the public a respectable Jeffrey Harper, an upstanding successful hotel developer. You'll again be a businessman everyone looks up to. The shareholders will have undeniable proof that you've settled down and are prepared to represent Harper Industries in this new venture."

"How?"

"With a legal contract signed in front of witnesses."

Jeff frowned. "What sort of contract?"

"The long-lasting, 'until death do you part' sort."

Oh, hell no.

Jeff sat heavily on his couch. "I'm not getting married."

"You can't be a playboy forever. It's time you settled down. Started a family."

"Like you did? How'd that work out for you, Dad?"

It was a low blow, thrown with force. Jeff would never forgive his parents for the hell they'd put him and his brother and sister through.

RW didn't respond. Not that Jeff had thought he would. The silence was a hammer pounding all the nails into the bitter wall lodged between them.

After a long minute RW said, "I'm hiring a project manager at the end of the week. When the hotel is ready, I'll hire a manager for that, too. You agree with my terms and you've got both jobs. Don't agree and you'll be scrounging on your own in New York."

I've been scrounging since I turned sixteen and you kicked me out of the house, old man.

"Think this through." RW's voice grew softer. "The hotel you create on Plunder Cove will be a family legacy. I don't trust easily, but I have faith you'll do it right."

Those words floored him.

He'd never heard anything like them before.

Jeff stared at his size twelve loafers. He wanted to believe what his dad said, but the reality of who RW had always been was too hard to forget—as was the "one condition."

"Come on, Dad. You can't expect me to get married."

"I'll give you a few days to think about it," RW said.

In a few days, another million people would share those damned GIFs and memes. The social media attack would never stop—unless he fought back.

Dad's ridiculous plan was the only thing that made a lick of sense.

It pissed him off, but still he growled, "Have your people start the search for a chef. A great one."

"You want to marry a chef?"

"No, I want to hire one. An exclusive resort needs a five-star restaurant. That's how we'll get the ball rolling. A restaurant is faster to get up and running than a hotel and the best ones get the word out fast. Find me a group of chefs to choose from. Lure them from the world's top restaurants and offer them deals they can't refuse. I'll assess their culinary skills and choose a winner."

"A contest? You'd pit them against each other?"

"Call it part of the cooking interview. We'll see which one can handle the heat. My chef has to be capable of rising above stress."

RW produced a sharp whistle through his nose, the one he used when he was not pleased. "You *must* marry, Jeffrey. That's my only stipulation. I don't care who as long as she makes you look respectable."

Jeff didn't want a wife. He wanted a hotel.

He needed to make Plunder Cove the best locale in the world, and then he'd have his dignity back. And a touch of something that might resemble a survivor's victory.

A plan started to form.

The producer of *Secrets and Sheets* had hounded Jeff for years to do a segment on the Spanish mansion and its pirate past. He'd always said no. Why glorify a place that still gave him nightmares? But now, his childhood home could be the only thing that would help him reboot his career.

"Fine. My crew can film the ceremony in one of the gardens or down on the beach. The reception will be filmed inside the new restaurant. You can't buy better advertising for the resort." The press would eat it up.

"Now that's thinking big. I like it," RW said.

Yeah? Well, hold on because it's only the first part of the plan.

Dad didn't have to know that Jeff was going to dangle the televised wedding to his producer in exchange for something far more important—the final, edited episode of *Secrets and Sheets*. Jeff wished for the fiftieth time that he hadn't given the raw footage to the show's producer. He hadn't thought to keep a copy and now he was empty-handed against Finn. But not for long. Once Jeff had the recording, he'd release it on every media outlet possible. The blackmail would stop and the world would finally know what Finn had done to his customers, and to Jeff.

No one attacked the Harpers and lived to tell the tale.

For the first time that week, Jeff actually smiled.

Michele Cox snuggled next to her sister on the twin bed at the group home and softly read Cari's favorite picture book. *Rosie's Magic Horse* was about a girl who saves her family from financial ruin by riding a Popsicle-stick horse in search of pirate treasure. Michele didn't know which Cari loved more—the idea that a girl could save the day while riding a horse, or that something as small as a used Popsicle stick could aspire to greatness. Whatever the case, Cari insisted that Michele read the book to her at bedtime every night.

Tonight, Cari had fallen asleep before Michele got to the part about the pirates. Michele kept reading anyway. Sometimes she needed her own Popsicle make-believe. When she closed the book, she slipped out of the bed carefully so as not to wake her snoring sister.

Kissing Cari's forehead, Michele whispered, "Sweet dreams, cowgirl."

Michele's heart and feet were heavy as she went down

the hall to the staff station. "I'll call in and read to her every night," Michele said to one of Cari's favorite caregivers. "You've got my number. Text immediately if she gets the sniffles." Cari was susceptible to pneumonia and had been hospitalized several times.

"Don't worry, she'll be fine. She knows the routine and is getting comfortable here. We'll take good care of her."

The pit in Michele's stomach deepened. It had taken six months for Cari to learn the ropes at this home. Six long, painful months. What would happen if Michele couldn't pay the fees to keep her here?

"Thanks for taking care of her. She's all I've got." Michele swiped the tear off her cheek.

"Oh, hon. You go have a good time. You deserve it."

Deserve it? No, Michele was the one who'd messed up and lost the money her sister needed. She was heartsick over it.

She drove to her own apartment, poured herself a glass of wine and plopped down at the table in her painfully silent kitchen. God, she felt so alone. She was the sole provider and caretaker for her sister after Mom had died six months ago. Her father had passed when Michele was only ten. Cari needed services and health care and a chance to be a happy cowgirl, all of which required funds that had been stolen by her so-called partner.

There was only one way to fix the horrible mess she'd made.

She picked up the envelope sitting on top of her polka-dot place mats. "Harper Industries," it said across the top in black embossed letters. Pulling out the employment application, she reread the lines, "Candidates will cook for and be judged by Jeffrey Harper."

Her stomach flopped at the thought.

Michele wasn't a fan of his show. That playboy attitude of his left her cold. She'd had her fill of arrogant, demanding males in her career. She'd given everything she had to the last head chef she'd worked with and where had that left her? Poor and alone. Because of him, she'd lost her desire to cook—which was the last connection she had to her mother.

Mom had introduced her to family recipes when Michele was only seven years old. Cooking together meant tasting, laughing and dancing in the kitchen. All her best memories came from that warm, spicy, belly-filling place. While the rest of the house was dark and choked with bad memories—cancer, pills, dying—the kitchen was safe. Like her mother's embrace.

As a young girl, Michele had experimented with dishes to make her mom and Cari feel better. Mom had encouraged Michele to submit the creations in local cook-offs and, surprisingly, Michele had won every contest she entered. The local paper had called her "a child prodigy" and "a Picasso in the kitchen." Cooking had been easy back then because food was a river of color coursing through her veins. Spatulas and spoons were her crayons. All she had to do was let the colors flow.

But now she was empty, her passion dried up. What if her gift, her single moneymaking talent, never returned?

If Michele Cox wasn't a chef, who was she?

She tapped her pen on the Harper Industries application. Could she fake it? Jeffrey Harper was an infamous critic who publicly destroyed those who didn't meet his standards. Would he know the difference between passionate cooking and plain old cooking? If he did, he'd annihilate her.

But if he didn't...

The Harper chef job came with a twenty-thousand-dollar up-front bonus. Twenty thousand! With that kind of money, Cari could continue riding therapy horses. Hippotherapy was supposed to be beneficial for people with Down syndrome but Michele had been amazed at how her sister had come alive the first time she'd touched a pony. Cari's cognitive, motor, speech and social skills had blossomed. But riding lessons weren't cheap and neither were housing and medical bills. Michele's rent was two weeks late and she barely had enough money in her account to pay for Cari's care.

Her options were slim. If Harper Industries didn't hire her, the two of them might be living on the streets.

She signed the application and went on to the final step. She had to make a video answering a single question: *Why do you want to work for Harper Industries?*

Straightening her spine, she looked into the camera on her computer and pressed the record button. "I want to work for Harper Industries because I need to believe good things can happen to good people." Her voice hitched and she quickly turned the video off.

Shoot. Where'd that come from? She'd almost blurted out what happened at Alfieri's. "Get it together, Michele. If you spill all the sordid details, they'll never hire you."

She scrubbed her cheeks, took a giant inhale and tried again.

"I am Michele Cox, the former chef at a five-star restaurant, Alfieri's, in Manhattan. I will include articles about my awards and specialties but those highlights are not the most important aspect of being a chef, nor are they why I cook.

"Food, Mr. Harper, is a powerful medicine. Good cuisine can make people feel good. When the dishes are excellent, the patron can ease loneliness with a bite of ricotta cannelloni. That's what I do. I make patrons feel happy and loved. I can do that for your new restaurant, too. I hope you'll give me a chance. Thank you."

Well. That wasn't so bad. Before she could change her mind, she pressed Send on the video and sealed the application packet to be sent by overnight mail along with the glowing newspaper articles she'd promised. Today was the day she'd put Alfieri's behind her and search for her cooking mojo.

A good person should catch a break once in a while.

All she needed was one.

Two

Michele ran as fast as she could through the parking lot while trying not to break her neck on her high heels or snap the wheels off her luggage. She'd arrived in Los Angeles yesterday and spent the night at a nearby hotel to be on time for today's flight to Plunder Cove. The taxi driver had dropped her off in the wrong wing of the airport, making her late. He didn't seem to believe that a woman like her actually did mean she should be dropped off at the private jet terminal.

Her heart was pounding out of her chest when she arrived at the guarded gate. "Please tell me... I'm not...too late."

"Name," the guard said

"Michele Cox. A jet from Harper Industries is supposed to take me to—"

The gate opened. "You're expected."

"Over here." A woman wearing a blue suit waved to her. "Oh, dear. Your cheeks are pink. Come, there's ice water inside the private suite but there's no time for a shower Mr. Harper is ready to leave."

Her first thought was *A shower in a private suite in the airport?* The second was *Jeffrey Harper is inside?* She could only guess how she looked after her panicked run in the Los Angeles sunshine. No doubt her cheeks were more scarlet than pink. She finger-combed her blond hair and hoped for the best.

A door opened and Michele found herself in a ritzy lounge complete with cream-colored sofas, hardwood floors, recessed lighting, deep navy curtains, game tables and a cherrywood bar. Five women were chatting and drinking champagne.

"Miss Cox?" A deep voice called out from the end of the corridor. "I almost left without you."

Her heart skipped a beat until she realized it wasn't Jeffrey Harper. The man was handsome—of the tall, dark, broad-shouldered variety. He was also married, with a shiny new band on his left finger. Other than that, she had no idea who he was or why he knew her name.

"Sorry!" And…there went the wheel on her luggage. She grabbed the suitcase by the handle and kept hustling toward him. "Thanks for waiting. The International Wing was full of people and—" Her heel broke and she nearly twisted her ankle. "Shoot!"

"The International Wing? That's a good mile. You ran that whole way?"

"Only one?" She struggled to catch her breath. "Felt like two."

"Let me take that." He handed her luggage to an agent while she collected her broken heel.

She scanned the room. When she saw a beautiful woman speaking French over by the bar, her heart plummeted. It was Chef Suzette Monteclaire, the queen of French cuisine. What was she doing in the Harpers' private suite?

"Now that we're all here." The man raised his voice above the chatter. "Let me introduce myself. I'm Matt Harper, Jeff's brother and your pilot to Plunder Cove. Before we get on the jet, do you have any questions?"

The women looked at each other. A bad feeling slithered into her belly. Michele raised her finger.

"Yes, Miss Cox?"

"Are we *all* applying for the chef job?"

Matt shrugged. "Looks like it."

"I don't understand. I thought there was only one position open."

"Me, too," another woman agreed. "Why are we all here?"

A woman in the center of the group chuckled. She had thick dark hair and hooded green eyes. "Isn't it obvious? It's a contest. The winner gets to work for sexy Jeffrey Harper." She winked at Matt.

"Is this part of his show? I have not seen this on *Secrets and Sheets*," a soft-spoken woman said. Michele thought she was Lily Snow, the chef from Manhattan's upscale Chinese restaurant—The China Lily.

"He's creating a cooking show, no?" another woman asked, in a Swedish accent. Her hair was strikingly white-blond. Her large eyes were like sapphires against a milky pale complexion. She was tall, svelte and gorgeous. Everything about her screamed perfection and wealth. Lots of wealth.

Michele tried to inconspicuously wipe the sweat off her upper lip. Jeffrey Harper was going to turn her misery into a cooking show. Would she be able to pretend she was the chef she used to be not just for him but with all of America watching?

Matt shook his head. "I don't know what the hell this is, I'm only supposed to fly you all into Plunder Cove. If this is not what you signed up for, I'll give you the chance to back out gracefully. I'll arrange for a driver to take you back to your terminal and I will pay for your return flight."

Seeing all the talent in the room, Michele's legs twitched to start running back to New York. But she needed this—for Cari, for herself.

She didn't move. None of the other women did either.

"No takers?" Matt shrugged. "Right. Follow me to the jet."

Three hours later, a stretch limousine filled with six chef candidates turned up a long lane. Beautiful purple-flowered trees lined a wide driveway. Michele had never seen trees like that before.

"There it is!" One of the women squealed. "Casa Larga."

Michele looked through the tinted car window and saw a mansion straight out of a magazine spread. It was way bigger in real life. Imposing.

The women all started talking at once—something about Jeff's sister being Yogi to the stars—but Michele could only swallow hard. Why did she think she belonged here with these famous chefs and celebrities? She should've listened to Matt Harper and walked away gracefully. On her broken heel with her broken luggage.

"Jeff is a seriously hot man," one of the ladies said.

Michele didn't disagree but what did it matter? She didn't want to be hit on. And she didn't want a playboy or an arrogant critic for a boss. She needed Jeffrey to hire her and stay out of her kitchen. It hadn't gotten past her that Jeffrey Harper was only interviewing women. Why wasn't there a male chef candidate in the bunch?

The limo parked and the women piled out.

"Welcome to Casa Larga at Plunder Cove," a woman wearing a yellow skirt said in a voice that was soft, melodious. "I'm Jeff's sister, Chloe Harper. It's my job to get you settled inside. You'll be sharing. Two ladies to each room tonight. Tomorrow…well, we'll see how it all plays out. Follow me and I'll give you the tour."

They walked through large double doors and into a huge entryway. Michele looked up at the largest chandelier she'd ever seen.

Chloe continued, "I'll give you a schedule for when you will be called to the kitchen to cook a meal. It should be a signature dish that highlights what you do best."

The woman with the white-blond hair held up a perfectly manicured finger. Michele had learned her name was Freja. "Wardrobe and makeup, first, eh? My fans will be seeing me in Sweden. They can vote, too, no?"

An avalanche of panic made Michele's limbs weak. She hadn't suspected this would be a competition, much less a televised one. She didn't know if she could cook a masterpiece and if she failed with the entire world watching, her career would be over.

Chloe looked startled. "This is not a reality show, it's a competition. At the end, Jeff will choose one of you as his chef. Fans will not be voting."

Michele's heart started to beat normally again until Chloe went on to add, "We'll have a television crew in here once the restaurant is completed. Whomever Jeff chooses should expect lots of cameras that day."

Even knowing that, Michele wanted to be the chosen one. She had to be. This job was the path to financial stability, the only way she knew to make sure Cari was healthy and happy. It was the kick in the backside that she desperately needed. She had to convince Jeffrey Harper that she was the right one for the job. Somehow, she had to get her cooking mojo back.

Jeff stood shoulder-to-shoulder with Matt on the upstairs landing and watched Chloe lead the women through the downstairs corridor. They all had one thing in common—they were fantastic chefs. That's all he really cared about.

"You sure about this plan, bro?" Matt asked. "You're getting married when the restaurant is done?"

Jeff grimaced. "I don't have much of a choice. That's the deal."

"You and Dad are big on deals. It's stupid. Marriage is not a business contract. When it's right, you connect on a deep level, deeper than you'll believe. Julia touches me in places I didn't know existed."

"Sounds like good sex to me."

"Shut up." Matt socked him in the shoulder. "You should give yourself a chance to find love, man. That's all I'm saying."

Jeff could take all the time in the world, but he'd never find the sort of connection Matt had found with his wife, Julia. Jeff wasn't wired for it.

The chefs walked below him, a slow parade of beauty and talent, chatting as they went. They seemed oblivious to him standing above them. He was fine with that. He really didn't want to make contact until he judged their dishes. Why waste time with small talk if he wasn't impressed with their culinary skills?

As the last woman passed by, she stopped and looked up as if she'd sensed him. Her eyes met his. She tipped her head to the side slightly, and the light on the chandelier sparkled like diamonds across her long blond hair.

She raised one hand.

He raised his in return.

She smiled and hell if he couldn't see her dimples from where he stood. It was the purest sight he'd ever seen. If he had to choose one word to describe her in that moment it would be *sparkly*.

All too quickly she turned and hustled to catch up with Chloe's tour. She was gone two full beats before he looked away.

Matt thumped him on the head. "Earth to Jeff."

Jeff turned to face his brother. "Was she limping?"

"Did you not hear a word I said? That's what I was telling you, yes, she's limping because she broke her shoe running to catch our jet."

Jeff was still thinking about her smile. Can't fake dimples like that, right?

"She ran at least a mile in those high heels. I don't know about the other women in this competition, but that one has strength. A backbone." And then Matt butchered a handful of Spanish words.

"What?"

Matt grinned. "Good, huh? My wife is teaching me Spanish. It means 'she has the heart of a bull.'"

"You like saying that word, don't you?"

Matt tipped his head. "Which one?"

"Wife."

Matt had that look on his face—the "sneaking cookies and eating them in bed before Mom caught him" look. "Oh, yeah. You could enjoy saying the word, too, if you allowed yourself to find the right lady. You don't let anyone get close, Jeff. Start putting yourself out there. Be real and you'll find love. I swear it."

Jeff exhaled deeply. "Lightning doesn't strike twice in one family. And I'm not like you. Never was. You and Julia were meant for one another, you've known it since you were, like, ten. Another woman like Julia doesn't exist."

"You haven't found her because you need to open up. Show her who you are without the smoke and mirrors. No stage lighting. No props. Just two real people being...normal."

Did he want normal? What did it even mean?

"You could start with the lady you were making goo-goo eyes at. Along with her backbone, and pretty face, there's something sweet about Michele Cox."

"That was Michele Cox from Alfieri's? She made me one of the best chicken cacciatore dishes I've ever tasted. I still have daydreams about that chicken."

"Can I pick 'em or what?" Matt grinned and threw his arm over Jeff's shoulder.

"You've got it wrong. I'm not marrying any of these women, but I might hire Cox. I watched her on a cooking show once. Hell, she handled her kitchen with such passion, such flair. Spice and color all mixed together. I've never seen anything like it. She was poetry in action."

Matt cocked his head. "Poetry in action? Seems like you've thought about her a bit."

Had he? Sure. After seeing her on television, he'd made a point to visit her restaurant a few times. One night he'd even asked Alfieri if he could go back to the kitchen to meet the chef, but she'd left before he got a chance. The next time he'd gone in, he was told Michele had left the restaurant altogether. He'd been disappointed.

"I see it on your face. You like her," Matt said.

"I've never met her."

"So now is your chance. Ask her out. I dare you."

Jeff shot him a dirty look. "What is this, middle school? Dares don't work anymore. I'm not interested in searching for love. I just need a chef, and a wife who'll satisfy Dad's terms."

Matt shook his head, his voice sad. "You'll never feel it that way."

"Feel what?"

"Lightning."

Three

Michele scoped out her beautiful bedroom. It had a sitting area, a desk, two televisions, two queen-size beds, Spanish tile and a balcony. The decor was tasteful and lightly Mediterranean. The room was twice as big as her bedroom at home. Heck, maybe it was bigger than her bedroom and living room combined. She opened the French doors and stepped onto the balcony.

"Oh, hello!" The petite chef from The China Lily was sitting on the veranda. "Lovely view from here."

Michele looked out over the gardens below and let her gaze drift out to sea. "It's beautiful."

"And overwhelming. This bedroom is almost as large as my flat in Manhattan."

"Mine, too." Michele stretched out her hand. "We weren't formally introduced. I'm Michele Cox, from—"

"Alfieri's." Lily took her hand. "I know. May I say I love your lasagna? It's the best Italian dish I've ever tasted."

"It's my own recipe. The secret's in the sauce." Michele brought her finger to her lips. "And your dim sum is to die for."

"Ah, we're a mutual admiration society." Lily motioned to the other lounge chair. "Join me?"

Michele sank into the plush cushions and exhaled deeply. She was tired, jet-lagged, and her feet hurt from running in heels. "It feels like I haven't sat down in years."

"It has been a long day. I didn't know there would be a competition. Did you?"

"No. I might not have applied," Michele said softly, thinking about how the competition complicated her plans. "Do you know any of the other chefs?"

"Not personally, but I recognized Freja Ringwold, the gorgeous tall blonde? She's very famous in Sweden with her own cooking show. Tonia Sanchez, the curvy brunette with green eyes, owns three high-end Southwestern restaurants in Arizona. Suzette Monteclaire is well-known for—"

"French cuisine. Yes, I know." Michele felt like a fish out of water. A really small, unqualified fish. "What about the dark-haired chef with amazing skin? Nadia something."

"I've never seen her before. But—" Lily held up her finger and took out her cell phone "—Google will know." A short time later, she smiled. "Nadia is an award-winning Mediterranean chef in Saudi Arabia, oh, and her father is a sheikh. There's a picture of him and RW Harper taken about fifteen years ago. So, she might be a shoo-in, with her connections."

Great. What were Michele's chances with this group? "That's all of us, then. An eclectic bunch. What is Jeffrey looking for?"

"A fantastic chef. Any of us would fit the bill," Lily said.

Except she wasn't the chef she used to be.

"If you do not mind me asking, why did you leave Alfieri's? It seemed like you had a good situation there. I read there was some sort of—" Lily ran her slender hand through the air— "shake-up?"

Michele sighed. "You could call it that."

"Sorry. I shouldn't pry."

Michele studied the woman who was her competition and didn't feel any sort of maliciousness in her. It had been a long time since she'd had a friend to talk to. Mom was the person she had confided in her whole life and now that she was gone... God, her heart was so heavy.

"It's okay. Alfieri was—" how to describe the man who'd destroyed her? "—difficult. I couldn't stay. Don't get me wrong, I owe him my career. He took me in as a young apprentice. He was a great teacher, a fabulous chef who took a chance on me. When things were good, they were really good. I miss what we had together. What we created." That last bit came out choked.

"Oh," Lily said softly. "You were in love with him?"

The creative genius? She adored that part of him, but the rest terrified her.

She shook her head. "He is fifteen years older than me and so full of life and experience. I was an innocent girl from Indiana who ventured to New York to hone my cooking skills. Alfieri became my mentor. Because I owed him so much, I overlooked—" she winced, remembering the night he'd tried to scald her with boiling sauce because it was too salty "—I tried to ignore his faults. Until things got too intense."

Her throat was dry. She reached for the mineral water on the table with trembling fingers. Damn that man! He still got to her. She tried to wash the memories down.

"What happened?" Lily's eyes filled with concern.

She didn't know if it was the fact that she was so far from home and missing her sister—and, of course, Mom— or because Lily had such a gentle way about her, but Michele felt like she could confide in her. Now that she was talking, she couldn't stop. "I threatened to leave because parts of me, the best parts, were disappearing." Now, thanks to him, she still second-guessed herself every time she stepped into the kitchen. Alfieri's caustic words had dammed up her colorful river. "He apologized for his behavior, promised to go to anger-management therapy, and begged me to stay. Then he offered me a partnership. He was opening a second restaurant and said I could be the head chef there. We'd rarely have to see one another and I'd have full reign over the second location. It seemed like a dream come true. I agreed and gave him my life's savings as my share of the partnership. I trusted him." She looked Lily in the eye. "Fatal mistake."

"Oh, no."

"Long ugly story cut to the chase—he hired another chef for the second location without telling me." Another young woman to idolize and belittle. "I quit and demanded my money back. He said he didn't know what I was talking about but I could hire a lawyer if I wanted. He knew I didn't have money for lawyers. I was such a fool to trust him."

Michele didn't realize she was crying until Lily got up from her lounger, went inside and came back with a wash towel.

"You poor dear." Lily handed her the towel. "I hope Alfieri gets his just deserts for treating you like that."

Michele wiped her face, grateful for the kindness. Lily was the first person she'd confided in about this. She didn't talk about Alfieri much, because she was deeply ashamed. She should've left his restaurant long ago but she'd been in such awe of his brilliant mind that she'd made excuses for his behavior. As if cruelty was acceptable, even expected, from a head chef.

What she hadn't realized was that cruelty would eat goodness and destroy beauty. It had wormed under her skin, stealing the special gift her mom had given her, and even after that, she'd believed Alfieri.

She should've known better than to put her trust in a condescending, egotistical man. She'd never make that mistake again.

The door opened to the balcony, making Michele jump.

"Here you two are." Jeff's sister stepped outside. "Lily, you're the first chef to cook tonight. Please come downstairs to the kitchen in thirty minutes. Michele, you'll be cooking tomorrow. Good luck to both of you."

Good luck she needed desperately, and she would work her backside off to get it.

* * *

Jeff paced the large kitchen.

What in the hell was he doing?

The first two chefs had created culinary masterpieces. He'd personally judged them both and gave them five out of five stars. Either one of the dishes would be perfect for his new restaurant. The chefs were both talented and intelligent. There wasn't anything wrong with either of them. The problem? He hadn't…*connected* with either one.

There was no poetry.

Who was up next? He looked at his clipboard and read the names. The second name from the bottom caught his eye. *Michele Cox.*

A tiny spark zinged in his gut.

He picked up his cell phone and dialed Chloe's number. His sister had come home recently, too, and was helping with the candidate selection. Right now, he needed a clear head.

"How's it going?" Chloe asked. "Ready for Tonia?"

"Skip ahead to Michele Cox."

"She's not up until lunch tomorrow."

He couldn't wait that long. He had to know if the zing in his core was real. "Move her up."

"Sure. I like her. She's so, I don't know…"

"Sparkly." The word left his mouth before he could shut it down.

"Yes! That's it. Her eyes, her dimples, there's a shine there. Do you know her?"

"Not really. Do not tell her I said that either. If her culinary skills don't match my expectations I'll send her home like the other two."

"You're dismissing them already? Don't move. I'm on my way." Less than a minute later, Chloe rushed into the kitchen. "Seriously? Just like that, they're done? You didn't give those first two chefs much of a chance and one of them was Dad's pick—the sheikh's daughter."

"Dad isn't making the decisions here. I am. Why waste their time and mine?" He leaned against the counter, crossing his arms.

"Because this is just another example of how you don't spend much effort getting to know people. Do you ever let anyone in, Jeff?"

"What's that supposed to mean?"

"I worry about you. When was the last time you made a real connection with someone? Anyone?" She pressed her hand to his chest. "Here."

Never. "I don't have time for real connections."

"You need to try or you'll wake up one day, grumpy, old and lonely. There's more to life than work, Jeff. More to relationships than three minutes in an elevator." She softened the zinger with a smile.

He wasn't going to discuss the sex video with his kid sister. It had been more than three minutes, but few people knew what had really happened in the elevator and he wanted to keep it that way.

"I'm fine."

"Are you?" Her gaze pored over his face, her expression sad. "After what Mom did to you? Of the three of us, you had it the worst. I still have nightmares about that night in the shed."

Suddenly, he felt cold, his heart pounding. "How? You were, like, three."

"I remember."

He squeezed his hands into fists. He was not going to talk about this. "I'm fine. You can stop worrying about me being old and lonely. Didn't you hear the news? I'm getting married."

She shook her head. "Not funny, Jeff."

He lifted an eyebrow. "Don't believe me? Ask Dad."

She mimicked his pose right back at him. His little sister never backed down from a challenge. It ran in the family.

"Stop teasing. When we were kids, you swore you'd never get married."

He shrugged. "People grow up."

Her eyes widened. "You're serious."

"As a heart attack."

"I can't believe it. This is great. Who is the lucky bride? Please tell me it isn't the one from the elevator."

"Hell, no." His insides shuddered. "No one from New York."

"A local sweetheart? Is that why you changed your mind and agreed to come home?"

He frowned. "I'm not Matt. No one has ever waited for me."

"Then who?"

"Beats me. Got any ideas?"

She cocked her head. "I don't understand."

"The great RW Harper proclaimed a marriage to be so and…" he raised his hands in surrender "…I'm tying the knot. Once a bride shows up and agrees to a loveless marriage."

"No. You can't get married without falling in love. That's…not normal."

"Must run in the family. Doubt Mom and Dad cared for one another."

"And look how that turned out!" She gripped his elbow. "Please, Jeff. Reconsider. I want you to be happy."

He patted her arm. "I don't have a lot of options right now. In case you didn't see it, there was another meme released this morning. It's brutal."

"I saw it." She leaned against his shoulder. "I'm so sorry."

Her small act of kindness tugged on the anxiety in his gut and made him question whether he should tell her what had really happened in the elevator.

Would she understand?

"You're a good person who deserves to be loved. I'll do whatever I can to help you find your soul mate, Jeff."

"That's not happening," he grumbled.

"All you need to do is open your fourth chakra—your heart space. I'll help you unblock it so you have a chance."

Did she think he was emotionally constipated? Hell, maybe he was. "Give it up, sis. I'm a lost cause. Besides, I've managed this long without love, why find it now?"

"Oh, Jeff." Her eyes were wet. "Managing is not happiness. I learned that the hard way. I can teach you how to let your feelings flow. To heal you."

He didn't want to offend her, but yoga wasn't going to fix his problems. She was lucky she hadn't acquired Mom's "incapacity to love" genes like he had. Damned lucky.

"I've got a chef to hire and a hotel empire to build. And on that note—" he pushed himself up off the counter "—tell Michele Cox to come down in twenty minutes. She'll be the last one tonight."

"Okay." Chloe started to walk out of the kitchen but turned back to give him a big hug before she left.

Jeff made sure no one else was around and then pulled up the application videos on his computer. He played the one labeled "Michele Cox."

"...When the dishes are excellent, the patron can ease loneliness with a bite of ricotta cannelloni. That's what I do. I make patrons feel happy and loved. I can do that for your new restaurant, too. I hope you'll give me a chance. Thank you."

Her voice and words were strong. Confident. So why did he get a sense that Michele was fragile?

He played it again. "I want to work for Harper Industries because I need to believe good things can happen to good people." He pressed Pause so he could study her. Zoomed in closer. There. In her light brown eyes, he saw a look he'd seen in his own reflection.

It made his heart beat faster.

Michele Cox was a survivor, too.

Four

Michele stood alone next to the island in the Harper family kitchen and pressed her palms against the cool marble countertop.

She closed her eyes and silently breathed in, *I am a cooking goddess. Amazing and talented.* And exhaled, *I will create greatness.* And then she threw her arms up in victory. It was a superstitious ritual, one she'd done before big cooking nights at Alfieri's to focus her thoughts. It used to work. Tonight? Not so much.

Bad thoughts kept rushing in. Broken fragments of anxiety looped through her mind like a terrible song she couldn't stop hearing.

Why do you think you can do this? You'll mess this up.

It was Alfieri's voice. She opened her eyes and squeezed her fists together.

She couldn't make a mistake tonight.

Biting her lip, she debated long and hard before she finally gave in and pulled up her recipe on her cell phone.

That's right, you have to cheat. You are nothing without me.

"Shut up, Alfieri!" she whispered.

Using her own recipe wasn't cheating. She'd created it after all, but she usually didn't need to look at it. She used to be able to cook by her senses, her mood and something she called "Mom's magic." Lately, though, she second-guessed herself about everything. Her mom and all the magic were gone.

Michele put the phone on the counter in front of her where she could see the recipes and began.

The sage-rosemary bread was baking and the pan with lemon, olive oil and Italian white wine and spices was heating up nicely. The kitchen smelled divine. She stuffed squid with prosciutto, smoked mozzarella and garlic cloves and gently placed them into the pan. Lightly, she drizzled the squid with her secret homemade truffle sauce. Her special linguine noodles cooked on the back burner and the arugula-basil-chardonnay grape salad with light oil and lemon dressing was up next. Everything looked perfect...except... something felt off.

She had a sinking feeling she'd forgotten to fill the last squid with garlic. It wasn't hot yet. If she hurried, she could snatch it back and fix her error. She turned the heat down and used a slotted spoon to carefully recover the squid from the pan. The truffle sauce made the darned thing slippery to handle and it plopped out of the spoon and into the pan again. She wasn't wearing an apron because all of hers had Alfieri's name on them, so when the oil splashed up, it spotted her silk blouse. The one people said brought out the amber color in her eyes.

"Gah! Thanks a lot, you slimy sea booger!"

"Miss Cox?" A deep voice came up behind her.

The surprise caused her to jerk the spoon and catapult the squid from the pan into the air. She lunged and caught it before it hit the floor tiles. Cupping the drippy squid behind her back, she straightened her shoulders and rose up to face...*him*.

Jeffrey Harper's large frame filled the space, blocking the exit. There was no way she could flee or pretend he hadn't seen her glaring faux pas. The way he was looking at her? He'd definitely witnessed her launch food into the air and catch it with her bare hand.

"Mr. Harper. You startled me."

He stepped closer and her heartbeat kicked up even more. He wore a white linen shirt—unbuttoned just enough so she could glimpse glorious red chest hair—and jeans that molded perfectly to his legs.

The casual version of the man was sexier than the one she'd seen on television.

"My apologies. I didn't mean to interrupt your conversation with…" He cocked his head toward the pan and a beautiful copper-colored bang fell onto his forehead. He tossed his head to move it back into place. "Slimy sea boogers."

Could a person die from failure?

She steeled herself to be the recipient of his disgusted look—the one he used in the episode when he'd seen rats running across a cutting board in a hotel's kitchen. Instead, she saw…*amusement*?

"I wasn't having a conversation with all of them. Just this one." She produced the squid that she'd been hiding behind her back. "He was behaving badly."

Instead of berating her and kicking her out of his kitchen—as Alfieri would have—the corner of Jeffrey's lips curled.

He had beautiful lips.

"I see. What are you going to do about him?" He kept coming closer.

He was so tall. She had to tip her head to gaze into his eyes, which were an amazing powder blue with a golden starburst in the irises. Simply mesmerizing. It was easy to understand why women lusted after Jeffrey Harper.

She looked at the misshapen squid. Alfieri would've scolded her. *That mistake will come out of your paycheck.*

"Throw it away?" she said.

"Why? Cook it up. I'll eat it."

Her hands were shaking when she shoved a garlic clove inside, rearranged the stuffing, dropped the squid in the pan with the others, and turned up the heat. The pan started sizzling, which didn't come close to the electricity she felt when Jeffrey stood so close. His woodsy cologne smelled better than the food but having him watch her cook made her nervous.

"I don't see chicken." He sounded disappointed.

Did he expect all the chefs to serve chicken? Had she missed that part of the fine print in the contract she'd signed?

"It's pan-seared and stuffed squid with my special truffle sauce. The linguine noodles and bay clams are almost ready," she said, her voice tiny.

He crossed his arms, his body language expressing disappointment. "Miss Cox, the chef position for my restaurant is highly competitive. I expect to be impressed by each meal."

Now *that* sounded more like Alfieri. The condescending tone stirred up her anger. "What more do I need to do, Mr. Harper? Juggle clams and catch them with my teeth?"

His mouth dropped open. She'd surprised herself, too, since she usually didn't speak up to a boss and never in a job interview. She waited for him to ask her to leave.

Instead Jeffrey Harper surprised *her*.

He laughed.

It was a good, hearty sound that rolled through her core, loosening the bitterness inside her. She couldn't help but smile.

He had a really great laugh.

"No, Miss Cox. Just excite me. I'm looking forward to being transported."

What did that mean? The way he looked at her, like they were sharing some sort of inside joke, was unnerving. She didn't get the punch line.

"Chardonnay?" he asked.

"Sure, if that's what you like to drink. But I'd probably suggest a nice light-bodied, high-acid red wine, like a Sangiovese, or perhaps a white Viognier?"

"I'll see what we've got in the cellar." Watching him stride out of the kitchen, it struck her that Jeffrey Harper was not as cocky as he seemed on television. She liked him better this way. Plus, he hadn't yelled at her.

She took the bread out of the oven, wrapped it in a colorful towel, and placed it in a basket. Checking the recipe again to make sure she hadn't forgotten anything, she plated up the meal. Four stuffed squid were dressed with the light sauce and adorned with a sprinkling of spices. The linguine and clams were cooked perfectly. The salad was a lacy pyramid of arugula and basil leaves and decorated with sweet chardonnay grapes. The dressing was another secret recipe that never failed. The meal was not a work of art, but it looked good, it smelled good, and she was sure it would taste good. That was the best she could do tonight.

She sighed. Good wouldn't cut it here, not by a long shot. The other chefs would be excellent.

"I have both wines." His deep voice rumbled behind her, sending shivers up her spine. "Which would you prefer, Miss Cox?"

She glanced over her shoulder at him. He waved two bottles at her. "Me?"

"I'm not drinking alone."

She folded his napkin into a flower shape. "Oh, okay. Um, I like white. Thank you." She carried his plate to the table.

"Viognier it is." He poured her a glass and placed it at the table across from him. "Sit."

Apparently, she was supposed to watch him eat. Was he going to tell her bite by bite how she'd messed up or how the food didn't *excite* him? Would he throw the entire plate at her head and order her to clean up the mess like Alfieri would?

She glanced at the table and realized she'd forgotten the salad. Another rookie move. What else would she mess up tonight? "I'll be right back."

When she returned with his salad plate, she was surprised to see he'd split his entrée onto two plates.

"What are you doing, Mr. Harper?"

"Join me. I hate to eat alone." His smile was more sincere than cocky and there was something about the look in his eyes that tugged at her. Sadness? Loneliness?

She hated to eat alone, too. Uneasily, she sat across from him.

He sounded relieved when he said, "Thank you."

She heard those two words so infrequently that she checked to make sure he wasn't being sarcastic. He wasn't.

"Eat," he ordered.

Huh. Somehow, she'd scored an impromptu date with America's Most Eligible Bachelor. It wasn't a bad way to go out after the worst job interview of her life. Not bad at all.

He lit two candles and moved them so he could look at Michele Cox's pretty face.

Jeff had never met a chef like her.

When he first came into the kitchen, he hadn't been impressed. There was no poetry in action. No color or fluidity. She seemed stiff and uncertain. And why was she looking at her cell phone so much? Was she using someone else's recipe?

Then she'd verbally threatened her food. That was strange enough, but chucking it into the air and catching it as if nothing had happened? Her cheeks had flushed with embarrassment and her gorgeous honey-colored eyes had sparked with worry, and still she'd sassed him. That took balls. And wits. Two things he wanted in his chef.

Two things that made him want to know more about her.

He cut through the squid and garlicky butter oozed out. He popped the bite into his mouth and chewed, slowly, deliberately. She met his gaze, and in her expression, he saw hopefulness. She wanted to win this battle. Badly. A flicker of something lit up in him, too, though he wasn't ready to name it.

He took a bite of the linguine and the salad, making her

wait for his verdict. Not because he was cruel, but because he wanted to savor this moment—his eyes locked with hers, the two of them eating together.

"Here, you've got a little—" He shook out the napkin she'd folded into a flower and wiped a bit of butter off her chin.

"Thanks." She gave him a taste of those deep dimples. Foreplay with the chef. He liked it. So much so that he almost forgot he was judging the meal.

"It's good," he said, chewing the last bite. The second squid, the misshapen one, seemed to have twice as much garlic as the first. Inconsistency was a bad sign.

"I know." She looked at the food on her plate and her dimples disappeared. "Good. Not magic."

She felt it, too. Something was missing. "I enjoyed it. Why didn't you make your signature dish?"

"My chicken cacciatore?"

"Hell, yes. I had it in New York. It was seriously one of the best dishes I've ever tasted." If she'd made it for him, she would've been a shoo-in for the job and yet she went with seafood? She didn't know how risky that was.

"I created that dish for Alfieri's. I won't make it anymore."

"Why not? It was fantastic."

"I'm sorry… I just…can't." Her voice choked and she gulped the rest of her wine.

Was it his imagination, or had her cheeks gone pale? Wait. Were those tears in her eyes?

What the hell had he said?

"Miss Cox, is there something wrong?"

She put her glass down and looked him in the eye. "It's nothing. Thank you for being so kind. I'm not used to it."

No one had ever called him *kind* before. "I'm honest."

She waved her hand over the table. "The candles? Sharing your food? Your wine? It's a sweet thing to do when we both know I'm not getting the job."

That gave him pause. Why was she trying to talk herself out of the position? "Have you changed your mind?"

"No! I desperately need…" She pressed her lips together, cutting off her thoughts. "I want to work for Harper Industries. I really do. I'm just…this is embarrassing. I didn't cook an award-winner tonight. I'm not sure I know how to anymore."

He couldn't fathom why, but his senses told him that whatever she was hiding scared her. Was she in trouble? "You're selling yourself short."

"No, I'm not." She bit her lip. Was it quivering?

Was she that sensitive about her food? Chefs needed to be creative and strong, bold and thick-skinned. Tears in the kitchen wouldn't work.

"If you'll excuse me, I'll clean up the dishes for the next contestant." She reached for his plate.

He stopped her by putting his hand on hers. "Miss Cox? *What* do you desperately need?"

She froze. Her expression seemed serious and troubled as if the answer was the key to everything. "To find what I lost so I can take care of my sister."

What the hell did that mean?

As he tried to decipher her words, she pulled her hand back and reoffered it as a handshake, "Thank you for the opportunity, Mr. Harper. I wish you luck in finding the perfect chef. I'm sorry I wasted your time."

Shaking her soft, delicate hand produced a stab of disappointment. He said nothing. He couldn't. She had the right to walk away from the job; people walked away all the time.

So why did it feel like she'd just quit *him*?

He watched her leave and drank his wine. Alone.

Five

Michele berated herself all the way back to the room she shared with Lily.

How could she have made such dumb mistakes in front of a world-renowned critic like Jeffrey Harper? One bad word from him and she would never cook again. He had the power to ruin her career for eternity.

Well, if *she* didn't ruin everything first.

She knocked on the door and was surprised to see Lily was already in her pajamas. "Sorry, did I wake you?"

Lily yawned. "No. I am getting ready to go to bed, though. I'm exhausted from jet lag. Aren't you?"

Actually, no. She was still pumped from her time with Jeffrey. A wild mix of emotions—disappointment, embarrassment and attraction—boiled in her blood. She liked Jeffrey more than she'd expected she would, which made crashing and burning in front of him even worse.

She walked into the room and snagged her purse. "I need to make a call before bed. I'll take my conversation somewhere else."

She'd promised Cari she'd read her the bedtime story every night over the phone. She would've done it earlier but she'd been called to the kitchen tonight instead of tomorrow. Hopefully, the assistant at the home had reminded Cari that Michele might be calling later than usual. Cari couldn't tell time, but she'd have a sense that it was late in New York.

"Before you go…" Lily sat on her bed. "Please tell me how your interview went. I was confused by mine."

"Why? What happened?" Michele came and sat on the bed, facing Lily. "Didn't he like your cuisine?"

"Oh, yes. He said it was excellent. The best dim sum he'd ever tasted."

A sharp spike of jealousy pricked Michele's insides. *Excellent.* Not *good.*

That proved it. Jeffrey hated her squid.

"What's confusing about that?" Michele asked. "Sounds like you impressed him."

"During my interview, Jeffrey was… I don't want to say cold, exactly. But very businesslike, almost as if his heart wasn't in it. He only asked me one personal question and then thanked me and left."

Jeffrey hadn't been cold during her interview. Remembering the way he'd smiled at her still made Michele warm and tingly. "Didn't he invite you to eat with him in the dining room?"

Lily's brown eyes widened. "No. He ate over the sink in the kitchen. Didn't even sit down. He didn't want me to leave until he was finished and then he excused me. He asked you to join him for dinner?"

"Oh, well, he must've felt sorry for me. I really bombed my dish."

"Jeffrey doesn't give me the impression that he'd feel sorry for anyone creating unsatisfactory cuisine. Incompetent service seems to really annoy him on the show."

Michele thought about it. Lily was right. The guy she'd watched on TV would've asked her to leave the moment she'd showed him the deformed squid in her palm. Alfieri would have thrown whatever was in his hand at her and ordered her out of his kitchen.

More confused than before, Michele hoisted the purse with the book inside over her shoulder. "I'm going to make that call. I won't wake you when I come in."

* * *

Angel Mendoza was the only woman RW Harper loved, the only one he couldn't keep. He poured champagne into her favorite crystal flute and seltzer into his own mug.

He'd stopped drinking the moment she'd come into his life. He needed to be alert, awake. He needed to not slip back into that nightmarish hole she'd dragged him out of. It was as if she'd fashioned a new heart for him out of dead, tattered tissue, and was teaching it how to beat. How to feel.

She'd come to him as a therapist, and her therapy had saved his life. Now he was doing everything possible to keep from screwing it all up. He had to make sure that she could live her life, too.

He joined her on the balcony. "To you," he said, handing her the flute.

Turning her face away from the orange-pink sunset, she melted him with her deep brown eyes. Damn, Angel was gorgeous. Sundowners with her were his favorite evening ritual, one he would sorely miss if she left him.

When she left him. Again.

He knew they were sharing a slice of borrowed time. It had taken a lot of coaxing to bring her back two months ago, and he suspected she'd given in only to bring Cristina and her young son to Plunder Cove for protection from the gang that was hunting all three of them. Her return had nothing to do with him.

Still, he didn't want to let her go.

Taking the champagne in one hand, she cupped his cheek with the other. Her hands were soft and cool. "You are an amazing man. Thank you for protecting them, RW. I don't know what I would've done—" She shook her head, banishing ugly visions that he didn't want to imagine, either. She took a sip as if to drown the quiver in her voice.

Right. As if he could not hear her fear and pain. He was hypersensitive to all things Angel Mendoza. Right now, her breathing was too shallow, her soft cheeks pale, her sexy laugh lines drawn too tight.

"How are our guests? Everyone settling in?" he asked, hoping to take her mind off the past that still haunted her.

"Do you mean my guests, or Jeffrey's?"

"I assume Jeffrey is getting acquainted with the chefs we located for him. Quite an amazing amount of talent out there. I have no idea how he'll choose one. Maybe he'll marry one, too."

Cool ocean breezes blew over the edge of the balcony. Angel wiggled under his arm for warmth. He loved when she did that. He pulled her in tight and hung on.

It might be the last time he touched her.

"Are you sure that's his intent? Maybe he simply wants the best chef for the restaurant."

RW inhaled, breathing in her scent. "How would I know? The boy has no bridal prospects in mind and always loved the kitchen. Can't tell you how many times I found him asleep in there as a child and had to carry him back to his bedroom. It makes sense he would marry a chef." RW didn't mention how much the staff had taken care of Jeffrey when his own mother wouldn't.

"You're still going to force him to marry?"

"That was the deal," he said firmly. "He needs to change his ways. Repairing his reputation is the only way I can save him from Xander Finn. Jeff knows it, too."

"Well, if that's the case, Jeff simply needs to let himself *feel* which chef is the right fit…for whatever he is planning," she said. "He should follow his heart."

"It took me four decades to locate that organ in my chest. What makes you think he'll find his and trust it in a few weeks?"

She smiled up at him. "Because we'll help him."

He doubted Jeffrey would listen to his old man when it came to affairs of the heart—not after RW had so badly botched things with Jeffrey's mother—but Angel was a force to be reckoned with. She was the only reason RW had learned to get in tune with his own emotions. Lately, she had been trying to teach him how to forgive himself for all the sins of his past.

He rubbed her arm, to warm her, yes, but mostly to touch her. He touched her every chance he could get.

"How about your friends? Are they comfortable?"

"From the dirty streets to Casa Larga is a mind-blowing trip. Cristina is still jumping at every shadow. It's hard for her to believe that she's safe here," she said.

Twenty years ago, Cristina had joined the gang because she was a young, filthy and hungry runaway. Angel, who had been a teenager herself, had looked out for the girl until Angel left the gang, in fear for her life. She'd begged Cristina to go with her but the young woman was too scared. Leaving Cristina behind had been tough. So, when Cristina called three months ago, Angel did not hesitate. She'd rescued the young woman and her four-year-old son and now she was doing everything she could to keep them both hidden and safe. If the gang found them, they would find Angel and her family.

Angel would not let that happen.

"Cristina and her son are safe. You've got to trust me." He spun her around to face him. "I won't let Cuchillo find her or you. I'm going to break that bastard."

Angel swallowed hard. "I know." There it was again. The worry in her voice was killing him.

He pulled her back into his arms, shielding her, hoping to prove that he would always protect her. He wasn't supposed to fall in love with his therapist—she'd made the rules clear from the start—but that new heart she'd given him? It felt things it shouldn't.

Even if she left, *when* she left, he'd still feel those things. He didn't have a choice in the matter.

After a long silent moment, he asked, "What about the little boy? Is he scared, too?"

"Sebastian is four years old and confused. Living with the gang is all he has ever known. He doesn't understand why we brought him here. He's too little to know we saved his life. He's throwing a fit to go back home and is driving Cristina crazy when she's already on edge." Angel let out a deep breath. "It's going to take some time."

"What can I do to make him happy? Can I give him something?"

"Hmm. Stock options are out of the question, but..." She lifted her finger. "I might know a way to help both him and Jeffrey."

He lifted his eyebrow. "*This* I've got to see."

She picked up her cell phone. "Hi, Jeffrey, it's Angel."

"Hey, Angel. What's wrong? Is everything okay?" RW heard his son's voice through the receiver.

"I was wondering if you could ask one of your chef friends for a favor?" she said.

"A favor?"

"Our little guest is sad. A grilled cheese sandwich might perk him up. Since the regular kitchen staff is on vacation while you're running the cooking competition, I was hoping you could get one of the chefs to help me out."

"Any particular chef?" Jeff asked.

"It doesn't matter, just pick a nice one."

"A nice one? What does that—"

"Thanks, Jeffrey. Appreciate it," Angel interrupted him. "Gotta go." She hung up.

Angel smiled at RW. "Let's see who he chooses to help that little boy. That will be the one closest to his heart."

"Devious." RW kissed the top of her head. "I like it."

Michele sat on a bar stool and stood the picture book up on the island she'd recently used to stuff her career-ending squid. The kitchen was one of the only rooms she knew how to find in this gigantic house without a map. Besides, it was quiet and warm and just as clean as she'd left it. Apparently, she'd been the last contestant to cook tonight.

She spoke softly into her cell phone. "You're still awake. Don't you know all cowgirls need their sleep?"

"Can't sleep good without my story," Cari whined. "Why were you so slow?"

"I'm working, remember?" *At least, I was.* "Are you tucked into bed?"

"Yepee."

Imagining her sister burrowed under the covers with a plastic pony in each hand warmed her heart. "Okay, then. Let's find out what that Rosie is up to tonight…"

Jeff ran his hand through his hair. "Pick a *nice* one?" he grumbled. Why did it matter? Any line cook or fry guy could make a grilled cheese sandwich.

Hell, I could do it.

That idea sounded more appealing than approaching six women and grabbing one for Angel's job. No wait, there were only five now since Miss Cox had bailed. He didn't know the first two chefs very well, and they were on their way out. He had yet to meet the last three. How could he possibly pick a nice one out of the bunch?

No, it was less stress to do it himself. *I'll show you grilled cheese, little man.*

He headed into the kitchen, but stopped short two strides in. Someone was sleeping with her head on the kitchen island. Long, blond hair draped over a thin arm that held… what? He leaned closer to see. A picture book?

That hair looked so damned soft. He lifted it off her face and whispered the one name he'd been thinking about all day, "Miss Cox."

Michele jerked up, her eyes wild with fear. "Cari!"

"It's Jeff. You're safe here." When he realized his hand hovered over her back, itching to comfort her—to touch her—he stepped back.

He shoved his hands in his pockets. "Was your bed not to your liking?"

Awareness came into her face. She rubbed that pretty mouth of hers and sat up. "Sorry. I had to make a phone call and didn't want to disturb my roommate. It's so warm and comfortable in here, I guess I fell asleep." She pushed her hair back, inadvertently making it stick up on one side.

Damn, she looked adorable.

He took his hands out of his pockets and sat on the bar stool beside her. "I used to do that all the time as a kid. When my parents were fighting, this was the best place in the house to get any sleep."

She faced him. "Your parents argued a lot?"

"Only every day and twice on Sunday. I grew up thinking all parents hated each other and cursed the day they had kids."

"I'm sorry. That must have been terrible for you."

People didn't usually say nice things to him unless they wanted something, like a job or a good critique. None of that was the case with Miss Cox. She'd quit.

And she was different. *Warm.* He didn't talk about his past, but something inside him slipped when her honey eyes dripped with concern.

"My brother, Matt, took the brunt of Dad's fury. It was bad. But Matt was tough and took the mental and physical abuse. Sometimes I envied him because Dad at least noticed him. I was the little redheaded kid everyone ignored. Forgot. I broke the rules and threw balls in the house in the off-limits areas in the hopes of breaking something just so someone would remember I existed. God, I broke Mom's Ming." He threw up his hands. Knowing about rare Chinese ceramics now, he wanted to punch himself in the nose for that stupid trick. "Who got punished for the vase destruction? Matt. He lied to protect me." His hands were shaking. He ran them through his hair. "Why did I tell you all of that?"

"I promise I won't tell anyone. I signed a nondisclosure agreement, remember?" And then she smiled.

Those dimples did it. He took her hand in his. Gently, he placed a kiss on her knuckle. "Thank you."

Her mouth opened in surprise and he released her hand.

"Um. Why did you come in here, Mr. Harper? Are you hungry already?"

"Jeff, please. You know my ugly secrets."

"Only if you call me Michele."

Michele. His mind rolled her first name around like a shiny toy.

"So? Fess up. You hid the squid under your napkin and now you're starving."

He laughed. "Why won't you believe me? I told you I liked the squid. Ate every last crumb of your meal, Miss, um, Michele. I'm only here to make a grilled cheese sandwich for a friend."

"For a friend, huh?" She acted like she didn't believe him.

"Yep. He loves grilled cheese." That's all he would say.

Only a few people knew about the mother and child hiding here at Casa Larga and Jeff intended to keep the secret. Hell, everyone in Plunder Cove could be at risk if someone leaked the news. And then he remembered Angel's request to find a nice chef to make the sandwich.

"Would you consider making it for him?" he asked.

"Of course." She rose. "Maybe I'll recover a little dignity after the flying squid debacle. Call it my finale. What do you want—the kid or adult version?"

When she stepped away from him, coldness rushed in like a wave. It was a weird sensation that reminded him of the time when he was ten and he and Matt had raced out to the buoy in the boating lane. Ocean temps were incredibly cold that day and it was a dumb idea to swim out, but a challenge was a challenge. Jeff never backed down.

With Matt far ahead, hypothermia had set in and Jeff's arms and legs didn't want to work right. He'd treaded water, gasping for air, as wave after wave dragged him under. The buoy he was desperate to cling to moved farther away. Matt had saved him that day, dragging Jeff back to shore as a lifeguard would. But it had taken days to really warm up. When he was low, part of him felt like a layer of frostbite was still stuck to his bones.

But not now.

Michele embodied warmth. How else could he explain it? Sitting beside her heated his blood. His cells, one after another, thawed. It was irrational and damned stupid, especially since she'd already quit on him, but one idea kept washing over him. Dragging him under.

She needs to stay.

Six

Jeffrey Harper really got to her.

Sure, he was as sexy as the day was long, and smart, and confident and…did she say sexy? But he was also sensitive. That story about his childhood made her heart hurt. She couldn't imagine breaking valuable artifacts just so her mom would notice her. Not that they'd had any valuable objects in her childhood home. They'd had bills. Lots of them. Mom's cancer medicines and Cari's special schools came first. She hadn't had a father for most of her life so there was no use waiting for a man to show up and save the day. If Michele wanted anything for herself, she'd worked for the money.

Making a sandwich for Jeff was a nice thing she could do before she went home. It was her way of saying thanks. It had nothing to do with wanting to hang out with Jeffrey Harper a bit longer. Nothing at all.

He followed her to the pantry, closing the gap between them again. Her insides took notice of the heat coming from him. Or was that coming from her? She always felt hot near the man. There was a slight curve to his lips. Most women would have to rise up on their tippy-toes to kiss that mouth.

"What's the difference?" he asked about the grilled cheese sandwiches.

"For children, I go with the sweet grilled cheese. For a guy like you…" The humor in his starburst blue eyes made her reckless. What did she have to lose? "I'd go with heat. Roasted peppers. Habaneros, maybe."

"A guy like me?"

She tapped his chest. "A spicy guy like you could take it."

His gaze followed her finger and then slowly rose up to meet her eyes. She saw what she'd done. She'd flipped a switch. The playfulness in his expression had become dangerously intense.

She had no business stoking his fire, so why did part of her really want to?

"I can go with sweet." The way he said it, deep and low, like she could be on the menu, made her throat dry.

"One of each?"

He nodded, crossed his arms over that broad chest of his and leaned against the counter.

"Okay, but you're going to want to step back. The fumes will make your eyes water," she warned.

"Then you'd better wear these." He put a pair of mirrored navigation sunglasses on her and combed her hair back from her face with his long fingers. She stood very still and enjoyed the sensation. She'd missed feeling wanted, desired. Something about Jeffrey Harper brought out those needs. She supposed she wasn't any different from the rest of the women in America who lusted after Jeffrey Harper.

"Now you're ready to fly," he said, breaking the moment.

She saluted him and began roasting the peppers in a little bit of olive oil. It only took a few minutes for the fumes to make her cough.

He reached over her and turned on the fan. "Better?"

"Much. Thanks." *And, yes, I was just imagining your arm around me.*

When the peppers were nicely blackened, she took them out of the pan and put them on a plate to cool, leaving the pepper-oil in the pan. She cut a thin slice from the pepper and minced it finely. She mixed it and raspberry jelly into the pepper-oil and spread the spicy mix on two slices of focaccia bread.

"What about the rest of the habaneros?" he asked. "Aren't they going between the slices of bread?"

"Do you have a death wish? They'd blow your head off in this sandwich. Save them for another day."

"You said I was spicy enough to take it."

She blushed. "No one's that spicy. Those things are wicked. This tiny slice and the spicy oil will give the right amount of kick. I promise."

She spread cream cheese on the bread and grilled the whole sandwich in a mixture of olive oil, garlic salt and rosemary.

"Looks great. Can I eat it now?" he asked.

She nodded and took the glasses off.

He took a bite, chewing thoughtfully. When his eyes rolled toward the ceiling fan, she knew she'd done her job right. It gave her a zing of pleasure, something she hadn't felt in months.

"That's the best grilled cheese sandwich I've ever tasted." Two seconds later, he went in search of water. "Spicy."

"Told you."

He took another bite. The sounds he made while he ate could have come from an X-rated movie. Wickedly, she wondered what sounds he'd made in the filming of the elevator video.

"I'll leave you to enjoy it." She made the second sandwich with mild cheddar cheese, grape jelly and plain white bread. He watched her every move.

"My sister loves this sandwich. Sans the crust of course." Carefully, she sliced off the edges.

"She's the one you were reading to. Cari, is it?"

Michele nearly cut her finger. "Yes. How did you know?"

"You said her name in your sleep."

"Huh."

He leaned over and pointed at the bread. "You missed a spot."

"Sometimes I leave a spot, you know for the pain-in-the-neck critic." She smiled at him.

"Great. Thanks. Go on."

"You don't take an exception to my description?"

"Nope. Entirely accurate."

She shook her head, smiling. Who knew making sandwiches could be so much fun? It had been weeks since she'd been this comfortable in a kitchen. It felt good. Right.

"Now for every kid's favorite. You'd better come a little closer. This is the tricky part."

"An apple?" He put his hand on her shoulder, as he leaned in. His breath lifted the hair on her neck, sending a shiver up her spine. Her core heated up shamelessly.

"You see an apple? I see a jolly red apple man." She picked up a knife.

Out of nowhere, uncertainty struck again. *You're going to mess this up in front of him. You can't cook anymore. Not without me.* Alfieri's voice was back. Her hand shook just a bit when she held the knife above the apple.

"Michele." Jeff's voice drew her gaze to him. "What's wrong?"

"I'm a mess." She put the knife down. "I shouldn't have applied for this job. You don't want me for your chef."

She turned away so she wouldn't witness the disgust on his face. Or whatever his reaction would be to her admission. Jeffrey Harper was not the kind of man who put up with weakness or failure.

"Relax," he said softly, without an ounce of his cocky television voice. "You're not being judged now. Just breathe. Let it out slowly."

She exhaled.

"That's what I do when the nerves catch up with me on the show. Again. Deep inhale."

She did as told.

"This time with the exhale say, 'This is what I do best. I'm going to kill this sonofabitch apple.'"

That did it. She laughed out loud.

He grinned. "Go get it, tiger."

Still chuckling, she picked up the apple and began carving the first eye. She made a pupil and even added a starburst to the iris. "You get nervous on the show?"

"The more nerves, the better the show." He leaned closer. "That's an eye! Amazing, Miss Cox."

"Michele," she reminded him.

The excitement in his voice delighted her. He liked it. She went to work on the other one as Jeffrey stood beside her. Pushing on, she used a piece of red apple skin to roll up into a nose. Carefully, she cut out a smiling mouth with sweet full lips. After adding the apple stem hat, it was done.

"I did this once for my sister so she'd eat her lunch. Now, she wants all her apples to become jolly red men." She placed it in his hand. "I hope your friend enjoys it."

"That's unbelievable." He turned it in his hand as if it was art. "I've never seen anything like it."

The words of encouragement were a balm to her damaged heart. No boss had said anything like that to her in... well, she couldn't remember.

Critical words were more common in Alfieri's kitchen than compliments. He was a powerful head chef who'd used despicable behavior and abuse to "train" her to become one of the best chefs in New York, second only to him. In truth, he'd ruined her.

She closed her eyes and blocked out Alfieri's angry eyes, his shaking finger, the cruel turn of his lips.

"Michele." She opened her eyes to see Jeffrey leaning in close, studying her. "I don't know what problems you're having, but you should trust your talent. You are amazing."

That did it.

She rose up on her tippy-toes and kissed his spicy lips.

* * *

Michele Cox was full of surprises. Funny, sexy, sweet, kind, smart and...insecure. That last one didn't match up with the rest of her personality. Something bad had happened to her, he was sure of it. He wished he knew what it was and how to fix it.

Without a word, she rose up and softly, gently, pressed her lips to his. Fully unprepared, he stood still, cautious after what had happened in the elevator. Given one more moment, he would have swept her up in his arms and deepened that sweet kiss. But before he could, she stepped back.

"Sorry." Her beautiful golden-brown eyes were wide with...what? Had she surprised herself, too? "That was unprofessional. I don't normally..." She was pressing her hand to her lips. "I'll just leave. Good luck!"

Before he could stop her, Michele Cox rushed through the kitchen door and out of his life. Again.

Seven

Michele awoke with the sense that something was wrong. It was the same feeling she'd opened her eyes to every morning since she'd left Alfieri's. This morning was worse.

All night, her mind did the play-by-play critique of every mistake she'd made in front of Jeffrey Harper. Including that kiss. She pulled the pillow over her head in embarrassment. He must've thought she'd lost her mind.

What was that sound? She lifted the pillow, pushed the hair out of her eyes and listened. Sniffling? Sitting up, she noticed Lily's bed was empty.

Tying her robe around her, Michele followed the soft sounds to the closed bathroom door. She knocked lightly. "Lily? Are you okay?"

The door opened. Lily held a tissue to her nose. "He doesn't want me. I've been asked to pack my bags and go home."

"No. When?"

"I was doing my early morning Tai Chi in the gardens and Chloe joined me for what she called sunrise meditation and yoga. After we were both finished, she gave me the news. She was nice about it."

"Oh. I'm sorry, Lily." Michele's heart sank. She really liked Lily. Since they were both New Yorkers, and had bonded quickly, Michele had hoped her new-found friend would win the competition. Jeffrey deserved to have such a kind chef working for him. "Maybe we can call a taxi and leave together. Let me pack up and—"

"Miss Cox?" Chloe called to her from the doorway. "You've been asked to join the remaining chefs in the great hall to discuss today's schedule and what happens in the next stage of the competition."

Lily shot her a surprised look. No one was more shocked than Michele.

"Um, I think there's been a mistake. I quit the competition yesterday," Michele said.

Chloe turned her head and her long blond braid fell over her shoulder. "You don't want to be here?"

Oh, she wanted to stay. Desperately. The bonus money alone would save her. And cooking those grilled cheese sandwiches was the first time she'd felt like herself in the kitchen in a long while. Plus, there was a gorgeous, red-headed hunk she liked, more than she dared tell his sister, more than she wanted to think about. She'd kissed him for goodness sake! That's why she should bow out gracefully before she made a bigger fool of herself in front of him.

"I don't deserve to be here with these other great chefs," she muttered.

Chloe smiled. "My brother disagrees. You impressed him last night."

When? Based on her performance with the squid, she wouldn't hire her; would he?

"It is up to you, Miss Cox. If you want to leave, we'll make the arrangements for your flight back to New York. No problem. Jeff wants you to be happy with your choice, whatever it may be. The other chefs are gathering in the great hall. Join us, if you decide to continue on."

Chloe closed the door behind her.

"Wow, that's just..." Michele sat on the edge of her bed. "I didn't expect he'd want me to stay."

"I'm glad. If I can't win, I hope you do. He should have a great, kind chef." Lily smiled sweetly. "I'm rooting for you."

* * *

Jeff waited for Chloe to come around the corner. "So? What did she say?"

"Who?"

He gave her his deadpan look.

She laughed. "Just teasing. Michele was a little surprised. She thought she'd quit the competition yesterday."

"She did."

Chloe cocked her eyebrow, a typical Harper expression. "Sounds like she doesn't want to be here, Jeff. Why don't you let her go and continue this challenge with the other chefs?"

"Is that what she said? Michele doesn't want to be with me?" He cleared his throat. *Damn.* "*Work* for me?"

Chloe's lips quirked. "If you want her, why don't you end this competition and go after her? Ask her out. Woo her. See what happens."

"It's not that easy. She's not like the other women I've dated. Michele is...different." And struggling with something he didn't understand. She needed to be treated with care. He understood more than he dared admit. "Did she say she wants to leave Casa Larga?"

"Not exactly. She feels like she doesn't deserve to be here."

"That's insecurity talking. She's a damn fine chef, just as good as the other ones here. Did you convince her?" He was pacing now. "Is she staying or not?"

"I left it up to her. We'll know what she decides if she comes to the great hall, which is where I am supposed to be right now." Chloe kissed his cheek. "Good luck!"

Luck. He didn't believe in it, otherwise he'd have to ask what he'd done to piss off the universe.

"Good morning, ladies," Chloe's voice echoed from the great hall.

Part of him wanted to peek his head in to see if Michele had decided to stay. The other part of him reminded himself to cool his jets. He didn't want to do anything that might scare Michele off. It was obvious she was conflicted about staying. But damn, he wanted to look.

A workout. That's what he needed.

He started toward the gym to burn off his frustrated energy. It was laughable. A week ago, if he'd felt like this, he would've asked a lady or two out on a date. Now he was trying to get away from them.

"Mr. Harper?" a voice called.

Damn. It was a chef he'd already excused.

She hustled to catch up with him. "It's Lily. May I speak with you?"

He ran his hand through his hair. "My decision had nothing to do with your dinner. You are a fine chef, Lily. I meant what I said. I loved your dim sum."

"Thank you. That means a lot coming from you. I've watched all your shows. Some of them three and four times." She wrung her hands as if she was nervous and her cheeks turned pink. "I feel like I know you."

He pinched his nose. Was this some sort of hero worship? He was no hero. "I'm not that guy from the show. I'm just…a guy."

"No, no. You are a professional. What happened to you and to the show was very unfair."

He agreed with her assessment. "Thank you for your support and for coming here. I'm sorry it didn't work out. Best of luck in your job search." He tried to walk away, but she stepped in front of him.

"You deserve success and happiness, Jeffrey," she said. "Be careful about who you choose. Some of these chefs might be here for the wrong reasons."

Hold up. Lily had roomed with Michele, hadn't she? What had they talked about? "I'm going to need more information."

"I don't have more to say. Just…be careful."

That told him absolutely nothing but triggered his internal warning alarms because he, too, was cautious. Michele said she needed the job but something had spooked her so badly that she felt she didn't deserve it. That flicker of fear in her eyes? It hit too close to home. As a child, his heart had been broken by people who were supposed to love him. Had Michele encountered something similar?

Hell, these thoughts were depressing.

He needed to sprint on the treadmill or pound the hell out of the boxing bag.

Before the cold seeped in through the cracks.

Eight

The next morning, Tonia cooked him breakfast, Freja made lunch and Suzette rounded out the day with dinner. His taste buds were impressed but none of the meals captivated him as much as that single carved apple.

Michele had an artistic flair rarely seen in any discipline. Hell, in a matter of minutes she'd created an iris in the apple's eye that shockingly resembled his own. Michele possessed something he'd never experienced before. Magic? Is that what she'd called it? Unfortunately, it seemed to come and go for her, which was bad news for his restaurant. A five-star dining experience demanded consistency and near perfection for every dish. Betting on Michele Cox was foolhardy and, still, he couldn't bring himself to excuse her. Not yet.

She seemed to have worked her magic on him, too, with one gentle kiss.

When he wasn't judging meals, he worked with the building contractor and crew. The goal was to have the restaurant ready to open in six months. It was an ambitious time frame, but he wanted the restaurant in full swing as quickly as possible so the Harper marketing team would have good news to release, to hopefully counteract all the bad news still going around about Jeff.

Even though RW's lawyers had sent cease and desist orders, Finn was still doing his damnedest to ruin what was left of Jeff's reputation. The woman from the elevator was threatening to speak out as well. Lawyers had been dispatched to her home to try to reason with her.

The universe kept dumping on him.

In the early evening, Jeff took off his construction hat and joined Matt in the guesthouse for one of their brotherly, cutthroat games of pool.

"Married yet?" Matt handed him a beer.

"Asshole."

"What? I didn't sign up for this gig. That's all on you, brother."

"It was Dad's idea, not mine. Forget about a wife, I'm having a hard enough time choosing a chef."

Matt put a hand on his shoulder. "You can end it now. Tell RW to take a flying leap and live your own life. Go be happy."

"Happy. Everyone talks about that, but what the hell is it?" Jeff sipped his beer. "I like what I'm doing here. The restaurant construction plans are ambitious and, if I sit on the crew, they'll be done on time. I like that I'm creating this place from the ground up. If I walk now, I throw away my chance to make the hotel all it could be. RW will find someone else."

And Finn would release the rest of the video and Jeff would be done.

"This is not your only chance at building your dream. It's a restaurant and a hotel, man. You can do that anywhere, anytime. Building a strong relationship, a strong marriage? That's a lifetime achievement. Give yourself a chance to get it right."

Jeff racked the set. "You going to keep chapping my balls or take your shot?"

Matt didn't understand. Jeff's brother had everything he wanted—a beautiful, adoring wife, a son and a job he loved. Jeff didn't have any of that. Might never have any of it. The career he loved was at least attainable, here and now. He couldn't let it go or he'd have nothing.

"Oh, I'm taking my shot. Be prepared to pay up. I'm feeling hot tonight." And as promised, Matt's first shot launched two balls into the side pockets.

Jeff rolled his eyes. It was going to be a quick, demoralizing game.

Chloe opened the sliding glass window and stepped inside. "Thought I'd find you two here."

"Yep. Boy Wonder is hiding out from four gorgeous chefs," Matt said, and missed his shot.

"That's Karma for teasing your brother," Jeff replied.

"Looked like Karma to me. No decisions on a chef yet?" Chloe hitched herself up on the counter.

"Nope." Jeff's ball exploded into the hole.

"Whoa. Take it easy. You want to buy us a new table?" Matt complained.

"Sorry." Jeff glanced at Chloe. "Why don't you choose one?"

Chloe shook her head and her long braid fell over her shoulder. "No way. That's not my specialty. I'm just helping out until the hotel is up and running. Dad promised I'd be the Activities Director once we have clients."

"You aren't going back to your yoga studio in LA?" Matt asked.

"No. I'm done with the fakeness of Hollywood. And I could use a break from Mom."

"Yeah, no kidding. Jeff and I have taken a decade-plus long break. What's she up to these days?" Matt said.

A shiver rolled through Jeff.

"She's on a yacht in Europe with…" Chloe started, and then seemed to notice something in Jeff's expression that made her pause. She shook her head. "Let's not talk about her tonight. Jeff, I say choose the chef that appeals to your tastes. You won't go wrong."

Tastes. Michele's lips came to mind. He shot the next

ball harder than he meant to. It careened over the felt like a missile and rocketed straight toward Matt's head. Matt ducked just in time. The ball hit the wall with a loud bang, knocking a chunk out of the wood paneling.

"Holy smokes. You trying to brain me?" Matt asked.

"Jeff, are you okay?" Chloe asked.

"I guess I'm a little…frustrated."

"Just a little? I'd hate to see you all worked up." Matt motioned for Jeff to sit on a bar stool. "Plant your ass before you bruise my pretty face."

Jeff exhaled deeply and sat with Chloe.

"What can we do to help you?" Chloe asked softly.

Jeff tossed his hair out of his eyes. "Either you guys choose the chef or I'm going with the eeny-meeny-miney-mo method."

"I hear they're all great, but don't you like one more than the others?" Matt asked.

Jeff did, but he couldn't have her. Michele might ruin everything.

He had three goals at the moment: choose a great chef, finish the restaurant, and find a wife who didn't love him. That was it. He just needed two women who didn't make his head spin or his heart ache. But with Michele… His head was spinning and his heart pounded.

He was drawn to her more than he should be for lots of reasons, not the least of them being that nice girls like her shouldn't make spicy sandwiches for a bastard like him. It was too much fun, too easy, far too hot. And shouldn't happen again, or he'd really start regretting that he'd promised Dad he'd get married.

Hell, it was Dad's fault that he was this conflicted.

Why hadn't RW chosen male chefs to judge? A bunch of guys would have made the choice far easier. "I don't know them well enough to make that decision yet. And time is running out. Help me, Chloe. Pick one."

She smiled. "I won't choose for you, but I can help. Matt, let's save this poor boy from his misery."

Matt cracked his knuckles. "Yep. We can do this. Who's left standing?"

"Refined Freja from Sweden, toned Tonia from Arizona, spicy Suzette from France." Chloe had nicknamed them all.

"Scratch the last one. She's not staying. Her food was amazing—probably the best of the bunch—and she knew it. She came off haughty and super conceited," Jeff said.

"Yep, she has to go. Can't have two people who are full of themselves in one restaurant." Matt sipped his beer.

"Shut up." Jeff slugged him. "I'm knowledgeable, not full of myself."

"You keep telling yourself that, bro."

"Oh, I almost forgot the last one," Chloe said with a twinkle in her eye. "Sparkly Michele."

"What, no alliteration for her?" Matt asked.

"No need. Jeff has his own description."

"No, I don't. Michele is out, too." He didn't want to diagnose why those words were so hard to say. He wanted her to stay, but deep down he knew that was not a reason to keep her. She was the wild card in the deck, too risky for such an important project. Why was he tempted to trust her and rely on her to make his restaurant great when she admitted she wasn't cooking as well as she should be? Just the fact that he wanted her to stay despite her inconsistencies was a red flag that his head wasn't on straight when it came to Michele Cox. He walked back to the pool table and lined up to take his shot so that his sister couldn't see the emotion swirling in his eyes.

Chloe put her hand on his elbow, stopping his shot. "I thought she'd decided to stay."

He spun around to face them both. "Yes, but I can't let her. She's insecure, inconsistent and I heard she's here for the wrong reasons."

"Wrong reasons, like…?" Matt motioned with his beer bottle for Jeff to go on.

"Hell if I know. She said something about needing to help her sister. I don't know what that means."

"I might," Chloe said softly. "Dad showed me the report. He did a background check on each of the chefs."

"Any reason why Dad didn't show *me* the report?" Jeff was livid. His father obviously *still* didn't respect him. He felt like a kid again, being ignored by the old man.

"Did you ask for the report? I assumed Dad's team would've researched the candidates during the selection process, so I asked. No way Dad went into this thing blind," Chloe said.

"Oh." And now Jeff felt like a dumbass because he hadn't asked for the report when he should have. He could only blame his whole life being upturned for the oversight. Blackmail could mess with a guy's head.

"What did the report say about Jeff's Michele?" Matt asked.

"She's not my anything," Jeff grumbled but he looked at Chloe and waited for her answer.

"Michele takes care of her sister, who has Down syndrome. Medical costs. Housing. Everything. Her sister lives in an assisted community for adults. That can't be cheap," Chloe said.

Jeff had not expected that. When he'd caught Michele with the picture book, he hadn't imagined she was reading to an adult with neurotypical differences. His heart melted a little.

"Oh, man. I knew I liked her," Matt said.

Jeff did, too. He more than liked her. But should that matter? No. "This is a business. The restaurant cannot achieve five-star status without a great chef."

"Miss Sparkle is not as good as the others?" Matt asked.

Jeff exhaled deeply. "That's the thing. I believe she is the best, or was. Something happened to make her doubt herself. She lost… I don't know…the passion for it?"

Chloe leaned in. "I've worked with artists and actors in my yoga studio in Hollywood who were just like Michele. Something crushes their spirit and it's hard to recover. Some never do. What happened to her?"

He didn't know, shouldn't care. "Not my business." But that look in Michele's eyes on the application video—the survivor's spark—made him want to find out.

Matt patted his back. "My two cents? Don't quit on Michele so soon. See if she can recover her passion."

"She quit on me." Jeff swallowed his frustration with the last sips of beer.

"But she came back. You said it was her insecurity talking, remember? I'm with Matt. Give her another chance," Chloe said.

The idea of keeping her around another day lit a fire in his chest. It's what he wanted, even though he knew he shouldn't. "Fine. I'll give her one more day in the competition. If she can't cut it, I'll have to let her go."

"Okay, where does that leave us?" Matt asked.

"With three potential candidates. Michele, Freja and Tonia. I'd be cautious of Tonia—she's got knockout curves and knows how to use them," Chloe said.

"You can't fault her because she's smoking hot," Matt said.

"We're trying to improve Jeff's image. It's too easy to imagine Tonia faking it in one of Jeff's elevator videos," Chloe explained.

Jeff's head shot up. "Wait! You knew the maid in the GIF was faking it?"

Chloe laughed. "Seriously? Doesn't everyone? I highly doubt she was a maid, though. Porn star?"

He hadn't stuck around to ask. "Someone hired her to jump me in the elevator. I'd never seen her before." Jeff put the cue stick down on the table so they wouldn't see his hands shaking.

"Jumped? As in a stranger groped you?" Matt asked.

"Don't...want to...talk about it." He ground out the words through his clenched teeth.

He'd been the brunt of daily internet jokes, but he cared about what Matt thought and wouldn't be able to take it if his big brother laughed at him. Jeff's muscles bunched, ready to throw a punch. If Matt so much as cracked a smile, he'd lose a tooth.

"Some woman just..." Matt shook his head. "Wow. That's jacked up. Does that happen to you a lot?" His tone was serious, not at all teasing.

Matt believes me. Jeff released the air burning his lungs.

Chloe covered her mouth in horror. Her eyes wide with shock and filling up with tears.

Dammit, he couldn't do this now.

"Next subject!" he barked.

"I'm sorry, Jeff. I didn't realize what happened or I wouldn't have joked about it." Chloe rubbed his back. "It would do you good to talk to someone about this. If not with us, how about Angel? She's really helped Dad."

"I don't need a therapist." So what that his heart was pounding and his forehead was sweating? Big deal that he had an urge to snap the cue stick in two. He was fine. Would be fine. "I need to work and put it all behind me."

A silent look passed between Chloe and Matt.

"Just remember we're here for you, bro. All the time," Matt said.

"Fine. Can we get back to the chefs?" Jeff said. "You two are supposed to be helping me choose one, not psychoanalyzing me."

Chloe nodded. "Sure. We were talking about Tonia. If she's the one you want, Dad's image people will do what they can to tone down her sex-kitten vibe a bit for the cameras. It'll be fine."

Did he want a toned-down employee working for him? Did he want fake and surface level? With every chef so far, he'd wanted a connection. He wanted real for a change. Michele and her dimples popped into his head. And then her curves, closely followed by her soft lips. Damn, he wanted to kiss her again.

No.

He couldn't fantasize about the way she sassed him with that pretty mouth of hers. Or how much he wanted to taste the sweet spot below her ear and see if she would shiver with delight. He'd agreed to give her one more chance, but if she couldn't get her act together, he'd send her home.

"Now Freja is tall, regal, elegant and supermodel gorgeous. She has a stellar reputation in Sweden. Her entrées are supposed to be amazing. But..." Chloe trailed off.

His sister's assessment was spot-on. Freja was a real looker and her Swedish venison meatballs were both sweet and savory. "But what?"

"Don't take this the wrong way, but why is she here? She's famous in her own right in Sweden. Freja has graced more magazine covers than you have, Jeff. Why leave all that to come here to work for you? What's in it for her?"

"Way to crush a guy's ego, sis," Matt said.

"She's right, though. And before Lily left, she told me to be careful. Maybe someone is here under false pretenses," Jeff said.

"Did Lily say who to watch out for?" Matt asked.

"No. I wondered if it was Michele, but I guess it could be any of them. Or all of them."

Chloe leaned forward. "Why don't we test each chef to find out their true motives."

"Test them? How?" he asked.

Chloe sat back on her bar stool. "Leave that to me. I'll arrange outings for each of them tailored to give you a chance to connect with them personally, to find out why they're really here."

Jeff pinched the bridge of his nose. "We already determined that I don't make real connections."

"Fake it until you make it. And trust me. This next step in the competition will tell you who you should choose," Chloe said.

Matt grinned. "Sounds like a dating show."

Jeff slugged him, just because.

Nine

Michele got up early and called the billing department at Cari's group home to beg for an extension.

Even with careful fiscal management, she'd come up short. She didn't have enough for the rent. If she didn't get the chef job, she'd have to scramble for something else and fast.

But when the bookkeeper told her that all of Cari's expenses for the month had been paid for by Harper Industries, she gasped. Jeffrey Harper was full of surprises. She had no idea how he knew about Cari's group home fees but she was grateful.

Rushing downstairs to thank him for his generosity, she ran into Chloe.

"Good morning, Michele. You're up early. Still on New York time?"

"I'm an early riser." And a night owl. Working at Alfieri's meant being the first to arrive and last to leave the kitchen.

"Well, you should relax today. I am organizing individual outings with Jeff so he can get to know each one of you a little better. To see if your personalities mesh. The other two chefs are going to be with him for most of the day. I'm planning something for you that might take place tonight, but that one is still sketchy. I'll let you know when it's all settled."

This was the strangest interview…process? Contest?

Competition? "Okay. So, I might not see Jeffrey at all today?"

Chloe cocked her head and studied Michele for a second. "I don't think so, unless he runs into you like I just did. He's very busy. You go and enjoy the day. Use the pool. Walk the gardens. Go to the beach. If you get hungry for good Mexican food, I'd suggest visiting Pueblicito and going to Juanita's Café. Give them Jeff's name when you order and tell them who you are. We have a tab set up for you ladies in case you want to buy any food in the market or restaurant. As long as you're here, everything is paid for by Harper Industries."

Michele teared up and hugged Chloe. "Thank you for my sister's rent, too."

Chloe pulled back and smiled. "That wasn't me. Last night Jeff mentioned he had some online banking to do before he went to bed. He must have paid your sister's rent then. He comes off cocky and gruff, but there's a mushy heart under all that muscle. I hope you give him a chance."

She blinked. Give him a chance? Wasn't it the other way around?

Somehow, he'd given her a second chance at the opportunity of a lifetime and she was determined not to blow it.

Chloe patted her shoulder. "Enjoy your day off."

It was her first vacation in the last five years. And here she was in sunny California, staying in a sexy billionaire's mansion. It was a little mind-blowing. Suddenly she wanted to kiss Jeffrey again and it wasn't just to thank him for paying for her sister's fees.

On her way back to her room, Michele saw Suzette dragging her luggage out the front door. Holy moly! Jeffrey had excused the queen of French cuisine. It made no sense that Suzette was going home and Michele was still in the running. Why was Jeffrey keeping her here? She had a sense that she was dangling by one thin rope and had better figure out how to climb.

Tying up her walking shoes and zipping her sweatshirt, she headed out to explore Plunder Cove. She had barely started down the long driveway when a sleek silver car came from the house and pulled up next to her. The driver, a balding older gentleman, rolled down his window. "Want a ride, miss?"

"I'm not sure. How long does it take to walk to the town?"

"For me? It's a good thirty minutes one-way to Pueblicito since my legs aren't what they used to be. It is mostly downhill. You'd make it in twenty."

"I'll walk, then. The sunlight and sea air might do me some good."

"May I make a suggestion? If you buy something in town—food and whatnot—call me to come pick you up." He handed her a business card. "I wouldn't want a nice lady like you exerting yourself walking back up the hill."

She read the card. There was a phone number on it, plus a description that made her smile.

Robert Jones, Driver Extraordinary for Harper Industries
For Pickup, Call Alfred's Batcave

"Thank you, Robert. Or would you prefer to be called Alfred?" she asked.

He seemed very professional, somewhat stiff and formal, but his lips twitched before he answered. "Whichever you prefer, miss. Jeffrey calls me Alfred. But if you do that, you must request the Batmobile."

Jeffrey was into Batman? She had not expected that. The realization made him even more tempting. She'd loved DC Comics as a kid. She'd pretended she was a superhero who had the powers to save her mother and sister from illness. Michele's mother had made Halloween costumes for both of her daughters until she was too weak to sew. Man, she was devastated when she'd finally outgrown her Cat-woman costume.

"Will do. I'm Michele, by the way."

"I know, miss." He saluted her, did a U-turn in the drive-way, and drove back to what Michele now knew was the Batcave.

Michele smiled, imagining Jeff and his brother chasing each other through the spacious rooms and running through the gardens playing caped crusaders. It should have been a fun house to play in but then she remembered Jeffrey had said his parents wished they'd never had kids. Maybe this wasn't such a perfect place to grow up in after all. She was honored he'd confided in her about his childhood. It touched her. She had a sense that he didn't like to talk about himself much and had surprised himself by opening up. His can-didness and kindness made her want to trust him and prove that she could do the job he needed. The more she thought about Jeffrey Harper—his grin, those blue eyes, his wide chest... Okay, maybe she was thinking about him far too much. But the more she did, the more she wanted to stay.

"What the hell?"

Standing next to his sister, Jeff watched Freja stroll down the boat ramp as if it was a model's runway. She wore long crepe-like pants, a flowery blouse, a silk scarf, a large hat over her platinum-blond hair and four-inch heels. It was the strangest fishing getup he'd ever seen.

Chloe gave him a tiny elbowing and mumbled, "Not a word. Have fun!"

Untying the rope from the dock, he started up the motor and pushed off. Less than an hour later they returned.

Chloe must have seen them coming into the bay from the house, for she rushed down to greet them on the dock. "That was fast. Did you... Oh, dear, what happened?"

Jeff offered his hand to help Freja off the boat. She

pushed it away with a huff. Her hat was soggy, her clothes dripping. His weren't any better.

To Chloe, Freja said, "A head chef does not hunt for de food. It ees brought to her!" She stomped past them both in her squeaky heels.

"She's not wrong about that." He tipped his head to get the water out of his ears. "You owe me a cell phone."

"What happened?" Chloe asked.

"I'll put it to you this way, if I ever start acting like a prima donna just because I've been on television, slug me."

She punched him in the arm.

"Ow. Not funny. I mean it. Freja acted as if there were cameras everywhere. She was constantly turning to present her 'best side' to the invisible lens. Hell, if she'd just sat still and held the rod like I taught her, she wouldn't have lost her balance and gone ass-backward into the drink. And I wouldn't have had to rescue her."

He could see his sister was trying not to laugh. "Does she think we are secretly filming the chefs?"

They walked back toward the house. "Apparently. I tried to tell her the truth but she doesn't want to buy it. She thinks she's the only one in the competition who knows what's really going on."

"So…you didn't get to connect with her on a personal level."

"I saved her life and her giant floppy hat. Does that count?"

Chloe shook her head. "No, but it does give us a little insight. She's here for the spotlight. That might not be a bad thing. She knows how to work the cameras to improve your image and promote the restaurant. Her fan base in Europe is substantial already. And she is beautiful. Unless you can't stand her personality, I don't think we should count her out yet."

"I didn't say I couldn't stand her," he grumbled. "It's hard to communicate with her, though. She doesn't listen to my stories and she sure as hell didn't make me laugh." He flipped his wet hair off his forehead and wanted to slap himself. Since when did those qualities matter in a chef?

Michele Cox was ruining him.

"Get a hot shower. You're meeting Tonia at the stables at one o'clock," Chloe said.

Up at dawn at the building site, the morning spent fishing and performing ocean rescue, and horseback riding in the afternoon. Was his sister trying to kill him?

"Fine, as long as I get to soak in the hot tub tonight. I haven't ridden in so long, I might not be able to sit for a week."

He had a vision of Michele joining him in the warm bubbles and shook it off. He shouldn't see her in a bathing suit or he'd never be able to send her home.

"Sure, after the dinner party," Chloe said. "Dad says he can't make it to the California Restaurant and Lodging Association legislative meeting and dinner. You'll have to do it for him."

He gave Chloe a dark look. "No way, I'm not going to that." He wasn't ready to get sliced and diced in public yet. He didn't have a stellar restaurant to speak for him yet and the hotel was still in the planning phase. It was too soon.

"Dad thought you'd say that. He had hotel mock-up brochures made for you to wave around. They're awesome, Jeff. And you are the perfect guy to talk up the resort. This will be good for you, to get out there and show everyone that the stupid video hasn't fazed you. You're running this show, just like you always do. You'll see."

Was he running the show? Sometimes, it didn't feel like it. What happened in that video had knocked him back, but he'd gotten up and was working to be smarter, stronger, unfazed.

Like Michele.

Ten

It had to be the smallest town she'd ever seen. The main road had a few stores, an old adobe church, a miniature post office, a gas station and a couple of mom-and-pop stores. There were zero stoplights. Three roads with Spanish names jutted off toward the residential section of town. She strolled down one of the side roads in search of beach access and passed quaint old houses that looked to be at least a hundred years old.

A man washing a motorcycle in a small driveway looked up when she passed. "Miss Cox! Are you lost?"

It was Matt, Jeffrey's older brother. He lived here? "I'm looking for the beach."

He pointed. "Go back a quarter of a mile and you'll find the access road. Follow the signs and stay out of the snowy plover hatchery."

"Will do. How about lunch? Any place you recommend?"

"Not to your caliber of fine dining, but the best Mexican food is at my mother-in-law's place. Juanita's. You can't miss it."

Mother-in-law? Interesting that a rich boy would leave Casa Larga to marry someone from this small town and then live here. "Thanks."

"Oh, and, Miss Cox? I'm rooting for you."

Her chest warmed. It felt good to have someone believe in her again. Maybe she could do this. "Thanks."

Walking back down the main street, she found Juanita's Mexican Market and Café. The smell of barbecued meat made her stomach growl. She hadn't eaten breakfast and it was already close to noon. There were a handful of tables outside on the patio, full with people laughing and eating. Each table had baskets of tortilla chips and bowls filled with what seemed to be homemade salsa. Michele's mouth watered. Since there were no available tables, she thought she'd have to order a meal to go.

"Hey, lady. Wanna join us?" An older woman called from a table.

"Yeah, come on, we don't mind sharing. Well, Nona does," a second woman said.

The third woman had just dipped her chip into a small bowl of guacamole. "I told you to order your own. I don't like double-dipping." She pointed to the one available chair and said in a demanding voice, "*Por supuesto, siéntate*."

Michele didn't think she had a choice. She sat down. "Thank you. I'm Michele."

"You're one of Jeffrey's fancy cooks. I'm Alana, she's Flora and the guac-hoarder over there is Nona. We're sisters."

"I like to keep my germs to myself," Nona complained.

"My sister and I used to fight over food, too," Michele sighed. "I miss that."

Flora's hand went to her mouth and Alana made a little squeak.

"We lost our sister once. Thank God she's back for now," Nona said. "May your sister rest in peace." All three women made the sign of the cross over themselves.

"Oh, no. She's in New York. She's fine." Sort of. "It's just that I am used to seeing her every day. This separation is difficult."

Alana nodded. "Don't know what I'd do without these two picking on me every day." She pushed the basket of chips toward Michele. "Eat up. We'll get the waitress to take your order."

"How's the competition coming? I hear it's down to three chefs," Nona said.

Michele chewed a chip and marveled at how fast word spread in a small town. "The competition is amazing. Though I don't have much of a chance."

"Why would you think that?" Nona said.

Without going into the long story, Michele said simply, "I seem to have misplaced my confidence and my talent."

"You should learn from Jeffrey. He's talented and self-assured. Amazing, no? After how his mother treated him, it's a wonder he didn't end up crazy like his father," Alana said. "Those two were the worst."

"*Cállate*," Nona admonished hissed Alana. "That is private business."

"Jeffrey told me his parents fought," Michele said.

"It surprises me that he shared any of it. He must trust you, but I don't think we should add fuel to the fire." Nona gave both of her sisters a strong look to keep their mouths shut.

"*Claro*." Alana lifted her chin defiantly. "We wouldn't want anyone to know the evil mother ignored that sweet boy for days and screamed at him for no reason."

"That's awful," Michele said.

"A friend in the Harpers' kitchen said she had to make sure Jeffrey had enough food to eat," Flora pitched in.

"That woman is the worst mother ever," Flora said. "She didn't deserve those three beautiful babies. And that Jeffrey was so adorable with his copper hair and freckles. Who wouldn't love him?"

Michele's heart broke. She'd always known her mother loved her. She'd even said so with her last breath.

Alana nodded. "Holy Madre, she is terrible. I hope she never comes back here."

Nona's thin shoulders rounded and she seemed to cave

in. "She told everyone that I beat little Matthew. If I hadn't taken the brush from her hand, I don't know what would have happened..." Nona squeezed her eyes shut on the memory.

"Now I understand why that beautiful house seems so dark and cold. I'm glad his mother is no longer in the picture," Michele said softly.

"We are all glad of that. Things are getting better." Nona brightened. "Angel is there to help RW heal. She's convinced him to seek forgiveness from everyone he's harmed in the past. Believe me, it is a long list. But because he wants to change, he has asked the three kids to come home. We'll see if they forgive him or not, but it is great to have them all here."

Michele didn't know who Angel was or why RW needed healing, but she kept those questions to herself. What she really wanted was to know more about Jeffrey. Maybe she could help him before he sent her home. It was the least she could do after he'd paid her sister's expenses.

Michele ate the last chip and said, "It's amazing to me that his childhood was bad because he is so—"

"Handsome," Flora interrupted.

"Strong," Alana added.

"Smart," Nona said.

"Yes. All those things, but I was going to say 'sure of himself.' I wish I had an ounce of his confidence."

"Sure, sure he is confident but he is alone. He needs someone to take care of him, like his family never did. If we could only find him a wife—"

Three heads swung toward her.

Michele lifted her hands. "I'm just trying to be his chef."

She needed the job Jeffrey was offering, not a husband. Her sister depended on her to provide a stable income and life for the two of them. Getting romantically involved with a playboy who'd publicly declared he'd never get married? That would be the opposite of stability. Besides, she was not ready to trust any man with her heart after Alfieri had betrayed her.

The three women meant well, but marrying sexy Jeffrey Harper was not in the cards.

Besides, with all the women Jeffrey dated, how could he ever be alone?

RW stood on his balcony and looked out over his estate. It was beautiful, no denying it. His thousands of acres of gardens, pastures and grassy knolls all stretched out gracefully to the private beach that dipped into the sea. In the distance, he could see his nine oil derricks formed into a horseshoe in the sea. They were lit up like Christmas trees. Some would say he was successful and had created quite a legacy for his kids.

RW knew better. None of the toys, land or business meant a damn. The only things that truly mattered were setting things straight with his kids and winning the heart of the woman he couldn't seem to live without. And protecting them all.

Angel knocked on his open door and came on in. "Is everything okay?"

"Hell, yes. Now that you're here."

"Your text said come right away." She studied his face in her subtle way, looking for signs of distress. He knew all her tricks.

He grinned. "I figured you needed a break from that screaming kid."

"Cristina's boy is a bit of a handful. But I don't blame him. He misses his little friends and…" she swallowed hard "…the others."

He knew her dark spots, too. It killed him every time her sweet expressions twisted in momentary panic, which happened only when she thought about her ex-boyfriend, Cuchillo, and his gang. She had barely escaped those killers when she was a pregnant teenager. She'd been on the run, hiding in Plunder Cove for years with a secret identity and job as the local Mexican restaurant owner. Since she'd helped Cristina and Sebastian to escape to Plunder Cove, Angel was thinking about her ex more often. RW would fix that. He picked up the remote and pressed the button. Mexican music started playing.

Stretching his hand toward her he said, "*Baila conmigo*."

"Randall Wesley Harper! You're speaking Spanish."

Now that look of surprise was good. He loved impressing her. "People who call me by my full name are usually pissed off. I love the way you say it."

She turned her head, listening. "My favorite song since I was a little girl. How did you know?"

"A little birdie told me."

She smiled. "Henry."

"Yep, don't tell grandkids any secrets unless you want them broadcasted." He wiggled his fingers at her. "Come on, *bella. Baila conmigo*." She took his hand and he spun her into his embrace. "That's more like it."

She felt so good in his arms. Heart to heart. Body to body.

This meant something, though he didn't dare name it.

Angel was a dream he didn't want to wake up from. It was going to hurt in the end. He might not survive it.

Pressing her cheek to his, she played with the hair at the base of his neck. They swayed together in perfect rhythm. He sang softly in her ear.

"You know all the words?" She pulled back and he could see the shock of delight. "Do you understand them?"

He lifted his eyebrow and gave her one of his cocky grins. Jeffrey might have been famous for a grin just like it, but he'd learned the smug look from his old man. "I'm not just another pretty face, Angel."

She chuckled. "Go ahead, then. Translate."

He looked into her eyes and spoke the words he'd learned from heart. "Little mourning dove, my love, my heart. Do not fly away from me. I could not endure without your love. Cannot breathe without you with me. My heart beats only for you. You are my world. My everything."

Her eyes welled.

He kissed her with all the passion in his damaged heart. It beat strong when it was close to hers.

She held on to his neck and matched him kiss for kiss while he ran his hands down her lovely shoulders to her back. He pressed her against him and silently begged her to stay.

"RW." Her voice was breathy. "Close the door."

Eleven

Michele's hands were full of groceries. She'd bought all sorts of interesting and authentic ingredients at Juanita's Mexican Market and Café but had not gotten a chance to meet the owner herself. Too bad. She would've liked to have asked a few questions about the Harpers.

What those three sisters had told her seemed impossible. It was mind-boggling that a family so wealthy and famous could have such terrible troubles. Poor Jeffrey. She admired him for working to become successful after being raised like that and then being kicked out of the house when he was only sixteen. Her childhood had been a piece of cake by comparison. Even though her dad had died when Michele was only ten and her mom had to be both parents after that, she always knew she was loved. Her mother had been the best mom on the planet, even if cancer had cut her life far too short. The love her mother had given her made the situation Michele was in that much harder. She had to be the mom now for Cari and make sure her sister had everything she needed. She couldn't afford to get involved with Jeff or any man until she had her responsibilities under control.

Michele found a spot on the sidewalk that was out of the foot traffic to put the grocery bags down and dug into her purse for her cell phone. Smiling at the business card in her hand, she dialed.

"This is Michele Cox. Am I speaking to Alfred at the Batcave?"

A deep chuckle came through her phone. "Yes, yes, you are. Would you like a ride, miss?"

"I would. Thank you. I'm standing outside Juanita's," Michele said.

"Very good. We'll be right there."

We? Her heart beat a little faster.

Was Jeffrey coming, too?

She expected the long car that Alfred had been driving in the morning. She did a double take when a bright yellow Bentley convertible pulled up beside her with the top down. Alfred wore a plaid British ivy cap over his bald head while his passenger sat in the front seat with her long blond hair flowing in the wind. Chloe, not Jeffrey.

"Hi, Michele. Thought I'd tag along so we can stop at a shop along the way. I'll move to the back," Chloe said. "Alfred, take us to Carolina's."

Michele handed her bags to Alfred who loaded them in the trunk. "Carolina's?" She'd seen pretty much everything the little town had to offer but didn't remember that store.

"It's a one-stop dress store for baptisms, *quinceañera* parties, proms and weddings. Lots of color and yards of frill and lace but I've got my fingers crossed they have at least one gown that will work for you tonight."

"I don't understand," Michele said.

"For your outing with Jeff. It's been firmed up. Each one has been a different way for Jeff to get to know the chefs better. Freja, for example, went fishing with him this morning. And Tonia and he rode horses."

"I've never been on a boat before and love riding horses. Those outings sound lovely."

"Well, they were illuminating, that's for sure." Chloe smiled. "The other two chefs had adventures in Plunder Cove but yours will be up the coast in another little ocean-side town just south of Big Sur called Seal Point. Matt is flying Jeff up there for a meeting with the California Restaurant and Lodging Association. There is a dinner party afterward with lots of big shots and some press. He really doesn't want to go to this event, but it's important to get the word out about the Plunder Cove hotel. And let's face it, a conservative dinner party with a respectable date can help improve Jeffrey's public image. All you two need to do is show up for the dinner and then you both can leave. Alfred will drive you back home together."

Date?

She needed to keep her eye on the prize—the job, not the sexy man. Going on a date with him would be dangerous. Even as warning bells were going off in her brain, her lips were itching for another chance to taste Jeffrey's full lips. A real date could be more temptation than she could handle.

"This is an important night for my brother. Please say you'll help him," Chloe said. "We have to do something to fix his damaged image."

Schmoozing at dinner parties. Talking to big shots. Wearing a gown. All these things were so far outside Michele's wheelhouse that she didn't know where to begin. She was more comfortable behind the scenes and in the kitchen than outside where the VIPs ate. But she would go to this event to prove to Jeffrey that she could represent Harper Industries in any environment and convince him to choose her.

"Just tell me what I need to do." Her voice sounded meek, unconvincing. She cleared her throat. "I want to help him, any way I can."

"My brother likes you." Chloe touched her arm. "Be yourself, Michele. And have a nice time."

Trying not to yawn, Jeff shifted in his seat to ease off his sore backside. Tonia had sucked at horseback riding and had only wanted to ask him about his family—his brother, his sister, his father...and anyone else that lived at Casa Larga. Thankfully, they'd cut the adventure short before he'd had to come up with answers for her, or listening to the governor's speech right now would be even more painful than it already was.

He looked around the conference hall. It was packed with all the big boys in the California hotel industry plus a few tiny fish trying to make a splash for themselves. Where did he fit in? Jeff might be a small fish after having his reputation decimated, but he was working for one of the biggest companies in the world. When he made eye contact with some of the attendees, he could tell he was hated by some and idolized by others. Story of his life.

He checked his phone. No new GIFs. He should be grateful. Instead, it worried him. Had the lawyers convinced Finn to cease and desist, or was he working on the next series of damning videos?

Just then Chloe texted him.

Oh, brother of mine, you owe me. Big-time.

Why?

You'll see. How's the meeting?

Kill me now before the boredom does. What do I owe you for?

Tonight's adventure.

He frowned.

No more damned adventures today. I'm beat. As soon as this never-ending meeting wraps up, I'm going home and falling into bed.

You can't. Dad asked me to make sure you stay for the dinner party.

No.

His sister knew why he hated to eat alone. Eating with a group of strangers was not much better.

Come on. It's important for you to mingle and spread the word about our hotel. Show them the brochure. Talk it up. Besides, your date is on her way.

His pulse kicked up.

My date?

Don't worry, I packed your tux on the plane and Matt brought it to the hotel. They're holding it for you in the lobby. Have a nice time! Alfred will bring you both back to the Batcave when you're ready. Gotta run. You can thank me tomorrow.

Who's my date?

There was no response.

Chloe!

The texting had stopped. Dammit, his sister was toying with him. And now he had the rest of the meeting to wonder who would show up tonight. Was this supposed to be a real date or was it part of the interview process?

Hell, *who* was his date?

He'd already spent time with Freja and Tonia. Would it be pretty, sweet, kind Michele?

He'd missed seeing her today. She was the only chef he'd connected with on a personal level, and quickly, which made him wary. Plus, he couldn't stop thinking about the kiss in the kitchen. And how he wished he'd pressed her up against the kitchen island and kissed her back.

He honestly hoped it wasn't Michele because he would be distracted by her. When she was close it was hard to concentrate on anything but the light catching in her hair and eyes, and the way her smile crinkles tugged at a soft spot in his chest, the rise and fall of her breasts when she breathed... damn. He was in big trouble if his date was Michele.

Worse. If the big boys at the dinner party intimidated her, bringing out her insecurities, she'd be going home tomorrow. He had a job to do and couldn't make any more excuses for her. He'd have to cut her loose. And that would be the worst.

Michele felt a little funny sitting in the back of the limo while Alfred drove, but he said he wouldn't have it any other way. "You look like a movie star, Miss Cox. And you'll be treated like one tonight. You just relax. The drive up the coastal highway is beautiful."

He wasn't kidding. The highway meandered and curved along the blue-green craggy-rocked Pacific Ocean. It was breathtaking.

"And here we are. Seal Point," Alfred said, as he pulled up to the lobby of a two-story building.

She'd expected something larger, more ornate, and was pleasantly surprised by the rustic wood-sided lodge atop the rocky cliffs. Torches lit pathways through gardens and into groves of lacy dark green Monterey pines. It felt intimate, somehow. The sun was an orange ball of wax melting into the Pacific Ocean. The sea breeze softly caressed her skin. It was a beautiful night, fragrant and warm. The setting was so romantic. And inside the lodge was the man who had the power to make her professional dreams come true and tempt her into destroying everything. She wanted him and knew she shouldn't act on her desires.

Alfred opened her door. "Ready, miss?"

As I'll ever be.

She'd never had her makeup professionally done before today, nor her hair swept up so perfectly. The dress Chloe had purchased for her was pale pink and clung to her curves like a cloud.

For the first time since she'd left her hometown to work for Alfieri, Michele felt beautiful. Special. Even if it was just a fantasy for tonight. She was at a stunningly romantic place, but she wasn't here for romance. It was her job to make Jeffrey Harper look respectable, which meant she wasn't going to gaze into his pretty starburst blues or let his deep voice delight her, and she was certainly not going to kiss his full lips.

This was a business dinner, nothing more. She could do this because Jeffrey needed her. And if she proved capable here, perhaps he'd choose her for his restaurant.

You'll fail like you always do. You'll embarrass Jeffrey in front of everyone.

"Shut up, Alfieri!" she mumbled under her breath.

"Miss? Did you say something?" Alfred still stood by the door waiting for her to get out.

Her legs seemed unable to move. "If I asked you to drive me back to the Batcave, would you do it?" Her voice was shaky.

Alfred leaned closer and whispered, "Is that what you want, miss?"

If I leave now, I might as well fly straight home to New York.

She swallowed. "No. I'm just a little nervous. I'm not used to parties like this." Or being on a date with a famous, wealthy man. Who was she kidding? Any man. She hadn't been on a date in years. "Where do I go?"

"I believe the people in the lobby can direct you to the restaurant where the dinner party is taking place."

She nodded. "Sure, okay."

"Miss Cox? I'll be out here waiting for you and Jeffrey. Say the word and I will drive you back to Plunder Cove. But I believe you will be great tonight. Do as Chloe said and simply be yourself."

"Thank you, Alfred." She took a deep breath and walked toward the lobby, all the while wondering what word she needed to say to get a ride out of here should things go terribly wrong.

Michele didn't ask the people at the front desk for directions. She simply followed the sound of piano music and laughter. The restaurant was beautiful. Lots of windows, tables with white cloths and candles. She searched the room and found...*him*.

Holy wow, he looked great in a tux. His broad shoulders nicely filled out the jacket. The thin black tie dipped inside behind the single button he still had buttoned. The perfectly tailored tux highlighted his thin waist and long legs. Her mouth watered.

Jeff was scanning the crowd, too. Looking for her? When his gaze met hers, she lifted her hand to wave. His mouth opened in what seemed like surprise. He rose to his feet and lifted his hand back at her. His lips formed one word. *Wow.*

Her breath caught in her chest, her heart pounded, her lips turned up of their own accord. All the other people in the room, including the pianist, disappeared. There was only Jeffrey and that smile on his lips.

It was just like the first time she'd seen him. The way he looked at her heated up her insides.

Respectable business dinner, she reminded herself, even as she wondered what his kiss would taste like.

Twelve

At first, Jeff wondered if he'd been stood up. He suspected people were all asking themselves the same question he was asking: Where was his date?

The better question: Who was his date?

Dinner was about to be served and he was running out of small talk to use with the people at his table. He was disappointed by the lack of intelligent conversation and frustrated with the power plays. The organizers of the event had snubbed him and put him at a table with low-level hotel management—the flunkies. The big guys, the movers and shakers in the hotel industry, were all sitting together at the front of the restaurant next to the windows with the ocean views. They drank and laughed loudly, while he was at the back with these jokers, clenching his fists under the table. If his date didn't show up soon, he'd leave.

And then he saw her.

Michele walked into the room wearing an amazing pink dress that bared her shoulders and accentuated her breasts, waist and hips. Her blond hair was swept up into an intricate twist, exposing her sleek, long neck. One gold chain, with what looked like a heart, dipped into her cleavage. His gaze followed that heart and then traveled slowly back up to her parted glossy lips and smoky eyes. Lots of kissable skin.

"Wow."

She'd come to be by his side during a boring business

dinner. That was all. But he was aroused just by looking at her. His heart pounded out a distress signal, a warning not to get in too deep. And then she raised her hand and smiled and things suddenly got real.

Someone at his table asked him a question, but he ignored it. His aching body was drawn to her and he was striding in that direction before he realized he'd risen from his chair.

"God, you look gorgeous." He took her arm without even thinking about it.

"So do you." Her cheeks pinked and she looked at him from under her long lashes. Her voice was husky, and soft enough that only he heard her. No flirtatious tone. She said those words like she meant them.

Hell, he was going to have to sit down.

Guiding her to his table, he wished they could leave now and go somewhere quiet to be alone, but the food was arriving and she'd come all this way for him. To help him represent his dream to the industry movers and shakers. He needed to at least feed her before he whisked her away.

He pulled her chair out and she kept her gaze on his. "Thank you."

Sexy without trying. He was in big trouble.

He sat quickly and introductions were made around the table. Michele smiled and shook hands with each person and offered appropriate comments as she did so. Like she was really listening.

"I ordered steak for both me and my date. I didn't like the other option." When he scooted his chair in, his thigh bumped hers under the table. The sudden touch was electric. She didn't move away, so he kept his leg right where it was.

"Ah, so you were going to eat mine, too." She smiled. "I might share if you're good."

Michele looked at him for a beat too long and then, as if she had to collect herself, she turned back to the lady next to her. "Tell me about your hotel. Does it have a restaurant?"

The food arrived and Jeff silently chewed his steak,

watching Michele. Her whole body seemed to absorb what each person had to say. She laughed easily and gave restaurant advice. Calling each person by their first names, she seemed to remember what each one had told her about themselves. She interacted with them as if she was the one here to represent Harper Industries, not him, and she even added a few plugs for Casa Larga, as if she really cared about the place. The way she described the grounds and the private beach made *him* want to vacation there.

Hell, she was amazing.

Michele, in her gracious, easy way made him realize a cold hard truth—he was being a superior, egotistical ass. Like Finn.

And RW.

The thought that he was turning into his father made Jeff shift uncomfortably in his chair. He'd sworn to himself that he would never be arrogant, unfeeling and cruel like his father. He'd fought hard against those family genes for most of his life. That's why he'd created *Secrets and Sheets* in the first place— to stand up to the arrogant bastards who thought they owned the world. Sure, Jeff was cocky and funny on television, but he wasn't a superior jerk.

Was he?

Music started up outside and people left their tables and went out on the patio to dance.

She leaned over and whispered in his ear, sending chills bumps into his scalp. "Are you okay? You haven't said a full sentence in over an hour."

He scooted even closer and whispered back, "I'm an idiot."

They were eye-to eye, breath-to-breath. She blinked and he could see confusion in her expression. "Did I do something wrong?"

"No, sweetheart. You're doing everything right."

She studied his expression.

"I swear, it's not you. I'm just…off tonight," he said.

"You're allowed. I don't expect you to be perfect."

Damn. She'd done it again.

Michele had a remarkable talent for surprising the hell out of him. Most people he knew did expect him to be perfect—his agent, producer, fans, dates and RW. As a kid, he was never good enough. For the show, Jeff was supposed to be at the top of his game and improving his performance every episode.

Before this moment with Michele, he hadn't realized how exhausting his life was.

"It happens to the best of us," Michele went on. "If this party isn't working for you, we could leave now, or…" She cocked her head toward the music. "We could shake out the sillies on the dance floor. That's what my sister does when she's feeling…off."

He lifted an eyebrow. He'd never heard that expression before. "Oh, it might be a lot sillier than you think. I don't know if you've heard the rumors, but the truth is, only one of the Harper men knows how to dance and it isn't me. Sure you want that kind of embarrassment?"

"No worries. My standards are really low. The first and last time I danced was at my junior prom. And I'm not sure you could call that dancing."

He stood to pull her chair out and whispered in her ear, "A dancing virgin, then."

Her lips quirked. "I guess so."

When she rose, she gave his arm a squeeze, sending off an alarm that reverberated low and deep in his psyche. "I didn't have time to mention it before, but I want to thank you for paying my sister's fees. I will pay you back. I promise."

"That's not necessary."

"I think it is. But I am grateful for the gesture." She kissed his cheek. "Dance with me."

She turned to walk outside, expecting him to be right behind her. He wasn't.

Suddenly, he regretted agreeing to dance. What if he

couldn't hold her, touch her, feel her velvety skin on his, without wanting more?

Without wanting too much.

He exhaled slowly through his nose and stiffly followed her outside.

"Over here," she called to him. "I thought I lost you. Isn't this place beautiful? The Monterey pine grove and the moonlight shining on the water?"

He couldn't talk. All he could do was feel.

He wanted this, needed her.

The music slowed at that moment and he took Michele in his arms and held her close.

He didn't want to let her go. He had to keep reminding himself that this was business, not a date, not the start of something he couldn't finish. A woman like Michele would want more than he could give her. She deserved more than him.

Michele put her head on his chest and he pressed the small of her back, holding her against him. She felt good in his arms, really good.

"How do my moves compare to those at the junior prom?" he asked, his voice sounding surprisingly normal.

Gazing up at him, she smiled. Her dimples drove him crazy. "You, Jeffrey Harper, are so much better. This is definitely dancing."

Michele had one hand on his shoulder while the other was wrapped around his waist. As they swayed to the love song, he listened to her breathing, felt her heart beat against his chest.

Slowly, he ran a finger over her bare shoulder. Silky and soft. He wanted to kiss the curve of her there, the hollow, and work his way up to her delicate earlobe.

"Michele?"

"Hmm?"

"My closest friends call me Jeff."

Her breath caught. "Jeff," she said softly.

The sound of his name on her lips lit a fire in his groin. Feelings he had not felt in a long time burned through his blood.

He wanted this, to hold someone who was compassionate and real. He wanted to experience…something. Everything.

Was this what his siblings had meant by feeling a real connection?

"Remember when you kissed me in the kitchen?" he asked.

She stopped swaying and buried her face against his chest. "I don't know why…that was so…embarrassing."

"Yes. It was…for me." He tipped her chin up so he could see her eyes when he said, "I really messed it up. Will you please do it again?"

Her lips parted in surprise and then turned up into the sweetest smile he'd ever seen. "I promised myself I wouldn't kiss you again."

"Pretty please? What do I have to do, Miss Cox? Juggle clams and catch them in my teeth?"

She burst out laughing and then covered her mouth. She cut her eyes to see if she'd bothered anyone on the dance floor. He was sure she'd only bothered him.

Her laughter did amazing things to him.

"You got me," she said and smiled.

He liked the sound of that.

She put her hand on his cheek and rose up on her toes. This time, when her lips touched his, he kissed her back. Not gently.

It had been too long since he'd kissed a woman he cared about and his body reacted with a landslide of need, ache, fire. It felt good. Real.

He deepened the kiss, diving in, tasting, touching, wanting. He pressed her body to his. Enjoying the sensation of her breasts against his chest, her thighs touching his. He stroked her shoulder with his free hand. God, her skin was so soft, her lips perfect.

He'd come to this event to make a good impression on the other hotel owners and now he didn't give a damn about any of them. He kissed Michele as if he'd never kissed a woman before and still he wanted more.

He felt like he could never get enough.

The band played a faster song and he reluctantly pulled away to look at her. Her cheeks were flushed, her eyes hooded. Sexy. Her hips moved to the sensual beat. He liked it.

He liked her.

Putting his hands on her hips, he tried to follow along, not quite catching up. She raised her eyebrow and slowed the movement, rubbing against him as she did, pressing, teasing. Hell, he liked that more. Cupping her jaw, he kissed her again, soundly.

Out of the corner of his eye, he saw a woman dressed in a black sequined gown pass by, puffing on her cigarette. She turned around and took a long look at Jeff kissing Michele.

"You're disgusting," she snarled at Jeff. "First the maid in the hotel and now this? Stay away from him, honey. He's a pig." The woman threw her cigarette on the patio, ground it out with her heel and stomped away before either one of them could say a word.

Anger boiled inside him.

"Dammit!" How dare Finn's manipulations ruin this, too.

"Ignore her," Michele said softly. "She doesn't know you. People only see what they want to, not what's true. You are so much more than a stupid GIF."

He turned his head and studied her. Was *she* for real? Could she see him—past the show, the press, the GIF?

Matt's words rushed back to him.

Show her who you are without the smoke and mirrors. No stage lighting. No props. Just two real people being... normal.

And suddenly he wanted normal. Wanted real.

More. He wanted real *with* Michele. The thought alone

should have scared him. He should've pushed himself away because he knew he'd only hurt her in the end. But he was too caught up in the heat and her sparkle to do anything except pull her into his arms and kiss her like no one was looking. The little sound of contentment she made at the back of her throat went straight to his groin. He lifted his head to look at her. She still had her eyes closed and the sweetest smile on her face. This had nothing to do with the chef job—he'd have to figure that out later—it had everything to do with the sensations pulsing through him. He couldn't hold back the tidal wave of want that overtook him.

"Let's take this off the dance floor." His voice was little more than a growl.

Breathing heavily, she nodded.

"Tonight, the chef competition is on hold. Our date has nothing to do with that."

"I didn't believe it did."

"Good. I had activities with the other women, but nothing like a date. I wouldn't want you or anyone else to think this is how I operate."

"No. Of course not."

He led her down the torch-lit pathway, away from the restaurant and patio dance floor and past the Monterey pine grove. He was on the hunt for a quiet alcove far away from the dinner party and prying eyes, any place to be alone with Michele and not have to think or be judged.

"What's that?" She pointed toward the redwood structure perched like a beacon high above the rugged Big Sur coast.

"A wedding pagoda. Couples come from all over to be married under that canopy."

"It's lovely. I can just imagine the bride and groom standing there, gazing into each other's eyes, with the waves rolling in, whispering sweet promises below."

"You're a romantic."

"And you're not?"

"Not about weddings, no. My parents blew that institution sky-high."

"Ah, so that article I read about you was true. You will never get married."

"Don't believe everything you read. I will get married, but it sure as hell won't be for love."

Her jaw dropped. "What would it be for? A business arrangement? The trading of camels? A joining of kingdoms?"

She was joking. He wasn't.

"Something like that. I wouldn't want my bride to fall in love with me. I'd just hurt her like my parents hurt each other."

"It doesn't have to be that way. My parents married for love and rarely argued. They raised me and my sister in a great home before they passed away. What if you fall in love with your bride and you both live happily ever after? It could happen."

"Not to me. I don't have the chemical makeup for it."

She blinked. "You can't fall in love?"

"No. And I won't hurt anyone because of my screwed-up DNA."

"I don't believe that."

"That's because you aren't like me. You're warm and caring. Sweet. I see you going for the wedding pagoda and the happily-ever-after, Michele. I hope it sticks for you. I'll take the no-drama, no-stress business contract in front of a judge. It's better that way."

"That seems so…unfeeling."

Yeah, that's what he was trying to tell her. No matter what was happening between them tonight, he didn't have any of those feelings. Never would.

He was cold.

"Let's find a fireplace," he said.

He didn't tell her that he'd already agreed to a loveless marriage when the restaurant was completed.

Why ruin the best date he'd had in years?

* * *

Michele sat beside Jeff on a couch in front of a rock fireplace. They were alone and far from the dinner party. An owl hooted in a tree nearby.

"Cold?" He took his tuxedo jacket off and wrapped it around her shoulders. Not with him sitting this close. Her body was still humming from his kisses.

She put her head on his shoulder and looked up at the stars. "So beautiful."

"Got that right." He was looking at her.

It surprised her. He'd dated so many gorgeous women, did he really think she was beautiful?

She laced her fingers with his. She really wanted to touch him. All over.

With her head still on his shoulder she whispered, "Can we just stay here forever?"

"What about the restaurant I have to finish? And the world-renowned recipes you're going to create?"

She sighed. What if she couldn't create any recipes anymore, world renowned or otherwise? She knew the answer. This would be her last night with Jeff unless she could find the magic.

"Well, if we have to go back to reality tomorrow—" she started.

"Let's make this a night to remember," he finished and punctuated the thought by cupping her jaw and kissing her lips.

He was such an amazing kisser. When he sucked on her bottom lip she moaned with delight. She turned her head so he could have better access. He gripped her hair and pinned her in place. His tongue thrust in and out. In and out. She imagined that tongue doing wicked things between her legs and she moaned again.

"Pull up your dress," he growled. "I want to touch you."

She hesitated. The man had just told her that he couldn't fall in love. He wasn't interested in a real marriage, only one that was advantageous to his business. He was a play-boy who dated anyone he wanted. And he was right, she wasn't like that at all. She wanted to love, to feel every-thing, and to make a life and family with her soul mate, like her mother did.

But the expression on his face—dark, determined, needy—was her undoing. No one had ever looked at her like that before and she longed to feel sexy, just once. She stood and crinkled up the material from the hem of her dress until her legs were exposed.

"More," he said.

She swallowed and pulled her gown up further until he could see her pink panties. They matched the dress and probably looked almost nude in the light of the fire.

"Come here, sweetheart." He crooked his finger at her.

Her brain kept trying to tell her that Jeffrey Harper was the opposite of her soul mate. He was sexually experienced and hot enough to burn her to ash. He was a one-night guy and she didn't do one-night stands, and she didn't sleep around at work either. It wasn't in her chemical makeup to shut feelings off and walk away. And it certainly wasn't like her to hook up with a take-charge kind of a guy who had the power to hurt her professionally and personally. But part of her was drawn to the sadness in Jeff, the deep pain he tried to hide.

There was a heart in that wide, muscular chest. Jeffrey just didn't know it. Maybe if she could show him how to love…

She came toward him and he pulled her on top of his lap. She straddled his legs, the only thing between them were her panties and his tuxedo pants. He was so deliciously hard. He ran his hand up her leg starting at her calf and going higher, higher.

"Kiss me," she whispered.

"Oh, babe, your wish is my command."

He kissed her shoulder, her neck, along her jawline.

When he finally made his way to her lips she met him with her tongue. He opened to her, letting her lick his lips, taste, explore. He sucked in a sharp breath and she knew she was doing something right.

One of his hands rubbed, petted, traveling up her legs, driving her wild. Their tongues danced. She'd never been kissed like that before. When he got to her glutes, he gave them a squeeze. Her heart pounded hard in her chest. The world was spinning around her. She gripped his shoulders to stabilize herself, enjoying this man and his incredible lips. His finger ran underneath the elastic of her panties. She stilled in his arms. Was he really going to—the thought was cut off when his hand was suddenly touching her inside her panties.

"Okay?" he asked.

She nodded. More than okay. She hadn't felt like this in years.

He petted her, making her wet.

A voice in her head tried to remind her that she was outside a party where anyone could walk by, anyone could see what he was doing to her. But what he was doing was far too good.

Her own moans blocked out any inner voices.

"You like that?" he asked.

"Oh, yes."

He kept petting. Kissing. Driving her wild.

His finger went inside. He tugged gently, hitting a sweet spot she didn't know she had.

"Oh. " Was all she could muster. He felt so good. Before she knew it, her hips were moving with his hand's movements. Her breath and heart beat racing.

"Come for me," he growled against her neck. "Let go."

The words, hoarse and encouraging, undid any reserve she'd been clinging to. She threw her head back and rode him up and over the abyss. Moaning as the feelings—raw, rich, delicious—rolled through her.

Just then, a flash went off.

"Thanks, Harper!" a man shouted and ran off.

She blinked in surprise.

Jeff cursed while quickly lifting her off his lap. "Head down," he said in a clipped sharp tone. He brought his jacket up to cover her face. But it was too late. A photographer had snapped a picture of them in a decidedly unrespectable dating moment. And…there was the fact that she'd oh-so willingly flown over the abyss with her potential boss. No one would know that they mutually agreed this date had nothing to do with the chef position.

She'd thrown gasoline on his already damaged reputation, setting fire to everything.

Jeff pounded his pockets, coming up empty. "Do you have a cell phone?"

She handed him hers.

"Alfred, come to the side lot and get Michele the hell out of here," Jeff barked into it.

Paparazzi *here*? In the middle of freaking nowhere? Why wouldn't those bastards leave him alone?

He glanced at Michele. She was pale and still had his jacket held up to her neck as if she wanted to disappear. Hell, she looked so…beautiful. He'd never seen anything more gorgeous than Michele letting go in his arms. He longed to pull her back, nuzzle against her neck and whisper how much he wanted to have her come again and show her how much he still wanted her. Damn the paparazzi! He'd lived with the press long enough to know that the one night would have consequences for both of them. Sweet Michele—a woman who was already fighting insecurities—was about to have her reputation destroyed, too.

Unless he did something.

"Stay here. When Alfred arrives, climb in the limo and lock the door. He'll get you home safely," he told her.

"What about you? Where are you going?" Her voice was

small. Hell, he'd messed this up for her. He was pissed at himself for wanting her so much. He should have had better control, been stronger. But even now he wanted her and was nearly desperate to throw caution to the wind.

"I'll stay here as long as it takes to find that photographer and make him delete the photo. I'll get my own ride home. Don't worry, Michele. I'll handle it."

Her eyes widened. "How will you handle it?"

He wanted to beat it out of the guy, but he knew how these things worked. Jeff couldn't afford an assault and battery charge on top of everything else.

"The way Harpers do. With money." He spat those last words out. He really was becoming his father.

The limo pulled up. Alfred raced out of the car faster than Jeff had ever seen the old guy move and was quickly opening the door for her.

"Get her home safely," Jeff demanded.

"We can figure this out together. Please come with me." Michele reached out to him, but he stepped back.

"I can't." He was stepping back because he didn't want to hurt her. And he would, he was sure of that. A lady who wanted to get married for love would eventually hate him.

He couldn't love.

But his thoughts got messed up around her. He wanted to make love to her more than anything he'd ever wanted and wasn't sure why. He'd been with many women. Why was Michele different? Why did he need to touch her so badly? As if to prove the point, his hand was already on her shoulder before he could stop himself.

"Let Alfred take you back. This is my fault. I'm sorry."

Her crestfallen expression ripped a hole in his chest. "I'm not."

Damn. He wanted to kiss her so deeply that she'd never doubt how special she was. She made him want to be more than he could be. He wanted to feel. To be real. To fall in love. To love Michele deeply with everything he was not.

He exhaled slowly. "Don't misunderstand. I'm not sorry for our time together. That was…amazing. No, I'm sorry that I can't be a better man. You deserve more.

"Go. Now," Jeff finally managed.

"Jeff, please!" Michele called after him, but he didn't stop, wouldn't turn around.

He didn't understand why all the pieces he'd held together for so long were shattering like a bashed-in chandelier. Only one thing was crystal clear—he needed to protect Michele.

From himself.

Thirteen

Michele got up early to find Jeff. Had he come home at all?

She wanted to tell him that she wasn't mad at him. Concerned, confused, yes, but not angry. He'd given her the best night she'd had in a long time. She wanted to be with him again, in spite of everything, and she wanted to help him. If she could find him.

He wasn't anywhere in Casa Larga.

She wandered outside and found both Tonia and Freja sunbathing by the pool.

"Look who's here, Miss Sex Kitten," Tonia said.

"What?" Michele asked.

Freja pointed to the newspaper. "You made de front page."

Michele snatched up the paper. Sure enough, there she was on Jeff's lap with her dress hiked up to her thighs with the caption, "Who is Jeffrey Harper's New Sex Kitten?"

"Oh, no." Her heart sank. She sat on a lounge chair and read the scathing article. It painted him in a terrible light but the writer didn't know who she was.

"Good chefs win by their talents," Tonia snarled. "I can understand why you would try sleeping with the boss."

"A bad picture. Ees you, no?" Freja asked.

"Of course it's her. She wasn't here last night." Tonia gave Michele a withering look. "I demand you be disqualified from the competition. I guess Jeffrey won't do it, so I'm going to look for RW right now."

Tonia grabbed her cover-up and marched into the house.

Freja tsked. "Too bad. I like you better than that one, but she ees right. Ees best if you quit."

They were both right.

God. She'd messed things up. She really, really liked Jeff. A lot. And she'd let him down. The one night she was supposed to help improve his reputation, she gave in to her desires and let herself go on his lap. Even though it was one of the best dates of her life, she'd hurt his reputation even more. She'd been selfish and lost the job that would save both her and her sister while hurting the first guy she'd dated in a long time. Who does that? Feeling terrible, she decided she'd go clear the air with him, make sure he was okay, and then…she'd leave.

Angel was heading down the hallway in RW's private wing when she saw a woman opening doors and peeking inside each room.

Who was she? What was she looking for? And where was the guard?

Cautious, Angel stepped back inside RW's room and closed the door. The woman didn't seem to be dangerous. She was barefoot and wearing a pool cover-up, for Pete's sake, but Angel couldn't take any chances. Not with Cristina and her little boy hiding here from Cuchillo's gang. Angel had made many mistakes in her life, including trusting the wrong man and staying with him when she should have left. She wasn't that girl anymore. She was a woman who had escaped all of that. Now she had to protect everyone—RW's family and her own.

She called security. "A young woman is wandering the halls in RW's private wing. Please escort her back to wherever she is supposed to be. And make sure the guard is stationed at his post in the next thirty seconds, or RW will fire him."

Not even a minute later, Angel heard a commotion in the hall.

"*Idiota!* Get your hands off me," the young woman yelled. The voice sounded familiar. Was she one of the chefs? Had Angel made a mistake by calling security?

Angel was about to go and correct the situation when her phone rang in her hand. "*Hola?*"

"Oh, Angel. Good, I'm glad you answered." It was Chloe. "Can you come to Matt and Julia's house? Dad's here, too."

RW left Casa Larga and went to Julia's house? Something was wrong. With her heart in her throat she asked, "RW... is he...okay? Is Julia? What's going on?"

"It's about Jeff. Another picture has popped up in the newspaper this time. I'm worried this will convince Jeff that he can't have a real relationship and he'll marry for the wrong reasons. We need to figure out a way to convince Jeff that he is not like Mom and Dad. Please come here so we can talk. We need your help."

Jeff was on the restaurant work site, hammering nails with the rest of the framing crew.

He didn't want to think, or talk; he just wanted to pound nails. Over and over until his muscles screamed louder than his brain. He couldn't stop seeing the anguish on Michele's face after he'd forced her to walk away. After he'd given in to temptation and landed them both on the front page.

He hadn't been able to find the jerk who'd snuck up and interrupted the best thing Jeff had experienced in years. He still craved Michele more than anything. A cold shower, two cups of espresso and a terrible night's sleep hadn't dampened his desire for her. If anything, time had made his need for her grow, like an unquenchable thirst. The intensity of his desire for him scared him.

But that was too freaking bad because he couldn't have her, especially not now.

Everyone had seen the photo of Michele in his lap at the convention. They would assume he couldn't keep it in his pants. And they'd take Michele down with him. He was glad no one knew who she was and he planned to keep it that way. He wouldn't tarnish her career with his own smutty one.

This whole fiasco only proved his point about how different they were. This was why he couldn't marry someone who loved him or love them in return. No matter how good Michele felt in his arms, how amazing her lips tasted, he couldn't touch her again. He'd only ruin her.

He pounded nails as hard as he could.

By midday, Chloe showed up at the work site. She was about to duck under the chain when Jeff called to her, "You can't come in here without a helmet. Construction site rules."

"Then you come out!"

Hell, no. "Can't. Busy."

She gave him the stink eye. "Hey, can you throw me your helmet?" she asked a worker who was taking his lunch break.

"Sure, pretty lady. As long as you bring it back."

Plopping the helmet on her head, she swung her leg over the chain and stomped toward Jeff. "You aren't returning my calls. What's wrong with the new phone I bought for you?"

"I turned my phone off. Too many crazy women calling for a good time." He wasn't joking. He held a nail between his teeth while he hammered another one.

"Come on, Jeff. Stop, so we can talk about what happened. I feel terrible."

She looked terrible. Hell, he didn't mean to hurt her, too. He put the hammer and nails down. "It wasn't your fault." No, this whole thing started and ended with him.

She pulled him away from the other workers before saying, "I'm worried about you. You've got to stop thinking you can't connect with people. Feel. By that picture in the paper, it looks like you feel something with Michele."

He narrowed his eyes. "You don't know what you're talking about."

She put her hands on her hips just like she used to do when she was a little girl. "That might be the official story, but I know it's bull. You did make a real connection with her. I can see it in your reaction."

He couldn't look her in the eye. "Everything is fine."

"Really? Then talk to Michele. The poor girl doesn't deserve to be ignored."

He looked down at his hands. They still ached to touch her. They still belonged to a man who could turn Michele's life into a media circus. "I can't be near her right now."

Chloe let out a deep breath. "Because you like her. A lot. And you're scared."

He didn't respond.

"So, what are you going to do about the chef competition? Those three women are waiting for your answer. Which one will you choose?"

He still had no idea. He knew which one he wanted, but was she the best one for the job? Everything was even more confused than before.

"I haven't decided."

"Fine," she huffed. "One more event. We could invite the townspeople from Pueblicito to view the plans and the building site. The chefs can prepare their finest hors d'oeuvres and we'll see which one comes out the best."

It wasn't a terrible idea. The sooner he decided who the chef would be, the faster the marketing team could start the promo machine and drum up interest.

The sooner Michele would be gone...or permanently a part of the dream he was creating. "Okay."

"This coming weekend Dad has something going on,

and he'll want to be at the event. How about the weekend after that?"

"Yeah. If the chefs are okay with staying that long. I suggest having Dad increase their bonus." Twelve days. He could throw himself into his work and not have to think about anything until then. Not even Michele's soft skin. The memory of her on his lap crept into his thoughts. Since he didn't have a nail, he pounded his thigh to obliterate the vision.

Chloe shielded her eyes from the sun and studied him. "You should talk to Angel, or…someone. I really think it would help."

"I'll keep that in mind." He rose to go back to work, but then turned around. "Check in on Michele. Make sure she's doing okay. I didn't mean for any of this to happen."

"Or you could talk to her yourself."

He walked away.

He'd find someone else to date tonight. Someone he couldn't hurt.

It was time to start looking for a bride.

Michele was coming to grips with the fact that Jeff was avoiding her. It hurt.

She thought they'd had something special, but apparently, she'd read the situation incorrectly. She'd only been a one-night fling for him. And it hadn't even been a full night.

Part of her had known that truth at the time and yet she'd climbed on his lap anyway, because his lips and touch had felt oh-so good. She'd allowed herself to believe she could heal a playboy's heart. She'd risked her dreams and responsibilities on that hope.

Playing with fire only seemed to make her burn for more sizzling kisses, more caresses, more Jeffrey Harper.

He was the opposite of what she should be focusing on— taking care of her sister, learning how to cook again, finding a man to love her, starting a family.

But what she felt for Jeffrey didn't matter. She needed to put her energy into the one thing that *did* matter—landing this job.

There was one final competition, a sort of winner-take-all. She'd been asked to prepare hors d'oeuvres for a large party to show off the restaurant project. She knew this was a big deal for Jeff and was determined to do her best.

Sitting in her room, Michele scoured the internet looking for good Italian recipes, not finding anything that grabbed her. Nothing was good enough for Jeff's special night.

Closing her eyes, she whispered, "Help me, Mom. I need a little magic."

A light breeze came in through her window, lifting her hair off her face. Suddenly, she smelled sage, and rosemary. Opening her eyes, she squealed.

She knew what she was going to make.

Michele spent most of the next week in the Harpers' kitchen. It wasn't easy cooking meals next to the two other chefs she was competing against. They kept bumping into each other and fighting over the utensils, stove and ovens. All three chefs were making practice foods, getting them right.

Michele noticed that Freja was making a seafood cioppino. "You might want to rethink that one. Jeff hates seafood."

Freja pulled her white-blond hair up in a beautiful twist. "How ees dis possible? He took me fishing, said he loved water. He even swims like a fishy."

"Don't listen to her," Tonia said. "She's just trying to get into your head."

"I don't lie," Michele said.

Tonia shrugged. "We all know how you cheat."

Michele shook her head. "Suit yourself. Make all the fish hors d'oeuvres you want."

Freja looked at her ingredients, bit her lip and then put the fish back in the refrigerator. "I make something else."

The day of the event finally arrived. Michele had prac-
ticed enough. It was as if Jeff had flipped a switch inside
her. All that sensual energy he'd awakened had to be chan-
neled somewhere and she poured it into her cooking. She
sampled each of her hors d'oeuvres. They were fantastic.

She went upstairs to get ready. Would it be the last time
she'd see Jeff? She was incredibly sad at the thought. But
he'd moved on, apparently, and she should stop driving herself crazy and move on, too. They were two different people
who wanted different things.

He'd said it by the wedding pagoda. *You aren't like me.
You're warm and caring. Sweet. I see you going for the wedding pagoda and the happily-ever-after, Michele. I hope it
sticks for you. I'll take the no-drama, no-stress business
contract in front of a judge.*

Well, she hoped he was wrong. She wanted him to find
happiness and love someday, too. Even if it was with someone else.

Michele showered, applied her makeup, dried her hair
and put on her flowing black pants, pale blue halter blouse
and matching strappy sandals. Jeff seemed to like her bare
shoulders. And she liked when he kissed them.

Shut up, Michele! she yelled at herself. Jeff wasn't going
to kiss her anymore. And she shouldn't be wanting him to.

She was here to be a five-star chef. Period.

Downstairs, people had started to arrive. She hustled to
the kitchen and found Freja and Tonia had plated up their
trays and were outside feeding the guests already. Darn it!
They'd left her the two smallest, least attractive trays. She
hurried. The first tray was for the fried giant ravioli stuffed
with Italian sausage, spinach, parmesan, mozzarella, cherry
tomatoes and a mixture of fresh Italian spices. In the center
of the tray she had a tomato-and-red-wine-based dipping
sauce that was to die for.

On the second tray, she placed her crostini, made with
her homemade Italian bread. She'd kneaded savory fragrant

spices, some of which she'd purchased from Juanita's, into the dough and had toasted the slices perfectly. She'd spread a thin layer of olive oil and goat cheese on top of the toasted bread. Purple and black dry-cured olives with rosemary and orange zest came next. The crostini were gorgeous and reminded her of a midnight sky. They made her think of the stars she and Jeff had looked at together. Arugula topped the olives. Around the edges of the tray, she carefully placed delicious prosciutto-, mozzarella-and risotto-stuffed fritters.

Everything smelled good, looked good, and would taste great.

Her magic was back.

She was ready.

Angel sat on the couch in Cristina's bungalow and checked the watch RW had given her for her birthday. They were late. RW and his family had already gone downstairs for Jeff's restaurant unveiling. Angel's sisters were coming, too, but Julia and Matt had stayed home because Henry was sick. Angel thought about Jeff's predicament. Chloe, Matt and RW had all told her about Jeff's childhood. Jeff had refused to join what he called "an intervention" and claimed he didn't need their help.

From what the others told her, it was clear that Jeff did need some sort of help. Therapy was not a bad idea. Each of the Harper kids had their own crosses to bear because of the way RW and his ex-wife had raised them. The only role models Jeff had growing up were two adults who acted like they hated each other. Jeff had never known love and therefore thought he was incapable of giving love. But Angel knew differently. Hadn't RW proved that he was a loving man to her? Jeff could do the same. He just needed a gentle hand to guide him toward the feelings he was bottling up. Maybe Michele was the nice one he needed.

Angel glanced at her watch again. If Cristina didn't hurry, they would miss Jeff's big speech.

"Come on, Cristina. What's taking so long?" Angel's patience was growing thin. It was stressful having the woman and her child staying in Casa Larga. Protecting so many people kept Angel on edge.

Cristina walked out of the bedroom and closed the door behind her. "Sebastian doesn't want to go. Maybe I should stay here."

"No, you need to get out of this bungalow and have some fun. I'll get someone to watch Sebastian so you can take a break."

Angel instructed one of the maids to babysit. She knew Cristina needed more than just a break for one night. The young woman craved the same things Angel did—a free life with her family outside the gang. But Cristina and her son *could* go somewhere else and be happy and safe. Over time, Cuchillo would lose interest in wanting to make Cristina pay for deserting the gang. And since Cristina hadn't personally witnessed Cuchillo's sadistic crimes, not like Angel, she wouldn't be a strong witness for the prosecutor. Cuchillo wouldn't have to hunt Cristina down and seal her lips forever.

Angel wished she could be that lucky.

Fourteen

"Thank you all for coming." Jeff stood next to the newly framed restaurant, the sky peeking through the bare wood bones. He lifted his voice so everyone in the crowd could hear him while searching the faces for Michele.

Even though he knew he shouldn't.

He wanted to see her.

There had to be fifty people from Pueblicito there to take a look at the new building and taste the food from the competing chefs. *Shareholders*, Dad had called the townspeople. It appeared that RW Harper was going to donate a percentage of the hotel and restaurant profits to them after all. At least, Jeff hoped that was the case, otherwise his father had suckered him into lying to these people.

"As you can see, the restaurant is coming along nicely. We expect to be open for business right on time." It was going up fast and even in its early stages, it looked amazing.

The crowd cheered.

Pride bloomed in his chest. This was what it felt like to be proud of his accomplishments. Damn, he'd missed this feeling. It surprised him that he was so thrilled with a project that involved the home he used to hate. Working with his father had been better than he ever dreamed possible.

"The plans for both the restaurant and the hotel are pinned up on the wall for you to review at your leisure, but let me set the mood first. Pretend you have just arrived in Plunder Cove, weary and hungry. You walk up those steps…" He pointed to a grassy hillside. The steps had yet to be made. "…and see this wood-sided building, both rustic and charming, with views out to the Pacific Ocean. The shape, the wood, makes you think of—"

"A pirate ship!" someone in the crowd interrupted.

He nodded and one of the old women in the crowd, called out, "Knew you'd do this right. We've got faith in you, Jeffrey."

He pressed his hands to his chest and made a tiny bow. Then he went on to describe his vision for the restaurant. Freja passed by him with a half-empty tray. Tonia was on the other side of the patio surrounded by a group of hungry people. "And please, eat up. We have three of the finest chefs in the world here with us tonight. Enjoy."

He scanned the crowd.

And then he saw her.

Standing off to the side holding her tray, Michele was watching him. The look on her face resembled pride—in him. It made him want to grab her, press her up against the wall and kiss those pretty lips. Ignoring all the warnings going off in his brain, ignoring everything he'd told himself as he'd stayed away from her for days, he strode toward her, determined to pull her away and get a taste.

He'd drink until he was full and then he'd think about the reasons why he shouldn't have her.

A man bumped into him. "Water!" the guy choked.

Another person started coughing, and another. Someone behind him said, "We need flan, or milk. This stuff is too spicy!"

Jeff looked around. One guy had tears running down his face while his wife tried to console him. What was going on?

"I thought it would be sweet." A woman walked up to Michele and pointed. "My husband can't eat spicy peppers. He might have to go to the ER because of you!"

Michele blanched. "What?"

The three sisters from Pueblicito came to her aid. Nona said, "I love the sauce. Habaneros are my favorite."

"Me, too," Flora nodded.

"Just the right kick," Alana added.

"Habaneros?" Michele looked at Jeff, her face pale. "I didn't put peppers in the sauce."

"Are you sure?"

"No, I...don't think I did..." She bit her lip, indecisive. She tasted the sauce and her face went eyes widened. "There are peppers in this sauce."

Jeff ran his hand through his hair. Every molecule in his body, especially those below his waistline, screamed at him to ignore the mistake and give her a chance. Let her stay. No, make her stay. But would he let Tonia or Freja continue in the competition if they messed up as badly as Michele had with the sauce when it wasn't her first mistake? Maybe not.

Deep down he knew he wanted to forgive any mistakes Michele made because he wanted her. He couldn't be objective about Michele. With her he was in a constant state of need. He shouldn't feel needy when he was supposed to be in control. She was ruining him in more ways than one. His gut burned as if he'd swallowed a whole habanero chili.

He had to grow up, be the boss he was supposed to be and let her go. He turned to the serving staff and asked them to bring water and milk right away.

"Michele, I don't know what in the hell happened, but this is unacceptable. You know how important this night is for me," he said. "I need a chef who is consistent." Disappointment and sadness gripped him. He had to cut her out of the competition, which meant he might never see her again.

"I know, Jeff. I'm sorry. This won't reflect on you. It's not your fault, it's my responsibility. I'll clean it up before I go." The sparkle he loved so much was gone. She raised her voice. "Ladies and gentlemen, I apologize that the sauce was too spicy. Anytime there is a mistake in the kitchen a good chef always makes it right. Please do not leave yet. I will create something special for you to cool your tongues."

Before she ran back to the kitchen her gaze met his. "I'm sorry."

The three sisters from Pueblicito cornered Jeff.

"You were too hard on her." Nona eyed him ferociously.

"Yeah, she's a nice lady who makes great food," Alana agreed. "Did you try those giant ravioli? I'm gonna be dreaming about them for weeks."

"I like the ball things and the olives. Michele was my favorite. Those other two chefs?" Flora shook her head. "Not even close."

"I can't have a chef who makes mistakes like that," he said to them. "It's business."

"I see. You never made any mistakes." Nona's expression was all too knowing. As if she'd witnessed some of the hell he'd lived through. "No one ever counted you out? Treated you like you were dirt and then kicked you to the curb?"

His jaw dropped. How did she know all of that?

"Nona's right. Give her another chance," Flora said. "She's the one for you."

Alana smacked her lips. "You think she has any more of those ravioli in the kitchen?"

The old women were right. Michele's food tonight was sparking with magic. She was consistent with every dish except the dipping sauce.

Why had she messed it up? It didn't make sense.

Michele was beside herself. What had happened? She hadn't used habanero chilis since the night she made the grilled cheese sandwich for Jeff. Someone had put those peppers in her dish.

She quickly rushed to make a specialty that the crowd would love. The only secret ingredients in the dessert would be the love and grief she was feeling right now. The passion for cooking had come back to her because Jeff had brought the magic back into her life. She was full of gratitude for that fact alone. But it was more than that. She was falling for him, hard. She knew he didn't think he could give her what she needed, but part of her wanted him anyway. Okay, most of her wanted him anyway. Even if she couldn't have him. And now she wouldn't have the job she needed, either. Jeff was sending her home.

She blinked back tears. How had things gotten so messed up?

At least the dessert was delicious. She tasted it to make sure and decided it was time to bring the guests in. The only number at Casa Larga that Michele had in her cell phone was to the Batcave.

Alfred, will you please tell Jeff to send the guests to the great hall?

Sure, Miss. I'll send up the Bat Signal.

The group came into the hall, filling it quickly. She was relieved that they'd all stayed because she was scared she'd ruined things for Jeff. She'd been so proud of him as he talked about his project. It was clear he was meant to create hotels, just as she'd been meant to create great food. Even if she'd lost track of herself along the way.

Michele stood behind the long table and encouraged the crowd to come forward to take a bowl. "This dessert is called 'zabaglione.' It is an Italian custard with some of my own special spices and marsala wine. Don't worry, nothing hot in this, just sweet and—"

"*Delicioso*," a woman said after taking her first bite. "This is amazing."

People started talking at once.

"Oh, my."

"This is the best thing I've ever tasted!"

"Fantastic. You've got to try this."

The rave reviews continued until someone in the crowd clapped and soon the room erupted in applause. They loved her dessert. Her heart melted. She'd made something everyone loved.

"Hey." Jeff stepped up to the table. "Can I talk to you?"

Her eyes welled. She blinked quickly, determined to keep things professional even as she walked out the door. She'd gone from needing this job financially, to wanting to help Jeff succeed in his grand and wonderful adventure. And now all of it was over.

"Of course. Take a bowl of zabaglione, too."

He took a bite. The look that spread across his face was mesmerizing. It was like a wave of happiness and joy. She wished he always looked like that.

What she didn't see? Shock. It was as if he'd known she could cook like this and had just been waiting for her to figure it out.

"Tastes like light, creamy heaven. Simply poetic. Welcome back."

She blushed with delight. "Thank you."

He took her hand. "Come with me."

It seemed like they were leaving the great hall. Was this it? Jeff was escorting her off the property?

They passed Tonia eating a bowlful of zabaglione in the corner. Her pretty face twisted with white-hot anger.

"Wait for me," he said to Michele. "I need to talk to Tonia."

Oh. Michele understood what this meant—Tonia had won the chef's competition. Michele was heartbroken. She wanted Jeff to have the best chef but something about Tonia made her feel like she had to watch her back. She'd lost the chance to be Jeff's chef. It was over. Did this mean she would never see him again? Never touch him. Listen to his deep voice, his laughter. Kiss his beautiful lips.

Walking over to Tonia, she heard Jeff say, "You don't like the zabaglione?"

"Not one bit. Why did Miss Nicey-Nice get a do-over?" Tonia spoke loudly to ensure that Michele heard her.

He crossed his arms. "My competition, my rules."

She scowled. "I didn't mess up my hors d'oeuvres, and yet I didn't get to make a dessert. She gets special treatment, has since night one. That's not fair."

"You mean fair like when you lied to me about being able to ride horses? It was clear you'd never been on a horse and yet you told me you rode them on your grandfather's ranch every summer." His tone was loaded with sarcasm.

"That was different. I explained it had been a while. I was rusty. I thought you understood."

"About the horses, yes. Not the habaneros."

Tonia put her hands on her hips. "Excuse me?"

"How did you know to use those specific peppers to sabotage Michele's dish?"

Michele could see the hardening around Tonia's eyes. She was furious. "What are you implying?"

"I don't imply. I state. You spied on us 'night one' when I had Michele make the grilled cheese sandwiches."

Tonia blustered. "That's ridiculous. It wasn't me."

"Another lie. The cameras caught you on tape. I wanted to give you the benefit of the doubt for I, of all people, know how that feels, but it sure seemed like you were spying on us. Whatever the case, you did see Michele use those peppers and you'd know that I'd remember, too. It was easy to frame her that way."

Michele stood beside Jeff, facing Tonia. "You did it? Why?"

Tonia's dark eyes flared with anger. "Why do you think, Sex Kitten? You clouded his vision, made it so that no one else had a chance to win."

Jeff faced Michele. "She's right. You do cloud my vision so that I can't see anyone but you. You're my choice, Michele. Please, stay."

* * *

Angel and Cristina were on their way to the building site when RW texted.

Come to the great hall.

Okay. We'll be right there.

"I guess the party was moved inside," Angel said to Cristina. They were just about to enter the hall when Cristina grabbed her arm and pulled her back into the corridor.

"Oh, my God. Antonia is here," Cristina whispered.

"What? No, that's impossible." Poor Cristina was so frightened that she was seeing gang members everywhere she looked.

"Look over there. The woman with the dark hair in the corner talking to that tall redheaded guy. That's her. I can see the *cuchillo* mark on her from here."

Angel leaned over carefully and peeked. It was the same young woman Angel had seen snooping around in RW's wing. She'd thought she recognized her voice. And sure enough, the woman had a knife tattoo behind her ear. She gripped Cristina's shoulder as if her ex-boyfriend's blade had stopped her own heart.

"What do we do?" Cristina asked.

There was no question, Angel had to protect the ones she loved. Where was RW? Taking out her cell phone with trembling hands, she texted him.

The woman talking to Jeff is Cuchillo's sister!

Jeff was furious. How dare Tonia sabotage Michele.

"We're done here. Tonia, pack your things and—" Jeff began.

"Don't move!" a guard said, his gun drawn and pointed

at Tonia. Two more guards joined him. Several people in the crowd cried out in fear and everyone scattered behind him.

"What are you doing? This is unnecessary," Jeff said. "Put your guns away."

Seeing guards and guns, Tonia lunged and grabbed Michele. Before Jeff had blinked, Tonia had a knife to Michele's throat.

"Get back," Tonia yelled. "All of you."

Michele's eyes were wide and pinned to him. The fear in them slashed him.

"Everyone, calm down!" Jeff lifted his hands and willed Tonia to look at him. "Let Michele go and you can walk out of here. No one will stop you."

"Sorry, son, but she can't leave." Suddenly, Dad was beside him, whispering so that only Jeff could hear, "She's one of Cuchillo's gang members. She'll kill Angel."

Jeff stopped breathing. His Michele was in the arms of a killer.

"I walk out of here now. Understand me?" Tonia snarled. Her blade looked deadly.

Jeff's heart hit the floor. "Don't hurt her!"

To Tonia, RW said in an incredibly controlled voice, "We don't even know why you're here. Why pull this elaborate charade in my home?"

"I told you in my application video. Family is everything. Something was stolen from my brother a long time ago. He wants it back."

"I know you're looking for Angel. She's not here," RW said.

Tonia's gaze swung from Jeffrey's to RW's and back again. "Liar. Your PI said you're hiding her."

Jeff swallowed hard. RW's private investigator had been killed by the gang. Had they made him talk?

"Angel's here. I can feel it. Since she liked horses, we thought she might be working in your stables. The chef interview was the opportunity to snoop around. Plus, I wanted to win."

"Get the hell out of my home!" RW roared. "Tell your brother to leave my family alone or I will come for *him*. Got that, Antonia? Cuchillo has never met a man like me. I'll send that bastard straight to hell."

Tonia's eyes widened at the threat. She released Michele and ran out the door. Michele slumped to her knees.

"I've got you, sweetheart." Jeff scooped her up and carried her to the couch. She'd been nicked. "Get me a clean cloth!" he yelled to the crowd. "Someone call the doctor."

RW sent one of the guards to follow Tonia and find the rock Cuchillo was living under. Cuchillo's gang had a knack for slipping off the grid and RW had lost the trail when they murdered his private investigator.

"Where's Angel?" one of the sisters said.

"Oh, Jeff. Did I ruin your night?" Michele's voice was so soft.

"No, sweetheart. You did everything right," Jeff held the cloth to Michele's cut and applied pressure. His heart was pounding so hard he thought it might explode. After a few minutes he checked the cut and was relieved to see it wasn't bleeding badly. "You're going to be okay, sweetheart." He wanted to carry her out of there and straight to his bed. He'd been so afraid for her and now he just wanted to touch her everywhere. Taste her. Feel her heart beating strongly against his bare chest.

"I was so scared," Michele said softly. She reached up and put her hand on his cheek.

"I know. Me, too." He ran the pad of his thumb along her cheek. He kissed her then, deeply, filling up all the dark wounds in his thundering heart, and let the world fall away.

Fifteen

Jeff had canceled his date for last night. No great loss. He hadn't been too excited about it anyway.

Right now, he was concerned about keeping Michele safe. He could have lost her and that thought alone terrified him.

After the doctor had checked her out and determined the flesh wound didn't need stitches, Michele said good-night and Jeff walked her to her room. He wanted her in his bed but didn't say so because she seemed exhausted. He bunked down in the room next to hers in case she had nightmares or needed anything. He didn't sleep a wink because he was replaying the whole evening, trying to figure out what he would have done differently. He wasn't impressed with his performance but Michele had been strong, courageous and thoughtful from the start of the catered event to the dramatic end. Her food, other than the sabotaged dipping sauce, was artistic and delicious.

Chloe had been right—the best chef had risen to the top. There was no doubt in his mind that Michele Cox was the chef for him. She'd proved that she was ready for the job and had bravely conquered her insecurities.

Jeff, on the other hand, was even more worried because the closer he got to Michele, the more he realized he was the wrong man for her. Hell, he and his screwed-up family had almost gotten her killed! He wouldn't have forgiven himself if Tonia had hurt her badly. He cared about Michele, wanted her, needed her more than he dared admit, but she couldn't fall in love with him. He wouldn't let her. It would kill him to hurt her like his father and mother had hurt one another. He wouldn't allow that to happen. He would have to get married to someone else.

When he heard her rustling around in her room, he knocked on the door.

Her expression was a mixture of happiness and surprise. "Jeff! Good morning."

He leaned against the door frame and breathed in her freshly showered scent. "Are you feeling okay?"

She touched the small Band-Aid on her neck. "Yes, I'm fine. It was just a scratch."

He breathed a sigh of relief. "Good. I've got plans for you. Thought we'd better get an early start."

Her brow creased. "Am I cooking or are we going on another outing?"

"Neither. You deserve a break. Plus, it has come to my attention that you've never been on a yacht before. And, as far as I can tell, you have not spent the day on the Harpers' private beach up the coast."

Her smile was so damned beautiful. "I can't say I have done either of those things, no."

He shook his head. "We'll have to rectify the situation immediately. Wear something warm for the morning and pack your bathing suit and a towel. I'll provide the picnic lunch. We need to celebrate your new job, Chef Cox."

Her mouth opened. "You really meant it last night?"

"Of course. I mean it this morning, too. I choose you, Michele. You're my chef."

She squealed and threw her arms around his neck. He stumbled backward, emotion warring inside him. Finally, he wrapped his arms around her and hung on. He kissed her right there in the hallway with her feet off the ground.

It seemed as if he couldn't stop kissing Michele Cox.

His new chef. The woman he wanted but couldn't marry. What in the hell was he going to do?

His yacht was amazing. So much rich, dark wood and shiny metal. It looked like it was brand-new. It was the biggest boat she'd ever seen and she was surprised when he called it "the small one." Apparently, RW had several yachts all over the world. She couldn't fathom it. But she did love being on the gorgeous vessel and was lulled by the movement and the peaceful sea.

They'd been cruising up the coastline for twenty minutes already, close enough to shore so she could see the jagged edge of the bluffs and the coves. She wished they could keep going to San Francisco, or Hawaii, until she remembered she had a job to do in Plunder Cove. She didn't have to dream of running away anymore. She'd be living in paradise and working in the career she loved again.

She'd figure out a way to bring Cari to Plunder Cove, too. Surely, there was a group home nearby who could take her. It would take Cari a while to readjust to the new place but Michele was sure her sister would love digging her toes into the sand and meeting the horses the Harpers owned.

And getting to sail on the blue Pacific with Mr. Sexy was a nice perk. She understood why he had pushed her away for a week. He was busy with the restaurant, and the competition had been difficult. Plus, he was distancing himself because they were two people who wanted different things. She agreed it was best they didn't spend too much time together because her silly heart always wanted more. She kept reminding herself that Jeff didn't want to, or was unable to, give her more of himself. She needed to be realistic. This connection they had wasn't going to last.

"Want to drive?" he asked.

"Can I?" She felt like a kid being handed the car keys for the first time.

"Come on over." He stepped back and made room for her. Tentatively, she put her hands on the wheel.

"Relax. It's easy." His deep voice rumbled in her ear, sending delicious shivers up into her scalp. And then he put his hands on her shoulders.

Relax? Her body heated up and her thoughts zeroed in on the way his large hands felt on her. Why had she worn a sweatshirt? She wanted his hands on her skin. He pressed into her and she could feel his hard stomach muscles against her back. How she wanted him. She closed her eyes and breathed in his scent. Her eyes flew open again when she remembered she was driving his expensive boat.

Besides, she had no business enjoying his hands on her body or daydreaming about his lips. She was going to be working for him and didn't have any idea what impact their new working relationship would have on their...situation. She didn't really know what to call their relationship.

They had smoking hot chemistry but that was the *easy* part. The dangerous part. When she was close to him she wanted to climb into his lap, let herself go, and take him with her to ecstasy. It was going to be hard enough working for him and wanting to kiss him every day, but she couldn't *relax* and let down her guard or she'd fall hard for him. She was already tilting heavily in that direction with her feet slipping. One more of his sizzling, mind-melting kisses might topple her defenses.

Giving in to her desire for him again could only end badly for her. He'd made it clear that he wouldn't fall for her. She'd be a fool not to believe his warning. No matter how many times she fantasized about Jeff Harper, he wasn't her dream man. He'd eventually marry someone else and she...she'd have to let him go. Which was going to be incredibly difficult now that she would be working for him.

Jeff directed her to pull into an alcove. He dropped anchor and turned off the engine.

He stripped off his sweatshirt and for the first time she

got to gaze at his lean, hard chest, arms and stomach in person. The pictures in magazines didn't do justice to his amazing physique. Her fingers itched to touch the red curls on his chest and trace each muscle all the way down the dark V into his shorts.

"Ready?" he asked.

Nope. Her defenses were crumbling. She was in serious trouble here.

He rowed the dinghy to the shore and she helped him pull it up on the sand. It was a pretty little beach with white sand and clumps of rocks at the water's edge.

He tossed his bangs out of his eyes and grinned like a kid. "I haven't been here in years. The old firepit is still there. And the inner tube Matt and I used to float around on. This is like a blast from the past. Let's see if we can catch a crab in the tide pools."

"Okay. Let me just put this blanket down and I'll catch up."

He gave her a thumbs-up and jogged to an outcropping of rocks. She smiled as she stretched the blanket on the warm sand. She liked seeing him like this. Boyish, not so intense.

She needed to watch herself.

She had no business playing with fire.

But she really, really wanted to. Once again, she had the desire to show him what love looked like. If only he could see how easy it was to let himself go, to allow himself to feel, then maybe he could open his heart to her. She believed a loveless man could learn to love. She wanted to give that gift to him.

And today—with the chef job lined up and her sister taken care of—she felt brave.

So when he jogged back and sat beside her she said, "Is this a real date?"

He ran a finger down her shoulder. "As real as it gets."

He hadn't seen anything yet. "I seem to recall our last

date was rudely interrupted. Can we pick up where we left off?"

He grinned. "You want to sit on my lap?"

"Yes. But, no. I have another idea." The last time she climbed on his lap things flew out of her control too quickly. If she was going to show him how to feel loved she would need to slow things down a bit.

"Lie back on the blanket."

His gaze was intense—curious and cautious—but he did as she asked.

"Now put the towel under your head. I want you to watch me touching you."

She didn't know what she was doing, and it was probably a really bad mistake, still every inch of her begged to get close to him.

He tucked a towel under his head and watched her.

Starting at his fingertips, she made slow, sensual circles around the nail beds and gently petted his knuckles. She traced each bone and vein she could see under the skin.

He had a fine sprinkle of freckles across the back of his hand. She rubbed his skin softly, slowly, feeling the hairs on his hand lift with her touch.

He had large, strong hands. Turning them palm up, she traced every line. She looked at him, silently asking permission to keep going.

"It feels good." His voice was rough.

She was feeling things, too. Lots of heat. Tons of want. She'd never touched anyone like this before, never wanted to. She couldn't seem to get enough.

She massaged his fingers, pressing deep into the pads of his thumbs. He curled his fingers around hers, giving her hand a squeeze, like a hug.

"Your arms now." Why was she whispering? They were alone on a private beach.

She circled his wrist bones, dragged her nails up his forearm and then softly rubbed her way back down toward his wrists. Goose bumps rose on his arms. She pressed harder and smoothed them back down. Squeezing his biceps, she marveled at the muscles beneath her hands. Turning his arm over, she used her nails and soft touch along the length of the underside of his arm. His skin was smooth, not freckled on this side, silky. The bend of his arm was a kissable spot and she put her mouth there, pausing.

"Don't stop. Keep going." The growl in his voice made her look up. His gaze was intense.

She felt an answering zing in her core.

"Shoulders." Her voice was huskier than normal. She squeezed, massaged and ran a feather touch over his shoulder muscles.

God, he was so beautiful.

She ran her palm over his collarbone and dipped her fingertip into the hollow of his neck. She could feel his pulse beating fast there. He was breathing faster now, too, as was she. This slow, burning touch was working her up quickly.

Honestly, she'd been burning since that incomplete night on the coast. Maybe longer.

She caressed his neck. She ran the back of her fingers over his strong square jaw and chin.

She didn't want to miss one inch of him.

His eyes watched her every move. That sexy look was giving her goose bumps of her own. She wanted him. Inside her. She'd never felt such a desperate heat before her.

His lips twitched as if he knew what this was doing to her. If he gave her his signature cocky grin it was game over.

She cleared her throat and pressed her legs together against the ache building there and placed both her palms on his pecs. She made circles over the muscles and played with the nipple.

"Michele." Her name came out as a sexy growl that turned the heat to full melt-level. "Don't stop."

She rubbed the nipple again and twisted his chest curls. "I love your red hair."

"There's more to play with."

She lifted her eyebrow and looked down. *Oh.* He was fully aroused.

She was losing control of herself.

Very slowly, she caressed each stomach muscle of his gorgeous six-pack, working her way down. His breathing was fast now, almost as fast as hers. She circled his belly button with her middle finger and gently tugged on the hairs below it. Those were fun to play with, too, but she wanted more. Lifting her head, she saw heat and desire in his expression.

Good, she wasn't alone.

She ran her hand over his shorts, pressing against his erection.

He sucked in a sharp breath.

"Jeff?" she said quietly. "I want to kiss you."

The groan he made was music to her ears. He reached for her. Running his hand through her hair, he made a loose ponytail and gave it a gentle tug so that her chin tipped up.

She was looking into his eyes when he said, "Oh, babe. I want you."

It was as if she'd waited her whole life to hear those words. She pulled his shorts down and took him in her mouth.

This she needed.

Michele was touching him in a way he'd never experienced before.

With reverence.

With smoking heat.

Like she adored each millimeter of his skin and couldn't get enough of him. It was driving him wild. He was hard and wouldn't be able to hold on much longer. All this from her touch? Hell, what would it be like if he was deep inside all that heat? He needed to make love to this woman right now.

When she put her lips around his erection and sucked, a light show went off behind his eyeballs.

"Michele, stop," he somehow managed to say.

She pulled back, quickly.

"I'm too close. And I want to be inside you."

"Oh," she said softly.

He sat up and slid the bathing suit straps off her shoulders. He nuzzled the hollow of her neck and her moan almost made him lose it. "Sorry, sweetheart. This is going to be faster than I'd like but I want you too badly to wait. Take your suit off and I'll get the condom."

Thank God he'd decided to bring one.

She nodded. Her eyes were hooded with desire.

They were both ready. She was on her knees on the towel and beautifully naked.

"Hell, you are so damned gorgeous," he said and pulled her on top of him.

Skin-to-skin, her breasts to his chest, thighs pressed together, hearts beating hard, and he had one thought—*she's perfect*.

When she eased him inside and all that slick heat encased him, he closed his eyes to memorize her touch, everywhere.

And then she started moving and all thoughts left his brain.

She gripped his shoulders and her pace was fast. Apparently, she was close, too. He eagerly joined in the race to glory.

Cupping one of her beautiful breasts, he had the fleeting thought that he wished he could have spent time sucking and kissing her warm body.

Next time.

He sucked her nipple. She arched her back and cried out, coming quickly. He smiled and flipped her over so that he was on top. She wrapped her legs around him. Holding on to her thighs he went deep.

"Oh, yes, Jeff."

He kept going, loving the sexy smile on her face.

A few more thrusts and she cried out again, sending him over the edge. The light show going off behind his eyelids was better than Independence Day.

Michele and her gentle touch—her sparkle—was exactly what he'd needed. For the first time in a long time, he was free.

Sixteen

She didn't know how much time had passed, but she was hungry. Apparently, Jeff was, too.

"What do we have here?" she asked, rolling over to examine the picnic basket. "Did you make us lunch?"

He nodded. "Ham and cheese. My specialty."

"Can't wait to try it."

They sat side by side, legs touching, chewing in silence. Something had shifted between them, more than just giving in to sex. She could almost hear him thinking. But she didn't pry. Didn't ask the questions burning on her tongue.

He took his last bite, rolled the plastic wrap into a ball in his hand, and that's when the words poured out. "When I was six years old, I only ate mac and cheese."

"My sister was the same way! We had to trick her to try other foods."

"No tricks in my family, just demands. 'Eat your food, Jeffrey.'" He raised his voice to sound like a woman's. His mother's? "'Clean your plate or you won't get any food tomorrow.' That sort of thing."

"That's harsh."

"Sometimes I preferred to *not* eat. Like seafood night. Hell, I really hated squid."

She pressed her other hand to her heart. "I knew it. You didn't like my first dish! I wish I had made chicken."

He swallowed hard. "You didn't know. What happened

to me when I was a kid wasn't reported in the gossip rags. Families don't talk about crap like this. They cover it in dirt and pretend it's dead."

She didn't dare interrupt.

"So yeah, back to the story. I was a picky kid and one night when I refused to eat, my mother said she'd had enough of my whining. Seafood pasta was her favorite dish and by God, her son was going to eat it without a peep. Dad wasn't there, but she made everyone else pretend that I wasn't there, either. After several minutes of being ignored, I threw my plate. Shrimp and noodles slid down the wall. I'd never seen my mother that angry before. She grabbed my arm and dragged me outside. I whimpered, but she said, 'Don't be a baby!' and pushed me inside the toolshed. 'Cry and I'm never letting you out.' And then she locked the door.

"Matt had told me to stay away from the shed because snakes crawled under the crack in the door. It was dark. The cold seeped in. I screamed until my voice was hoarse and my throat was raw. I tried to find a tool to dig out, but they were too high for me to reach. I dug in the dirt with my hands, but the ground was hard. It was freezing cold and I believed I was going to die in that shed all alone."

"Oh, Jeff!" Michele covered her mouth. She'd been psychologically beaten down by Alfieri, but she had been an adult at the time, one who could walk away from her abusive boss. Jeff had been a small child. She couldn't imagine what his mother had done to him deep down inside. She quivered with the need to touch him.

"When did she finally let you out?" Her voice cracked and her eyes burned with tears.

"Mother?" The chuckle he produced was sandpaper rough, humorless. "She didn't. She wanted to teach me not to be a crybaby. Emotions were a sign of weakness in her world. I understand now that something was broken in her genetic makeup that made it impossible for her to love anyone. She passed that broken gene to me."

A person incapable of loving? Michele still didn't believe it.

"I'm sorry, Jeff. No one should ever treat a child like that."

"You're crying." He gently wiped her cheek with the back of his hand.

Softly she said, "Emotions are human, normal. Especially for a little boy. Your mother should've known better. What did your father do when he found out?"

"Mother told him she'd ordered the staff to bring me in and they refused. It was a lie. Donna, the cook, heard me crying the next morning and found me curled up on the dirt floor of the shed. I'd wet myself from fear. When she opened that door, I ran to Donna and held on like I'd never held anyone. The staff banded together and told my mother that if she came into the kitchen, they'd all quit. Since my mother had no idea how to cook for herself, she agreed. I was safe from her in the kitchen." He tossed his hair off his forehead. "To this day, I don't like to eat alone or be in small dark places. That's why I don't usually take elevators."

She frowned. "But the GIF. You were in an elevator with a maid."

"Right. I was getting to that. The GIF was orchestrated by the hotel owner to ruin me." Absentmindedly, he stroked her hand. She hoped touching her calmed him as much as it did her. "Finn had threatened physical harm if we filmed his hotel. It was the first time a hotelier had been so aggressive. It made me wonder—what was the guy hiding? I took my own camera inside. Michele, I could bury Finn with the negative press on the kitchen alone. You would've been horrified."

"So, you got it all on film?" She watched his finger make lazy circles on the top of her hand and felt the touch all the way to her bones.

"And then some. Employees told me about bad workplace conditions. Safety violations. Codes ignored. Cover-

ups and payouts. It was going to be the best episode ever."
He let out a deep breath. "It'll never see the light of day
because Finn stationed guards near the stairs, forcing me
to take the elevator. I didn't have a choice. I had to get the
tape to my producer. Stupid, rookie move. I should've expected Finn would pull some sort of devious stunt but this
was…" He shook his head.

She was starting to understand. "Because you are uncomfortable in small places."

He laced his fingers with hers. "Yeah. I was already
shaking when I got into the thing but there was a maid
inside, so I tried to act cool. But when the elevator got
stuck…" He shook his head. "It was one of my nightmares
coming true."

She could feel his palm sweating and gave his hand a
gentle squeeze.

"Then the maid removed her blouse."

"She *what*?"

"Yeah, that seemed strange, but women do weird things
for celebrities. I was still pressing buttons to get the elevator going when the woman grabbed me and kissed me."

Michele's mouth dropped. "No! She was a total stranger!"

"It happened so fast. Nothing seemed real. When she
started grinding against me, I woke the hell up. I tried to ex-
tricate myself. Gently. And then the lights went out. Blackness inside a box with only a slight crack of light under the
door… It was like the shed. I was disoriented, terrified.
When something grabbed my ass and pinched… I fought.
The elevator lights came back on. The maid was on her butt,
cussing up a storm. Her bra was torn. Her hair a mess. She
had a red mark on her cheek."

The torment tangled in his starburst irises made her want
to hug him, but she didn't move for fear he'd stop talking.
She sensed he needed to get this out.

"Finn had tampered with the elevator, turned off the
lights and paid the maid to come on to me while recording

the whole thing. Releasing the first part, the sex scandal bit, ruined my career. He's holding the second part—the section that looks like I attacked the maid—as blackmail," he growled.

"She kissed and grabbed you! How can he use that against you?"

"Blackmail works best when the victim is caught on tape. People believe what they see, even a lie."

Shame heated her cheeks. Even she had believed Jeff was having sex in that elevator.

"This isn't fair! If a man had grabbed me in an elevator, I would've fought back, too, Jeff. Don't be ashamed. You did nothing wrong."

"Sweetheart, I'm six foot three and over two hundred pounds. Lots of muscle. She was tiny. You are tiny."

Something in his tone worried her. She cocked her head, trying to read his expression. Why did he mention her?

"I'd never hurt a woman, Michele, I swear." He looked at his hands as if he had weapons attached to his fingertips. "I have bad genes. I'm not good at relationships or connecting with people the right way. What if I am exactly like my mother?'"

Now she understood. "Oh, Jeff." She touched his face tenderly. "Have you talked to anyone about this? A doctor or therapist?"

"This is the first time I've told anyone this stuff. You don't understand. I'm trying to improve my reputation. If any of this gets out—my childhood, what really happened in that elevator—the Plunder Cove hotel will be done. I need to see this dream to the end. I need it to be the best it can be."

"It will be."

It had to be.

For both of them.

They didn't talk any more about his past—or his fears of what his future held—instead they had a nice day on the beach, exploring the tide pools, bodysurfing in the waves, walking on the sand. They held hands, kissed and talked. It had to be the best day she'd had in years.

They were making out like teenagers on the blanket when a speedboat pulled into the cove. Jeff started to sit up and Michele turned to look, too.

And saw a telephoto lens pointed at them.

"Get down," Jeff told Michele as he covered her head with his arms.

But it was too late.

The camera had caught him and a woman in a compromising position. Again.

Seventeen

They scrambled to grab their stuff and hop in the dinghy to make it to the yacht and catch up with the photographer. Jeff didn't care as much about his reputation as he did Michele's. Everyone already thought he was a playboy. Michele didn't deserve to have her name and personal details dragged through the dirt. If he could catch the guy, he'd talk some sense into him and pay whatever it took to kill the shot. "Hold on," he told Michele, glancing over his shoulder to make sure she was safe before he floored the yacht across the waves. He drove the boat like a madman for a few minutes before he acknowledged the truth.

It was too late. The cameraman had a speedboat and knew how to use it. Jeff slowed the vessel. Running he hand through his hair he faced her. "Sorry. There's no chance."

Her chin was high but he could see the worry in her eyes. "What will he do with the photos?"

"It'll be okay. Come here, sweetheart." He took her in his arms.

She lifted her head and the usual sparkle in her eyes had turned to flashing fear. "Those private pictures of us were...intimate."

Dammit. He saw all too clearly how he was messing up her life. "He'll sell them to the highest bidder. I'll get the PR team on it, see if we can buy them before someone else does."

"And if they can't buy them? What if Finn did this as another way to destroy you? He'll post them everywhere."

Yeah, he would. A firestorm raged inside his gut. How could he protect Michele?

"We have to stop Finn," she said with fierce determination.

He ran his finger down her cheek. "This is my fight, not yours. I shouldn't have dragged you into it. You shouldn't be with a guy like me."

She wrapped her arms around him and pressed her cheek to his bare chest. "What if I want to be with a guy like you?"

He sucked in a breath. Her words were a soft rain on the fire in his chest.

"Even with all my past?"

She rose up on her toes and pulled his lips toward hers. "Yes."

That night, Jeff slept alone. He'd kissed Michele goodnight and told her he had work to do. He'd worked with the PR team until dawn to no avail. They couldn't find any information on the photographer in the speedboat.

He'd never really worried about the women in his paparazzi shots before. This time he did care and would do anything he could to keep her out of his press.

What was he going to do about Michele?

Being with her had changed him.

Despite the paparazzi interrupting his and Michele's last kiss on the sand, he felt like he'd become a new man overnight.

He'd never found a woman he could talk to like her. Hell, he'd told her things he'd been afraid to admit to himself. Yet she hadn't run, hadn't judged. And she'd touched him like no one ever had—with reverence, kindness, and heat that had rocked him to the core.

Damn, they had sizzling chemistry. Even though he hadn't slept the entire night and had to get his head into the job at the restaurant site, he was still aroused thinking about their time on the beach. He wanted her now.

He slipped a note under her door.

"Please join me for dinner tonight. Yes, it's another date. Say yes."

He couldn't wait to see her naked again and drive deep inside her maybe in his shower and then in his bed. Maybe twice in his bed.

At dinnertime, he called it a day at the building site and headed back to the house to find Michele. Since the chef competition was over, Donna and the rest of the cooking staff had come back to work. He was happy to see them, but a little disappointed that Michele wasn't in the kitchen. He'd grown accustomed to seeing her sweet face screwed up in concentration as she cooked. Not to mention her cute ass bending over the oven.

He was getting hard just thinking about her.

Only one thing to do…bound down the hall, take her in his arms and show her how much he'd missed her. When he got to her room, she was talking on her phone and sitting on a lounge chair on the balcony. The setting sun framed her in golden light and the ocean breeze lifted her long hair. He watched her stare out over the gardens.

God, she was stunning. His heartbeat sped up and there was a strange warmth filling him. He'd never felt anything like that before. It both scared and awed him.

"Yes, I see why you were in total lust with Jeffrey Harper," she laughed. "I get it. Boy, do I get it."

He grinned. She was talking about him, huh? He liked that more than he dared admit. Would she talk about his blue eyes, his red hair or his six-pack? Those were the three things most articles mentioned about him.

"He's a good man," she said.

Her words stunned him like a flash of sunlight on a black day. No one had ever called him a good man before and hearing it from her lips melted something hard that had been lodged in his chest. It also worried the hell out of him.

He wanted to be the man Michele thought he was. But there wasn't anything good about him. That wasn't going to change. He'd sleep with her for a while, make sure she had a good time, but then he'd have to follow through with his promise to his dad and find a wife.

The idea didn't sit well with him anymore.

"It happened fast, but yes," she went on softly. "I'm falling for him."

Warning bells rang in every part of his psyche.

She can't be in love with me.

Michele went on, "Please, don't let Cari see the picture of us at the dinner party. She'll think I'm marrying him and that's not going to happen. We want different things."

That knocked him back.

Michele didn't believe they had a future together, either. It was the truth. He needed to marry someone he couldn't hurt.

So why did her words sting so damned much? He turned around and walked away.

Michele was disappointed when Jeff hadn't come to collect her for dinner last night. One of the staff had dropped off a note that said Jeff had work to do and she should eat without him. He seemed to be extremely busy working on the restaurant.

The next morning, still dreaming about that beach encounter, she went into the kitchen and found the regular staff in place. She smiled and introduced herself to them. When an older woman with white hair named Donna stepped forward to shake her hand, Michele hugged her instead.

"Thank you for taking care of Jeff," she whispered in Donna's ear. "He told me about the shed."

Donna pulled back with wide eyes. "He told you?"

Michele nodded. "The secret is safe with me."

"Oh, sweet girl. Jeff has needed someone like you his entire life." Donna pulled Michele into a huge bear hug.

They nodded at each other, insta-friends.

"What can I make you?" Donna asked.

"Actually, I was hoping I could jump in here with you and make a lunch for Jeff." Her brain was overflowing with recipes. Her cooking muse was back.

"Of course! He'd love that."

"I won't get in your way. I'm leaving in a few days anyway."

"What? No, you can't go."

"I've got to go back to New York to collect my things, pay rent and figure out how to bring my sister to California. But I want to do something nice for Jeff before I go."

"Sure, hon. My kitchen is your kitchen."

Later, Michele went down to the job site. The framing was finished. The restaurant seemed to be coming along faster than Jeff had said it would. It made her realize that she had a lot to do to be ready for opening night. She'd ask Donna if she could use Casa Larga's kitchen to create new recipes for the restaurant. Her brain was bubbling over with ideas.

Jeff came out of the building. He wasn't smiling and he didn't come close enough to touch.

Why the distance?

"Michele, what are you doing here?"

"I brought you lunch."

"That wasn't necessary."

She frowned. His vibe was all wrong. Was he mad at her?

"I know. I wanted to…" *See you. Touch you. Kiss you.* "…feed you. That's all."

He took the bundle from her hands. "Thanks."

She stood there, wondering what was going on with him. "So…"

He waited.

Okay, then.

He was busy or in a bad mood. She rushed on. "I won't take up any more of your time. I just wanted to know if I could go home for a couple of weeks to check on my sister. I miss her terribly. You know, if there was one thing I could change it would be to have her live with me. She needs round-the-clock care but I am sure there must be group homes in California, even if I have to drive a ways to get there."

She saw a subtle shift in his demeanor, a softening. But it passed quickly. He crossed his arms over his chest, closing himself off. "Fine. Distance between us is probably a good thing right now."

She blinked. "Jeff, what's the matter?"

He stepped closer and she could feel the intensity rising off his body in waves. "You can't love me, Michele. I won't allow it."

Her mouth opened. "Excuse me?"

"I told you. I'm broken, just like my mother. I sure as hell don't want to hurt you, of all people. God, Michele, you're special. Sweet. The gentlest person I've ever met. It'll kill me to cause you any pain. That's why we should stop seeing one another, except professionally."

You can't love me. She didn't know how he'd known, but it was the truth. She was starting to fall for him.

She couldn't help it.

"Jeff..." She reached for him but stopped, not wanting to see him recoil from her touch. "Maybe if we give it a little time—"

"I'm almost out of time."

"What do you mean?"

Instead of answering her question, he said, "Go home and see your sister. I'll give you three weeks to decide if you still want to work for me, knowing that I have to marry someone else."

Her heart broke. "You have to? Or want to?"

"It's not my choice. My father has made it part of my

work contract. I have to marry someone when the restaurant is finished."

If her jaw could have hit the dirt, she would be tripping over it. "That's…months away."

The muscles in his jaw flexed. "I keep hoping I can change his mind, but he's a stubborn bastard."

None of this seemed real. He'd slept with her knowing he would be marrying someone else? "Who…?"

He lifted his hands. "I haven't found a bride yet."

"This is crazy! Your father can't make you do this."

"He can. I promised I would abide by the contract. I signed it." He exhaled through his nose. "Listen, I'm sorry. Not for what we had, that was amazing, but I can't get you messed up in my family drama, because you are too important to me."

"As your chef," she clarified.

"And I hope as a friend. But I leave the decision up to you. Think about it while you are in New York. If you don't want the job, I'll call Freja. I never wanted to hurt you."

He turned and walked away.

The kitchen stoves and appliances arrived that same day.

Jeff was busy directing the installations and didn't think about Michele, much. But when the sun went down and he had to eat dinner alone, their discussion weighed on him. The hurt look when he told her he was still marrying someone else tore him up, especially knowing that he'd put that sadness on her beautiful face. He cared about her, more than he should. Letting her go was for her own good. Once she was in New York she'd see he was lousy boyfriend material. She deserved so much more.

God, he should've chosen Freja for his chef. At least then he wouldn't torture himself every time he stepped into the kitchen. He wasn't good about abstaining from treats he couldn't have. Not being able to kiss Michele would be hard. That is *if* she decided to return. For her own good she should never return. But for *his* good? He still wanted her beside him. What a selfish bastard he was.

Even now he wanted to see her, touch her, inhale her sweet perfume. He went to find her to apologize for being so harsh earlier and beg her to stay. But he found her room empty. She'd already left.

What if she didn't come back? Had he lost his best chef? The only woman he'd ever cared about?

This was RW's fault. Dad was the one making Jeff get married. If he didn't have that stupid cloud over his head, he could date Michele and not worry about the future. They could simply enjoy one another for a while. Be together for as long as it lasted.

He didn't want to think about his own role in creating this heartache.

He stomped into RW's wing determined to make his father change his demands. He passed the guard and stepped into a dark hallway.

"Dad?" he called. "You in here?"

No answer. Frowning, Jeff turned on the hallway lights and knocked on RW's door. Music was playing inside. A strange foreboding came over him. Something wasn't right. He opened the door and stepped into total blackness. He fumbled around to find the light switch and was startled to see his father sitting at his desk drinking bourbon while a Mexican song blasted.

His father didn't drink. As far as Jeff knew, he didn't speak Spanish.

What the hell was going on?

"Dad? What's wrong?"

"Angel left. She took Cristina and the boy and drove away. How can I stay here and…breathe? I can't do this, any of it, without her. She was the only person who saw past this…" RW slapped his own chest "…this stupid man."

Jeff had never heard so much pain in his father's voice, in anyone's voice. "Where did she go? Is she all right?"

The look in his father's eyes was heart wrenching. It reminded him of the pain he'd been pushing past since he'd ended things with Michele.

"I don't know. How can I protect her when she won't let me? She said she couldn't put me at risk. Me! As if I wasn't dead before she started treating me."

Jeff ran his hand through his hair. "Let's go after her."

"No, dammit! Cuchillo will expect me to follow her. It's too risky." He grabbed Jeff's collar. "Swear you won't go after her."

Jeff gripped his father's wrist. "Fine. We'll wait for her to contact you."

"I'm not a patient man."

Jeff snorted. "Yeah, I know. But unless you have a better plan…"

RW shook his head and lifted the bottle to his lips.

Jeff pulled it away. "That's not helping. You stopped drinking, remember?"

"For Angel. She told me I couldn't see what was right in front of me from the bottom of a bottle. But without her… I lost my family and now my…angel. I'm alone." RW slumped over his desk.

"You're not alone. I won't leave you." Jeff hoisted RW up from under his arms. "Come on, Dad. Let's walk it off."

The next morning, Jeff woke up and cracked his back. He'd had a lousy night's sleep in the chair beside his father's bed. But at least his father's problems had kept Jeff's mind from lingering on Michele.

RW opened his eyes and cursed, gripping his head. Jeff handed him two aspirin and a bottle of water.

"Glad Angel isn't here to see me like this," RW said, his voice gravelly.

Jeff shrugged. "One bad night. Put it behind you and do better."

RW lifted his lips in a half grin, half grimace. "You

sound like her. Of you three kids, she worried about you the most."

"Angel worried about me? Why?"

"Chloe told us about what your mother did to you in the shed and Matt told us that you worry you can never fall in love."

Jeff bolted up. "What the hell? You all sat around talking about me behind my back?"

"To help you, son. That's what families do." RW rose, too, swayed a little and put his hands on Jeff's shoulders. "I swear, I didn't know your mother left you out in the shed."

When RW grimaced that time, Jeff wondered if it was hangover pain or from imagining what his little boy had gone through. Part of him wanted his father to feel real pain. A white-hot poker of justice.

Something to block out his own pain over mistakes made.

"Bullshit. How could you not know how she was? Why didn't you stop her, Dad?"

RW nodded. "You're right. I should've been there to save you. It was my fault, Jeffrey. That's another thing on me that I need to make amends for, a bad one. Give me the blame and let your shame go."

Weakness seeped into Jeff's legs. "I need to sit down." He'd never heard his father accept the blame so quickly, and then apologize. It knocked him back, and he crumpled into the chair.

"Listen to me, son. You're nothing like your mother. You are ambitious, thick-skinned and strong. That's why your mother took her anger out on you. Not because you're like her, but because you are like me. She probably didn't even know that's why she picked on you so much."

Jeff blinked. RW had never been this open with him before.

"Another thing, I know you think your mother was incapable of loving. That's bull. Your mother loved me until I got sick. Something broke inside me and I couldn't love her anymore. I got mean and hurt her, too. Together, we raged World War Three on one another and destroyed…everything. I was too deep in my own hole to understand at the time, but I see now. Angel showed me the light."

Jeff hung his head between his knees. His limbs were heavy. "I don't know what to say."

"Say you're done hiding from your own damned feelings. Your mother and I hurt you badly and you don't want to hurt like that again. I get it. Trust me, I do, because you are like your old man. But if you don't let yourself feel, you'll never truly live. I want you to live, son."

And then, without any warning, RW wrapped his arms around Jeff.

For the first time in his life, Jeff buried his head in his father's shoulder and held on.

Eighteen

Michele flew to New York like a regular person—no chartered jet, yacht or limo. It was strange to be in New York again. Nothing had changed, except her. Days passed and she still felt out of place in her own home.

During the day, she stayed with her sister and answered the hundreds of questions that Cari's caregivers asked about the Harpers. They all wanted to know what Jeff was like in real life. The more Michele talked about him, the more she missed him. It was a sweet ache that wouldn't go away.

Did he think about her?

When she was back in her tiny apartment, she whipped up recipes one after the other. She kept a pad of paper on the countertop and by her bed so she could write down the rainbow of flavors that fired inside her brain.

Joy. That's what it felt like. Her cooking anxiety was gone.

So, apparently, was Alfieri's voice. Cooking for Jeff had silenced the negativity inside her.

She was free.

Man, she couldn't wait to create some of these dishes for Jeff. He'd love her mildly spicy chicken parmigiana. She smiled, thinking about how much he'd loved the grilled cheese sandwich she'd made for him. That was the first time she'd kissed his spicy lips and he'd asked her to eat with him.

Who was eating dinner with him now?

A horrible thought stopped her pen—what if he was married by the time she returned? Could she work for him then? She honestly didn't know if she could. It would hurt too badly. Her pain would be bad enough but watching him self-destruct with a person who didn't care about him, who maybe only wanted his money or fame? She couldn't bear the thought.

A friend. That's what he said he wanted her to be. Would a friend let him do something that would end up harming him?

No, she had to stop him from marrying a woman who would not love him. Because, heaven help her, *she* loved him. Desperately. Without question. She'd never loved a man before but she understood that love was about risks and she was willing to risk it all for Jeffrey Harper. She wanted him to be happy. She wanted to make the rest of his life sweeter than he could ever imagine. To do that…she would have to be brave and go for what she wanted—him.

Biting her lip, she knew what she had to do.

She called him and was disappointed when his voice mail picked up. How she'd wanted to hear his deep voice.

"It's Michele. If you still must get married…" Screwing up all the courage she could muster, she said, "Marry me. We're good together. Really good. Friends with benefits. I want you to be happy and I can make you happy. I know what I'm getting into. Please, call me back and we can…" she laughed "…plan a wedding. Call me."

She hung up and stared at her phone. Did she just ask a man to marry her?

Falling back on her bed she laughed out loud. Yes, she did.

Jeff was busier than he'd ever been but he couldn't stop thinking about Michele.

Would she come back?

And if she did, would he be able to keep his hands off

her? He didn't think so. All he'd thought about, dreamed of, imagined since she left was Michele. He was glad he didn't have his cell phone with him at the site. He couldn't stop checking social media or searching the web for pictures of her. When he found nothing, the hole in his heart widened. He turned his phone off and buried it in his sock drawer.

RW showed up at the building site, looking ragged and drawn. Like a strong California sundowner wind would blow him off his feet.

"Hey, Dad. Have you heard from Angel yet?"

RW shook his head. The muscles in his jaw flexed. "I'm working another angle so she feels safe to come back once and for all."

Alarms went off in Jeff's head. "What sort of angle?"

"Taking the fight straight to the bastard himself. Cuchillo invaded my home. Now he'll see what that feels like."

Jeff didn't like the sound of this plan. "Ah, that sounds dangerous. I'm not sure you're up to that sort of fight, Dad."

The flash of fury in his father's eyes startled him. "I'm exactly the one for this fight. He hurt Angel and will pay for that. Don't worry, I'll make sure our family is protected."

Now Jeff was thoroughly worried. He would talk to Matt and figure out what the old man was planning.

"Dad..."

"I'm done discussing this." RW ended the conversation by walking around the building to check out the progress. Typical Dad move—walk away when he didn't want to hear any more.

Matt and I will figure it out.

Jeff continued working. It was all he could do with so much on his mind.

When RW reappeared ten minutes later, he said, "It's coming along."

"Yep. The kitchen will be fully functioning by the end of the week. Just have the rest of the dining area to finish up."

It was the first time he'd seen RW smile since Angel

left. "I'm proud of you, son. This project is just what we both needed."

Warmth spread inside Jeff's chest. "Thanks, Dad."

"I haven't seen anything online from Finn lately." RW frowned. "I wonder what he's up to."

"Maybe our lawyers scared him off."

"Doubtful. I'll check into that, too. Okay, son. I'll leave you to your work."

Jeff watched his father walk away and wondered what *he* was up to.

Almost two weeks had passed since Michele left. It felt like a thousand. When was she coming back? Would she? The questions haunted him night and day. Jeff and Matt were insulting each other and playing an extremely aggressive game of pool when RW stomped into the pool house waving a newspaper. "What in the hell is this!"

Chloe rushed in behind him. "Dad, some of those go back to the start of the year before Jeff came home."

Jeff walked around the pool table to see what they were looking at. The headline read, "Jeffrey Harper's Harem." Below that were two pages filled with pictures of him on dates.

"No way. Are those women you've dated *this* year?"

Chloe bit her lip. "I have our image guys on it. But I'm not sure what they can do to help you, Jeff. These appear to be real pictures."

Matt cocked his head. "Oh, look, there's Michele Cox. And there she is again at the beach."

Jeff pressed his fingertips to his temple. "Finn did this."

Chloe nodded. "Sounds like something he'd do."

"I don't care who took the pictures. I've already gotten angry calls from shareholders. You're supposed to be building a respectable image, Jeffrey. Not—" RW slapped the page "—a harem."

"You told me to find a bride!" Jeff yelled.

"I didn't tell you to date every female in the northern hemisphere. You're sabotaging your career and hurting the family in the process. It's time to choose. Marry one," RW ordered.

Jeff wasn't ready to discuss it. He didn't know when he'd ever be ready to marry.

The only woman he'd made love to recently was Michele. She saw through the television celebrity image, the rich Harper prince, the cocky hotel critic, and saw the real him. Messed up childhood and all.

No one else got him like she did.

He didn't want to think about what that meant.

"What are we going to do about Finn?" Jeff asked instead.

"Leave him to me. I'll settle the score but we need him to come here. I can't go to New York, in case Angel needs me here. Plus, I'm working on something."

Jeff and Matt exchanged looks. So far, they hadn't figured out what RW was planning to do to Cuchillo.

Chloe studied RW's face. "How will you get Finn here?"

"I'll invite him to come see how the restaurant is coming along. Jeff, make sure your chef is ready to make him a meal he will never forget."

"When? Michele is not due back for another ten days."

Jeff's gaze went to her picture. The one on the beach was his favorite. He traced her jaw with his finger.

"Michele Cox is not coming back. She tendered her letter of resignation this morning. To me," RW said.

Jeff turned around so quickly that the room spun. A low hum of despair started at the base of his tailbone. "She quit?"

"That's what happens when you let people down. She called you several times and you refused to call her back. Don't you understand what I am trying to teach you with this project?" RW's voice was raised but there was a thick undercurrent of sadness in it. "The townspeople. Our employees. People we care about. Harpers don't get to crap on anyone anymore. You lose good people that way…for good. I expect better of you."

Jeff slammed his hand on the pool table. "I didn't get her calls, Dad."

"Jeff, I bought you a new phone. Is it not working?"

"It's fine. It's just…my phone is… I turned it off. Social media was destroying me." He didn't explain that it was more the lack of seeing Michele anywhere than seeing his negative posts that were killing him.

Chloe said. "Did you bury it in your sock drawer like you used to?"

"Hey. How did you know I hid things there?"

Chloe smiled. "You're still the same. You know that? You always hid the good stuff there. Candy bars, comic books… I'll go get the phone."

Matt patted his shoulder. "Explain it to Michele. It's just a misunderstanding."

"Is it?" RW's nostrils flared. "Did you treat her badly, son? Could she have seen this two-page spread this morning and decided she didn't want to be another notch on your bedpost?"

Jeff opened his mouth. No words came out.

"If you want to be respected, you have to treat people with respect. Why can't you learn from my mistakes instead of making the same ones? This is yours to fix. Figure it out." RW stomped out the same way he came in.

Matt shook his head. "We really need to find Angel. Are you okay?"

No.

His mind was spinning, searching for answers. Jeff scrubbed his face.

She quit?

He'd really thought she'd come back, even if they couldn't be together anymore.

"I'm fine." His voice was full of gravel.

Matt rubbed his shoulder. "Of course, you are. Hey, you know what's different in these pictures? I just figured it out."

"You're still looking at those? Give it a rest."

Was Dad right? Had Michele seen this, too? Did she feel like just another woman in his bed? Hell, he could see her sparkle even in the grainy black-and-white shots. Could feel her touch way down deep.

She was nothing like the others.

"No way. Look. This is too good to pass up." Matt sounded amused.

Jeff didn't want to look. He'd forgotten many of their names already.

"It's a bunch of women I dated, so what?" Jeff snarled.

"No, jackass. Look at *you* in the pictures. Here's your ugly mug with all these women. Serious, glum, bored, practicing your multiplication tables in your head…" He pointed across two rows. "Now look at you with Michele. Both pictures. See the difference?"

Jeff leaned in closer. "I'm smiling at her."

"Bingo. A real smile, man. Like you feel it down to your toes. You are into her, totally and completely. At least, that's what I see in those two photos and not in the others. Hell, if I didn't know better, I'd say that guy in those two pictures with Michele—" Matt grinned. "That dude is in love."

Jeff looked closer and saw what Matt recognized. He seemed like a different person in the photos with Michele. A person he'd never seen before.

He *was* different with Michele.

A surge of heat flooded his gut. It wasn't love, it was… hell, he didn't know what to call it. But it was…something.

Chloe raced in, out of breath, and shoved the shiny new phone toward him. "Here. Play the voicemails and call her right now. Tell her…tell her anything, something. She's good for you. Get her back, Jeff."

He stepped away from them and listened to the messages. All ten of them.

The air was sledgehammered out of his body. He slumped onto a bar stool and listened. A lump was in his throat when he closed the cell phone and faced his brother and sister.

"Matt, can you fly me to New York tonight?" he asked.

Matt raised his fist to the air. "Hell, yeah! Let's go get her."

"No. I have a score to settle with an asshole named Alfieri. That's all."

Chloe's eyes were full of concern. "What did Michele say?"

He swallowed but the damned lump wouldn't move. "She asked me to marry her. A few times. Eight, I think. Then waited for my answer. When I didn't call, she told me she never wanted to see me again. Another man had stolen her joy once, and she wasn't going to go through that again."

Matt sucked in a hiss of breath. "Go talk to her, bro. You can fix this."

The heat in Jeff's gut begged him to race after her, grab her, kiss her until she changed her mind and came home with him.

But his mind knew otherwise.

"She's right. I'd only break her beautiful sparkle. Crush her joy. I don't deserve her."

Matt made a half grunt and used one of his little boy's catchphrases. "No, duh."

"Matt!" Chloe slapped Matt's arm.

"What? He *doesn't* deserve her. That's a given. We Harper men are totally screwed up. But here's the thing..." Matt wrapped his arm over Jeff's shoulder. "The right woman can make you a better man. I'm proof. I wake up every damned day amazed that Julia sees anything in me and go to bed praying, begging, that she never stops. Without her, I'm nothing. With her, I'm Matt on steroids, a flipping superhero." His grin was full of awe. "With all the powers."

"Go to her," Chloe said. "Love her, Jeff."

He couldn't. He didn't know how.

Nineteen

Michele was moving on. That's what she told herself.

What choice did she have, since there was no going back?

She'd laid it all on the line for him, and he hadn't even called her back to blow her off.

She owed Jeff a lot for helping her to see clearly and get her cooking mojo back. He'd taught her that she didn't need any man to tell her who she was. Michele Cox was still a kick-ass chef. The voice in her head was her own. She was small, but she was also mighty, and she had the power to take care of herself and her sister now.

She was alone, yes, but she didn't have time to dwell on it because she had three good job offers already. She would decide which one to take by the end of the week. Her goal now was to save enough money to start a restaurant of her own. A small one. Nothing like the posh restaurant Jeff was going to have, but it would be great. It would be hers. Stickerino's, she might call it—after the horse who carried the heroine to the pirate's treasure.

How she wished she could have kept the pirate as her treasure.

But he didn't want her, or at least, not enough.

So, she was moving on and she would stop thinking about *him.*

Eventually.

That was her plan anyway, until that two-page newspaper article hit all the stands with two pictures of her kissing Jeffrey Harper and her short-lived romance became the topic of conversation everywhere she went.

And the paparazzi found out where Cari lived.

Jeff had intended to come to New York for Alfieri, and Alfieri alone. He hadn't planned on seeing Michele, but now he had to. Because he had her money in his pocket and had a question to ask her.

Or that's what he told himself.

About seventeen times.

But his insides were thrumming with heat and excitement at the thought of seeing her again. *Just to give her the money and ask her the question*, he reminded himself for time number eighteen.

He didn't dare get too carried away. She probably hated him for not calling back after her emotional, heartfelt messages. And he knew he'd done the right thing by letting her go.

And yet, he still wanted to kiss her.

When he pulled up in front of her flat he couldn't help but notice the photographers. They were like a committee of hungry buzzards waiting outside. She didn't appear to be home. Good. He pulled up directions to the group home where he'd paid her sister's rent and sped off.

Dammit, reporters were parked outside the group home, too. Why in the hell were they bothering Michele's sister? Putting on a baseball cap, he walked inside.

The attendant at the front desk looked up warily. "Can I help you?"

"Hope so. I'm looking for Michele Cox."

When she saw who he was she squealed and then told him he'd just missed her. Michele had taken her sister to horseback riding lessons. The woman gave him the directions.

The vultures had beaten him to the stables, too. Police

had been called and they and the stable owner were pushing the photographers off the private property. When an officer asked him what business he had at the stable, he said he was there to pick up one of the riders—a woman with special needs and her sister.

"I'm the owner," a woman said. "I'll let you pass if you tell me the name of the rider you are here to pick up."

"Cari Cox," he replied. "Her sister is Michele."

The woman grimaced. "Oh, good. Michele must've texted you, too. I was just getting ready to call one of my stable boys to come back to work and go rescue them."

"Rescue them?"

"One of the photographers opened the gate and went into the ring to get a picture of Cari, which, as you probably can guess, didn't go over well. She doesn't like strangers. She started screaming, the horse spooked and ran out of the gate with Cari on its back. Michele ran after them and then she got injured—"

"Michele is injured?" His heart just about exploded in his chest. "Where is she?"

"She texted that she twisted her ankle and can't walk. She can't make it to where Cari's horse is because the terrain is steep."

"Where? Can I drive there?"

"No. Can you ride?"

"Yes."

"Then take my horse. She's saddled up and ready to go. I'd do it myself but I have to make sure these nutballs don't sneak back onto my property—"

"Text Michele. Tell her to sit tight. I'm coming." He would fly if he had to. He stopped telling himself lies about why he'd come to New York because he needed to hold her and kiss her pain away.

"That was fun! Really fast. I was like Rosie," Cari squealed and giggled in delight.

"Sure, laugh. It's all fun and games until your sister nearly breaks a leg running after you."

"You dance funny."

That's because Michele had stepped in a hole and twisted her ankle. "I wasn't dancing."

Out of nowhere came the memory of Jeff's hands on her hips at the dinner party. Now those were real moves. She shook it off. She didn't have the time or the stamina to be heartsick. What did it matter that she missed him like crazy? He'd made his feelings clear by not returning her calls.

"Can you give your horse a little kick and steer him toward me? I can't hop on one foot that far. And this other one is…" She looked at her leg. It was terribly swollen already. Oh, God, was it broken? "It's not good."

"My horse likes the grass here. He's hungry."

"He gets plenty of food in the stables. Let's take him back there where he can have a proper dinner and I can get some ice for my leg, okay? Come over here so I can ride with you."

"No. You are too heavy. Only one cowgirl on each horse."

Michele cursed under her breath and tried hopping on one foot. It was no good. The path was rocky and steep. Cari's horse had found a grass-covered mesa at the top of the hill. How was she going to make it up there? Crawl?

"Ahoy, there. Need a lift?" A voice called behind her.

She couldn't see the man, but she was overjoyed that the owner had sent someone to rescue her and Cari.

"Yes! But please, don't spook my sister's horse."

It took a small feat of balance to be able to turn her body on one foot without slipping down the steep embankment. By the time she did, the horse and rider were already beside her.

"Did someone order a cowboy from California?" he asked.

She blinked. No. It couldn't be.

"You're not real."

He laughed then and her heart did funny things in her

chest. "Tell that to my horse." He slid down and stood beside her. His starburst baby blues seemed to take her all in. "Are you hurt?"

She pressed a hand to her heart.

Oops, did he mean her ankle? "It might be broken."

He bent over and checked it out. When he touched her leg, she bit her lip to keep it from quivering, not entirely from the twisted ankle pain either.

Jeff is here.

Why? What does it mean?

"I don't think it's broken, but you twisted it good. Let me help you up on the horse so we can have a doctor look at it. Do you want the front or rear seat?"

She realized there wasn't much room for him to sit behind the saddle. "Rear."

Once he got her situated on the horse, he swung his leg over and sat in front of her. She had a sudden dilemma. Should she touch him? For the moment, she kept her hands to herself.

"My sister is over there." Michele pointed. "She's pretending to not see you."

"I can see that. What am I supposed to do?"

"Cari, this is a friend of mine named Jeff. He's very nice," Michele called out.

"The pirate!" Cari clapped her hands.

Oh, dear. "Um. Yes." Michele leaned over and whispered. "Sorry. Someone must have mentioned your family history. Cari's favorite book has pirates in it."

He grinned. "So, Cari, how would you like to go with me and your sister on an airplane back to a pirate's castle?"

"Yay!" Cari cheered. "Right now?"

"What?" Michele said. "You can't just tell her things like that."

"Listen, sweetheart. It's not safe for you two to be here by yourselves right now. I saw the paparazzi. They're everywhere because of me. Let me fix it. If you aren't around here, they'll leave after a while."

"But, I have a life here. A job to accept."

"It will all still be here if you want it, but I was hoping you'd change your mind about the resignation and come back to Plunder Cove. For good. If...you'll accept my proposition. But first, let's go get your sister, okay?"

She stared at his back. *Proposition?*

"Okay?" he asked again.

"I...don't know what I'm agreeing to."

"Fair enough. Tiny bites. First, we rescue your sister and that fat horse."

"I agree."

"Great. But I'm not moving until you wrap your arms around me. Safety first."

Tentatively, slowly, she wrapped her arms around his waist. He took her hand and pressed it against his chest. Capturing it next to his heart. She could feel the strong beat beneath her palm. He felt so good in her arms, even when she knew he didn't feel the same way about her. Her heart was cracking from the bitter sweetness of it all. She wanted to stay like this forever, touching him, breathing in his manly cologne, listening to his deep voice. Holding out hope that he wouldn't say he didn't love her. Again.

"That's better." His voice was hoarse. "Hell, I missed you so hard. Please, say you'll come back with me."

Her inhale caught in her throat. The only word she could muster was, "Why?"

"I'm miserable without you. I still need a chef, and that job is still yours, but you deserve more. Which reminds me..." He reached into his pocket and pulled out a thick envelope that seemed to be full of...money? "This is yours. I had a little chat with Alfieri. He was overcome with the desire to pay you what he owed you. With interest, of course."

"That's...no. Now I know you're not real. I must have hit my head when I twisted my ankle."

"Does this feel real?" He lifted her hand and kissed her knuckle. Then he turned her hand over and kissed her palm. "Or this?"

"Yes," she said softly. She felt those kisses all the way down to her throbbing ankle. It was all she could do to not beg for more. "I'm so ashamed. I should never have let Alfieri treat me like that."

"Sorry, sweetheart, but that's pure bull." He swiveled around and pinned her with his gaze. "He assaulted you with his words and actions and robbed you. You have nothing to be ashamed of. I'm glad you got away from him and I told him so…in something like words."

"You didn't hurt him, did you?"

"Hell, I wanted to. But I think my old camera crew will hurt him far more than I could unless he agrees to change his ways. They'll pop in on him and interview the staff on a regular basis just to make sure he's a kinder, gentler Alfieri. So that he doesn't do to others what he did to you."

"Thank you."

"There's more. I found out he'd promised you a partnership in the restaurant and that's when the coincidence hit me. I need a partner in *my* restaurant while I build and run the hotel. Someone I trust. That's my proposition. Will you be my partner?"

She cleared her throat. "In the restaurant?"

"What do you think? We can get the finest care for your sister and you two can live together again. It's perfect."

Almost.

"What about your wedding plans?"

His shoulders stiffened. "RW may not like it, but if you agree to come back as my partner, I'll break my agreement with him."

"You won't get married?"

"No." He swiveled so she could see his face. He went on, "And you and I can focus on our careers. I can take care of you and your sister and together you and I can create the best restaurant the world has ever seen. Say yes."

"And we, the two of us, will be real partners? Nothing more?"

He stiffened again. "You are much more. You are important to me, Michele. I hope you see that. I don't want to jeopardize our…relationship, or our restaurant, in any way. I need you."

She sighed. He would never love her. "I see."

It wasn't the partnership she'd been hoping for—it wasn't the one she'd bet her heart on when she'd left him those voice messages—but she'd get to be with him and she'd be doing what she loved.

She'd spent too long without what she wanted and even if he never loved her back, she would take everything he'd give.

"I say yes."

She put her head on his back, breathed in his most excellent manly smell and took a second to notice all the places they were touching.

Just then Cari's horse decided to come down and join theirs

"Weeeee!" Cari said. "Let's go to the pirate castle."

Twenty

The day arrived. Finn had been invited to Casa Largá to see the restaurant and taste some of Michele's new creations. RW knew the bastard would come. Finn owed him.

RW met him in the circle of the driveway. When Finn got out of the limo with a swagger, RW's blood boiled.

"Hello, old friend." Finn held out his hand.

RW took it and shook, but then he squeezed, dug his nails in and refused to let go until he had Finn's full attention. "You were only supposed to threaten him. Convince him to leave the television show and come to work for me. That was the deal."

Finn squinted and yanked his hand back. "It worked, didn't it?"

"I didn't tell you to attack my son," RW snarled.

Finn shrugged. "Attack him? I sent my best girl in there. Jeffrey was the one who went ballistic. What in the hell is the matter with him?"

"Nothing," RW said.

The problem is mine.

All RW wanted was what was best for his son. Creating hotels was in Jeffrey's blood, in his heart. RW had done everything he could to convince Jeff to design the hotel at Plunder Cove, but that damned show, *Secrets and Sheets*, got in the way. RW had taken drastic measures to put an end to it by asking Finn to nudge Jeffrey in the right direction.

That had been a mistake.

RW was heartbroken to see that he'd been responsible for Jeffrey's internal struggles. It all stopped now.

"I want the videos and the photos to end. Hear me? You are done," RW said through gritted teeth.

"I hear nothing but hot air whistling in my ears, Harper. I'll stop when I have the episode he filmed of my hotel. That's my deal."

RW's hands clenched into fists. Rage pounded behind his eyeballs.

Chloe came out the front door, effectively ending the clandestine meeting. "Mr. Finn! Welcome. Please follow me to the restaurant. It is not finished yet, but the kitchen is fully functional and we have seating in the courtyard." She guided him to a comfortable table next to the firepit. "Enjoy!"

Jeff walked outside to the patio. "Finn, I can't say I am happy to see you."

There was a loud crash inside the unfinished restaurant. A drill, somewhere around the back of the site, made a horrible grinding sound followed by cussing.

The commotion made Finn grin. "Your restaurant is just as I imagined it."

"We're still getting the kinks out."

"I can only imagine that your hotel will be just as kinky." Finn picked up his cell. "I'm going to film this meal and Tweet it."

"Great." Jeff hoped Michele was ready. "Red or white wine?"

"A glass of each."

"Of course." It was a struggle not to grab the man by his collar and throw him out, but Dad had a plan—something he hadn't completely shared with his sons.

Imagine that.

Finn was working on both of his wine glasses when Michele softly called, "Order up."

Jeff picked up the plate. Michele had made her signature chicken cacciatore but the sauce was better than Alfieri's. Michele had fed him an early spoonful and he thought it was the best thing he'd ever tasted—next to Michele's lips. He missed her mouth and running his hands over her body.

Finn took a bite and rolled his eyes. Overwhelmed, he mumbled, "Holy crap. It's better than sex."

Jeff lifted his eyebrow and Michele nodded. They'd heard Finn all the way in the kitchen, since RW had bugged the table.

"Round two," Jeff said before he left the kitchen.

"Give him a knockout punch for me." Michele winked.

Damn, she was amazing.

Having her as his partner in the restaurant should've been a dream come true. She was the perfect, hardworking professional who created the best meals he'd ever eaten. If anything, she was too perfect, too dedicated. He was the one who had trouble focusing with her so near. He longed to sweep her away and find quiet moments for just the two of them. But he didn't, because they'd made a deal and he was determined to hold up his end of it. No matter how much he hated it.

A professional relationship with Michele wasn't enough. For the first time in his life, he wanted more. Something big was pounding inside him, burning to get out, struggling to have a voice to tell her what he probably knew all along—he wanted Michele. Forever.

He doubted she'd ever want him. Not after he'd let her walk away. He should have fought for her, begged her to stay in his life, instead of offering her a simple partnership. It wasn't enough. He'd blown it.

To Finn, Jeff said, "How's it going? More water? Another bottle?"

"More food. This is the best damned meal I've ever had."

Finn shook his head, his eyes already having trouble focusing. "You did something right. Your chef is brilliant."

"I agree. But she is more than a chef. She's my partner. The best part of me." He hoped she heard that.

"Bully for you. What's for dessert?"

"Get ready, because Michele's tiramisu is the best, sweetest thing you will ever taste. She has her own secret spices from Italy plus a rare organic cocoa from a small farm in Ghana. You will swear you have died and gone to heaven."

"Enough jaw-flapping, Harper. Bring it on!"

Absolutely, you arrogant prick.

He went back into the kitchen. He'd done his job sparring with the man; it was time to let his dad deliver the final blow.

RW sat at the table across from Finn. "Enjoying your meal?"

"I have never tasted anything like it. Such a pleasurable surprise. Where did you find your chef?"

"Jeffrey found her, not me. But I'm going to tell her not to serve you anything else unless you stop releasing clips from Jeffrey's sex tape."

Finn snorted. "You call *that* a sex tape?"

"What would you call it?"

"I don't know. A Photoshop masterpiece? It's flawless. I dare you to find anyone who can tell where I sliced the sections together."

"What about the woman? Is she really a maid?"

"No. She's one of my best hookers. Gorgeous tits. Sweet ass. She really brings in the dough, so I only charge her a small referral fee."

"Pimp commission, you mean."

Finn sipped his wine. "Tomato, tomato."

Listening in the kitchen, Michele sucked in a breath. "Did you know Finn ran a brothel in his hotel? "

"Some of the employees I interviewed hinted at something going on behind the scenes," Jeff said. "He's a real creep."

"And he made it look like you had the sex issues! I can think of stronger words than 'creep.'"

They continued to eavesdrop on the conversation outside.

"Interesting discussion," RW said. "So now that I've fed you a great meal by Chef Michele Cox and let you be the first to experience this amazing up-and-coming Plunder Cove restaurant and hotel, I want to ask you nicely to stop blackmailing my son."

Finn shrugged. "No can do. I haven't gotten what I want yet. Wait until you see what I do with the next segment of video. With a little cut and splice wizardry, the world is going to think your son is one twisted sucker."

"Why are you doing this?" RW growled.

"You know why. He still hasn't televised how fantastic my hotel is. I need people to believe it's perfect. There's a lawsuit breathing down my neck."

"You want Jeffrey to lie to the public."

"Well, damn, RW, I can't have Jeffrey telling the truth! I watched what he filmed on my own security cameras. That episode would bury my hotel. I'd be run out of New York. That's why I had to create the fake sex tape. Your son has too damned much integrity to be pressured into turning over that episode. He wouldn't listen to reason."

RW crossed his arms. "And that's where he and I differ. Integrity? Not so much. Fierce determination to protect what's mine? You haven't seen anything like me. Guards! Take this scumbag off my property."

Finn laughed. "Right. Good one. Where's my tiramisu?"

RW picked up the tiny camera stuck to the flowerpot. And pointed to the recording device on the bottle of wine. There was another one under the table and a third one under his chair. "Seems like you are the one caught on tape, Xander. It's going to be a great commercial for the restaurant."

"You wouldn't dare."

"I'm releasing the part where you talk up the food. That's good stuff. If I see even one more shot, video, GIF—*anything*—on the internet about Jeffrey, I don't care who posts it, I'll release the entire video shot tonight to the press. All of it. Understand me?"

"But…" Finn sputtered. "I thought we had a deal."

"We do now. Good luck, Xander. Do not cross me."

Michele stood in the kitchen beside Jeff, listening to every word. When Finn started demanding his dessert, she fed it to Jeff bite by bite. She had absolutely no intention of giving anything more to that vile Finn.

He'd blackmailed the man she loved to try to force him into lying. How preposterous was that? Jeff didn't lie.

"Holy sweetness, Batman. This is amazing," Jeff said with his mouth full.

"Catwoman. I had the costume and everything."

He cocked his eyebrow. "Babe, I'd love to see you in that costume." He waggled his finger for her to feed him more. With each spoonful, his eyes rolled back in pure delight. The look did wicked things to her. How she wished they were still dating.

When they heard the guards throwing Finn off the property, Jeff said, "I don't need to have my producer give me the Finn hotel episode now. Finn just sealed his own fate."

Michele cheered, "We did it!" And jumped into his arms.

The kisses on his cheeks, jaw, neck and lips? Well, she couldn't stop them if she tried.

And she hadn't tried.

Somewhere in the back of her mind, she sensed that it was a mistake. They had a deal to be partners only and she'd kept her side of it until tonight. But his lips were an intoxicating mix of dark chocolate, cinnamon and rum. Everything began to spiral out of control. His hands dove into her hair and held her head as they devoured each other's lips.

God, he tasted and felt so good.

She barely registered that he'd sat her down on the counter. All her thoughts were centered on this man. His tongue plunged inside her mouth. His hands roughly grabbed her butt.

She wanted more, needed more. Wrapping her legs around him, she pulled him closer until she could feel his thick erection pressing against her panties.

"Michele." The way he growled her name melted her.

If this was a mistake, she was going to make it big-time.

He was hard and she was desperate. She ground herself against his zipper. "Please," she begged. "I need you."

His groan of desire made her wet.

He cupped her through her panties, pressing his thumb against her nub, and nearly short-circuited her brain. She tossed her head back and arched as he rubbed in circles. Panting, she was in a frenzy to get him inside her.

She wanted to come with him. Biting her lip, she unzipped his pants.

His eyes were blue pools of hot desire. "Condom." He yanked his wallet out of his back pocket and took out a silver packet. When he was ready, he lowered her until he filled her.

This. Was. Perfect.

He started thrusting and she held on to his shoulders, rolling with him. Taking him in as deep as she could. "Michele." That growl again.

With each thrust, he said her name, never breaking eye contact. "My Michele."

He took her higher and higher until her body screamed for release and yet she tried to hang on so they could come together because she'd wanted him for what felt like forever. She needed this one moment to last for as long as she could stretch it out and save each second of it in her memory. She'd keep it locked away in her cracked heart, safe, perfect for the times when she was lonely. Alone. Love with Jeff was beautiful and so hard. It broke her even now as she knew he'd pull away again, needing to push her out of his arms because he couldn't feel what she did. He didn't know how to let himself fall for her.

"Sweet Michele," he said with a contented sigh against her neck. He was spent. She let herself sail away with him.

A few minutes later he said, "Don't move."

Move? How could she? Her body was a puddle of happy pudding.

He disposed of the condom and came back to wrap his arms around her. Against her neck he said, "One of these days, I want to take my time with you. Go slow."

Tears pricked her eyes. He was thinking of a future with her. "Slow, fast, I'll take you any way I can get you." She still meant it. She'd risked it all over and over for him, and she'd do it again. There was only one thing she craved in return—his whole heart.

Her body pulsed with her need for Jeffrey Harper and because she couldn't contain her emotions any longer, she let them out. "I want to be with you, Jeff." She loved him. Pure and simple.

"I'm right here, babe." He nuzzled her neck. She sensed that he was distracting her, trying to steer her away from the discussion to come. He knew what she was going to say.

Her insides crumbled because she thought she knew what he was going to say, too, still she pressed on because she had to hear the words. "Are you? Or will you push me away again and tell yourself you can't have a real relationship?"

That's when she saw it— something sharp and raw twisted his beautiful face. He stepped back. "What do you want me to say?"

"The truth."

He swallowed hard, as if his throat was coated with sand. "I've always told you the truth."

"Not about your feelings. Those you shield, protect and bury deep. Say what you think about me, about us. Not what you worry we'll become but what we really are."

He shook his head, his blue eyes clouded. "I don't want to hurt you, Michele. I never did."

"The only way you'll hurt me is if you don't let yourself hang on to what is real and special, standing right here in front of you."

"Michele, this isn't easy for me." A thread of warning rumbled in his voice. He didn't want to talk about his feelings.

She couldn't stop now. "Remember when you said you wished you could feel something real? Feel this." She pressed his hand to her chest. Her heart was pounding hard. "Please, Jeff, I need you to see the man I see—an amazingly gorgeous guy who is worthy of love. Don't you see that, too?"

He didn't answer for a long moment. Tipping his head toward the ceiling lights, he let out a deep exhale. She could tell he was struggling. "When I look at myself, I see a guy who has a restaurant that needs attention and a hotel to finish." He rubbed her arm, slowly, sensually. "Standing next to a beautiful and amazing chef who is going to put our restaurant on the map. I don't want to screw this up."

Damn. He just did.

She'd wanted to believe he cared for her so badly that she'd ripped her heart out of her own chest and handed it to a man who'd warned her he couldn't love her. She couldn't do this anymore.

A tear dripped down her cheek. "Being the head chef of a five-star restaurant isn't enough. I want more for you and need more for me. I wish you could see us like I do."

Until Jeff was brave enough to trust himself and her, she had to step away. She wouldn't give up the job she loved, but she needed to let the man she loved slip through her fingers. She had to let him go.

Everything hurt. It was almost as bad as the day Mom died. She couldn't breathe, but her legs, they could move. She fast-walked outside.

"Michele, wait!" he called after her.

She kept going because she didn't want to see him or hear any of his pretty words. Especially not the way he said her name. None of it was as real for him as it was for her. It never would be.

"Stop!" he called. "Please don't leave. I don't want to lose you."

She turned around and was surprised by the sadness she saw in his eyes and the tenseness of his jaw. "I'm not leaving. I love what we're creating together in the restaurant. I just… I can't date you anymore if you don't care about a real future with me. It's too painful."

He kneaded his neck, as if trying to release the tension she could see in his body. "I'm not any good at this, Michele. I've never been in a relationship before and I don't want to fail you. Hell, I wanted to protect you. From the press, my family, from me."

"From you?"

He stepped closer, his gaze boring into hers. "Yeah. I don't deserve you. I never did. But the truth is that I want you, Michele, more than I can say, more than I ever thought possible. I started crushing on you the first time I saw you on television cooking with such finesse and poetry in action. I've fallen hard every second after that." He wrapped his hands around her waist. "I'm not me—the real me— without you. Please, give me a chance to show you what I feel."

He pulled her to him and kissed her then and the whole world started spinning around her like she was flying. After several minutes he finally pulled back, pressed his forehead to hers and gazed into her eyes. "Did you feel that?" he asked. "I love you, Michele."

She blinked and tears sprang off her eyelashes. "You love me?"

"Hell, yes, with everything in me." His voice choked with emotion. "I'm a mess, sweetheart. I've never felt like this before." His words flowed out like the breaking of a dam. "This—you and me—it's intense. Consuming heat, burning need, but good, too. Warm and sweet. Your touch heals me. When you left, every part of me ached. I was ill with the need of you. Starved for your touch. The wanting of you tore me up inside. I love you so damned much that I can't think straight. I was afraid to admit it, afraid of who I'd become if I let you love me. I don't want to hurt you like my parents hurt each other."

Her heart was so full it hurt. "That won't happen because you are not them. You, Jeffrey Harper—" she held him as tightly as she could, their hearts pounding together "—are mine. We'll figure this all out together." She wrapped her hand around his neck and pulled his lips to hers.

When they finally came up for air she said, "I love you, too."

He exhaled. "Hell, that makes this next part easier." He linked his fingers with hers and kissed her wrist, sending shivers up her arm. "I had a whole thing planned out for to-night. Been working on it for days, but you sort of messed up my timing. Not that I'm complaining about how you preempted it."

"What thing?"

"Sunset yacht cruise up the coast to our beach. Bonfire. Champagne. This." He pulled a box out of his pocket.

She gasped.

He cupped her cheek with his big, warm hands. His gaze bored into her soul. "If you'll let me, I'll be the guy by your side, your partner in life. The one who encourages you and touches you as deeply as you touch me. I want to fall asleep to the rhythm of your breathing and wake up wrapped around you. You inspire me and make me laugh. You heal me and warm all the coldness inside. I want to do all those things for you and more. Much more. Let me be the man who makes *you* happy. Please let me love you for the rest of our lives. I promise I'll get better at it. I'll talk to a therapist, do whatever it takes to get brave for you."

He dropped to his knee in the grass. "Michele Cox, will you marry me?"

She squealed, "Yes! Oh, Jeff, yes!" And then she dropped to her knees and kissed his spicy lips.

Epilogue

The small crowd filed in, taking their seats in chairs by the wedding pagoda at Seal Point—the place where Jeff and Michele had their first date under the canopy of stars. The waves crashed below and a mocking bird sang an artistic medley while Jeff snuck around the back of the restaurant to steal a peek at the bride.

Cari was in the doorway shifting her feet side-to-side, watching her dress swish with her movements.

"Hey, pretty lady. Where's your sister?"

"In there." Cari pointed to the dressing room. "Michele said you aren't supposed to look."

He grinned. "Aw, come on. Just a quick peek. Maybe a big old kiss."

Michele's voice came from somewhere inside. "Tell that sexy man out there to save his kisses until he says, 'I do.' And no peeking!"

Cari screwed up her face in confusion, trying to remember all the words. "She says, um…"

He pulled Cari into his arms. "I heard the bossy woman. I can give you a kiss on the cheek, though, right?"

"Yep. You're gonna be my big brother."

"Can't wait." When he kissed her cheek, Cari giggled. "Okay, tell my love to hurry up. I'm dying out here. She needs to come out and be my bride right now."

Chloe rounded the corner. "Get out of here! It's bad luck.

And you don't want to smudge her lipstick. We just got it right." Then she kissed him on the cheek. "Love you. Now get up front."

"Fine. So many bossy women in here. I'm going."

"Jeff!" Michele called out.

He didn't stop to wonder why she'd called his name. She needed him and that was all that mattered. Screw bad luck. He ran past his sister and Cari and into the bridal room.

Gorgeous didn't begin to describe Michele. She was so beautiful that he couldn't breathe right and his lips felt wonky and his eyes were too full. His legs were full of sand.

"Do you still want to marry me?" Michele asked. "Now's your chance to call it off."

He forced his sand-filled legs to wobble toward her. Her eyes scoured his face, stopping on his lips. Did she see them trembling?

"Sweetheart, I have never wanted anything more. I love you, Michele. With all my heart. Please don't doubt that, but…"

Her lip started to tremble, too. "But?"

"You are so much better than me." He swallowed. "Do you really want to marry *me*?"

She let out a long breath. "Hell, yes."

He kissed her then and smudged her lipstick all over the place.

The wedding was running late, but he didn't care. He'd kissed his bride. All was well with the world.

When he was standing by the pagoda, butterflies of anticipation filled him. Michele was finally going to be his.

Matt bumped his elbow. "You've got this, bro. Just keep your eyes on her. She'll pull you through. I knew she was the one for you. Knew it all along."

RW nodded at him. "We all knew it."

Sure you did, old man.

Jeff took an extra moment to assess his father's demeanor. His eyes were clear, but there was still tightness around his mouth and eyes because Angel hadn't come home. No one knew where she was. Dad was dealing with it by "working the angles." Jeff was only starting to understand what that meant.

Matt had friends in the Bureau who'd slipped him intel that RW was working with the FBI to go after Cuchillo. That scared Matt but Jeff understood that a man would do what he had to do to protect his woman and bring her home safely. Besides, RW knew what he was doing. Jeff had a strong sense that the thing with Finn had started out as RW's devious plan to bring him home. The man was a scheming genius.

If Jeff hadn't met Michele, he'd be furious instead of grinning his fool head off right now.

The music started up and Jeff squinted to see the love of his life. If this wedding didn't happen soon he was going to combust. He was desperate to start his life as a married man with his sparkly bride. He was going to love her with everything he had and then learn how to love her even more.

Just then, a car roared up to the parking lot and the back door flew open. Jeff couldn't see who it was but he sensed the sudden tension in the air. Red heat covered RW's face and his eyes fired up with an intense, unnamed emotion. Matt's face was pale and his body rigid.

Who was it? Jeff still couldn't see.

A figure stepped out of the car, walking toward them with clipped, deliberate movements.

And then he knew.

"Oh, hell." Jeff turned to Matt. "Who invited Mom?"

* * * * *

COMING SOON!

We really hope you enjoyed reading this book. If you're looking for more romance, be sure to head to the shops when new books are available on

Thursday 7th February